Praise for Xenure Station

Praise for Xenure Station: A Billion Light Years

Book 1

Sequel please! – 5 stars

I don't normally read science fiction but found this to be a very interesting little story. Hope the author decides to publish a follow up to this as I would like to know what happens in the future!

Clare, amazon.com.au

Dystopian – 4 stars

I received this copy through voracious readers and now leaving a voluntary review. This is a short read of only 49 pages. The world building is written nicely. For a short story It keeps you gripped until the end.

Natalie Power, amazon.co.uk

Interesting short read, enjoyed – 4 stars

I don't read a great deal of sci-fi but found the description of this intriguing so thought I'd give it a go, and I was glad I did. The story was well written and kept my interest, and the characters were interesting and well described. A good portrayal of a dystopian future.

Bigfishybob, amazon.co.uk

Maria P Frino, well done you!

Xenure Station: A Billion Light Years is a short story. Well, what an imagination, however in time, scary to imagine, but possibly a truism. Well done again and I enjoyed the story so much that I completed it in one go.

Yours in reading,

Aldo Barnaba, via email

Praise for XENURE STATION TRILOGY

Xenure Station was the first Science Fiction I had read since my teenage years. It transported me to a future world with technology so advanced, travelling the universe was no longer a dream but a reality.

Notably, power struggles and human frailties transcend the centuries. Humankind is still under the powerful control and force of but a select few.

I found it a great portrayal of some complex characters.

Veronica Stolfa via email

July 2021

XENURE STATION TRILOGY

MARIA P FRINO

MPG Communications

Xenure Station Trilogy

Xenure Station: A Billion Light Years Book 1

Xenure Station: The Revenge Book 2

Xenure Station: The Return Book 3

This is a work of fiction.

Titles:

Xenure Station: A Billion Light Years Book 1

Xenure Station: The Revenge. A novel. Book 2

Xenure Station: The Return. A novel. Book 3

Author: Maria P. Frino

Cover Photo: Joseph Todaro

Cover Design: Mark Drolc - http://onthemarkdesign.com.au/

Visit the author's website at https://mariapfrino.wixsite.com/authorwebsite

All inquiries should be made to the author – mariapfrino@gmail.com

ISBN: 9780648894605

✿ Created with Vellum

For Tony,
My ever-patient husband

VOLUME ONE

Xenure Station: A Billion Light Years

Book 1

Characters and places

Dawa – Lead female. Partner to Zenac

Zenac – Lead male. Partner to Dawa

Teegue – first born son to Dawa and Zenac

Aria – daughter to Dawa and Zenac

Braxton – youngest son to Dawa and Zenac

High Priest – Leader of The Enforcers

The Enforcers – Twelve men who do the High Priest's bidding

Eldane – High Priest's main security man

Kiane – Teegue's school friend, male

Trisia – Teegue's school friend, female and love interest

Braceon – football player and school bully, male

Krosy – Best football player and school bully, male

The Luminaries – Zenac and Dawa's advisers
    Luminary 1-Sheabz – Dawa's father
    Luminary 2-Tanjaz
    Luminary 3-Xzackry

Soldiers who protect Zenac, Dawa and The Luminaries
    Commando1-Zaydin, female
    Commando2-Ringax, male
    Commando3-Blyzin, male
    Commando4-Amallin, female
    Commando5-Anorea, female
    Commando9-Fletchar, male
    Commando10-Kriska, female

Taaz – head of security for Arisis

The Mechanic – Organises a citizen's army and becomes part of Taaz's security team

Trisear – Zenac and Dawa's assistant

Breex – Engineer. Escapes Arisis with Leyna and Eween

Donnelle – Psychologist. Escapes Arisis with Leyna and Eween

Sanuel – one of Leyna and Eween's engineers

Thadd – High priest enforcers son (died 2290)

Leyna – Thadd's love interest. She is a vexperson

Eween – Leyna's lover after Thadd dies. Also a vexperson

Fixor – a vexperson and colleague of Leyna

Asheel – soldier for Leyna and Eween, female

Flaiwyn – soldier for Leyna and Eween, male

Karim – market seller in Morocco

Respil/Whore – confronts Thadd in his room. Helps Dilvant

Shadear – owner of The Bunker, illegal club

Todfa – Eween's father, he adopts Eween

Nable – Teegue's friend at The Vatican

Mayiss – Nable's love interest

Jzinta – High Priest's illegitimate daughter. Teegue's other love interest on Earth

Marzeen – High Priest's servant and lover. Later Breex's love interest and wife

Vimara – High Priest's first wife

Quinan – Brother of Felida and Ruler of Crete

Felida – Sister of Quinan. Dilvant's love interest

Quinan Jr – Son of Dilvant and Felida

Wilkern – Head of GIS – Global Initiative for Sustainability

Sayen – Deputy of GIS – partner to Wilkern

Galexia – Leyna and Eween's daughter

Edsel – Breex and Marzeen's son

Elvardo – old man who brings them to the King

King Setiago – ruler of Granada. Descendant of survivors from 2050 mission

Elira – Teegue's wife on Granada

Joaque – Elira's daughter adopted by Teegue

Chapter 1

Year 2270

We survived climate change. During the early 2000s there was talk of Earth overheating. There is evidence in the archives that this was happening and panic among humans at the time was rife. Since 2050 we have been taught never to let this happen again. The environment is protected. It was at this time that emissions were reduced enough to save Earth from burning up. The Climate Treaty was signed by every country and emissions controlled by a group known as The GIS –The Global Initiative for Sustainability.

Harmony reigned as each country concentrated on saving Earth and its environs. The GIS and Governments worldwide worked together successfully for two hundred years. Global warming became a thing of the past, and humans were all the better for it. Technology thrives, people are employed, food is distributed evenly, and clean water is available in every country. Many countries prospered.

Our lives are now filled with practical robots and machines, our technology grows ever stronger with inventions to make our lives easier. Space travel is popular, and holidays can be spent on Earth, the Moon, or Mars. Space stations protected by the GIS allow us to research and expand the possibilities of living on other planets. Thousands of people work for the GIS and they protect us all.

However, this prosperity was only for the developed nations, it became an issue for five countries that still struggled with poverty and political corruption. From these countries came a group who were to blindside the GIS and the governments. They disrupted the harmony and were determined to rule.

Chapter 2

Year 2290

Things were different back in 2270. Time was a luxury. We were all too busy to notice what was happening. We were enjoying life, full of work, play and laughter. We were joined in a common goal, to achieve for us; to prosper. We produced sustainable products; we enjoyed the products we produced and distributed them wisely between countries. We were busy and happy with our lives. Time wasn't something we thought about.

Now time is the only thing we have left. Time for them. To do what they say. Do not think; do not suggest, do not do what you want. They froze the Licdan, the world's common currency. No one has their own funds; no country has their own currency. The Enforcers tell us they know what is best for everyone. They control what we spend and how we spend it; what we eat, where we go and who we see.

The Enforcers are twelve people, although we don't consider them people. They are power-hungry, sadistic individuals who think only of themselves. The tentacles of their power invaded our world with promises of further prosperity under their regime. Their believers infiltrated governments and greed became the staple of their rhetoric. Corruption began to enter established governments as this greed took hold. The High Priest Enforcer, with his mix of religious fervour, charisma and antiquated values of ultimate leadership, ordered computers to be disabled. What wasn't disabled was blown apart during the war. Technology died under this self-indulgent regime.

Those of us who did not follow or did not believe their warped ideals kept quiet in the beginning. We underestimated the power of the High Priest's charisma teamed with power-hungry avarice. When the war started, it was too late to speak out. We have curfews now. Our time is to be spent only for them, to do what they enforce. The rest is idle time, but we have nothing to fulfil the idleness. The war devastated everything; technology has stood still for twenty years. Prosperity is for a select few and we have to accept what we are given. Food and water are metered out depending on your status. The Enforcers tell us when to do their deeds. Refuse and you will pay the consequence.

We who remember the time before we were forced into submission. We have nothing left of us. We remember when it was revered to be your own star. To make something of yourself, to achieve. We have time now, but we are not allowed to shine. What we do is for them, to benefit them, we are cogs in their machine.

Chapter 3

I arrive home in time to hear Zenac. His authoritative yet gentle voice comforts our children. Everything will be alright. He will protect them. They are mesmerised by his words. It is his voice keeping their focus only on him. Zenac has a voice of reassurance. He smiles towards me. However, his smile does not reassure me because even he will find it difficult to protect us now.

Braxton is the first to hear me. "Mummy," he screams running towards me, his pudgy four-year-old hands outstretched, "Daddy will protect you too." Smothering him with kisses after scooping him up, I walk towards Aria and Teegue, kissing both their heads. The twins' faces are vanilla as they look up towards me. Aria's eyes plead. How I wish I could give them hope.

"We will get through this. Your mother and I are formulating a plan," he says, reaching out towards me with his hand.

My partner, the father of our three children, is forever emboldened. We do have a plan and Zenac will make it work. I have to have faith in him, for us, for humanity. But at this point in time, we have to follow The Enforcers. We have to listen to them. We have to survive on the few Licdan they allow us. The 20-year war is over. The Enforcers are in power whether we like it or not.

Twelve commanders led by the charismatic ultimate High Priest Enforcer rule the world. They care little for their people, those of us who are left. They are blinded by power. This power they use to keep everyone subservient, so no one can vanquish them.

Power given to them by selfish people who wanted more than what they had. They voted The Enforcers into power. Their power came from a series of social media posts promising prosperity for all. People believed and fell under their spell. Some governments also believed in their lie: "Believe in us and we will protect you."

They started a war that rivalled all wars, devastating every country and now they rule. From seven billion people we are now two billion, many of whom are maimed and living in desperate poverty. We and our followers have withstood the worst of their tyranny. But no one is immune, everyone must follow The Enforcers' machine.

Chapter 4

I am Dawa. I do not follow the machine. Neither do Zenac, my father and our tribe of non-believers. There is a plan, it is Zenac's and my father's vision for humanity. We, the Three Hundred all know the plan and have formed this underground group to salvage what we can. But we fear this vision, our vision, will not come to fruition because The Enforcers will try to stop us. They know of the fractious murmurings but have no idea how close we are to perfecting our escape.

This spurs me on, it spurs us all to achieve our goal. I will not let us fail. Zenac is by my side, our followers want the same as us, to be free again. To be human again. Their rules are barbaric. We all wear the same brown uniforms, skirts for women, shorts for boys and a shapeless shift dress for girls. Be seen without a spotless and perfectly ironed uniform in public and you will be placed in shackles, sometimes for weeks. There is no talking back or giving your opinion or the same will happen. The severity of your crime determines the length of time you are shackled. We, the Three Hundred, follow their rules in public areas. We do not want any attention and keep our heads down.

Education was banned, books were burned, and only one school and library remain. The library is where their offices are housed. Security around these buildings is tight, their army of guards have machine guns at the ready. No one is sure, but we suspect the High Priest Enforcer and his twelve commanders reside in one of these buildings. They have not been seen since the end of the war.

We will risk our lives to be free of The Enforcers. Now is our time. The plan is set. Our family will be the first to leave with our security team. The others will follow. They know their instructions. Is it safe? We will make it safe. For all of us, the Three Hundred. The ones who remember the time before.

In their haste to take over, The Enforcers destroyed indiscriminately. Many robots, cars and jets lay strewn where they were bombed. Useless and abandoned.

The war left something behind to help us with our plan - jets, useless to many but not to us. We restored three jets, we improved their capacity and speed, and we are ready. Our jet, the Salverz is ready to take us to Xenure Station.

The Enforcers did not take our intelligence, nor our skills.

Chapter 5

Year 2290
The Arrival

"Welcome to all of you. You are here because you believe in us. This is the start of something bigger and better. We have come too far with this mission to fail."

I listen to Zenac. We all listen. The arena on Xenure Station is alive with the murmurs of the Three Hundred. His voice booms throughout the arena. Their faces believe. The Enforcers will not rule us again.

The arena is the cavernous bunker at the bottom of the station. It houses jets, machines, equipment and what ammunition we were able to smuggle out. Each person yet to be rescued will bring more supplies. This space is still a vacuous void, we only fill a small section at the front near the podium where Zenac and I are standing. Our dream is to have it filled with our followers, those who want a better, prosperous world again. Zenac and I have ensured everyone's safety. This is our paradise. Away from The Enforcers and their draconian rule.

"You are all safe. This station has room for more. Others will follow when it is deemed safe for them to do so. It is time for us all to achieve, to produce and to grow. We will no longer suffer under the antiquated rules and greed of The High Priest Enforcer and his henchmen. We will rebuild, and not only survive, we will prosper for the good of all."

Zenac's words inspire us. Applause reverberates throughout the arena. The Three Hundred have survived. Zenac and I hold our hands high looking out towards them. Our time has come.

Chapter 6

We are in the communications room focusing on our screens. A voice startles both of us.

"Sir, there is a signal"

Zenac leaves his station next to mine and stands next to the commando, "I'm sure I don't have to ask where it's from?"

"It is Earth, sir."

I turn to see how Zenac reacts to this information. We have been keeping vigil since our arrival three years ago. Concern etches his face as I turn away from watching the screen in front of me. Commando1-Zaydin is right. The signal is weak, but we know it is definitely from our enemies who still rule Earth.

This is the first time a signal, any signal, has reached us. We have been rescuing people with the utmost care not to be detected. My hope is that our security commander is wrong about the signal. The Enforcers have no way of tracking us, our security team are the best technicians. We selected them ourselves.

"How far?"

"One Billion, sir."

"Keep an eye on it. Don't do anything until Dawa or I give an order. They may not know our position yet." He turns to face me, "Dawa, come with me."

I turn and follow. I know we have a problem.

We are in our sealed room. No one will hear us here.

"Thadd is on his way."

"The Enforcer's best pilot? Zenac, he will find us, he is a good navigator." The Three Hundred is growing and thriving. We are humans again. Thadd must not find us. "The encryption shield, why has it failed us now?"

His head bows, "I don't have an answer for you. We have to work on it again. Are they still trustworthy?"

I know who he means, The Helpers. Those who assisted us in planning our escape and keeping it from The Enforcers. They did not come; they did not believe we would make it. Have they betrayed us?

"We must be prepared. This will mean war."

No, not again. This is not what I want. I will do everything in my power to make sure it does not come to this. "Zenac, I will organise The Luminaries. The Sanctuary Treaty will be executed. The encryption shield will be fortified."

The look on his face tells me otherwise, but The Luminaries and I will not fail. I will not live under The Enforcers rule ever again.

Chapter 7

I keep my promise to Zenac and our followers. With the help of a select few, our greatest minds, we are safe.

"Luminary members, the Sanctuary Treaty has kept us from being invaded. Zenac and I thank you." I am at the head of the Ovalaz Luminary Room's oval table. Thadd and his crew of Enforcers, the enemy army, came within three hundred thousand miles of Xenure Station, our home.

The Ten Luminaries murmur amongst themselves. It was close, too close. They were concerned when I convened the initial meeting to discuss how the encryption shield failed. We all thought it was strong enough and guaranteed to protect us.

"You were both right to warn us Luminaries as soon as you heard of the threat. You and Zenac saved us again."

"It was our promise to all of you when we left Earth that there would be no wars on our home soil. This is my promise to you again. As long as I live, Xenure Station and any other home we inhabit will be a sanctuary for all who share our ideals."

The Ten Luminaries clap their hands. A polite clap showing their support. I know I have their respect, but as their leader, I am wary. A leader can be ousted.

Thadd had tried to do this to his own father, a man he had grown to detest. He led a coup against his father, the High Priest Enforcer. An ultimate betrayal. This is why Thadd was sent to find us. He betrayed his father, so the High Priest Enforcer sent his only son to his death. We were informed of this by those of the enemy army who were captured. They will be dealt with by Commando1-Zaydin and her team. There is no room for leniency on those who wish to harm us. True leaders always watch their backs and Zenac and I will always be wary of any signs of discord amongst our followers.

The Ten Luminaries leave just as Zenac calls me to our sealed room. Another problem? Here we go again.

Chapter 8

"There were more arrivals today Dawa."

"How many?" I ask without emotion. These arrivals need to be security checked before they will be trusted to live amongst us. We must ensure there are no spies amongst them, we have learned many lessons since arriving on Xenure Station.

"Twenty. Many are from the original group of helpers. I think we can trust them."

I smile at his spirit. Zenac believes in trust, but I am more sceptical. "Let us see what our security team says first." They were our helpers while we were on Earth. Now, who knows where their allegiance lies. Did one of them betray us to The Enforcers? This is all the more reason to have them screened first.

He nods in agreement and continues with another important issue. We have to find another planet, the station will not hold more than three thousand, we are already at fifteen hundred refugees. We know of many more who wish to escape the tyranny of Earth's High Priest Enforcer and his army of sadists. He is a dictator, the ultimate leader of Earth. Why did no one see this coming?

I keep listening as I sink into the air-chair. Everything on the station is space ready, including the smattering of furnishings. Once we find a suitable planet, we will settle and have a real home, not this temporary situation on what was once a satellite before the war. These stations were meant to detect groups such as The Enforcers, their stealth is now known and despised. This is why we are vigilant, because if we let down our guard it will spell disaster for all of us.

Our dream is to have a home again, a free home where everyone can prosper. My greatest wish is for humans to live in harmony with leaders who care about their people and the environment they inhabit.

"There are two planets we are considering at the moment. Mars, as we know, is suitable but too close to earth. The Enforcers have already tried twice to conquer Mars. We need to be further away from Earth, where they will not bother us. Our scouts have found a dwarf planet, Arisis. This one is suitable because it is three billion light years away from earth, has water but little vegetation. Oxygen is limited, we can only spend a few hours outdoors, not days. We will be able to improve this once we settle."

"Do we have enough power to reach that far?"

"We are working on it now. Progress is swift because we brought the best space engineers with us."

This is true, the Three Hundred, the first to leave Earth with us, were the brightest scientific minds available and willing to risk everything to leave the tyranny of The Enforcers.

Agreeing with him I say, "We are making progress, I applaud this. The scouts must keep exploring this planet," I say as he nods indicating this is already happening. "Now, is there anything further? I need to check the children have completed their studies."

"That's it for today. I will go and see the security commandos for a debrief then join you and the children."

Lifting myself from the air-chair I envelop him in a hug. "You are my rock Zenac, together we can do anything."

"I know Dawa, you have played a big part in this operation. Your years of psychology allowed us to find the people we could trust for our escape. Along with your father, you gave me the courage to believe in our dream."

Smiling, I kiss his cheek, "Thank you for your trust in me. We will discuss your meeting with the security commandos tomorrow." I press my left wrist to allow myself out of our secret room.

Chapter 9

Aria and Teegue sit at their desks, their books strewn in front of them. It is a sight I will never tire of. To see our children finally allowed to study is a bonus of us escaping the tyranny of The Enforcers. Braxton is collapsed on the air-lounge sound asleep. I brush his blonde locks away from his eyes. He looks up, smiles and turns over, falling straight back to sleep.

"He finished reading a few minutes ago. He did better today, Mummy."

I look into Aria's dark brown eyes and see her concern. But it is Teegue who speaks for the three of them, "We heard about the signal, are you and Father sure we are safe?"

"We are and I don't want you to worry. Please concentrate on your studies. And Aria, how was Braxton better today? Did he read both books?"

"One, but he read it without errors. And he didn't complain like he has before. Mummy he wants someone to play with, why can't we let him play with the other children?"

Without thinking I let out a sigh, large and heavy, full of a mother's concern. Their eyes bore through me wanting an answer. How can I tell them? Braxton is seven and should be playing with other children. All three of them should. Unfortunately, Zenac and I can't allow them to leave our section of the station. It's too dangerous. The encryption shield is at its strongest here, we are protected.

"There will be a time where you can all play with other children and it is not far away, I promise you this. For now, please concentrate on your studies. It is important for the three of you to be educated so you can keep us all safe in the future."

Teegue speaks again, "Aria and I are older and understand this Mother, but Braxton finds it hard to accept. He misses his friends."

"We all miss something of our past, but we are together and away from danger. I know Braxton is too young to understand what has happened, so when he wakes, I will explain things to him. Please believe me, everyone on this station is safe but we are in the section that is impenetrable."

Aria puts her head back into the book she was reading. She seems comforted, her face more serene than when I walked into their study. Teegue, however, stands up placing his arm on my elbow and walks me to the window whispering, "Braxton is different to Aria and me. He feels left out, he wants the company of kids his own age."

I am in awe of this teenage boy with the wisdom of someone twice his age. My son has a bright future, of this I'm sure. "As I said before, this is a temporary situation, the three of you will be with other children again. Your father, myself and our team are working on finding a planet for us to live on." My voice is low, just as his had been. I look over to see Aria still reading, "Be patient Teegue. Braxton looks up to you, show him how this is for the best. If you help him with his studies, just as Aria does, it will keep his mind active and he won't dwell on his problems."

He drops his arm from my elbow and walks back towards his desk, "As you wish, Mother. I will do my best."

Our three children have a bright future, but it is Teegue who has the special qualities to be a leader. As I am about to leave, Zenac walks in, and seeing Braxton asleep, he sidles up to me putting his arm around my shoulders.

"I see everything is under control here," he whispers, winking at Teegue who smiles towards us giving us a thumbs up.

Chapter 10

Ear-splitting alarms penetrate the whole of Xenure Station. Both Zenac and I summon the Ten Luminaries to the Ovalaz Luminary Room. I sit staring at my hands. I am panicking and absolutely distraught as I sit at the head of the oval table listening to Zenac address us. His exterior is calm and stoic, but I know inside he is a mess just as I am.

"Our twins, Aria and Teegue have gone missing. They are being held for ransom. There is a traitor among us."

Murmurs and whispers saturate the room. Horrified faces look towards each other and then back at us. I remain passive, I do not want them to see my fear. My worst nightmare has happened. Our children are in danger. This is the price we are paying for our freedom.

"Our highest commandos must be deployed. Zenac you have our permission to do whatever it takes to bring the twins back home alive."

"Thank you Luminary1-Sheabz, I appreciate your support. I will accompany the commandos in this rescue and then all of us will return to head towards Arisis, our new home. This planet will be our haven away from these madmen Enforcers."

My face now shows my fear. My breath becomes short. Zenac is going too? He did not discuss this with me, when did he decide such a thing? "Zenac, it is too dangerous. They will take you too. You are falling right into their trap." My words blurt out, I am not able to contain my anger.

"Dawa, my love. Do not fear for me. The Enforcers will not know I am on board. My shield will protect me. It is the commandos who will do the searching for the twins. Believe me, I will not let them harm our children."

His shield did protect us during the war. Its power to deflect all ammunition is now legendary. His authority is strong, but I am not convinced. "Then I am coming with you. They are our children and we will both rescue them.

"No!" he exclaims with reserved forcefulness, "I forbid it. We have Braxton who needs you here with him... I need you here. You will be in command while I am gone."

"Dawa, listen to him. He is right," reassures Luminary 1-Sheabz. His voice calm, and laced with fatherly affection.

I nod unwillingly, too distressed to fight. I will need all the energy I can muster to cope without my partner and my twins.

Chapter 11

Year 2291
Arisis

My plants are growing. The hothouses are working. Everything is going well since our arrival on our new planet, Arisis, six months ago. We are three thousand people now; we are growing in numbers and in strength. If we had spent another month on Xenure station, we would have had to build extra accommodation for the refugees being rescued from Earth.

Zenac insisted we leave. I wanted to wait for him, for our twins too, but he promised they would meet us on Arisis soon. He has assured me the three of them will return together. I have to believe he will succeed. But I am still waiting.

Braxton told us how the twins were taken. He was awake and heard a noise. Frightened, he hid in his desk drawer. He is lithe, his flexibility allows him to fit in places most children his age would never fit. Voices were muffled, but he heard someone say, "Don't bother with the little one, the twins will suffice." Their bedroom is partitioned so each of them has a separate section and he peers out from the drawer to see his brother and sister carried out. By who? He wasn't able to tell in the darkness. His voice caught in his throat as fear took over him. He has regretted not screaming out ever since.

Aria and Teegue are nearing their fifteenth birthday. They are still alive, for this I am grateful. The Enforcers want a ransom as well as Zenac in return for the safe return of our twins. They are not to be trusted; the 20-year war taught us this. We refuse to be blackmailed and will not bow down to their demands. Our commandos are closing in, Zenac has told us all to be patient.

My heart is broken, I miss them desperately.

Chapter 12

The Ten Luminaries have joined me once more in the Ovalaz Luminary Room on Xenure Station. Although Arisis has distance in its favour, we fear that signals may still reach Earth. It is safer to discuss issues on the Station, the encryption shield around it is impenetrable now. It was strengthened further after the twins were kidnapped. Now it covers the whole station, not just the section we resided in.

"The traitor has been captured," I inform them, "Commando1-Zaydin is interrogating her now."

"Why did she betray us? She was one of our trusted helpers."

Looking over towards Luminary 2-Tanjaz, I see a face of someone who wants to trust everyone we have allowed to be with us. I now know this is no longer possible. "People are motivated by different things. She was involved with Thadd back on Earth. The commandos found this out and said she wanted to avenge his death. Even though it was his own father who wanted him dead, not us."

The Luminaries whisper among themselves, a few of them angry that the traitor wanted to hurt the people who had rescued her.

"She will suffer her fate then, our security team will see to it," Luminary 1-Sheabz interjects, "Zenac and the twins' safe return is our priority."

My eyes drop towards the table, not wanting to show my fear to my father. "Yes," I mumble, "That is our only and most urgent priority." Then with a courage that empowers me from deep within, I raise my eyes and look towards all of them. They see my determination. The Ten Luminaries know what needs to be done.

Chapter 13

He finds me in the hothouse where I am tending vegetables. These will feed us all within a few weeks. The children will especially benefit from the nutrients, to grow strong and keep us safe for the years to come. "Father, you have good news for me I hope?"

Bowing his head, he takes off his headgear and sits with me on the ledge. "There has been some progress. Small, but it is progress," sighs Sheabz.

"Go on," I say apprehensively.

"The Enforcers holding the twins have been overrun by our commandos." I am about to speak, but he stops me, placing his finger to my lips. "Before they could escape back to the ship an army of a hundred Enforcers trapped them in the compound. They cannot leave but they are protecting the twins. The ransom is now that Zenac replaces the twins as well as one million Licdan. They have upped the ransom, but as you know we do not have enough Licdan for them. And they will not accept our new currency. It is worthless on Earth."

My heart deflates. "I forbid Zenac from leaving the safety of the Commando Mission People Vehicle (CMPV), you must relay this message to him. He is not to surrender to them. As for us giving them that ludicrous sum, there is no way..."

"Dawa we will do everything in our power for this not to happen, Zenac must remain on the ship. He knows it is a trap, The Enforcers will take all three of them and then come for you. It has been their plan all along."

I know this. We all know how The Enforcers work. I have never trusted them and never will.

"My trust is with the Ten Luminaries as always. Thank you for relaying some small bit of good news, at least Aria and Teegue are still alive."

I watch as he leaves. He has aged. His shoulders droop with the despair of missing his grandchildren, and like Zenac, blaming himself for this tragedy. The decision to flee Earth was Sheabz's and Zenac's brainchild, but we all agreed to the plan. What has happened is the fault of the power-hungry Enforcers, they will stop at nothing to retain power over all humans.

Chapter 14

I am walking towards him. His eyes flare with anger as he sees me. "What are you doing here? I told you not to come. It is too dangerous for both of us to be on this rescue mission," he barks at me, his face harsh and stern.

"Zenac, it has been too long. We work better when we are together." I fall into his arms and feel him soften against me. The CMPV is smaller than I remember. It was initially built to carry crew from space station to space station, but no more than fifty crew fit on this one. Many of the larger CMPVs were destroyed during the war.

Our new home, Arisis, has spoiled me with open areas and freedom to move around. Even though we wear oxygen-infused helmets outdoors, we are free. I have already forgotten how it feels to live in confined quarters.

Concern riddles Zenac's face as he holds me. I try to allay his fears, "Sheabz sent me. He too was not keen on this idea until I convinced him we work better together. He desperately misses Aria and Teegue too. Please Zenac, this has gone on far too long. I need our twins to be back with us, we need to be a family again."

Three commandos run into the communications area. "Oh, apologies. We saw you come in from the docking station Dawa. We are just checking everything is okay"

"Thank you, commandos, we appreciate your concern. Please leave us alone. We will summon you if needed."

"Yes Sir." The three of them bow towards Zenac and then shuffle awkwardly, still facing us, into the galley.

He turns his attention to me again, "Dawa, I have been on this mission for a year and we have at least located where our twins are, what more do you think you can add?"

"I am their mother and you are their father and we owe it to them to do everything we can to free them. Also, to free the commandos who are left with them. Now, if you will just listen, Sheabz and I have formulated a plan."

Reluctantly he offers me a seat. Before sitting down, I spread out the plan my father and I worked on before I left.

His eyes brighten as he peers over them. "I'm impressed. I have to admit this has not been tried yet. Commando1-Zaydin will be informed and she will implement this plan right away.

Chapter 15

"Mummy! Look Teegue... it's Mummy," Aria screams as I run towards her scooping her up into my arms. I kiss her furiously and then Teegue, with tears stinging my eyes. I let them flow, they are tears of joy. My twins are finally in my arms, they are thin but alive.

Teegue looks up into my face. He has changed, his face is one of a young man, there is a spattering of facial hair on his top lip. "Where is Father? Is he alright? How did you get here? I can't believe you are here."

His words tumble out. My ears suck in my children's voices. I look around the tiny hold they have lived in for twelve months. The stench is overwhelming, those barbarians let this happen. But they fed them. Not much food but it does not matter now. All I want is to have them home with us.

"Dawa, follow us. Stay close. Here, Aria and Teegue, put these suits on."

We follow the commandos as I embrace both twins, one on either side of me. The compound is in the middle of the Sahara Desert, a secret tunnel of warehouses where munitions were stored during the war. We managed to impregnate the outer area where The Enforcers army was stationed by deploying an incapacitating agent, but it will wear off in a few hours. We must hurry.

Zenac gave me his shield, but it will only protect one of us. I have to keep the twins close but even then, there is no guarantee they will survive if we are attacked. We have to avoid being attacked at all costs.

"Mummy, I'm tired. How much further do we have to run?"

"Aria hold on please. We are nearly there." I lie to keep her spirits up. We have another hour before we reach the support vehicle to return us to Zenac who remained on the CMPV. The commandos are in constant contact with him. He is keeping an eye on any movement from The Enforcers army and will deploy more commandos if he fears we are in danger.

Aria falters again. I gather her into my arms. She is so thin against my chest, I feel her bones.

"Mummy I'm sorry," she whispers.

"Don't worry Aria, I have you. We are nearly there." Within minutes she is asleep in my arms. Then suddenly, we stop.

I call Commando10-Kriska over to me, "Here you hold her while I go to the front to check why we have stopped. Teegue, hold your father's shield and wait here."

"No, I am coming with you. You should not go anywhere without this shield." His determined face is the last thing I see as he grabs my hand and pulls me towards the commandos at the front.

"Commando3-Blyzin, why have we stopped?" I ask when we reach him.

"We picked up a signal, Dawa and until we know it is safe, we cannot proceed. I have sent five commandos ahead to scout the area."

My fear is we do not have enough time. Aria needs medical attention and Teegue, as determined as he is, needs caring for as well. My heart pounds as I think. By my calculations we have twenty minutes to reach the support vehicle. We are close, I will not let The Enforcers stop us now. Sending Teegue back with Commando2-Ringax, he fights to stay with me. "Teegue go and protect your sister, that is an order."

As I watch them leave, his face wet with tears, I am more determined than ever to save us all.

Chapter 16

"Commando3-Blyzin, I order you to send a message to Zenac. Ask him to deploy a rescue crew. Aria and Teegue need medical attention."

"Dawa, my orders are to not bring attention to us. The Enforcers must not know our location. If Zenac deploys a rescue crew, he will send a signal they can detect. It is too dangerous."

A voice I don't recognise screeches from my mouth, I am beyond angry. Is it really me shouting at one of our trusted commandos? "I am in charge here. Stuff your orders! This is an emergency. If we stay here much longer, they will find us anyway. We have a better chance of escape if we keep moving. Give me that." I snatch the Answae from his hand and speak directly to Zenac. To my surprise he is not aware how close we are, Commando3-Blyzin had not contacted him since we left The Enforcer compound. Our trusted third commando has some explaining to do. The Answae was off when I snatched it from him.

Zenac was not able to get in contact with us, he had been gravely concerned. "It was stupid of me to leave you without an Answae, but we had to keep you and the children safe. The more signals The

Enforcers pick up, the more chances you would be captured. The support vehicle has already been deployed. I will give them your exact location; they will not be far from you. Stay safe my love."

We had argued about the Answae. I eventually agreed to only Commando3-Blyzin carrying communication equipment for safety reasons. He has now betrayed us both. The five commandos he sent to scout have not returned. I am sure The Enforcers have been informed of our position. "Why?" I turn to him, "What do you achieve by having us captured? All of us."

Commando3-Blyzin spits out a tirade of vitriol. "You and Zenac promised us a new world, a new start. Then you closed the doors to other refugees too soon. My loved ones remained here on Earth. I am alone while you have everyone you love with you. On Earth I had a name, I had a home to go to. My partner and children were waiting for me to have them rescued. Now they are dead. What do I have now? My loneliness. You took away my happiness, how are you any different from The Enforcers?"

"So, you have sold out to them, to our enemies? You disgust me."

"They offered me more status than I will ever achieve with you and Zenac. You are no different to The Enforcers. Once you have enough followers you forget who put you where you are. All leaders forget the people who got them where they are once they achieve their goals. Why did you not consult your people before closing the doors to your new world?"

I place my palm close to his face. I match his vitriol, my body shaking, "How dare you compare Zenac and I to the barbaric Enforcers. You make me sick. After everything we have done for you, you betray us. Why did you not come to us with your issues before running to the enemy?" Anger roars inside me. How long have The Enforcers known our position? We must get moving. Two other commandos standing near me take Commando3-Blyzin's armed belt, handing it to me. Then, placing his arms behind his back, they march him away. It took all my strength not to hit him.

Commando5-Anorea places her arm on mine, "We can deal with him later. We need to keep a look out for the support vehicle."

We head back to the others. I cuddle my children hoping the support vehicle is closer to us than The Enforcers. Have I failed them? Pushing this emotion aside I am determined we will not fail. I must believe in us and our plan or we will perish at the hands of our enemy.

Chapter 17

A sound wakes me out of my light slumber. Commando5-Anorea calls me over to her. Zenac runs towards me, "Where are the children? Get them quickly, The Enforcers are right behind me."

There is no time for questions although I have many. Why is he the only one? Where is the rest of our crew? Where are our reinforcements? But I cannot think about questions now, we must get everyone in the support vehicle as quickly as possible.

"Where is Commando3-Blyzin?" he yells back at me. I signal towards the three commandos towards the back. "Go, all of you. Head to the support vehicle now. I'll deal with this and catch up."

"Zenac..."

"Dawa, just go. Now!" He stands firm pointing towards the direction of the vehicle where the others are headed.

Collecting Aria into my arms and with Teegue's hand in mine, we run. Shots begin firing as we step into the vehicle. As I turn, I'm horrified. Many of our commandos are down, others are taking cover, returning fire, keeping us safe. Zenac had left this rescue crew near the craft knowing of this imminent attack.

I tumble the twins into the CMPV. "Stay inside. Do not move out of here. If father and I are not back, leave."

"No, we are not leaving without you." Teegue's determined look spears through my heart. This spurs me on, we will succeed for our children's sake. The medicos are pulling our children away from me, "Take good care of both of them." As I run down the ramp, Teegue is screaming, "... and come back with father." This the last thing I hear. The roar of The Enforcers shooting towards us drowns him out.

With Zenac's shield for protection I order two commandos to follow me. Flicking on the Answae, I try contacting Zenac. He answers but the signal is weak. "Keep The Enforcers at bay as best you can. I have..." the signal crackles... "commandos with me. They think we are all together near the CMPV... take them from behind."

I hear enough to know what to do. At least I know he is safe. With the few commandos I have left with me, we hold off The Enforcers until Zenac arrives with his reinforcements. They are taken by surprise.

I am in his arms. "The twins? How are they?"

"They are okay now. I left them with the medicos. Teegue listened to my orders and stayed in the craft. Aria was in a worse state, we made it here just in time. She was pale and weak."

We had staved off The Enforcers attack because they didn't expect us to hit them from behind. We ambushed them. Had Zenac not stayed to deal with Commando3-Blyzin, we would be in the hands of the enemy once more.

Some of our commandos are still checking for survivors and bringing back weapons into the CMPV hold. We stand on the ramp overseeing their progress.

"Leaving in five minutes, bring all the wounded, the medicos will care for them. Do not bring anything unnecessary with you, the CMPV will be at capacity. Well done to all of you," Zenac's reassuring voice booms out to them.

I turn walking up the ramp to check on the twins. "Thank you," he says.

Looking back towards him I smile, "We're a team Zenac, don't ever forget that. You and I are meant to work together."

With an imperceptible nod, he follows me up the ramp. "Two minutes," he yells to the remaining commandos.

Chapter 18

I am in his arms. "The twins? How are they?"

"They are okay now. I left them with the medicos. Teegue listened to my orders and stayed in the craft. Aria was in a worse state, we made it here just in time. She was pale and weak."

We had staved off The Enforcers attack because they didn't expect us to hit them from behind. We ambushed them. Had Zenac not stayed to deal with Commando3-Blyzin, we would be in the hands of the enemy once more.

Some of our commandos are still checking for survivors and bringing back weapons into the CMPV hold. We stand on the ramp overseeing their progress.

"Leaving in five minutes, bring all the wounded, the medicos will care for them. Do not bring anything unnecessary with you, the CMPV will be at capacity. Well done to all of you," Zenac's reassuring voice booms out to them.

I turn walking up the ramp to check on the twins. "Thank you," he says.

Looking back towards him I smile, "We're a team Zenac, don't ever forget that. You and I are meant to work together."

With an imperceptible nod, he follows me up the ramp. "Two minutes," he yells to the remaining commandos.

Chapter 19

Year 2295
Arisis

Our planet has many lakes, the largest, Lake Ilquarra, is near our headquarters. It glistens as I enjoy the pristine view from my office window. The lake's name is a reminder of where we once lived. Earth is still ruled by The Enforcers, who now leave us alone.

We did open our border again for two years after the twins' kidnapping with great success. Commando3-Blyzin was never heard from again. When a distant cousin of his arrived on Arisis he was surprised to find out what he had done. Why he placed us all in danger was beyond his comprehension.

Our children are safe, our people are safe, we are safe. This is what matters most. I have no desire to seek revenge, I do not want to start another war with The Enforcers. This is what I will discuss with the Ten Luminaries. Our security is of paramount importance.

"They are ready for you, Dawa."

I turn to see my assistant returning to her post as I head towards the Ovalaz Luminary Room II. The security of Arisis will be assured.

END of Book 1

VOLUME TWO

Xenure Station: The Revenge

Book 2

Chapter 1

Leyna

Things could be worse for her, but the anger keeps her focused on her mission. It was their mission; they were going to overthrow his father. The same father who sent him on the suicide mission to Xenure Station. Now she will revenge Thadd's death. His father, the ultimate High Priest Enforcer, along with Dawa and Zenac, are in her sights.

Dawa and Zenac thought they could escape The Enforcers. They have for now. They think they are safe on this planet Arisis, where they hold her prisoner. Leyna's crime was loving a man who was sent on a mission to return Dawa, Zenac and their 300 followers back to Earth. The High Priest Enforcer demanded their return. Earth was their home and he was their ultimate ruler. The High Priest knew his son was not ready for such a task, but he sent him anyway. Leyna's love for Thadd meant he was sent to his death. His father disapproved of their love because Thadd had Enforcer blood running through him, yet she was a nobody, a vexperson with nothing to offer his heir.

Leyna was the orchestrator of kidnapping Dawa and Zenac's twins, Teegue and Aria, while they were all still on Xenure Station. She had come onto the station as one of their trusted helpers. She wanted to avenge Thadd's death and hurt them as much as she was hurting. The twins were taken back to Earth as ransom to lure Dawa and Zenac back to Earth. Unfortunately, she was found as having orchestrated the kidnapping and after being captured, was thrown into prison. She had the unenviable trophy of being the first person incarcerated on Arisis.

She is in her own cell. There is a small window, too high for her to see out of, but it lets light in. At the moment a small sliver of moonlight seeps through it. Her bed is a thin mattress on metal slats flat on the concrete floor. They have given her two blankets, but she rarely uses them, there is no need. The temperature in this cell is always like the summer days she enjoyed back home. She misses those days, when life was carefree, and she would swim in the lake with her brothers as her parents watched on. Those days are long gone, and she grew up with the world changing around her due to The Enforcers.

This prison cell is comfortable compared to Earth standards. Thadd had shown her where the worst of Earth's criminals were kept. Prisons under The Enforcers rule were hellholes of square cubicles with a blanket and a bucket for a toilet. Prisoners' only saw daylight if their crime was minimal. A minimal crime, like not wearing your uniform correctly, or not wearing your appointed uniform, would land you in prison for a month. Once a week you were allowed outside for thirty minutes. Those who committed heinous crimes against The Enforcers never saw daylight again. Many never left prison alive.

Thadd had told her that a crime against his father or one of his twelve henchmen — a betrayal, a military coup or speaking out against The Enforcers values — meant those criminals lived in the cubicle all day long. They were then put to work at night making ammunition. This ammunition was used by The Enforcers to win the 20-year war. Now, it is used to keep the people left on Earth submissive to their draconian rules. Sitting on her prison bed, it is late, but she remembers meeting the son of Earth's most powerful man. This memory is keeping her awake.

Thadd came to a party, an illegal event under The Enforcers strict rules. These parties were underground gatherings of young influential people and were strictly invitation only. This event was in an underground bunker that was once a car park. Everyone at these parties risked punishment, Thadd even more so for being the son of the high priest. Many of the other guests were from the families who protected the high priest and his twelve. These young influencers have a code, which they use to allow entry to such events. Kept under secret scrutiny, the code is known to these select few. It is only revealed to a sibling once they reach the age of fifteen.

She was there serving drinks, even though she was not yet eighteen. No one noticed nor asked for ID. This gig was one she never spoke of. Anyone who worked at these parties was sworn to secrecy. Not that she had anyone to tell, her parents and two brothers were killed in the war. She is what is known as a vexperson, one who has no ties to any other human. Vexes or a vex, as they are called, live alone and keep to themselves. In the pecking order of The Enforcers new world, vexes are at the low end. Only the elderly and infirm are below them. Unless, of course, you happen to be an elder of one of the twelve Enforcers and their families. These elders are treated as royals, adored and admired for having the foresight to bring The Enforcers the power they now enjoy.

As a vex, she knows she is not to speak or make eye contact with the guests. These people are out of her reach. The Enforcers have instilled a hierarchy whereby only by birth can you be one of them. Even if you marry into the family, you are not considered to be a true blood. Everyone else, vexes or not, work for the regime. You are given a job depending on your status. With her status so low, her job is in the factory that makes their drab uniforms. She is a cutter, day in day out, six days a week she cuts the coarse hessian-like fabric.

This party gig was offered to her by one of the boys who supervises her crew of fabric cutters. Fixor, only two years older than her, had befriended her. She liked him because he reminded her of her brother, the older of the two. He has the same green eyes and dark curls. She feels comfortable around him, and even though he wants more, she likes him as a brother. This particular party was the third one she had worked at and Fixor was working with her that night.

"Keep your eyes peeled tonight. Apparently, a special guest is coming, and this could cause some chaos."

"Chaos as in fighting?" she asks as her eyes scan the room, "what am I supposed to be looking out for Fixor?"

"What I mean is this special guest is so high up in the ranks of The Enforcers, it will cause a riot of people wanting to be near him."

"Who is it?"

"I don't know, I was just told to be extra vigilant tonight. This is going to be a very different party."

And he was right. The minute Thadd walked into the bunker the whole area erupted in applause and people whistled and cheered. The cheers were so loud the music faded into the distance. Leyna wasn't able to take her eyes off him. She had to try extremely hard not to make eye contact, keeping her head down was not easy when someone as famous as the High Priest Enforcer's son asks for a drink.

At the end of the night, Thadd was by her side asking her questions as she cleaned the tables.

Chapter 2

Leyna

She hears voices. There must be other prisoners now. She had been on her own in this prison for the last three months. There are others on Arisis who are resisting Dawa and Zenac's rule. This pleases her.

Eween, another vexperson she had befriended before being sent to prison, was incarcerated for decrying how slowly things were moving on Arisis. He had the same ideals as Leyna. He believed there were so many more people to be rescued on Earth, why had Dawa and Zenac closed their mission again? When he tried to form a movement by speaking out, he had been quickly shut down and imprisoned. Some of his followers were in this prison as well. Eween and Leyna have formed an alliance, the two of them want the same thing, to be back on Earth to overthrow The Enforcers. But first, they must escape this prison.

They are sitting in the break room. This is where prisoners are allowed for an hour a day to eat, read, play board games and talk amongst themselves. "Has she been to see you again?"

"No, Dawa doesn't visit as often now. She sends her lackey,

Anorea. She's one of Dawa's commandos. Anorea believes I am reha-bilitated as much as Dawa does. I have gained their trust.

We are not far from succeeding Eween." Her voice rises slightly with excitement.

"That's good to hear but keep your voice down. Now is not the time to sabotage our plan by allowing others to overhear our discussions."

"You're right. But I'm already seeing it, it's so close it's hard not to be excited." They have been planning for the last year and every detail is imprinted in both their minds.

"When are you being visited by Anorea again?"

"In two days. I think this is the time to do it, I have the serum."

"Yes, okay. We are ready but please be careful. Only give her a few drops, we need some for the guards as well."

"I know. I have kept it safe ever since I was brought back to my cell from the infirmary. Being ill has turned out to be advantageous for our cause."

The bell chimes. It's time to return to their cells. She gives Eween a nod, "Two days and our escape will happen."

Back in her cell, Leyna goes over their plan in her head. She is a trusted prisoner and the guards treat her well because she has not given them reasons to do otherwise. She has listened and assisted in programs such as teaching other prisoners to read, write, and most importantly, draw, which is her main passion. Dawa, as part of her rehab initiative program designed these lessons. Dawa's dream is to have the prison empty, which is why she participates in the program herself whenever possible.

Leyna respects a leader who places priority in the welfare of their people. Dawa is a good leader, but Leyna will take her down anyway. The High Priest will be first, and once she deals with him, she will deal with Dawa and Zenac. They murdered Thadd as much as his own father did. Revenge will be hers. Thadd's memory will not be forgotten. With Eween by her side, she will assassinate the High

Priest and put in place the plans she and Thadd had discussed five years ago.

An army of recruits will be easy. Once back on Earth, they will spread the word of ending The Enforcers rule, to restore some dignity back into everyone's lives. Dawa and Zenac started a revolution, but running away to another planet doesn't solve the problems for those left on Earth. Arisis is a planet for a select few, what about those millions left on Earth? Are they to live under The Enforcers' sadistic rule forever?

Chapter 3

Dawa

She is in her office at Parliament Row where all parliamentary and legal offices are housed. Standing, she peers out of the floor to ceiling window, admiring Lake Ilquarra. The salt levels of the lake are three times that of lakes the same size on Earth. They have developed a process of clearing the salt, giving them fresh water. Because of this, the water level is now low and rain has been infrequent. This worries her as they have established a community on this planet, but without clean, fresh water they will perish. She and Zenac knew there would be issues with Arisis, both with the atmosphere and water. People are only able to stay outdoors for two hours a day. A day on Arisis is twenty-six hours with twelve of those hours being daylight. The best time to be outdoors without their special helmets is early morning. This is Dawa's favourite time of the day, her body relishes the fresh air and this makes her feel like she is back on Earth. They can breathe without a helmet at this time, but later the atmosphere thins. No one complains about wearing the helmets, but Dawa likes the freedom of being without one.

The water problem is a bigger issue. At the moment the only ones who know about it are Dawa, Zenac and the Ten Luminaries. There is no need to alarm the other fifty thousand residents yet. Unfortunately, because of the issues on Arisis, they had to stop their rescue missions to Earth. Until they know whether this water issue is long term, they are not able to house any more people from Earth on this planet.

They know of many people on Earth who are desperate to come and live here. Arisis is paradise compared to Earth's living standards. Dawa and Zenac have allowed their people to work and prosper. Technology is thriving, food is abundant and their monetary system, the Loope card, is much simpler than the Licdan that is used on Earth. The Licdan currency was used globally before The Enforcers took power. As a currency it worked well, there were no issues with currency exchange fees. The problem with this currency was the convoluted tax system attached to it. Each country had its own way of dealing with taxes so there were different tax rates depending on where you lived. On Arisis there is no such problem, everyone is taxed at the same rate.

This has allowed the whole population to prosper and be on the same level. The harder you work, the more points on your card. And working harder did not mean more taxes. This has allowed the mood of the people on Arisis to be one of contentment, everyone is living in harmony. Dawa is pleased with how they have all settled into their new lives.

Zenac is overseeing this meeting. They are all seated in the Ovalaz Luminary Room on Arisis. This room is larger than the one on Xenure Station and they only use that one if they want to discuss serious issues with only the twelve of them present. This meeting has their assistants and their ten commandos also present because it's an important one. Zenac is revealing the possible water issue to everyone and discussing their course of action. He wants their input; this is to be an ideas forum.

"So, you will see from this meteorological forecast of the next five years, Arisis will not receive the amount of rainfall we require. For those of us who do live here now, it will be sufficient as long as the forecast is correct. However, we will not be able to house any further refugees from Earth."

"How unfortunate. Our plan was to rescue everyone who wanted to leave Earth," says Luminary 1-Sheabz

"It is and if this forecast proves wrong, then this planet will no longer be viable for those of us who are already here."

"We have been discussing our options," says Dawa, "Zenac and I believe there are a few different ways of solving our water problem."

"That's right. We looked at the worst-case scenario – not enough water – and worked from there. With this option, we will need to look for another planet. I have been doing some research and will discuss this with some of you at another meeting. Next, we thought about how to ensure we have enough water for the long term. This would involve some type of transportation of water from other sources. The third option we discussed was to manipulate the atmosphere of Arisis to increase rainfall."

There were murmurs from the Luminaries as Sheabz speaks again, "Manipulating the atmosphere? I don't like this idea. It smacks of global warming and all sorts of things can go wrong. We learned that on Earth."

Many heads are nodding, and the faces of the Luminaries show concern.

"These are only some ideas Dawa and I discussed. We need more research and more meetings before any final decision is made. What I ask from all of you is to talk amongst yourselves and bring your ideas to our next meeting. Dawa's assistant will send the date and time. And Please remember, do not discuss this issue with anyone outside of this room, we do not want to cause alarm."

As everyone files out of the room, two Luminaries remain behind with Dawa and Zenac. They remain seated and Luminary 3-Xzackry starts the conversation again. "This is of grave concern. Our people trust us to keep them safe, they followed us believing in a better life."

"There will have to be many more discussions," adds Luminary 1-Sheabz.

"Father and Xzackry, we understand your concern," says Dawa, "but we have time. There is enough water for another three years, even if we receive no rain. Our meteorologists and scientists have confirmed this, we are not yet in any danger."

"This is the reason we called this meeting, to have an early start on a possible problem. If we receive more rain than forecast, then this water issue is not as dire as first thought."

"Zenac, you and I are responsible for us living on Arisis. We have to do everything in our power to keep everyone safe."

"We are all in this together now Father," Dawa interjects.

"Yes, you and Zenac formulated the original plan of escaping Earth to Xenure Station for us and the three hundred, but we now have fifty thousand people to watch over. Everyone that was in this room today has a responsibility to ensure everyone's safety. Let us discuss our ideas further at the next meeting."

"As you wish Dawa," says Luminary 1-Sheabz standing and kissing her cheek. He and Luminary 3-Xzackry leave the room, both smiling back at Dawa and Zenac as they exit.

They're both back in Dawa's office.

Zenac pours himself a drink. "Want one?"

She shakes her head, she wants a clear mind to tackle the work on her desk. Watching him as he remains quiet, staring out the window, she knows he is worried. They have done what they can for now, all of their top people know about the situation and they will work together to find a solution. The worst-case scenario is that they have to leave Arisis.

Zenac comes over to her and gives her a hug. Again, he is quiet and she knows by the look on his face he feels defeated. "Things are not so dire yet."

He bends to kiss her, "I know, but it would be nice to have a day where nothing major happens. I feel like we have been moving full blast since leaving Earth, my mind needs to slow down."

She cuddles closer into him, "You're right, we have. Try to think of all the good that has come from us leaving Earth. Our people are not complaining because they know their life here is better than they had on Earth."

Zenac nods and kisses her again. He leaves her without saying a word. He may seem to be a worldly leader who knows what people need, but deep down he is a complex man with a mind that won't shut off. She needs to stay close and keep him talking because the last thing she needs is for him to have a breakdown.

Chapter 4

Teegue

Sitting at the desk in his room, Teegue chats with his friends on his compupad. Next to him is his school cap with the logo of their school, Lakeside. They are discussing the actions of a group in their year at school and have been for two hours.

Kiane writes:

Do you blame them? Krosy and his cronies are stirring trouble. The tournament is for all of us to participate in.

Trisia writes:

That's right. He has no right to tell others not to play. Sport is for all of us, not only for those who are good at it.

Teegue writes:

Oh, I agree with both of you, but he says that a tournament should only be for the best players. He does have a point.

Kiane writes:

Well then it should be left to the sports coordinator to decide. Krosy should not be telling others, especially Braceon, what they can and can't do.

Teegue writes:

Braceon is a good player but his friend Krosy is better. I'll discuss things with the coordinator, we don't want Braceon and Krosy to become too heated over this. See you both in the morning.

He shuts his compupad then moves over to his bed. He places his head on his pillow with one arm behind his head. Krosy is a trouble-maker and needs to be controlled. He is a hothead, but he is one of their school's best football players and they need to harness that skill. The tournament is between their school and that of the other two schools, one of which is an all-girls school.

The game of football has been modified for the conditions on Arisis. The eighty-minute game they played on Earth is now only forty-minutes. With the thinner air on this planet, even the young cannot run for too long. And wearing helmets to play is not an option. The ball is still round but has a sensor added. When the play-er's foot hits this sensor right on target, the ball will enter the goal. The skill of learning to hit the sensor in exactly the right spot is what makes the difference between a good player and a mediocre one. Teegue can hit the sensor ninety percent of the time. Krosy hits it every time.

His compupad pings. Hopping out of bed he checks who wants to talk to him this time. A message appears, Braxton's text is unrecognisable. His text isn't visible, so Teegue switches to audio, "What's happening with your screen? I can't see anything."

Braxton voice crackles through the microphone, "Oh shit, not again. The hologram screen has been glitchy, I'm going to have to send it for repair. I'll sort it out with the school IT department on Monday. Any further progress on the Krosy problem? I heard that idiot caused a fight today."

"News travels fast. I'll talk to the sports coordinator and ask him to diffuse the problem. Unfortunately, we need Krosy."

"He's a good player. Not very well liked but everyone appreciates the fact he can play. Anyway, I wish you luck with the coordinator, the tournament is only a month away."

"Krosy has to pull his head in and focus on helping our school win the tournament. Making enemies in his own team is just stupid. Goodnight Brax, see you in the morning."

Braxton is the best player in his division and Aria is as good as Teegue. He wishes he could recruit them and get rid of Krosy, but the divisions are all set. Aria could play in his team, she is old enough, but Braxton is still too young. An idea comes to mind, maybe Braxton can play in his team for the Tournament? He will speak with the sports coordinator, this idea might give them the inaugural cup.

He hops into bed again, this time to sleep. When he looks at the time on his phone, he's surprised to see it's almost midnight. He will struggle to wake at six in the morning.

Chapter 5

Zenac

He is in the kitchen and watches as Teegue drags himself towards the bench. "Up late again?"

"I was discussing the Krosy issue with Kiane and Trisia last night. He caused a fight yesterday."

"Hmm, we heard about all this from Braxton," says Dawa. Braxton and Aria are already eating their breakfast on the other side of the bench.

"Can't keep anything secret in this place, can we!" Teegue scowls at Braxton.

"What secret? Everyone knows, it's all everyone is talking about since it happened."

"Teegue you need to conserve your energy for the tournament. Maybe not so many late nights from now on."

"Yes Dad," he says with exasperation.

Zenac knows that telling Teegue to stay off his compupad is probably useless. He's old enough to know what is good for him. He watches as Teegue wolfs down his eggs and by the look on his face, Zenac is sure he is going to be in a bad mood all day.

After breakfast, Zenac kisses them all goodbye. Standing at the front door, he says, "Enjoy your day everyone." He then turns to Dawa, "I'll be at the office as soon as I deal with the issues relating to our latest rocket."

Dawa looks towards Zenac and nods her acknowledgement. He appreciates her not saying anything. This rocket is still top secret. It is the craft they will use to find another planet as well as rescue more refugees. Whether they continue living on Arisis or find somewhere else, there are still people on Earth who want to join them. The Enforcers have added stricter rules since their departure to Xenure Station. The people left on Earth are being made to pay for the escapees succeeding in their mission. The High Priest has raised taxes and monitors the movement of all his citizens. Zenac vows to rescue everyone who has been left behind.

As he waits for his family to leave, he takes in his surroundings. This planet is serving them well and is greener than when they arrived. The seeds they brought with them from Earth include some bush and tree varieties. These have adapted to the thinner air. Whether these improve the quality of the air is yet to be seen. He turns and heads for his car, he has more important things to deal with today.

Commando1-Zaydin comes up towards him as he arrives at the Spacedrome. "I have good news. The problem we had yesterday is not as serious as we first thought."

"That's good to hear, Zaydin. Tell me more as we walk." She continues telling him the o-ring seal problem has been corrected. He is impressed with Zaydin, he knew his instincts were right when he promoted her to the Commando1 post. She is proving to be very valuable as the Head Production Coordinator on this rocket project. There is not much she misses, keeping him well informed. This makes his job easier, and to Dawa's delight, he does worry less.

As they reach the hundred-metre craft, still only a prototype, he sees the crew working on it are in a better mood than yesterday.

"Good morning. I'm happy to hear you found a solution. Now, is it possible to have more than one of these built if necessary?"

"We need to have this one right first," laughs Commando2-Ringax who is overseeing the whole project, "But yes, once we do, we can build as many as we need."

"We need another one the same size. These will be the ones used for rescue missions to Earth. Then we will need smaller versions for other missions, possibly twelve. Do you see any problems, Ringax?"

"Not at this stage Zenac. You will be the first to know if we do. As I said, once we have this one working the others will follow."

"This is all good news. All of you keep up the good work," he says as he walks out of the hangar leaving his commandos and their crew to their duties. As he drives towards Lake Ilquarra and his office, he thinks about how far they have come in the five years since they left Earth. They have saved many, found a new home, and escaped a draconian society ruled by sadistic leaders. So many did not believe they would achieve their goal, but they have, and they are thriving. His goal now is to keep the people of Arisis safe and happy, one he and Dawa seem to be achieving.

Chapter 6

Leyna

The break room is empty except for her and Eween. They still have a few minutes before returning to their cells. The room is a bland space with metal chairs and tables, no windows and one patrolled door made of steel. It's always icy cold in here, which is probably on purpose so inmates don't want to linger. She rubs her hands between her thighs.

"Are you sure you are ready? We can wait. I'd rather be more prepared than risk us failing."

"Eween, we have been planning this for a long time. I know I'm ready. Are you with me or not?"

"Of course I am. Then it is settled. Tomorrow morning..."

"Hey, you two. Break time's over," yells the security guard interrupting their conversation.

They both nod to each other and obey the guard. All the inmates that were in the room with them have already left.

Back in her cell, Leyna goes over the plan in her head. Although she isn't familiar with where they will board the ship, Eween lived as a free man on Arisis for a year before being thrown in prison. He will lead the way. Right now, she needs to sleep, they have an early start in the morning.

She is awake long before she needs to be. Adrenaline is coursing through her body as she again recites the plan in her mind. She has the benzobutyric acid oil ready for the guards. There is enough in the vial to knock out four of them. Eween has two knives he stole from when he was on kitchen duty. Cell checks are infrequent and not thorough, so it had been easy to keep these items hidden. One of the knives was used to fashion a place to keep the vial safe. They had crafted a hole near the window, just large enough for the vial to fit. Guards never checked up there. Eween had told her the knives were in a hole behind the cistern. She had been worried about how he was going to keep them hidden. One was a carving knife. "It took a week for me to make a large enough hole, but the carving knife was big enough for the job," Eween had told her. They made a good team. Eween is as passionate about returning to Earth as she is, they have this as a common goal.

Stretching her limbs, she gets up and begins her exercises. Half an hour every morning was a ritual she had begun from the day she was placed in prison. Keeping up her fitness had been essential because this escape was always going to happen. As she finishes her routine, she then proceeds to smash her elbow into the wall. She hits it hard enough to bring out a bruise but it's enough for her to need a guard.

"What happened?" asks the guard, "and what is going on this morning? Eween has cut his hand by accident too."

"I was exercising and felt dizzy. Next thing I know I'm on the floor and in pain," says Leyna. As he is examining her arm, she brings her leg up and smashes it into his groin. He lets out a powerful grunt falling to the floor. She takes the vial and drips two drops into his mouth. His groaning stops after a few minutes. He remains collapsed on the floor.

Eween is at her door. "Let's go before other guards notice. Follow me," he says handing her the smaller knife then she notices the gun.

"You managed to steal a gun as well?"

"Sure did. It was sitting in his holster begging to be taken."

Footsteps are coming closer. They hear guards yelling. "Close all the exits. They're still here. Capture them and bring them back to me."

"Leyna, go up the stairs. From there you can come down the fire stairs at the back of this block."

"What about you?"

"I'm going to cause a distraction. You go now! I'll catch up with you at the fence."

"But... we should stay together."

"I'm going to be fine. Now stop wasting time."

She listens to him although this wasn't part of the plan. Why has he changed the plan without consulting her? She hears gunshots and yelling as she runs up to the top floor.

"Stop. What are you doing here?" asks a guard

"Oh, good," she looks at the guard trying not to show how scared she is. She feels like a deer caught in the headlights. "You can help me. I'm lost. I was headed to the infirmary, but I don't remember where it is," she tells the guard, showing him her bruised elbow.

"Why are you on your own?" asks the guard with suspicion.

"I thought I could find it on my own. This early in the morning I didn't want to bother anyone."

With his hand on his holster, he comes close to her. Her arm is up hitting his neck before he knows what is happening. A groan and he's down. Two drops in his mouth and she knows he'll still be out when Eween arrives up here. She darts off to the fire stairs, hoping Eween is not in trouble. The fire stairs are empty, and she is down the three floors and outside in only a few minutes. She can hear commotion from inside, so she runs to the designated spot at the fence. Her heart is pounding when she hears the sirens. Where is Eween? More guards will be out looking for them, they have all been alerted.

She crawls under the fence and finds their backpacks. Taking out her clothes she discards the prison overalls. With fumbling fingers she ties her hair into a bun then places a cap over it. Eween had better show up soon, she knows the longer she remains here, the higher the chance of being caught. She has to believe he's on his way because they're in this together. Without him how is she going to find the Spacedrome?

The sun is beginning to rise. This is becoming too dangerous. She is vulnerable in daylight. *Come on Eween, where are you?* She scans the area hoping to see him running towards her. Then, she sees two guards scouting the stairs. It's her turn to cause a distraction. Picking up some rocks, she hurls them through the bush hoping they go far enough away from her. The guards turn and run towards the noise but stay on the prison side of the fence. She decides to go further into the bush and finds a large tree. Climbing it with both backpacks, she sits on a branch out of breath and waits.

After half an hour she sees him. He's running towards the fence. She can see him from her vantage point. Climbing down without the backpacks, she runs towards him. He is limping.

"Eween, oh no! You're hurt."

"I'm okay. The other two are worse off than I am. Come on, let's go. Someone is waiting to take us to the Spacedrome."

"What? Who? How did you get a message to someone else?"

"Stop asking so many questions. I managed to contact a friend and she's waiting for us. Now let's go."

"Umm, alright. The backpacks are still up in the tree. I'll get them. You had better get changed."

"No time. There are more guards out looking for us. I'll change in the CMPV."

"Your friend was able to organise a People Vehicle. She must know someone high up."

"She is someone high up. Now, help me tighten this tourniquet around my leg so I don't bleed to death."

Leyna dutifully does as she is told. Her heart has only just stopped banging in her chest, she thought she was going to have to do all this alone until Eween finally showed up.

Chapter 7

Leyna

The CMPV is waiting for them. Eween introduces her to Anorea, a woman twice her height with rippling muscles gleaming with sweat.

"Get in. The Salverz is ready for you."

"The Salverz? We're taking that one?"

"Leyna, I had to change much of the plan without telling you. After I was able to contact Anorea, she kindly offered to help us achieve a better outcome. Besides, why bother taking a rocket? It will take longer."

"That's right, the Salverz will have you on Earth in half the time. There are many of us who want to return, some are waiting for you two. They are coming with you."

Leyna is stunned. This was supposed to be their mission. Only the two of them were to know about this. Less chance of error, less chance of being detected. "I appreciate your help Anorea," she says taking in her stature, "but Eween and I agreed to only the two of us going. We don't want to put other lives at risk. The High Priest Enforcer is mine to take, I won't need anyone else to help me."

"Leyna, be reasonable. Do you really think you can penetrate the fortress he lives in on your own? We can do with some help with this and these people want to help."

She glares at him. How dare he make decisions without consulting her? This escape, the whole mission – it is all her idea. "We have much to discuss, Eween but right now we need to fix your leg. Anorea, do you have medical supplies?"

"Yes, and I have stocked the Salverz with essentials too."

"Good. Get me the supplies. Eween, I'll clean up and bandage your leg. And your hand too, how is that cut feeling?"

"It's nothing. Just a scratch really. It bled only enough for me to attract the guard's attention before I killed him."

She attends to his leg as Anorea fires up the CMPV and then Leyna realises who Anorea is – she's one of Dawa and Zenac's most trusted commandos. She is Commando5-Anorea. Only five places away from being the top commando. Eween does have friends in high places. A disturbing thought passes through her mind, *is she trustworthy?* And as quickly as the thought popped out, it disappears. Only time will tell.

They arrive at the Spacedrome and go to one of the hangars towards the back. With Anorea escorting them, no one asks questions. She and Eween look like any other personnel inspecting the spacecraft, it's a daily occurrence here.

She looks up at the Salverz. "What about the shield? Is it still working? We don't want to be detected entering Earth's atmosphere."

"It has been fixed. This is the reason Anorea suggested we take it. The newer spacecraft are not meant to travel as far as Earth. We would have been detected long before reaching Earth."

"Why did you not discuss these changes with me? Don't you trust me, Eween?"

"Things happened so fast. I only managed to contact Anorea two days ago and I wanted to be sure it was actually going to happen before I told you. Your plan was good, but this one is better."

She has to give him that. Without Anorea's help, they would have struggled to get to the Spacedrome safely. With Eween hurt, he would have slowed them down and now they had no time to waste.

"Commando5, you're required at Hangar 1. Teegue is ready for his lesson."

"Thank you Fletchar, I'll be there soon," Anorea answers Commando9. "I must leave you now, duty calls. The crew awaits you and I wish you much luck. I look forward to hearing the news we all desperately want to hear, that of the High Priest Enforcer being dead." She salutes them and leaves them standing ready to board.

She is at the controls, her fingers tingling as she runs them over the screens. Eween has taught her some flying techniques, but he doesn't seem concerned, the Salverz can fly itself if need be. They left as soon as everything was ready, in silent mode. The shield protected them; detection from Arisis is impossible. She is thankful security on Arisis is lax, they had no reason to fear an attack, nor would anyone think that someone would steal the Salverz to return to Earth. Not while The Enforcers are still in power. Someone stealing a ship was ludicrous, but then not everyone has the motivation that Leyna is carrying with her.

"Right, we are out of the atmosphere of Arisis. It should be all smooth from now on. In five days and ten hours we will be back on Earth." Eween announces this with pride.

She has forgiven him for taking over because his plan worked. Her plan was good, but having the help Eween was able to secure, well... she couldn't fault it. When you have someone in the know everything is easier. She should have known he had enlisted Anorea to help us, she was at the prison often enough for him to gain her trust.

"We'll be landing in the Sahara then make our way to what was once Morocco. From there we head to the High Priest's fortress in Vatican City."

Leyna is looking forward to being home. She was born to the south of the Vatican Library and knows the area well. She frequented the library on many school excursions and then as a university student. She remembers the smell of the books and the organised space, each book belonging in its space on the shelf. Much of the history she knows was learnt in this vast library. How she hopes The Enforcers have not harmed anything in the library, it would be a tragedy if the tomes held within its walls were destroyed.

Vatican City is the only part of Italy that remains intact from the 20-year war. The Enforcers claimed it as their own, along with all the riches that came with it. There is no way of knowing the value of everything that is contained within the Vatican walls. This is the only place books and scriptures survived and the only place where gold, art and antiquities are kept. There are rumours that the scriptures are from many religions, not only Catholic, but no one has been inside to confirm these rumours.

The Enforcers rule in strict, archiac ways. They are following the old testaments because hangings, whippings and beheadings are not uncommon. All Leyna wants is for the world to be back to how things were before the war. In fact, Arisis is close to how things were; Dawa and Zenac are managing their people with care and good leadership. Their people are happy even though many miss Earth. Leyna wants Earth to be her home again, this is where all her memories are. This is where she met Thadd.

Chapter 8

2270

Earth

Thadd

After arguing with his father for two hours, Thadd is out drinking with two friends. He had to leave his father's rooms before something drastic happened. Being the son of the High Priest Enforcer has many shortcomings, and he is sick of being treated like a child. Always being told what to do, what to say, what to think. He has ideas of how to lead the people that he relayed to his father and The Enforcers, all of which have gone unheeded.

Nothing. All his ideas have amounted to nothing. Now, at twenty-five, he is restless and wants his voice heard. He wants a say in how the world is run. His father refuses to listen and tells him to be patient and wait for his time. He doesn't know what is worse, the waiting or the not being heard. With his vodka shot in hand he raises his glass, "To the future," he says clinking glasses with his friends.

"To our future," they reply in unison.

Thadd, along with Fixor and Leyna are devising a plan to overthrow The Enforcers. They are doing this for the young, the ones who want more power to bring prosperity and make life easier for humans again. Thadd's view of leadership does not align with that of his father. People fear his father and the twelve Enforcers. What is the point of being a leader if you are not bringing the best out in your people? No, Thadd has a grander view of how to lead, he needs to topple his father's rule and show the people what a leader should be like.

"Do we have the numbers to do this?"

"Yes, Fixor. I have five thousand followers who I keep in touch with and all are ready to fight with us. Add yours and Leyna's followers and our army is doubled."

"Thadd, are you sure you want to go against your father? He is untouchable with the twelve Enforcers protecting him. What makes you think we have enough power to penetrate their security?"

"Leyna, I have learned many lessons from my futile attempts in the past. Talking does nothing because my father will never see my point of view. He sees me as a child and one that has to listen to him." He notices she doesn't seem convinced and understands her concerns because of his previous failures. However, this time he will not fail. There is a stirring within him, it grows stronger every day and with his followers he feels their determination too. This spurs him on.

They are at her apartment. He wonders how anyone can live in such small quarters. The kitchen has a portable gas cooker, a bar fridge and one sink. Two cupboards under the sink finish the kitchen area. Leyna has a chair and a shelf where she eats, although she has told him she rarely cooks at home. The next room has a single bed with a side table and two shelves. The bathroom is off this room and it has a one-person shower, toilet and a sink where you can barely wash your hands. He hasn't heard her complain, she says she is happy to have a roof over her head. In comparison, he lives in a palace. But he feels more trapped and confined there than he does here.

She hands him a beer and he doesn't ask where she was able to purchase it. Alcohol is prohibited unless it is bought and consumed in licensed premises. Even these are limited to designated areas. He takes a gulp of the cool liquid. It washes over him and he feels calm and happy to be with Leyna.

"I didn't mean to dismiss you earlier. I do understand your concerns. What we are proposing is risky and dangerous."

"Not to mention crazy. Thadd, I don't want anything to happen to you, I... well I think I have fallen for you."

His face can't hide the shame he is feeling. "Leyna, I have feelings for you too. I want you by my side and once we overthrow my father, we can be together." He holds her in his arms and kisses her forehead.

"Then you do feel the same. I thought you might think of me as below you."

"Don't! Please don't ever think that. I know there is hierarchy in our world right now, but this is one of the things I hope to change. The people who have no control over their own lives, like you and other vexes, will have the resources to change this if they wish. You are already doing this by working your way out of poverty."

"More resources would be good. It is a struggle living as a vexperson. I'm more determined than many not to stay living this way," she says, indicating with her hand her measly surroundings.

He remains quiet. How can he comment when his world is so different to hers? He has no idea what it feels like to go hungry, to have no money nor to have someone to do things for him. Feelings rise in him he has never felt before. This woman, five years his senior, has taken his heart and flipped it. He cannot imagine his life without her in it.

The night they met he could not keep his eyes wandering over to her as she worked. Her black hair pulled back in a severe tail high on her head, green eyes that flicked around to everyone who called for a drink. Her black uniform, tight against her buttocks, so sexy compared to the sacks vexes usually wear. He knew then that Leyna was different to any other women he had dated.

"What? Why are you looking at me like that?"

"You're beautiful and I want you," he says, taking her into his arms again. He sucks in her smell, a mix of sweat, cheap perfume and garlic from the chicken they had eaten. To him it is the sweetest smell, the smell of the woman he loves.

Chapter 9

Eween

They are sweltering. Their supplies are low, and they need to move quickly. This fetid heat is slowing them down. No one is talking to conserve energy but there is another reason for the silence. The anger at the mistake of landing in the wrong place is festering. Eween had managed to calm everyone by asking them to focus on their goal.

He is disappointed. How was he to know the Salverz had a guidance system requiring an update? He is in one of the five CMPVs finding their way to the tunnels. Once they find them, some of his team will return the CMPVs to bring the others to the tunnels.

He tries to keep positive; they are on Earth and have arrived undetected. This is important even though they have still further to travel to their destination. They landed three hours south of where they needed to be. The Sahara Desert is vast, hot and inhospitable. Being this far from the tunnels where munitions were kept during the 20-year war is disastrous. It means more time and more resources are needed to reach The Vatican.

Their water supplies are being rationed. He hopes they have enough to make it to the munition's depot. There they will find more supplies and the ammunition they will need to take The Vatican. This mission is dangerous enough without this problem giving him more headaches. Why had he not checked the Salverz before departure. When he had mentioned this to Leyna she told him he was being too hard on himself. Besides, there was no time to check anything, they needed to escape before the authorities found them. Zenac had begun the hunt to find the escapees, they had no choice but to leave when they did.

"Eween, do you mind if I speak? I know you're trying to focus on driving," asks Leyna.

"If you're going to ask me if we're going to make it, I can't answer that question."

"No, I wanted to say thanks for seeing us this far and to tell you not to give up. Once we arrive at the tunnels we can restock, refuel and after a short break, head to our final destination."

He stares out of the front windscreen at the vastness ahead of them and hopes her enthusiasm rubs off on him. Leyna is a woman on a mission, so entrenched is her desire to avenge Thadd's death, sometimes it scares him how much she wants to succeed. Having said that, he admires her tenacity. "I'm keeping as positive as I'm able. Failing being hit by a sandstorm, we might make it. All we can do is keep moving."

"We cannot fail Eween, it is not an option," she says. placing her hand on his shoulder. Her smile and raised eyebrow reassure him.

How did he arrive here? A year ago, he was barely managing to eke out a living and now he is heading a mission to overthrow the man who runs the world. Someone like him who had no prospects now might be part of something big, he will finally have a place in the world. Leyna is right, there is no other option.

Eween was born to a single mother who had two other children already. She couldn't feed the children she already had let alone feed him as well. She left him on a doorstep with a note asking someone to look after him. The man who took him in was as destitute as his mother, but he did look after him until he was eight years old. This was when Todfa, the man he called his father, told Eween he was dying. Cancer took him a few months later. Eween was on his own with no idea what he was going to do.

The spot they lived in, a tiny space above a dilapidated shop, was rented to a couple, and she was pregnant. *No*, they told the agent, they did not want to take Eween. They were already wondering how to feed themselves with another child on the way. This was when Eween packed his few belongings, was given a sandwich and some cookies by the pregnant lady, who sent him on his way wishing him luck.

The next ten years of his life he scrounged around the streets living with a gang of boys and girls in the same situation as him. They dabbled in stealing food, doing drugs when they could find them, and keeping each other's backs. They were the closest thing he had known to having a family. It was at eighteen-years-old when things began to change and the direction of his life led him to where he is now.

Chapter 10

Dawa

Teegue, Aria and Braxton are dragging the chain. "Will you hurry up, I have an important meeting this morning. What is going on with you three?"

"Yeah, we're coming," drawls Teegue.

She is worried about him. He spends too much time alone each night in his room on his compupad. They have argued many times about this with Teegue usually screaming about her suffocating him and storming off back to his room. No doubt venting to his friends about his nagging mother. When does parenting stop being so hard? Zenac is also concerned, but he did say Teegue is a teenage boy, it's normal for some rebellion at this age.

Zenac was right about the teen years, but having Teegue speak to her with disrespect is not something Dawa wants to endure. Tonight, she will sit her three children down with Zenac and herself to discuss a few issues that have been bothering her.

The last thing Dawa wanted after a long, hard day of meetings was to argue with Teegue. "Will you please sit and listen for a few more minutes," she asks Teegue, trying to keep the frustration out of her voice. They have all been sitting at the dining table since they finished dinner. No one had been allowed to leave. Dawa had ignored their protests and began discussing issues that were concerning her. Although the main culprit was Teegue, she wanted to send a message to Aria and Braxton as well.

The swearing had to stop, being locked away in their rooms for hours on end was neither healthy nor acceptable and they were to stop talking back. Being a parent is a thankless job and all parents navigate this task as best they can. Dawa draws some of her instincts from her own parents, but times have changed since she was a teenager. Not to mention they are living on a planet that is not conducive to children being outdoors. Apart from their sports and the short outdoor breaks at school, most of the time the children of Arisis are indoors. This is a source of frustration for many of the parents she and Zenac have spoken to.

Case in point is Teegue right now, refusing to place his butt back down on the chair. Zenac is standing with his hand on the back of the chair demanding he sit. His face stern, his threatening and ominous eyes scowl at Teegue. He is giving him an ultimatum without uttering a word. Teegue slips into the chair clasping his hands together. His eyes are down, and his cheeks are red with the teenage anger that comes with being forced to do as you're told. This is a tactic Zenac uses often when he wants someone to heed his warning. Dawa has witnessed Zenac use this skill over and over, it is one of the reasons he is a persuasive and admired leader. Teegue has much to learn from his father and he is yet to appreciate this fact.

Suddenly, Teegue is on his feet again and stares down his father with a stubbornness Dawa feels is becoming increasingly worse with each passing year. "I think I'm old enough to manage my own time, Father. You don't need to fret that I'm wasting away my youth. Now, are we done, I have homework to attend to and we have a maths exam tomorrow. I'd like to cram for that. I'm sure you appreciate how important it is that I study."

"Don't be so smug. It's this attitude that has brought you to this point. You are exasperating your mother and I with your moods, the way you leave your things lying around and... do you want me to continue? This is only a short list of annoying things you are doing."

Dawa intercedes, "Look, I think we've had enough discussion for one night. Teegue go and study. Your marks will reflect whether you are telling us the truth. Remember though, you will only hurt yourself if you don't do as you say. There is one thing I have to agree with your father though, this habit you have of leaving your things all over without any consideration of anyone else, has to stop. We will not tolerate sloppiness, it is a sign of a distracted mind."

Teegue walks away without commenting, grabbing his school bag on the way and throwing it over his shoulder with force.

"Well, I guess that's a start, one less item to be tidied," says Dawa. "Do you two have homework as well?" Both Aria and Braxton nod and slip away quietly.

Dawa fills her glass with wine asking Zenac if he wants some. He nods, holding his glass towards her to be filled. "Is this the same boy who worried so much about me during their rescue? He did not want to leave my side for fear something terrible was going to happen. Now, he hardly speaks to me."

"As I said before, enough for tonight," Zenac says, placing his arm around her shoulders. Let's enjoy this wine together."

She brings her glass to his and they clink them together in salute to leaving parenting behind for a few blissful hours.

Chapter 11

Leyna

Leyna is awake. She has not been able to sleep for a few nights. They are making progress and will be at the tunnels in two days, notwithstanding any severe weather change. They have had long, hot days, which are preferable to wind and sandstorms. She hopes they will arrive before the Sahara's unpredictable weather becomes angry. Once they arrive, the tunnels will be their encampment for as long as they need. This is a mission she does not want to rush.

Her mind goes to how Eween had changed their plan without discussing things with her. She is not quite sure why this is making her uneasy, but the fact that a high-ranking commando like Commando5-Anorea helped them is bothering her. She will have to find out more about Eween's relationship with Anorea, how well does he know her? The vision that comes to her mind makes her snicker; short and stocky Eween under the bulk of Anorea who is gawking at him with lovelorn eyes. Leyna shakes her head, she laughs this off as an impossibility.

She also wonders why Anorea risked her position to help with their escape. As a trusted commando she had taken a huge risk. Still, why would anyone find out they had help? No one took any notice of them when Anorea walked them to the Salverz, they were dressed in the uniform everyone wore at the Spacedrome. No, Anorea took a risk, but it was a calculated one.

Leyna knows Eween is stressing about whether they will make it. If she is being honest, these negative thoughts are clouding her thoughts too. She is using every fibre of her being to be positive. She repeats over and over, "I will not fail you Thadd."

Her memories and love for Thadd are still strong. She feels his presence; a tingle on her arm, a shiver of excitement down her spine and the feel of his caresses. These will never leave her, and this is the reason she will keep his memory alive. The people of the world will know what it is he wanted for them. They will know he was not the tyrant that his father is. She will ensure Thadd will be remembered as a leader who wanted the best for his people and was willing to die to prove his worth.

Eween walks into her tent, "You're still in bed, aren't you feeling well?" He sits on the edge of her sleeping bag brushing away her hair from her forehead and checking for fever.

She admires her friend who is now her lover. They are a couple and one that will be a power that no one expects. Eween is not handsome in the same vein as Thadd, but he has qualities that endear him to her. His vision for the world and its people is as important to him as it is for her. For a man, he is short, but his stockiness and brilliant mind make him a force to be reckoned with. Eween can battle wits with any of The Enforcers, or even the High Priest Enforcer himself. His knowledge of history, engineering, politics, his intuitive nature and his passion to right wrongs, will place him in good stead when they do finally eradicate this current regime. The people will band together under their team of leaders to bring the world back from the brink, this dystopia will be an era soon forgotten.

"No, I'm fine," she says, kissing him lightly on the lips, "I've been going over a few things in my mind before starting the day."

"Well, you're needed now so I'll meet you outside, okay?"

"Give me five minutes, I have lots to discuss with you," she tells him, swinging her legs out of the sleeping bag and preparing to start her day.

She finds them at the communications tent. Their concerned faces unsettle her. Eween sits at his compupad with Breex and Donelle seated at their own screens. These are two of the people who volunteered to help them when they left Arisis. Breex is an engineer with mechanical and electrical skills and Donelle is a psychologist specialising in change management. Leyna was pleased to have them on the team, they need as much help as possible. And by the look on their faces, there is more trouble ahead.

"The three of you look anxious. Please don't be, we will arrive soon."

Eween nods to Breex who says, "Umm, you're right Leyna, we are on track to arrive at the munitions depot in the next two days. However, I sent out a reconnaissance crew late yesterday. The Enforcers have guards there, at least one hundred. They remained after the kidnapping of Dawa and Zenac's twins."

"That many? What a waste of troops. There is nothing much left to guard. The ammunition left is either outdated or broken. But I guess I'm not surprised, the High Priest Enforcer does not leave much to chance," Leyna says as she takes position at her console and checks the screen. "I see the weather is on our side."

"We have that advantage, there is no dust storm forecast, but our problem is not the weather. We need to discuss how to deal with the guards."

Donelle shifts in her seat talking directly to Leyna and Eween, "If I may make a suggestion?"

They both nod.

"The guards are sick of being out here and have asked to be redeployed. My contact within their ranks has said they are almost to the point of rebellion. We could take advantage of this weakness."

"And do what? Convince them to join us."

"Is that so far-fetched, Eween? They are a hundred disgruntled soldiers who have been left here with nothing to do and they are guarding nothing of importance. It would be easy for me to convince them they will fare better with us."

They remain quiet, each pondering the issue. Eween taps notes onto his compupad, Leyna keeps her eyes on the screen as Donelle and Breex await a response.

Leyna is the first to break the silence. "It would be preferable to us losing anyone through force. Do you propose we walk in and just talk to them?"

"If only it was that simple," says Donelle, "no, I suggest allowing me to ask my contact to start spreading the idea before we arrive. I can glean their reactions from him, then we make a decision – we bring them onboard with us or take the depot by force."

Eween clears his throat, looks at Leyna for confirmation then says, "It's risky Donelle, but I'm willing to take the risk. Without the element of a surprise attack, we might be placing ourselves on the back foot. However, there will be enough bloodshed when we arrive at The Vatican. Donelle and Breex, I give you permission to put this idea into action."

"I do have one concern," says Leyna, "the High Priest will notice the loss of one hundred of his troops. How do we keep this quiet?"

"You have a point," says Donelle, "I will ensure the commander keeps in touch with The Enforcers as if nothing has changed. Do you agree this might work better?"

Eween looks towards Leyna showing his acceptance. After a few minutes contemplating other issues that may occur, Leyna nods her head in confirmation and gives Eween a simpering grin that shows a twinge of concern.

Chapter 12

____

Zenac

He is in his chambers having arrived only minutes earlier when the red light on his desk flashes. "Trisear, round up the engineers and security staff. The commandos too. Tell them I will meet them at the Spacedrome meeting room in half an hour." This light only flashes during an emergency. There are strict rules for when it is to be used. There had better be a good reason it was pressed.

He is seated at the head of the table with his twelve engineers, security staff and the ten commandos. Taaz, the head of security who pressed the red light is explaining.

"I came in for my morning shift as usual. Went about deactivating the alarm system, switching on the network and noticed this when it finally booted up," he tells them as he presses play. They all watch as the security vision plays on the large screen behind Zenac.

"There's a break in the transmission. What caused that?"

"The network security system was overridden, someone

tampered with it. So, then I went to check on the spaceships and CMPVs. Zenac, there are several CMPVs missing as well as the Salverz."

Zenac looks from the screen towards Taaz, "Do you know how this happened? How could they override our security system?"

"They had some inside knowledge. This is the only way it's possible."

"Who would want to leave Arisis? Where have they gone?" asks Commando10-Kriska.

"There's more. We know who has left and we assume they are heading to Earth. Why take the Salverz if they're not? Leyna and Eween are the two inmates who escaped from prison two days ago. The prison guards have searched a wide area, there is no sign of them. Also, fifty others went with them."

"Two days ago? Why am I only hearing of this now?" asks Zenac with an anger rising through his body. "Who are these incompetent prison guards that did not alert us when they escaped?"

"I have not had time to contact the prison warden yet. I thought it best to alert you first," says Taaz.

Zenac, annoyed with this delay, presses the intercom, "Trisear, call the head prison warden and ask him to meet us at the Space-drome. Tell him we need him to explain his actions." He stands and walks towards the window. He will deal with the warden when he arrives. Placing his hand on his chin, he speculates, "Leyna. She is the prisoner who was involved with the kidnapping of my twins. She and Thadd were an item. I suspect she has a reason to return to Earth and it will involve the High Priest Enforcer. He sent his own son on a suicide mission to us at Xenure Station, the son who was Leyna's lover."

Kriska says, "We are dealing with two prison escapees and fifty others here. Leyna is not the only one who is disgruntled."

"You're right Kriska, we need to focus on why these people went with Leyna and Eween. Do we have a larger problem here on Arisis? Are there more people unhappy living here?" says Taaz.

Murmurs fill the room as Zenac replies, "We have a few issues to tackle. The warden will arrive soon. We need to hear from him first. Let's break for fifteen minutes, by then he will have arrived."

Zenac and Taaz are the only ones left in the room. Neither is talking, both musing over their own thoughts. Zenac stares out the window still angry with the prison warden for not disclosing what happened. Why did he wait? He has the authority to alert others, especially with something as important as an escape. The intercom buzzes, interrupting his thoughts. It's Trisear announcing that the prison warden is walking into the Spacedrome now. Zenac's team is filing back into the room as he takes his finger off the intercom.

Once everyone is settled and quiet, Taaz speaks to the warden, "You have some explaining to do. Why have you kept something as important as this security breach to yourself?"

Zenac watches on as the warden scans the room before he speaks. Does he have any allies here? Even though he is sitting at the opposite end of the table, Zenac can see the warden is uncomfortable. His stiff, upright stance and his clenched hands are signs he is nervous.

"We were confident of capturing the escapees. Scouring the grounds up as far as this Spacedrome took time. It was hours before I was informed that they had somehow disappeared. My officers felt it best to chase after them before alerting me. Our dogs found a scent up to this building, but then nothing."

"That still does not explain why I wasn't informed until now," says Zenac who is standing again with his hands on the table. His voice is loud yet has a calmness he doesn't feel.

The warden coughs and fidgets before answering. His voice is barely audible when he says, "I umm, my fellow wardens and I are... how do I put this? Umm, these are the first escapees since we arrived, so we wanted to keep things quiet until we knew for sure they were not to be found. We made this decision as a team. Unfortunately, in hindsight it was the wrong course of action. My apologies Zenac."

Zenac looks down at his hands. He doesn't speak for a few minutes, trying to decide what to do. Punish the warden for his lack of leadership and foresight? Does he fire the whole team of officers –

all twenty of them? He needs to discuss this with Dawa and The Luminaries. "Thank you for your honesty. Leave and return to the prison, I will be in contact soon." The warden leaves the room, but not before Zenac hears him whimper.

He sits down running his hands through his hair. "We will need another meeting. Everyone is to send their ideas to Trisear who will collate them into an agenda. We have now finished here until the next meeting at a date Trisear will organise. Thank you all for your time." He watches on as they all file out and when he is alone, he stands at the window again. *Well Leyna, we certainly underestimated you, didn't we?*

As he walks back into his office, he asks Trisear to come in with his compupad. "I'm going to throw ideas at you, please start an agenda for another meeting in seven days' time. The others who were at today's meeting will be sending you similar ideas. Add theirs to mine and distribute the agenda to everyone."

"You look concerned, is everything alright?"

"Two people escaped our prison and stole the Salverz, CMPVs and some of our people left with them. Right under our noses. Now, the first idea I wish to put forward is that we need another Salverz, a bigger and better one. How are we to save more people from Earth without it?"

"Why would people want to leave Arisis? I understand the prisoners wanting to escape, but others?"

"I know. After everything we have done, there are still people who are unhappy and dissatisfied. But never mind them, we have to work at building better spaceships along with the rockets we are developing."

Trisear doesn't answer, he concentrates on documenting Zenac's ideas and leaves when he has finished.

Zenac sits at his desk contemplating what lies ahead. How many people living on Arisis feel the same way as those who left? It's time to discuss this with Dawa and The Luminaries.

• • •

The Ovalaz Luminary Room II has everyone who needs to be there: Zenac, Dawa along with the Ten Luminaries and the commandos. Zenac peers out of the floor to ceiling window overlooking the lake.

They will not leave this room until everyone has signed off on the requisitions he requires. Also, they are to discuss how to deal with the warden and officers for their lack of judgement. As he turns, Luminary3-Xzackry stands. "These requisitions, are they necessary? This is not only a lot of parts, we will also need more manpower."

"Yes, they are necessary. We need to build enough space equipment to combat what may come our way. We have been complacent believing everyone on Arisis is happy to remain here and we are not prepared for an invasion." He watches on as some of The Luminaries nod in agreement. Some he knows had not thought of being invaded. "You have all read the report Trisear has placed in front of you. The plan is we will begin building another Salverz, which is to be named Vespira. This will be an upgrade of the Salverz, as you can see from the plans already drawn by our engineers. We will travel even further with this ship."

"You have also requisitioned another ten CMPVs, as well as more rockets. How far do you plan to go? We already have ten rockets being built."

"Xzackry, as your leader and along with Dawa and The Luminaries, we know what is required to keep our 50,000-strong population safe. You will source the parts because this is what we ask of you. We have our reasons and they are all for the good of everyone living on Arisis."

Luminary 1-Sheabz and Luminary 2-Tanjaz both applaud. The other Luminaries follow as Xrackry sits down. His defeated look dissipates into that of acceptance.

The meeting ends and they had not discussed the warden and any punishment but now Zenac felt this was a small issue compared to the requisitions, the warden will be pardoned.

Chapter 13

Dawa

Dawa and Zenac are heading towards the Ovalaz Luminary Room II. They are quiet, having already discussed what they believe to be the best option going forward. The water issue on Arisis is not yet at crisis level and they want to make sure it does not become any worse. This meeting with The Luminaries will shed some light on what they think about this option, or whether they have better ideas. As they walk in, The Luminaries are already seated as they all acknowledge their entrance.

"Thank you, Luminaries for meeting with us at such short notice. Also, so soon since our meeting with the Commandos. We, Zenac and I, feel this problem of fresh water is as important as the building of more space craft."

"The requisitions have been approved. This is progress and I have enlisted more manpower, both intellectual and technical, to produce what we need at record speed. The water issue was our only concern until the escape. Now we have two issues to deal with and it is good to have one under control. We do not have a problem building the new Vespira, the CMPVs and the extra ten rockets." Dawa is beaming the plans she and Zenac devised over the table. The Luminaries begin to see how important it is for them to find a solution to the water problem.

"Last time we spoke, you said we had enough water to last a few years. From what you are showing us here, we have less time."

"Sheabz, unfortunately it is the case. Our modelling was incorrect as the rain forecasting for Arisis is not as sophisticated as what we had on Earth. What we require from all of you is to digest this latest information and either agree to what we propose or suggest something better."

Sheabz nods and The Luminaries spend some time taking in what is in front of them.

Dawa asks Zenac to follow her over to the window. As she looks over to the lake, she says in a whisper, "It is clear from this vantage point we have less water than first thought. The lake is shrinking each day." It has been three months since they had good rainfall. It was only sufficient to raise the levels of the three lakes by an inch. This added another ten months to their total water use according to their meteorologists. At the most, the water would last eighteen months. Lake Ilquarra is the largest of the lakes and it looks fine to the untrained eye, but Dawa watches it every day and knows what is happening.

"I agree, Dawa. We can both see this lake from our offices. Let us give The Luminaries another few minutes before we make any final decisions."

She looks at him. He is the man she loves with all her heart. His dark brown eyes show concern and he is feeling the weight of current issues on his broad, toned shoulders. Coming through the ranks as a commando, Dawa met him when he was promoted to the rank of Commando1. As a young soldier, he fought valiantly with his troops during the 20-year war. So, at 27-years-old, he deserved the recognition of being the top commando. However, when The Enforcers came to power, all commandos were stripped of their rank and they were no different to the rest of the population. They were to do the bidding of The Enforcers. Ten years later, as a family and along with her father's help, they are now in power together. She trusts Zenac implicitly and they will overcome this hurdle the same way they have the others. Together.

Zenac is already at the table discussing their idea with The Luminaries. She smiles to herself knowing her trip down memory lane has to stop, the future of their planet is at stake.

"The rockets will be ready soon. I think we should send a crew out on at least two of them to search for water on nearby planets," says Xzackry, "this is a good plan that needs to be implemented quickly."

"I agree with him," says Sheabz with Luminary 2-Tanjaz also giving his approval.

Other Luminaries nod in agreement too.

"Good. We will test a rocket next week. If all goes well, we can deploy twenty men on two rockets. There are three planets near us they can explore."

Dawa and Zenac listen on as The Luminaries discuss the other areas of their plan. They have tweaked a few things, which improved the way water will be imported to Arisis. Pipes can be laid to pump fresh water to a station where rockets will be ready to bring tanks back to Arisis. These freight rockets will only need a pilot and co-pilot so weight can be kept to a minimum. The tanks will hold fifty thousand litres of water each.

The other part of the plan, to find another suitable planet will also go into action. The importing of water is an expense they cannot keep going for too long. However, it buys them time. They need to discover a more suitable planet and this extra time will help.

Chapter 14

Leyna

Donelle's plan to recruit The Enforcers' soldiers watching over the munitions' depot had worked. Her informant was correct in saying they were bored and uninterested in a mission that had no purpose. Why were they keeping watch over old ammunition no one was interested in? The one hundred soldiers agreed to come on board peacefully and give their allegiance to Leyna and Eween. They were also able to give information and suggestions about how to enter The Vatican without detection. Donelle ensured her contact kept this new allegiance from The Enforcers.

Leyna is lying on her front with her arm over Eween's chest as they lie together in her sleeping bag. The space is snug but she likes being this close to him. "I wasn't sure Donelle's idea would work. We've been given more than we bargained for."

Eween stretches and props himself on his arm looking down towards her, "Hmm, maybe we've been lucky this time, but there is more danger ahead. Let's not become complacent."

Giving him a light peck on his lips she says, "I know. We have been given a boost to our numbers, more information and have replenished our supplies, so I feel our troops are ready and able to do what they need. Entering the Vatican under stealth, a few of us at a time, will give us an edge. Donelle's idea to blend in as families and nomads who are passing through is brilliant. She has certainly been an asset to our mission."

"I agree. There is still much planning to do," he says moving closer, "But right now I have other plans."

She smiles, "Oh, now this is the sort of plan..." Eween's mouth is caressing hers before she can finish speaking. "Arrrh, yes," she moans as he moves down her body.

Leyna is walking through the main tunnel over to where Breex is working on what looks like a discarded weapon. "Is that what I think it is?"

"Good morning. Not many of these around anymore, I'm surprised to see one here. It is a Carbon Dioxide Laser with diamond windows and lasers. If I can have this working by the time we leave, we can target the Vatican efficiently. The beam is powerful enough to cut through block walls without any noise coming from the laser."

"Great Breex. There is more useful ammunition left here than we first thought. Take whatever time you need, all the weapons we take with us must work at their best."

"Understood Leyna," he says as he heads to find more tools.

She remains in the tunnel rummaging through the discarded weapons. These tunnels were here long before they were used as a munitions' depot. Nomad tribes and warriors built them in ancient times. The blocks were fashioned similar to the ones used for the pyramids. They were used as shelter from ravaging weather conditions and warring tribes. The positioning of them is perfect for hiding away. No one in their right mind would venture into the middle of the Sahara looking for tunnels that supposedly don't exist. There are many theories as to why they were built here. One is that it is where the blocks to build the great pyramids were formed. If this is the case, then why build it this far from Egypt? As Leyna keeps sifting through the rubble, she stops suddenly when she sees a uniform.

Her heart thumps with desire. It is Thadd's space uniform. His name is embroidered on the right-hand side. She had seen him wear this many times, but what is it doing here? Picking the jacket up gently, she puts it to her nose. "Achoo!" She rubs her nose, the dust having furled up into it. What did she expect? Did she really believe his smell would still be on the fabric? Slowly she collects the pants, shirt and belt as well. Under more discarded guns she finds shoes but is not sure they would be his so leaves them. She is not sure why she wants to keep the uniform other than the fact he is gone, and she needs something of his. With this uniform, she feels closer to him.

She walks out of the tunnel towards her tent where she places the uniform under her duffle. As she folds it, dog tags fall out of the shirt pocket. They are his dog tags. She clasps them lovingly to her heart. *Thadd you are watching over me.*

Chapter 15

2270

Earth

Thadd

He and Fixor are at the Bunker. They are discussing another illegal party with the owner.

"This one will be different, Shadear. I only want people to attend if they are willing to sign up for the mission. They will not be told what the mission is, we will only tell them it will benefit every human on Earth. Poverty will end, the social class system will fall, and people will again prosper if they put in the effort."

"Thadd, I admire your conviction. However, without knowing the reason, many will not want to attend. Should you not divulge the real reason?"

Fixor intervenes, "And risk someone going to the High Priest? If our plan is exposed, both Thadd and I are dead."

Thadd nods in agreement. The three of them remain quiet until

Shadear breaks the silence, "So be it. I will send out my informers. The date is set for next Friday."

"Thank you. Now Fixor and I will go and inform Leyna. She will tell her followers. All going well we should fill the Bunker with thousands of people ready for change," Thadd says and indicates to Fixor that they are leaving. Once outside, Fixor bids Thadd farewell telling him he will inform his followers.

Thadd heads back to his rooms. As he walks into his main bedroom, one of his father's whores is sitting on his bed. "Go, I have no need for your services."

She walks towards him, throwing off her robe. She runs her finger gently under his chin licking her lips, "Are you sure, the night is young."

This is the last thing on his mind right now. "I said go," he demands, pushing her away.

"As you wish sire," she says, picking up her robe and sashaying out of the bedroom.

He hears her opening the fridge and take something out before she leaves. Deciding to let her have whatever she stole, he has more than he needs. He won't bother reporting her. His father has a habit of sending one of his many whores to his room. When he was younger it was fun to play around with these meaningless women, occasionally he would have a few of them and ask Fixor to join them. That was when he had nothing on his mind, just a frivolous privileged kid with a lot of time on his hands. Right now, he wanted to think through what needs to be done before next Friday. He will go to see Leyna in the morning and discuss things with her further. She will be pleased with the progress he and Fixor have achieved.

Thadd is walking down the Great Hall when he sees her. She is dressed in her day clothes and looks younger than she did last night.

"Sire. Your father was curious to know why I was back in my quarters so soon last night. I told him you were not feeling well."

"Thank you but this was not necessary. I have told my father before that I will tell him if I want someone in my bed. Please do not worry yourself, I am able to handle my own father."

"Sire," she says, bowing her head and walking away from him.

As he walks towards the grand exit he thinks about the whore. Why would she make a point of telling him this? It's not the first time he has refused to sleep with one of them. He will keep an eye on this one because his shoulders prickle with uneasiness. Does she want something from him? He breaks out into a sprint towards Leyna's apartment trying to clear his head, he is probably reading too much into this thing with the whore.

"Good morning," she says, giving him a kiss.

"Hi, umm we need to discuss the plans for next Friday but first I need to speak to you about something that happened last night."

"Sure, are you okay?" she asks, sitting down while he paces.

"When I arrived in my rooms last night there was a whore in my bedroom. You know, the ones my father has on hand when he needs satisfying. Well, I sent her away."

She nods, everyone knows about the High Priest and his predilection for young women. His wife, Thadd's mother, knows all about them too, having her own selection of young men.

"I saw her this morning in the Great Hall and she told me Father was concerned she was back in her chambers early. Why would she make a point of telling me?"

Leyna twisted in the chair thinking before answering, "Is it a warning? Why would your father be concerned that you said no?"

"That's the thing, he wouldn't. She's not the first I have sent packing. I have no interest in casual sex, especially since meeting you."

She smiles towards him and rises from the chair. Placing her arms around his neck, she pecks his cheek, "Maybe keep an eye on her, she may be an asset or a hindrance. We'll find out when the time is right. But honestly, stop worrying about her."

"With the fact she spoke to me I am assuming she will be an asset. Now, we need to discuss more important issues." He continues with the agenda for Friday night. The security around this event has to be flawless because if the High Priest finds out their plan, both she and Thadd are dead.

"The extra security Fixor and I have organised will help. This time you will not fail."

"We must not fail. We are in this together. And I look forward to the day you and I are beside each other ruling a very different world." Leyna gives him a broad smile, her eyes sparkling, which confirms she is with him all the way.

The High Priest Enforcer will never accept her because a vexperson is below his family's status. He spends no time worrying about this because while his father has his women, he prefers the love of one good woman.

They are in the Bunker. There are no lights, no music is playing, and everyone is listening to Thadd. He has them in the palm of his hands. This audience of more than three thousand wants what he wants. He is pleased to see more people here than he had imagined. They all want a world where people are happier, can achieve more and are not subjected to the torments of a sick ruler.

"You all know I am as dissatisfied as you about how my father is ruling the world. This dystopian society of beatings; being sent to prison for minor offences, people disappearing if they speak up and a world with little economy to project us forward. This will come to an end and the social class system will also fall. Together we will all make it happen."

The crowd cheers and claps, some fist-punch the air.

"Ok, now you all know what to do. Each of you has the responsibility to recruit others who want this world to change. Once we are ten thousand strong, we will dethrone The High Priest Enforcer," says Fixor with his palms face down indicating them to calm down, "for now keep it down, we do not want to attract attention tonight."

As the crowd files out carefully, a few at a time, Thadd is more than pleased with the turnout. "There are many who are disgruntled Fixor, they turned up without even knowing what we have planned."

"People want something different. They are sick of being treated like animals and many of them know you are better than your father. They want to follow you, not him."

Thadd smiles at his friend and taking Leyna's hand they head towards the Bunker's back door. "Take care while going home tonight Fixor, we have unleashed the beast. We really don't know how many people who attended tonight are fully on our side."

Chapter 16

Leyna

Leyna and Eween are on the Salverz. Eween had asked the engineers to fix the issues and find a way to move it closer to the tunnels. They are discussing this when Breex walks onto the control deck and asks them to follow him, "I have good news. The Carbon Dioxide Laser is ready."

Leyna looks behind making sure no one is listening, there are a few engineers with them. Until everything is ready, she doesn't want others to hear their plans. Maybe she's paranoid but she wants to execute the plan with precision, nothing must stop this from happening.

"That is good news. Can we see it?" asks Eween.

"This is why I asked you to follow me. At this stage I left it in the same tunnel where I found it. We can move it into the storage bay on the Salverz after we've tested it."

"Ok, I don't have a problem with that. Lead the way to the CMPV," says Eween, indicating to Leyna and Breex to walk ahead of him.

They arrive at the tunnel and again Leyna checks behind them. No one is around so she indicates they can keep going, "How many engineers worked on this with you, Breex?"

"Just me. There is nothing too complicated about lasers as you both know. The light emitted by this one was only pulsing whereas we need the laser to be coherent so it will cut through large areas. I want the precision to be perfect. What I have done is made the laser stronger by narrowing its aim, which makes it faster as well."

They reach the laser and Eween is surprised by the size, "Oh, it's smaller than I thought. This is good, it will be easier to conceal."

"Yes. I thought it might be a problem as it may not have been powerful enough, but I was able to fix it to work better than the larger ones."

Leyna looks toward Eween and nods knowing he will agree with what she is about to say. "I'm impressed with what you have done and that you have kept this to yourself, Breex. If this laser were to fall into enemy hands, they could use it to destroy indiscriminately."

"Which is why I have kept this between the three of us. I have an idea where we can test it too. There are more underground tunnels, we can do the tests in one of those and only store the laser when we are satisfied it will work well." He picks up the laser and as they walk towards the smaller tunnel, Breex tells them how he sees this laser working on the Vatican walls. The size is a bonus, no one will see him smuggling it into the city. When they arrive at the tunnel both Leyna and Eween agree this is where the laser will be tested.

This tunnel is filled with discarded weapons, filing cabinets, desks and discarded computers and looks no different to the main tunnel. However, it is the walls they are interested in. Leyna asks, "Are you able to show us how it works now?"

"Yes, but first place these glasses on. The infrared light emitted by this laser is strong, I have done this deliberately."

They do as he asks and then wait while he makes some adjustments. Leyna pulls her shoulders back feeling such pride at how this mission is coming together. She is sure Thadd would be proud of her as well.

•   •   •

Back in the control area, it is only the two of them. She stretches because crouching in the tunnel for hours has made her body stiff and sore. "I liked what I saw Eween. The laser will serve us well."

"It will and I know we will put it to good use. Imagine, we can sneak out some valuables if we want," he says with a cheeky grin.

"Once we dispose of the High Priest and his henchmen the Vatican valuables will be ours and we can share the riches with the rest of the world. Do you want to keep some for yourself?"

"Why not? We're risking everything so I intend to keep something for myself. Who knows, I may want to share the spoils with my kids one day"

"It's good to see you in a joking mood," she says, moving towards him and pulling him close by his shirt collar, "shall we keep this good mood going?" She kisses his neck and he responds by pulling her onto the console. She feels the familiar flutter in her body as he savours it. She arches back bringing him with her, his mouth burrowing into her breasts. Her groans are deep and guttural and after a day that has shown her their plan will work, she drinks in his power. Eween is a force she needs next to her and together they are invincible.

A noise startles them. Someone is coming so they tidy themselves, both staring at their screens when an engineer comes onto the deck.

"We are ready to transport the Salverz towards the tunnels. Do you give us permission to do so?"

Eween looks up from his screen, "Of course, please go ahead. I've had enough of sleeping in tents."

The next morning, Leyna is sitting in front of her compupad when Eween and Breex come onto the control deck. She asks the two commandos sitting with them to please leave and thanks them as they do so. She waits as Eween and Breex take their seats.

"It's time to start."

"I know Eween. We have planned and waited for this moment. It's definitely time."

"A word of warning first," says Breex, "we need to start slow. If we all barrel into Vatican City together suspicions will be raised. Too fast and we are doomed to fail."

"I absolutely agree. Here is my plan timeline," she says as she deploys her screen and the hologram is in view, "as you can see, I propose we send our troops in as groups of a few families, some singles and others as nomads of say six? They will then survey the area for us and find safe havens."

"Still once safe havens are established let's not rush into this. Don't forget the security in the city is high and if one of us is captured, the whole plan is doomed."

"Understood Breex. We also need to train everyone up with the other weapons your team has worked on, this will take time."

"Yes Eween, I'll have the commandos start tomorrow. I suggest I go with the first of the troops with the laser concealed. Then I can test it in situ. We will take minimal other weapons. Once we establish our safety, then others can bring more with them."

Leyna is listening to them and wondering how much longer she has to wait. Her timeline shows an earlier start date, she is becoming frustrated. The training will take weeks. "So how much longer? I thought we would start sending the first people through by next week. And yes, I think it's a good idea that you go with the first lot."

"Have you not been listening to me?" says Breex exasperated, "we have to take this slow and I'm not risking sending anyone in before they are ready."

"How long?"

"Another month at least. We can start heading towards Morocco now, this way I can start training more troops while we are on the ground there."

Leyna nods, accepting his timing and shuts her compupad. Her timeline has been added to by one month, but for the good of everyone's safety she will listen to Breex. He walks towards the exit saying that things are moving as they should be.

Not fast enough for me. She sighs and Eween gives her a hug, "Be patient, Breex is right. Everyone has to be ready, we don't want to jeopardise anyone's safety."

Looking into his caring eyes she knows he is right.

Chapter 17

Teegue

Teegue, Aria and Braxton are sitting on the sideline. Teegue and Braxton's soccer match is next. Teegue managed to secure Braxton to his team by convincing their sports co-ordinator he would be an asset. It was bending the age rules, but it would be worth it. The inaugural Arisis Soccer Tournament started today and will run for the next week. Four teams will compete, these are the teams that qualified. Only the best players were chosen from each school and Krosy was also chosen. Teegue wonders how he will play without his friend Braecon protecting him on the field. These two are always together, but Braecon is an inferior player and didn't qualify. Now, with only four teams left, they are playing the best of the best. The four schools – Arisis East Public, Lakeside, Southwest Public and Northlakes – have all competed in the trials that led up to this tournament week. Teegue is becoming anxious, he just wants to be on the field.

"Did you hear about the prison breakout?" asks Aria.

"No, what happened?" asks Braxton looking at both his siblings. Teegue has a blank look on his face.

"I overheard Mum and Dad discussing it after dinner a few weeks ago. I thought you would have heard by now." When neither of her brothers answer she continues, "Apparently two prisoners escaped and ended up at the Spacedrome. They stole the Salverz, CMPVs and other equipment. They even took hostages. Dad thinks they are back on Earth by now."

"Really! How fascinating. Why would anyone want to go back there? Life here is much better."

"Who knows Braxton? Dad is upset about it all and I heard him say someone helped them and it must be someone high up in the ranks because not everyone has access to the storage facility at the Spacedrome."

"There's a traitor amongst us. Ooh, this is juicy."

"Another traitor, that's all we need," says Teegue, "we already had one. That Leyna woman, remember her Aria, the one who had us kidnapped?"

"How could I forget? And it was her, she is one of the prisoners who escaped."

"Oh wow, now this is news. I bet I know why she's gone back to Earth. I'm sure there are some people she wants to deal with. I wonder how many people know about this. Did Dad mention any more?"

"I think it's still a secret. Dad will probably want to know who the traitor is before this gets out. We had better keep this story amongst ourselves," says Aria as both the boys nod in agreement.

An announcement calling the four teams is sounded over the speakers. Teegue and Braxton head over to meet up with Krosy and the others in their team.

Dinner is a quiet affair. Dawa and Zenac look at Braxton who is shuffling his food around the plate. Teegue is also in a foul mood, it was his fault Braxton has a broken arm.

"Now come on you two, there is nothing that can be done. Teegue it was an accident, you didn't do it on purpose."

"Mother," he says, "I pushed Braxton over. I should have looked down and checked who was near me."

"And I should have called out," says Braxton, "we are both at fault."

"Boys eat your dinner. Braxton's arm will heal, and he will still be able to play soccer. There will be another tournament next year."

Teegue gives his parents a smirk knowing this year's tournament is now lost. Braxton is the best player on their team, without him their chances to beat the best team, Arisis East Public, are now a lot less. It doesn't matter what anyone says, he is the reason his little brother has a broken right arm. "May I leave the table?"

Both his parents nod. He scrapes back his chair and heads to his room, it's time to chat with his friends, they will make him feel better. Firing up his compupad he sees everyone from his team is already chatting.

Kiane writes:

It's awful what happened. Teegue was looking up at the ball, how was he to know his brother was near him?

Teegue writes:

Hi guys. Thanks Kiane, but even you know we are supposed to know who is around us on the field at all times. I feel bad, he's my little brother and our best player.

Kiane writes:

Hey there, Teegue. Yes, sure, but mistakes happen.

Teegue writes:

I still feel bad. It's not only Braxton's arm, but this will also cause us to lose the tournament. I know we won today's game, but Braxton had already scored the two goals before I pushed him.

Trisia writes:

As usual you are being too hard on yourself. Brax's arm will heal and you don't know whether not having him in the team means you will all suffer a loss. Be positive and do your best out there this week.

Teegue writes:

And as usual Trisia you are the voice of reason. I need more friends like you and Kiane because you keep me sane. Besides, how can I not be hard on myself, look at who my parents are. I have to keep up their standards.

Teegue reads on as others weigh in on the conversation. They all agree with Kiane and Trisia, which does make him feel a little better. With both his palms on his neck, he pulls his head down to stretch it. He feels the stress that tightens his muscles release then his arms are out in front of him as he stretches his shoulders. His thoughts go to the conversation about the prison breakout, and he is about to open a discussion when he remembers it's still a secret. That Leyna woman is one tough person, first she kidnaps he and his sister and now she steals the Salverz. He admires her spirit.

Chapter 18

Leyna

Eween is tickling her arm with short, affectionate kisses. They have made love twice, once last night and now again this morning. Both are expending nervous energy because it's been five days since Breex headed to the Vatican City with fifty of their troops and still no word.

They had arrived in Morocco three nights ago expecting an abandoned city. What they found surprised them. Descendants of the nomadic tribes had set up shops in the main streets, like the ones that were there before the war. They were thriving and people seemed to be living well. How is the High Priest Enforcer allowing this to happen? Leyna sees this as a sign The Enforcers are losing their hold and are becoming complacent. She feels a slight zing of triumph, this is also another sign that their plan might just work.

"I'm going to head to the market again today, want to join me?" she says looking into Eween's eyes wondering if he feels the same about their plan.

"No, but thanks. I'm going along to supervise more training. With Breex gone I'm the one who is keeping the training going."

"Of course, yes. A question before you go, do you think the fact Morocco's market is thriving is a sign that our plan will work?"

"If you mean people have had enough of The Enforcers and will back us up, then yes."

"Oh good, I thought it was only me. This is a positive for us and I'm heading down there to scout about and see if anyone wants to join us."

Eween kisses her saying, "Fine but be careful who you choose to speak to, I'd say these people are suspicious of strangers."

She rolls out of bed heading for the shower, "I did receive some strange looks yesterday, so I will take care." Eween is risk averse, which is strange for someone in his position, but she understands he wants the best for her. Being loved is something she doesn't take for granted, she knows how easily it can disappear.

Walking around the area that was once Morocco's capital, Rabat, there are remnants of the war scattered about. In some areas the locals have piled up the rubble to make room on the main street for this market. The smells of the herbs and spices caress her nose as she passes stalls with rosemary, mint, coriander, cinnamon and cumin. The heady fragrances transport her to more pleasant times when she was with her family. These memories caress her as well because she knows the world will be a safer place again. With this thought she asks a seller she saw yesterday how much for his freshly ground spices

"You are not from here? Why are you in our market?"

"I'm passing through with my family. My partner's father died, we attended his funeral. We are now returning home," she lies. Until she befriends this seller by visiting him daily, she won't ask questions of how this market came to be. There must be a reason the High Priest Enforcer is allowing it to thrive.

"So sorry for your loss," he says bowing with his hands in prayer.

"Thank you. He is at peace now, unfortunately he was very ill for many years."

"Then please, choose something special to soothe your partner.

Here, this one has been made with calming herbs." He hands her a small vial of oil with the lid off.

The calming smell of orange blossom, mint and thyme wafts up her nostrils. "This will be perfect, thank you," she says, handing it back to him. He wraps the vial for her then hands it to her. She moves along to other stalls.

Further down the street, it narrows and there are laneways branching off it. She heads left down one of the lanes memorising where she is as there are no street names. This lane has more of the same spice sellers along with fruit and meat sellers as well. The overpowering offal smell of the meat drowns out the more pleasant spices. Leyna places her scarf over her nose. She is startled as one of the sellers comes out from behind his stall holding a wild boar's head.

"Special for you," he says, brandishing the foul-smelling carcass in her face.

"Ahh, not today. thanks." She hurries from him but finds many other sellers in the lane just as aggressive. Maybe they have to be because this area is not as busy as the main section where she was earlier. Deciding to go back, she is stopped at the entrance to the lane. The stocky figure in front of her is menacing and asks where she is going.

"I have finished my shopping, so I am on my way home," she tells him with her hand on the small knife in her pocket.

"You do not have many bags like other women here, how can you be finished?" The look in his dark eyes show distrust and Leyna knows she is in trouble. He lunges to grab her, but she sidesteps and plunges the knife into his leg. His screams bring others running to help him. She charges up the main street towards the seller who served her. He grabs her arm and pulls her into the back of his stall pushing her down.

"Stay there and be quiet."

She does as she is told and hears the commotion as the men chasing her run past.

"Okay, they're gone. Who are you and why are they chasing you?"

"Umm, thanks for your help. Tell me your name and I'll explain."

He obliges by saying his name is Karim. "I am Leyna and I am here with some people who will help the world." Even as she says this, she realises how unbelievable it sounds.

Karim laughs, his green eyes lighting up. "A little woman like you is going to save us?"

"Look, I've said too much. Thank you for helping me but I must go. My partner will be wondering where I am."

"Okay, little Leyna. I hope to see you again, stay out of trouble."

She walks into the training area to find Eween in a wrestling hold with one of the soldiers. "I see training is going well."

"It is, you should have seen my last contender." Both Eween and the soldier laugh as the soldier bows his head and leaves them alone.

"You look a bit frazzled"

"I am, I had a close encounter at the markets..."

"I told you to be careful," he says before she can finish.

"I know you did. Everything was fine, I even bought you some calming oil from Karim, one of the sellers."

"And he turned on you. Let me go and sort him out."

"Eween, there's no need, it wasn't Karim," she says as she explains what happened in the laneway.

He places his hands over her shoulders, "I don't want you going to the markets on your own from now on. Maybe not at all, we don't want to bring attention to ourselves from the Vatican."

"Hopefully once we hear from Breex we won't be here much longer. But I will bring an escort with me if I go again. Now, do you need some help with training?" she says, pulling his arm around his back.

Eween places a kiss on her cheek, "I'm fine, thanks," he laughs. "I think you might be needed up on the control deck."

Listening to him, she walks away and heads to the deck via their bedroom. She places the vial on the dresser hoping to be able to go to the markets again despite what happened today.

With her compupad open, she hears a message ping. It's from Breex. She opens the Answae app to answer him and writes:

You are safe. It's good to hear from you.

Breex writes:

We are all safe. I didn't want to call until I knew we had a safe haven for all of us. We're all housed in a ruin not far from the Apostolic Palace. The area is large enough for maybe half of us. We will need to find another safe haven near here.

Leyna writes:

Well done, you found an area for you all for now. Are you sure we won't be detected? We are over ten thousand.

Breex writes:

This area is abandoned as are others nearby. No one ventures out of the Vatican walls. Besides, we surveyed the area, there is no sign of others being here for years. It will be tight and many will be on top of each other, but it is only temporary. Once the High Priest Enforcer is dead, we can all move into the city and the greater surrounds.

Leyna writes:

Good. I will speak with Eween and let you know when the others will follow. Is there anything we should know about entering? Did anyone have trouble?

Breex writes:

We took things slow and blended in with other travellers. It seems The Enforcers are allowing markets to trade here.

Leyna writes:

That's interesting, the same thing is happening in Morocco. There is more to this but I will come back to you after speaking with Eween. Again, well done.

Breex writes:

I was surprised too. Obviously, The Enforcers feel they have nothing to fear. I await your instructions.

She closes the app and is gratified to hear the first party of troops had no problems. However, she can't shake the thought that The Enforcers are up to something, and she knows Eween will agree with her.

· · ·

They are in their bedroom and it's late. Eween had kept the troops training having heard of Breex's message, he wants everyone at the safe haven as soon as possible. The Enforcers can't be trusted. "Leyna, this may be a trap. It was too easy."

"That is a possibility. But we've come too far to back out now."

"No, I agree. I'm not suggesting that. What we need to do is infiltrate The Enforcers homes, see if we can pick up any clues."

Leyna remains quiet for some time. She fiddles with the oil bottle, turning it around and around. "I guess we could send in domestic staff, one in each house. Breex can organise twelve soldiers to go undercover."

"Hmm, that oil bottle gives me an idea. Do you think the seller could mix up some type of truth serum?"

"He sells herbs and spices, Eween. What makes you think he can whip up a truth serum? Anyway, there is no such thing."

"Not a truth serum as such. The Enforcers don't drink right? Well, maybe Karim – that's his name isn't it? Maybe he can make a concoction with alcohol instead of oil?"

"And because they don't drink, if the alcohol is pure enough, they will be intoxicated quickly and probably talk. Eween, this could be possible, but it doesn't mean they will talk?"

"We only need one of them to spill what's behind this change of policy. Since when do The Enforcers allow people to earn their own money?"

Chapter 19

Teegue

The soccer whistle blows and the team from Arisis East Public School holds up the inaugural cup. Teegue had been right, without Braxton they could not win. Still the Lakeside team will receive trophies for coming second and there is always next year's tournament.

All the participants enter the club house for the presentation. Realising how hungry he is, Teegue heads to the food platters and piles his plate. Braxton and others are following behind him doing the same. They find a table and he helps Braxton place his plate down. Another four weeks and the plaster will come off. They all sit discussing the events of the day, each going over how things could have been different had Braxton played.

Once the presentation is over and they return home, Teegue enters his bedroom placing the trophy for coming second on his desk. It's a bummer his team didn't win the inaugural trophy, but they can train harder and do better next time. For now, he should concentrate on doing his homework, this being his last year at school. Only one term to go and his schooling will be over. He looks forward to starting work as a mechanical engineer at the Spacedrome. His flying lessons with Commando5-Anorea will ramp up too. *The day I am at the controls of a spacecraft will be the happiest day of my life.*

Chatting with his friends on the compupad, he is in a good mood until they start talking about the prison break.

Kiane writes:

So, we all know the news, right? Two prisoners escaped and are now on Earth.

Trisia writes:

It's all over the news. Of course we know. They stole the Salverz too, that's a brave move. How is your Dad, Teegue?

Teegue writes:

He's very quiet actually. It's only been mentioned once in front of us, but I'm sure my parents are discussing what needs to be done with the Luminaries.

Kiane writes:

Is it true the woman is the one who kidnapped you and Aria?

Teegue writes:

I'm not sure. I know that's what is being said in the papers, but nothing is confirmed. It's all alleged.

Kiane writes:

She's one brave woman if she had something to do with this. If your parents capture her again, she is done for. They should throw the book at her, what if she has placed us all in danger again?

Teegue writes:

If she's on Earth, how does that put us in danger? The Enforcers have no idea where we are.

Kiane writes:

Teegue, if she is captured by The Enforcers, don't you think they will torture her until she tells them everything?

Trisia writes:

If I was her, I would kill myself before I said anything to The Enforcers.

Trisia is right, even he would do the same. She has a lot of sense for a nineteen-year-old. Teegue decides to tune out and lets his friends battle this one out. He doesn't want to discuss the escape with them. He knows how much his father is embarrassed that two prisoners along with others escaped right under his nose. Again, his thoughts turn to Leyna. He should dislike her for taking part in his and Aria's kidnapping, but she made sure no real harm came to them while they were in the tunnel. Whenever she spoke to them, her voice was calm, and she assured them they were not at fault. She even promised they would be back with their parents as soon as her demands were met. He thinks all this has something to do with Thadd; she was his lover after all.

He wants school to be over so he can concentrate on working at the Spacedrome. The other thing he will concentrate on is finding out exactly why Leyna has returned to Earth. She is in more danger there than she ever was here on Arisis.

Chapter 20

Zenac

Zenac completes his inspection of the rockets. Two are ready to scout nearby planets for water. "Well done to all of you for fast-tracking these rockets. The first two rockets will launch next week and will go a long way to solving the water issue. Commando1-Zaydin, is there anything further you wish to add?"

"Thank you Zenac," she says taking the microphone, "I have statistics of the other spacecraft we are working on." She fires up the hologram as she speaks.

Zenac watches and listens along with the engineers and technicians gathered in the research and development hangar. The numbers are good and on track for him to go on a mission to track down the prisoners. He is not going to allow Leyna to beat him. With Zaydin and a few more of his most trusted commandos, they will track her down along with the others who escaped with her. He burns with anger whenever he thinks of Leyna, she didn't get away with the kidnapping, so he won't allow her to win this time either.

There is applause, enthusiastic and protracted as Zaydin

completes her speech. Everyone returns to their positions as Zenac and Zaydin walk out towards his waiting CMPV. "Thank you for speeding things along, I am keen now for you to concentrate on the Vespira, I have plans for Leyna and Eween."

"Are you asking me to coordinate the spacecraft as well as the rockets?"

"Yes, you're doing great so keep going."

"Thanks Zenac, I appreciate your support. I will ensure this project is kept to the deadline as well."

"I know you will, Zaydin. Let me know when I can inspect the first stage of the Vespira," he says as he enters the back seat of the small CMPV. He rubs his neck as they zoom towards Parliament Row where he has a meeting with Dawa and the Luminaries. He has to shake this tiredness because he wants to be alert as he delivers his report.

"I welcome you all here again," he says as the Ten Luminaries take their seats at the oval table. Dawa is already seated next to him. "I have a report for you from the rocket and spacecraft development. It is good news." He continues filling them in with what he and Zaydin had inspected earlier.

"This is indeed good news," says Luminary 1-Sheabz, "our need for more water is becoming dire every day. Your team on these projects are dedicated, please make sure they are compensated."

"They are already well compensated. We did this also to keep a lid on the projects, they have all signed non-disclosure agreements." Other Luminaries ask questions and the meeting heads into two hours before Luminary 3-Xzackry asks about the escapees.

"Is there any more news about them and what is being done about having them returned?"

"I have the Vespira being fast-tracked for this mission. I will travel to Earth and I have my team in mind. I will report more about this at our next meeting. Now, if there are no further questions, Dawa and I have further work to discuss."

"We look forward to hearing about the Earth mission when we

next meet," says Xrackry as he stands along with the others and files out of the Ovalaz Luminary Room II.

He walks into his office with Dawa behind him. At the bar he turns to her asking, "I'm having a scotch, what would you like?"

"Isn't it a bit early to be drinking? It's only 4 o'clock."

"I have a lot to nut out with this new mission, I need this drink to help me focus."

"Well then I'll join you and help you with your planning. I'll have ice in mine please."

"Really? You're telling me how you like your scotch?"

"Just checking," she says as he hands her a glass, "now tell me your thoughts."

They sit at his stainless steel desk with dark timber inserts, Zenac's design. He wanted to make a statement with the furniture in these offices, wanting bold and practical, which has been achieved.

"We managed to capture Leyna the first time, I see no reason not to do so again. I suspect the reason she has gone back is to seek revenge against the High Priest Enforcer, possibly wanting to kill him."

"That is a big ask, how will she get past The Enforcers, they protect him with their own lives."

"I know Dawa, but Leyna loved Thadd, she has a reason for revenge. The prisoner she escaped with, Eween, is helping her and I am sure they both have followers on Earth who will want to avenge Thadd's death as well. Remember, Thadd was well-liked."

She nods and he keeps explaining what he is thinking, "I will take Commandos 1 to 5 with me and Taaz along with some of his security team. This leaves you and the Luminaries here to protect Arisis in case of attacks if The Enforcers hear I am on Earth."

"Sheabz will want to come with you."

"I know, but it is too dangerous. Your father is of an age where placing him in danger is not responsible because his reaction time is slowing."

"He will want to be there to guide you with his wisdom, not his strength."

"Still, I think it is better if he stays here to protect you and the children. Everyone on Arisis respects him, he is an asset and will be useful here."

She nods in agreement as Zenac keeps discussing his plan. He listens to her input and the more they talk, the more he knows Leyna will be recaptured.

The next morning Commando1-Zaydin walks into his office, "Good morning. The rockets are ready to be tested. They have been manufactured to do five missions as you know, so I suggest as we only have two ready at this stage and that we test both only once over the next two days."

"I will take your lead on this, Zaydin."

"Well, if you'd like to follow me, the engineers are waiting for us to start."

He rises from his chair and follows Zaydin down to the waiting CMPV. They arrive at the Spacedrome and within minutes they are standing in the communications room watching the launch of the first rocket. Zenac knows each rocket can house four people, however, for this test the rocket is on autopilot.

"Now we wait, Zenac. We have programmed the rocket to search three planets near Arisis. It should take three days to return."

"Excellent work to all of you. Zaydin, please return to Parliament Row with me to discuss further my plans for the Vespira and the mission."

The next day, Zaydin is about to leave Zenac's office after another long meeting when Zenac receives a call. He answers and after a couple of murmurs he pushes the receiver button ending the call. "I'm afraid we have a problem, Zaydin. The rocket lost course and blew up outside of Mazadon's atmosphere."

Chapter 21

Leyna

Leyna is at the Moroccan market once again. This time she has a bodyguard and is only here to see Karim. He has agreed to make up the concoction of herbs with alcohol, "I have perfected this mix. There is no smell so placing a drop in a drink or food should be easy, they will not detect anything."

"Well done. I will take two vials for now to be tested. The recipe, may I have it?"

Karim is silent for a few seconds then slowly says, "You are a trustworthy person and if I was going to give the recipe to anyone, it would be you. I will be keeping this to myself as I may use it for similar purposes."

Leyna nods agreeing, "I understand, but I do hope you will not need it in future. With this we hope to secure enough information to know what the High Priest Enforcer is up to. As always this is to remain secret, the whole mission as well as the recipe."

Karim gives her the vials placing his hands around hers, "You are my friend Leyna and I do not betray my friends. My wishes are only that you achieve your dream of changing this world back to what we had."

With her bodyguard in tow she returns to the tunnels wondering if Karim is indeed to be trusted. If this recipe of his works, what is stopping him from selling it to others? Although, if he does, he is being a good businessperson. *Let him be, it will not change the outcome of what we need to do.* No, she decides to trust Karim and begins to think about who to test this potion on. Who doesn't touch alcohol within her team?

She is in the bathroom when Eween walks in. He looks exhausted from training. "Another tough day? How many more need training?"

He doesn't answer, he kisses her instead, "Hi, I'm not in the mood to discuss more training. Besides there are many more who need it, we'll be at it for some time. Breex only left me with two others who can help."

Recognising he is too wired up to talk, she walks over and slips into bed. "I went to see Karim today. He gave me two vials, are you up for talking about this?"

"Give me a minute and only as long as you do all the talking."

When he is comfortable in bed with her, she explains how Karim suggested the potion is to be used. One drop in food or drink at first, then keep adding until it reaches the desired effect. She also explains how Karim is not sharing his recipe and how he might sell it to others if the test works. "Now, who should we test this on? Do you know someone who doesn't drink?"

"Yeah, there's a few people that I know of," he yawns.

She looks at him, placing a kiss on his forehead, "You're wiped out. Let's discuss this in the morning." He closes his eyes and pats her arm. He is snoring soon enough, and she knows he will be more focused in the morning.

When she wakes Eween has already left. Knowing where he is, she readies herself and goes to find him. He is at the training centre and waves her over when he sees her. With hundreds of soldiers training, the smell of sweat mixed with leather and muscle cream is overwhelming.

"Good morning. I was awake early, so I didn't want to disturb you. I've started testing the potion with the two who are sparring over there."

She looks over to where two soldiers, one male, one female are boxing. The female is swaying, "Has she been hit too hard or is that the potion working?"

"Maybe a bit of both," says Eween as they walk over to the boxing area. "Flaiwyn, that's enough for now, go and have a shower. Asheel, may we have a word with you?"

Asheel, clearly wounded and grateful for the rest, walks unsteadily towards them. Eween helps her to sit on the bench and asks to check her over. When she agrees he checks her bruised eye and asks whether she has a headache. "No, but my eye feels like it's going to burst," she says touching it gingerly.

"We'll get a medic to check that soon. Do you feel anything else?"

"Lightheaded, I think. But not in a bad way, if that makes sense. If it wasn't for the pain my eye is giving me, I'd say I'm fine. Although, I have this sudden urge to drink lots of water, my mouth is so parched."

"Ok Asheel, I've called the medics, they are sending someone to look at that eye. Wait here," he says, going to fetch her a bottle of water. He hands it to her and with that he and Leyna leave.

They head into the communications area discussing the amount of potion Eween gave Asheel. He started with one drop and then gave her two more. Her speech was not slurred, she was a little unsteady and was thirsty. He didn't see these as side-effects they should worry about. "Her unsteadiness may have been the result of the hit to her eye and being thirsty isn't a bad thing after drinking alcohol. How potent is this alcohol? Three drops and you're thirsty?"

"Who knows what Karim has used, but at least we know it is effective. Three drops per person is not a lot, these two vials will go a long way. We only need a couple of the High Priest's staff or family to talk."

"Until we use it on one of his people, we really don't know how effective it is. We have to wait and see. I'll have the next group take the vials to Breex and we'll wait on his report."

Leyna agrees with him and sits down in front of her compupad. She wants to do some research on how many of their people they can send into The Vatican before raising an alarm. Ten thousand extra people in the city will be noticed at some point.

A few days later Breex sends in his report of how the situation with sending people undercover is going. Leyna reads that he managed to secure positions for three of them, two men and one woman, the men will work as bodyguards and the woman as a maiden to one of the High Priest's wives. It won't be necessary to send twelve. It wasn't an easy feat to have these three soldiers undercover, which is why he hadn't reported earlier. The Enforcers have strict rules on who can work for them and they vet everyone with suspicion. The three people he sent are seasoned spies and after three interviews they were accepted.

The feedback has been good, especially from the maiden. Wife number three is bored and is happy to chat, so the potion has not been used yet. Apparently, she doesn't get on with the other five wives and tells the maiden they are bitchy and are trying to oust her. Paranoia runs rife throughout the wives' chambers, and this will be an advantage, Breex has written in the report.

Leyna is pleased. She rubs her neck releasing some of the tension as she had not been sure this potion idea of Eween's was going to work. When they escaped the prison on Arisis they had used a known prescription drug, this time the potion contents is unknown. Only time will tell and from this report it looks like they will have the information they need soon without the use of the potion. It will be their backup if necessary. The High Priest Enforcer isn't allowing the markets to thrive for no apparent reason. Leyna has never and will never trust that brutal man.

Chapter 22

Eween

Eween is walking towards her and is pleased to see she has a smile on her face. Leyna is still apprehensive about all ten thousand of their followers entering the city and he understands this, he too has some concerns. A blast of wind throws up sand and she is obscured from his vision for a few seconds. The heat sears through his coveralls and he wishes he had taken them off and left them at the training area.

"Oh, it is you. I wasn't sure through all this sand being whipped up. What's the issue? When you called you sounded anxious"

He places his hands on her face and after wiping the sand away, he kisses her. "Hello you. I feel like we haven't spoken this past week. I've been busy training and you with the research, we have no time for us. I'm not sure I like it."

She places her hand on his face, "I know, it is stressful trying to run this operation, but do we have a choice?"

"No, I guess we don't. I wanted you to know how I am feeling. Now, let's go into this tunnel out of this windstorm."

Leyna follows him and sits on one of the ammunition boxes as he explains his concern about everyone being sent into the city. "The Vatican is already populated and I'm sure The Enforcers have a handle on who comes and goes. We have sent in fifty people without detection. At least this is what Breex has reported back to us. You and I both know that when we all descend on the city it will make them suspicious and then we are in trouble."

"This is what I've been thinking too, Eween. Do you have a solution? Is this why you called me out here?"

"I wanted to tell you alone because the idea I'm formulating may be risky but not as risky as all ten thousand of us entering the city," he says, moving onto the box next to her. "Breex has his fifty people organised well, they are safe and soon we will know what the High Priest is up to. So, to keep the rest of us safe I propose we move to an area outside of the city walls, further to the north. I will send a reconnaissance crew out tomorrow to see how populated that area is and what control The Enforcers have over the people living there. If it is safe, then we move there and coordinate our attack, having Breex closer to the inside. What do you think?"

Leyna places her hand on his knee, "You have been mulling this over more than I have, and I think this will work. I wanted us all within the walls because we would have safety in numbers, but your idea means we can use stealth, and this will be more effective."

He nods saying, "I thought you would agree. My mistrust of the High Priest and his Enforcers made me look at our situation in a different light. I'm glad we haven't rushed into moving everyone too soon. We make a great team, Leyna." He takes her hand kissing it then he leads her onto the sandy floor and his mouth is on hers with a passion that is all consuming. This woman, this powerhouse of a woman, has him stitched up. He has eyes only for her.

She is not a woman he would be attracted to had circumstances been different. Eween dated buxom blondes and one girl, a young fifteen-year-old, was his girlfriend for two years. She towered over him; he only reached her shoulders. But despite her height, she was insecure and needy, something Leyna is not. Leyna is his height and they are the same age, something he finds attractive because Leyna's way of thinking is like his. The days of him wanting a vacuous blonde to play around with are long gone.

He is kissing her and savouring her taut body, her smell arousing him. She moans and arches her back. He hears and feels her desire. This urges him on as he thrusts himself into her, his moans matching hers. Slowly and rhythmically they enjoy each other as he professes his love for her. She looks into his eyes, smiles and lets his words hang in the air.

They are on the communications deck with ten of their most trusted soldiers. Eween has explained their mission and they have agreed to leave before dawn. "Keep aware of each other and remain inconspicuous. The area of Borgo, although not always patrolled by The Enforcer's army, is prone to raids by them. My research has shown this area is populated by artisans and many of the city's workers live here. It's positioning on the west bank of the Tiber River gives views of St Peter's Basilica and the Vatican Palace. The perfect place for us to enter the city is on Triumphal Road via the Stone Bridge. The Ponte Sant'Angelo would have given us better access, however, this bridge was destroyed during the war as you all know. Now, I thank you for your time and look forward to positive information from you as soon as possible."

The head soldier bows then turns ushering the other soldiers out. Eween and Leyna watch them go with Eween hoping he has not sent them on a suicide mission.

"Your face shows concern, Eween. Don't worry, this is a good plan. The fact you have chosen an area where ancient Roman soldiers entered the city walls after triumphant wars means we will not fail," says Leyna, placing her hand gently on his shoulder.

"I do hope the old Roman soldiers watch over our followers and keep these ten soldiers safe. It may be a sign, who knows Leyna? I'm glad you see it as a good sign."

"Eween, we have come this far with victory now in our sights. The High Priest Enforcer is not long for this world and this is what we have come back to Earth to do. I want my revenge and once he is dead, together we will bring a future the people of this planet have not even dreamed of."

Leyna's courage galvanises him with strength and this helps to push his concerns to the back of his mind.

Eween sees two of the soldiers from the reconnaissance crew walking towards him in the training area. They are both hobbling with their armour in tatters. "What happened? I didn't expect to see any of you back so soon."

They both collapse onto the bench as one of them speaks, "There is only the two of us left that we know of. We arrived at Borgo in the middle of a raid, some workers were rebelling and protesting about their conditions. Although we were hidden in the outskirts on the river's west bank, Enforcer troops captured us as they were heading in to break up the raucous. Flaiwyn and I managed to escape. The others were taken prisoner. Whether they are alive we don't know." Her breathing is erratic as she blurts out the words.

"Asheel, you seem to be in only slightly better shape than him. I'm calling the medicos," says Eween, as he presses the medic button. "Our timing could not have been worse. I don't suppose you were able to see if there is a safe area?"

"We kept to the west bank and I noticed there is an area to the east of Triumphal Road that may be safe. We would have to send another crew out to check again."

"That's a start and well done, both of you. Let's hope the others are still alive and we will be able to rescue them," says Eween as the medicos attend to their wounds.

Eween enters the communications deck and asks the three engineers to leave them then he turns to Leyna, "Flaiwyn and Asheel have returned, injured. The medics are treating them now. The reconnaissance crew was ambushed, and the others are either dead or imprisoned. We will have to send others because we need more information about the area."

"Ten soldiers and all of them were ambushed? Although, two of them managed to escape, which is a good thing."

"The Enforcer's army were already doing a raid and patrolling the river. It was bad timing on our part. Asheel did say there is an area near the river that may be good for us, but she was concentrating on escaping so wasn't doing the job we sent her to do."

"That's understandable. Once they are well enough, Asheel and Flaiwyn can take others with them and scout around that area. Only this time we will check with Breex whether another raid is imminent."

"Yes, from now on we use our three spies to help keep everyone safe. Now, you said you wanted to share your research findings with me?"

Opening up her compupad she says, "Well with what has happened with the crew we sent out and my research findings, it is a much better idea to find a safe haven to the north of the city. With no more than one thousand residents in the city at the one time, we have already taken a risk with sending in the people we have under Breex's watchful eye. The safe haven they are currently in will only house maybe a thousand, and even this number is too many as Breex pointed out in his report. We need the bigger area for the rest of us."

Eween knows what to do. He will contact Breex and ask him to check when it will be safe to send another ten soldiers out to scout for the larger area. Sending the first crew without checking was a mistake he will not make again.

Chapter 23

Dawa

Sitting opposite Zenac they both watch the footage of the rocket that blew up entering Mazadon's atmosphere. When the footage is finished, Zenac powers down the hologram. Placing his hands on his desk, he says to Dawa, "I have ordered the engineers to rework the steel used, we need to harden the outer surface to withstand harsh atmospheres like that of Mazadon."

She nods and tells him she agrees before returning to her office. She knows Zenac and his team will find a solution, they have to because again the rain is alluding Arisis. There are two things they must concentrate on – finding water or finding another suitable planet to live on.

Zenac has been preoccupied with having the spaceship Vespira ready for the mission to return to Earth. Leyna and Eween's escape has him fixated on capturing them. She worries about anyone else from Arisis returning to Earth and ending up living under dystopian rule again. The Enforcers will not forget what they did, they will want revenge. Zenac has tried to appease her by saying their shields will protect them, however, his personal shield has not been in operation for five years. The technology in that shield may no longer work. She will have to make sure the engineers test it before anyone leaves on the Vespira mission.

Trying to allay her fears she concentrates on her work. Opening her compupad and bringing up the water files, she continues her report for the Luminaries. After the disaster with the first rocket, they will need convincing that looking for water over finding another planet is the best way to go.

"Will you please stop," says Dawa, putting both hands in the air. "Teegue apologise to your sister, there was no need to speak like a spoiled brat." Aria is in tears after Teegue yelled at her for embarrassing him in front of his friends.

"She needs to learn to keep her mouth shut. I am not interested in Trisia, she is my friend and that's all."

"That's not what Trisia has told me," sniffles Aria.

"You believe her over me, your own brother?" he yells again.

"Okay, enough. It doesn't matter whether you like her or not. Aria from now on check with Teegue before you say anything in front of his friends, and Teegue, it's your turn to clean up these dishes," says Dawa, indicating to Zenac that he follow her.

Walking into the bedroom she starts turning down the bed then sits and sighs, "I'm over the two of them fighting all the time. Ever since the soccer tournament, Teegue is angry more often than not."

"He has a lot on his plate with exams and wanting to work instead of being at school. He told me he is looking forward to working at the Spacedrome next year."

"Fine, but that's no reason to take his frustrations out on his sister. Please talk to him again."

"Will do, I'll speak to him when he finishes the dishes as long as you promise to relax. Have an early night."

She looks into his eyes and sees his concern, "Yes I had already planned to do that. Good luck with Teegue. I hope to see him in a better mood tomorrow morning."

. . .

Placing her breakfast on the table she hears laughter down the hall. Teegue and Zenac walk in both saying good morning in unison. Zenac places his hand on her shoulder giving her a reassuring tug, "Teegue has something he wants to say to you."

"Sorry Mum, I was out of line yelling like that last night. I know there is no excuse, but I am stressed out with exams and stuff."

"You're right, it isn't an excuse, but I'll take the apology," she says as he sits at the table.

She sits listening while he and Zenac discuss the issue with the exploding rocket. They talk about what the engineers have in mind to fix the weakness and Teegue's animated face shows his interest. He will do well at the Spacedrome and for this she is thankful.

Rising from the chair she wishes them both a good day and heads to the bedroom to finish getting ready for her day. The report for the Luminaries is ready and she knows she has a strong case for continuing with the water search. Actually, she has devised a plan where they can also search for another liveable planet as well. Pleased with herself, she hopes Zenac and the commandos will also agree.

When she arrives at Parliamentary Row, she is surprised to see her father waiting for her in the car park. "Father, is everything alright?"

"Good morning my darling," he says, kissing her cheek, "I wanted to see you before you went into the lion's den this morning. To wish you luck. A few of the Luminaries are out for blood, that rocket disaster cost too much as far as they are concerned."

"Thanks for the warning. I appreciate you doing this, but I already had some idea," she says as they head to her office continuing the conversation.

The Luminaries are musing over her report. She is pleased with their reaction, and even though most of them were against sending more rockets to their possible doom, they understand the importance of the water mission. They realise that Arisis is not being abandoned when they find another planet, both Zenac and Dawa hope to populate a few planets in this part of the universe. She was applauded when she finished her presentation, and her father gave her a wink and a lauded smile.

"That went well."

She is back in her office with her father. "Yes, better than I thought. It does make sense though to invest in both water and finding other liveable planets. I know Zenac has this fixation on returning to Earth to capture Leyna and Eween, but I think it's a waste of time."

"Maybe, but he has to win. There is no way he wants to let them get away with what they did. It is humiliating for all of us, don't you think?"

She pulls up a chair near the lounge and invites him to sit, "I was embarrassed at first, but we have more important issues. If they want to go on a suicide mission to kill the High Priest, then let them. They are actually doing us a favour. But I do understand where Zenac wants to go with this, he wants to make them pay for betraying all of us on Arisis."

He agrees then says, "Dawa it's been a long day, so I'll leave you to get back to work and I'm heading home. You did well. I congratulate both you and Zenac on wanting to focus on the future of the human race, there are still millions of people on Earth to be rescued."

She stands and gives her father a hug, "Thanks, I'll relay the message." As he leaves, she notices he is stooped more than usual, her father is ageing in front of her eyes.

Chapter 24

Dawa

She and Zenac are walking out of the Spacedrome after another inspection of the rockets and the Vespira project. Entering the car, Dawa places her head back onto the headrest.

As their car proceeds to take them home he says, "I'm exhausted too. We've made progress though. I'm pleased with what we saw today."

"Hmmm, but the rockets are yet to be tested. Let's not get ahead of ourselves. I heard you talking about more planets in this system, are any of them worthwhile Zenac?"

He proceeds to tell her there are three planets they are considering including Mazadon. If the next rocket makes it through the atmosphere, then the water issue will be solved. We know there is enough water on this planet, it has a tropical climate, which we will take advantage of.

Dawa had already heard about this good news and hopes their engineers have done enough to strengthen the outer shells of the rockets. Zenac tells her about the other two planets, one, Heredan, is similar to Arisis so helmets will be required. This is fine because the inhabitants of Arisis are used to wearing them. The other planet is the better of the three, its atmosphere is like Earth's, however, this one is the furthest away. At two billion light years, Xeradyn will be the most difficult to colonise. It will be at least ten years before they will be able to send a team there. For now, they are concentrating on Mazadon and Heredan. Arisis will have a sister planet giving many more people on Earth the chance to escape.

They arrive home and Zenac's phone rings, "I'll take this in the study, won't be long." Dawa stretches her aching body wondering who is calling at this time. Zenac has been on his phone late many nights since he began the rockets and Vespira projects. When he returns, she asks who called.

"The Vespira will be ready next week. I'm having a meeting with the crew to discuss when to leave. Leyna is not going to know what hit her."

"We were at the Spacedrome all day, why didn't Zaydin tell us when we were there?"

"She wanted to be sure, they were doing some final tests after we left."

Dawa is not sure how she feels about Zenac going back to Earth. He is placing himself and everyone else in danger and for what? Revenge for some embarrassment that no one will even remember. Lately, no one has spoken of the prison escape. Of course, she will not stop him, but she hopes he realises he is leaving her with a lot of responsibility when he does eventually go. She is about to speak when Braxton comes into the kitchen followed by Teegue and Aria.

"I'm starving, what's for dinner?" he asks.

Dinner was the last thing on her mind and Zenac saves her having to answer Braxton. "You know what, we've only arrived home a few minutes ago, who's up for some takeaway?" The three children cheer and each asks for their favourite. "How about we go with burgers?"

Dawa nods towards Zenac, happy not to have to make a decision and Braxton punches in their order as each of them tells him what type of burger they want.

They're sitting at the dining table within half an hour with Teegue asking what happened at the Spacedrome today. "Well, actually we only found out when we walked in that the Vespira will be ready next week. I'll be leaving for Earth soon."

"Wow, how awesome," says Teegue.

"Yes, it is good news, but a lot more than that happened today. We were shown the progress with the rockets and we now have three planets to explore," added Dawa.

"Three more planets, that's even more awesome," says Braxton. "Dad, are you going to the other planets too?"

"I will once the issue on Earth is settled. It's been a great day with a lot of progress, and we will rescue many more people once Mazadon, Heredan and Xeradyn are explored. We hope at least two of these planets can be colonised."

Dawa listens as her children ask their father more questions. This is their family, loved ones they placed at risk when they left Earth. Their safety is her utmost priority, she doesn't want Zenac's return to Earth to place them in danger. The Enforcers are never to know where they live.

She sits at the head of the Ovalaz table with Zenac. He is briefing his crew on the mission to Earth. It is Friday and the Vespira is due to launch on Sunday, depending on the weather. If the predicted storm does arise, then the launch will be two days later. Nothing is going to stop Zenac, he is determined to capture Leyna and Eween. He does not want them to set a precedent.

"This launch is an important one. Not only will it be used for this mission but also for us to commence rescuing people from Earth again. There are still many willing to leave as we all know. The Vespira will serve us well for many missions to come."

"Where will we house these people? We will need to construct more housing," asks Commando5-Anorea.

"As you know we are investigating three planets for possible colonisation. If two of them are suitable, we will be able to construct enough housing for anyone who wants to escape The Enforcers."

The five commandos nod and acknowledge this new information. Zenac moves on to brief Taaz and his security team. Dawa had argued with him that he was light on with this team, how is he to find Leyna and Eween with less than twenty? Zenac had said he didn't want to take too many with him as he knows this means there is less chance The Enforcers will notice them. She understood his reasoning and decided not to argue further. He understands why her fear remains, the chance of someone within The Enforcers army finding their home is possible. Zenac promises her and the others in the room he will do everything in his power not to divulge their new home.

Chapter 25

Teegue

Exams are over, their graduation is finished, and his class of 2295 is ready for what their future holds. Teegue is with his friends outside the ceremonial hall discussing where they want to keep partying. Eventually they decide to return to Trisia's house because her parents are with Dawa and Zenac at their own parents' after party. Twenty-five classmates descend on Trisia's place and party into the wee hours of the morning.

Trisia is looking at him with a crazed look, the veins in her neck protruding. "What? Are you crazy? You're going back to Earth for what exactly?"

Teegue is wondering why she is so upset, he thought she would be happy that he wants to return to Earth and help his father. "Wow, I thought you would be excited for me. I want to see this Leyna woman and find out why she returned. If the rumours about her wanting to kill the High Priest are true, then I want to be part of this historical event," he says, waiting for her to see how important this is to him. Teegue had been thinking about this since finding out about the prison break, and he also wants to make sure his father remains safe. He is not taking a large crew, so Teegue figures an extra hand on deck will be handy.

He watches on as Trisia paces around her bedroom. He is lying on her bed, the smell of their lovemaking still on the sheets. Admiring her lithe body, which is even more taut as she is visibly angry, he likes her impish look. She has a shapely but small arse with athletic legs, and he has nuzzled those perky boobs many times in the past year. But now he stares at her face, imploring her to calm down.

"You're risking your life and possibly placing your father's life in danger too. I can't accept this, Teegue, it's a fool's errand."

He hadn't thought of his stowing away as placing his father in further danger, he wants to help not hinder. "I will support my father in this and make sure we return safely to Arisis. Besides, I want more of you. Isn't that a good enough reason to return?" he asks, rising up and taking her by the hips, throwing both of them onto the bed.

"How can you think about making love again when you have announced you're leaving on a crazy mission?" she says pushing him away, "I will worry about you until you return. That is, *if* you return."

"I'm going to be with twenty others who are all trained in avoiding trouble, I know I'm going to return to safety and especially to you."

She softens saying, "Nothing I say will stop you. Please stay safe and I promise I won't tell anyone where you are. I'm sure your mother will be asking all your friends when she finds you missing. Now, you had better leave, it's four in the morning."

"That's my girl," he says, dressing himself, "I knew you would see reason eventually." She glares at him, so he decides to not say anything further and leave before she shouts at him again.

He creeps around in the darkness, not wanting to use his torch until he is closer to the Vespira. There is no one else in the hangar, the launch is not for another five hours. The engineers, crew and compupad personnel, along with his father, will arrive at dawn.

With his knapsack empty save for enough snacks for a week and a spare set of clothes, the heaviest thing he is carrying is his helmet, having removed it when he entered the hangar. Walking to the back of the craft, he unlatches the cargo bay, finding it filled with ammunition and supplies for a trip that will take a week to arrive. Then, they will have enough supplies to keep them going for another month. He doesn't think they will be on Earth for that long, Zenac will capture Leyna and Eween and they'll all be back on Arisis before The Enforcers know what has happened. This is the plan he has heard his father discussing with his mother over many nights. Dawa is not pleased with this mission, which makes him think of Trisia, who feels the same as Dawa. He will do everything he can to make both the women he loves proud of him.

Creeping into the cargo bay, he scrambles over boxes as he heads towards the back. They won't find him here until they begin emptying it. Even then, they won't take everything out at once, so he'll remain hidden for some time after they land. His father will be angry but there is nothing he can do and he will get over it. He won't be sent home and Teegue will make his father proud as well.

Chapter 26

Eween

Eween calls Leyna up to the communications deck. He is checking the coordinates on the hologram the engineer has activated. "I think you're right Sanuel. Let's discuss this further when Leyna joins us."

When she arrives, she takes in the hologram, "What's going on? Is everything alright with Breex?"

"All good there, this is a bigger problem. Zenac is on his way," Eween explains, pointing his finger to the approaching spacecraft.

"Well, well. We're going to have some company. I was wondering how long it would be before Zenac or Dawa paid us a visit."

"The spaceship is still two days away. Their trajectory shows they are headed for the Sahara, which isn't surprising," informs Sanuel, the engineer.

"We'll be ready for him," says Leyna, "Please keep us informed. Eween, a word in private please."

He follows her to the same tunnel they were in during the windstorm. "What is so secretive you couldn't speak in front of Sanuel? She was the one who identified the threat."

"It is a big threat too, Eween. We must organise ourselves to evacuate to the Borgo area sooner, Zenac can't find us. He will take us back to Arisis."

He understands her concerns because there is no other reason for Zenac to be returning to Earth. Placing his hands around her waist he says, "We could try and maybe send most of our people to Borgo. The area has been scouted and there is room enough for all, but to send everyone within two days will raise suspicions."

"Do we have a choice?" she says her worried eyes seeking his, "I don't want to return to Arisis, especially not before I have exacted my revenge. I say we try to send as many people as possible."

"Let's have a meeting with our team and include Breex via video. He will advise us, and I will ask him to ready the area for everyone."

"Now! I say we round the team up this minute, there is no time to lose."

He has another thought, which may work in their favour. Telling Leyna they could convince Zenac to work with them to capture the High Priest, and this may convince him not to take them back to Arisis. He places his forehead on hers and agrees, "You're right to be worried. We can discuss my idea to join forces with Zenac, but ultimately we listen to what Breex advises, okay?" She kisses him and he feels her disquiet as she thrusts her tongue into his mouth seeking a solace he knows he can't give.

Two thousand of their people are headed to Borgo. They were able to organise this late-night journey as soon as Breex gave the all clear. Tomorrow night another two thousand will leave, led by Leyna who has agreed to let Eween remain and sort out Zenac. She has asked him not to hurt Zenac, only to let him know that Eween and Leyna will never return to Arisis. They are no threat to him nor anyone else on Arisis and Earth needs them now.

He is holding her, taking in her smell, her strength and her angst. Leyna is as wound up as a cat on its nightly prowl ready for a feline brawl and is now second-guessing herself. She wants to stay with him. "It is not safe for you to stay here. Zenac wants you captured so

I have to keep him away from you. I've promised you I won't hurt him and will use all my negotiating skills to persuade him to join us in this cause."

She nods, giving him an ardent kiss then saying, "I await your good news."

"Take care and don't be tempted to take any shortcuts. Follow the route Breex has set out. I know it will take you longer to arrive, but it is better if you stay on track. As you near Borgo, Breex's troops will be patrolling the roads and river. Stay safe my darling, I will be with you soon," he says not wanting to let go of her hand. As she leaves, he watches until she is out of his view, hoping Zenac will see reason.

He snaps down the lid of his compupad. They made it safely to Borgo. Leyna had joined with Breex the morning of their arrival and they are now in a conversation with Zenac via their answaes. Everyone is staying in the ruins of the area and much of it is suitable for them to hide out. Leyna has asked Eween and the rest of them to leave the tunnels and join them saying there is no need for him to fight Zenac. Eween had told her he will organise to be with her soon, not giving a specific time. He wants to deal with Zenac and be sure he agrees to join them, or he must return to Arisis. If Zenac stays on Earth without joining them, then Leyna will remain in danger.

Sanuel says, "They will land tomorrow somewhere near the perimeter of the outer tunnel."

"Okay, then it's time we send troops to the area. I'll ask them to leave tonight so they will be ready to bring Zenac to me as soon as he steps foot on the Sahara."

"You don't think it's better if you go to him? Why do you want him to know where we are?"

Eween ponders what Sanuel has said, "I had thought to do that, but he will be expecting either Leyna or myself and may set a trap. Our resources here will give me options, I have not decided what I am going to do with him yet."

Sanuel nods, "I'll leave you to it then, shall I? If you need me, I'll be in the dining area."

He acknowledges Sanuel and keeps going through what he wants to happen. He wants to face Zenac alone to convince him to return without repercussions. He and Leyna mean no harm to Zenac nor his family. In fact, he and Leyna are doing everyone a favour by ridding Earth of the High Priest Enforcer. This is the only reason they escaped and returned to Earth. Zenac should understand Leyna's reason for revenge.

Pressing the intercom on the console, he summons Flaiwyn and Asheel wanting them close by for protection. Zenac is not one to be underestimated.

Chapter 27

Zenac

Watching the monitors and checking the hologram, Zenac along with Taaz and five commandos, are keeping a close eye on when they will land. The Sahara being so vast, it is easy to end up hours away from your intended destination.

"Here, this is where we will land," says Zaydin.

"Are you sure? We can't be too close to the tunnels, we want to land undetected," asks Commando 4-Amallin.

Zaydin gives her colleague a challenging look, "You distrust my judgement Amallin?"

"Only making sure we all understand," says Amallin, holding her head high.

Zenac smiles inwardly at the competition between his two senior female commandos. Amallin is a threat to Zaydin and isn't afraid to upstage her at every turn. "We all understand and have trust in Zaydin's abilities," he says, not wanting to escalate this feud. They all need their energy to find Leyna and Eween, this is what they should be concentrating on.

. . .

"How long now?"

"Three hours and counting, sir."

"Thanks, Zaydin. Everyone, prepare your stations and check all ammunition. Be ready for docking and your next instructions." His answae buzzes as he finishes speaking. "Dawa, we are about to land... what? Are you sure?" He listens as she explains Trisia has told her how Teegue stowed away, he's somewhere on the ship.

Later, Teegue is unceremoniously brought into Zenac's quarters. It's a few minutes before Zenac speaks. "Are you nuts, what the hell are you doing here? Shouldn't you be studying more about mechanical engineering?"

"Dad, there is plenty of time for that. I want to be part of seeing the High Priest assassinated. Besides, like Mother, I thought you might need more help."

"I appreciate that, but this is a dangerous mission, maybe you should have discussed this with me first."

"Oh, sure and you would have let me come along. Look, I'm here now so let me help. Remember, I spent a year with that woman, I know how she thinks."

He admires his son's innocence, knowing how she thinks might come in handy but not right now. Even though Zenac is angry Teegue has stowed on board, he has to accept he is here. One of Taaz's men will look after him, Zenac wants him safe at all costs. "Well now young man, I'm sure you're hungry after being in the cargo bay all this time. Let's go to the dining area, cook will have something nourishing for you. I hope you like food that has been hydrolysed."

As he is sitting eating, Teegue is finding out he doesn't enjoy this type of food. "Umm it's bland, isn't it? The snacks I ate in the cargo bay tasted better."

Zenac laughs, "We didn't bother bringing fresh food, apart from having to store it in specially designed fridges, we can survive on this dried stuff for this short mission."

"You hope it will be short. I don't think you should underestimate

Leyna, Dad"

"You're probably right, she is certainly a force, isn't she?"

"I admire her wanting to rid Earth of the High Priest, although how she is going to get past his henchmen is beyond me."

"She has a good track record. Earning our trust on Xenure Station; kidnapping you and Aria, escaping our prison and she is now on Earth with what I assume is a large following. I have never underestimated her, and I never will."

They continue discussing what will happen once they land with Teegue promising not to go anywhere and especially without his bodyguard. Zenac tells him how he may assist Leyna and Eween to kill the High Priest and his Enforcers if necessary, then make them return to Arisis for trial.

"Really? They are doing a good deed and you are still going to punish them. Don't you think you should wipe the slate clean, Dad?" "They made a fool of me, and your mother as well. For this they should pay, we have to make an example of them. The people of Arisis expect a fair leader and one who doesn't allow criminals to not pay for their crime."

They are congregated at the opening of the cargo bay listening to Zenac when there is a blast of fire.

"You are surrounded. Put your weapons down and don't put up a fight. This way no one will be hurt." The voice comes from a megaphone, it's robotic and reverberates around them.

Zenac orders everyone back into the cargo bay, "Stay low, my shield will protect me. I'll go and confront them." He sees Taaz is about to protest as he leaves. He tells him to watch over everyone else.

"I'm here to discuss helping Leyna and Eween with their mission. Take me to them," yells Zenac with his hands in the air. "We mean you no harm."

Two people approach him, both with arms as thick as blocks of wood, the girl is taller than the man, but both fill the space in front of him like a huge black box. "There is only you?" asks the male.

"Only me," replies Zenac, not confirming there are others in the Vespira.

"Follow us. Don't think about trying anything, there is a whole army surrounding your space craft."

Zenac has no intention of doing anything stupid, all he wants is to see Leyna and start negotiations.

The blindfold is taken off him and as his eyes focus, he sees Eween standing in front of him. Looking around he recognises the Salverz; it looks like it has had some upgrades done.

"You were expecting Leyna, I'm sure. She has been called away on another mission, you will have to deal with me."

"I take it you're Eween, we've only met once when you were on trial. Yes, I was expecting to see Leyna, I have an important proposal to put forward. We've come here to help you destroy the High Priest and his Enforcers."

"How admirable of you. So, you are not here to return us to Arisis?" says Eween with a sceptical look. "Whether you speak to Leyna or me, the result will be the same, we make decisions together."

"Very well then, this is my proposal. We, myself and twenty of my best crew, will assist you with whatever is needed to accomplish this mission. Afterwards, we will return to Arisis with everyone who wishes to return. You and Leyna are welcome too."

He watches as Eween rubs his chin, pacing and in deep thought. Zenac knows he is not a leader like Thadd, who made decisions with ease and was usually correct in whatever venture he entered. The only one he failed in was overthrowing his father, but this was due to inexperience and youth. Had he lived, it would be Thadd he would be negotiating with right now.

"I will not give you an answer yet. For now, you will be taken and guarded until I decide what is best. Asheel, take him to the cargo bay and chain him by his legs. Stay with him until I call you."

Asheel grabs Zenac by his shoulder and shoves him forward. He moves without complaint, the strength of this woman is intimidating.

Chapter 28

Zaydin

The other crew members left at the Vespira lock the cargo bay and head to their quarters. They know Zenac won't be back tonight.

Zaydin enters her room stretching her limbs, releasing some of the tension. She sighs as the muscles loosen, the burning as she pulls the tendons and their release is therapeutic. Still thinking about Amallin, that girl needs to be taught a lesson. Ever since she was promoted to Commando4, Amallin has had her sights on the Commando1 post. Zaydin is not ready to give up her posting yet and she will make this known to the young upstart at their next meeting.

She readies herself to rest when her compupad pings.

Dawa writes:

What is happening, Zaydin? I'm not able to contact Zenac.

Zaydin writes:

Hello Dawa, we are waiting for him to contact us. He is with Leyna on the Salverz trying to negotiate. An army of her followers ambushed us and Zenac made us return while he went to negotiate.

Dawa writes:

On his own? Why didn't he take someone with him?

Zaydin writes:

He didn't say why, but I think he wants to speak to them about helping with the mission. He wants the High Priest killed as much as Leyna does.

Dawa writes:

This is crazy. If Leyna wants to go on this suicide mission, then let her. Why do we have to be involved?

Zaydin writes:

You will have to speak to Zenac about that, Dawa. Please try not to worry, I'm sure Zenac will contact us soon and we will return with Leyna and Eween. They must go to trial and be returned to prison.

Dawa writes:

I appreciate your support Zaydin, thank you. Please keep me informed, but I will try to contact Zenac again later.

Zaydin writes:

Of course, Dawa. I wish you a pleasant evening.

She closes the compupad after signing off. Dawa must be concerned if she decided to contact her. They have a complicated relationship. Zaydin is not Dawa's favourite person and she feels her angst whenever Dawa is in close proximity. When Zaydin was promoted to the level of Commando1, it was Zenac's choice to do so. She knows this because Dawa has always been curt with her, maybe due to jealousy? She is not sure. Although why the most powerful woman on Arisis is worried about someone like her is a mystery. As far as she knows, she has not given Dawa cause to be jealous. Surely, Dawa knows she is not interested in Zenac? Men are not her preference.

She and Zenac work in close proximity, which is to be expected for the Commando1 post and one of the heads of Parliament. She shakes her head wondering why Dawa feels this way towards her. Maybe when this mission is over, she will try to speak with her, it's not a good idea to be on the wrong side of Dawa because Zaydin's position needs the support of both leaders.

. . .

She wakes to the crackle of her answae, Zenac is contacting her. "Yes, I can hear you," she says, listening to his command. "I will organise everyone and we will await the two personnel whom you followed yesterday. It's good to hear you are not in trouble." He continues telling her that negotiations have gone well, and they will be helping with the mission. He wants everyone with him so they can be briefed on what to do. Completing the call, he asks that Teegue be brought to him as soon as he arrives on the Salverz. "I will personally deliver him to you," she says as he clicks off from his end.

After they all arrive, Teegue is sitting on the air-chair in the tiny quarters Zenac has been assigned after the agreement between he and Eween. With his arms crossed, Teegue scowls at his father. "You're leaving me here with that oaf of a bodyguard? Wouldn't he be of better use to you out there? And me too? I can help somewhere, I know I can."

"You can help here on the Salverz. Keep watch that none of The Enforcers finds it while we are in the city walls. This is a useful job for you actually, an important one."

"I want to be part of the action. The reason I stowed away was to be witness to this event, an event that will go down in history."

"Teegue," sighs Zenac, "I understand your enthusiasm, but your safety is my biggest concern. Who knows how many will be killed trying to capture the High Priest? No, you are not to join us, your job is here and that is the end of this discussion."

Zaydin leaves with Zenac to attend the briefing she has organised, but not before hearing Teegue scream in frustration, "I'm not a child, Dad."

Chapter 29

Dawa

She is lying in bed. This is a luxury she rarely has, but with Zenac away, Teegue with him and her other two still peacefully asleep, she is being self-indulgent on this cool Sunday morning. Winter is only two weeks away and the crisp air invites her to stay in bed. She is still seething with Teegue, how dare he place himself in danger by stowing away on the Vespira. Her headstrong son has gone too far this time.

When Dawa confronted Trisia about Teegue's whereabouts, at first she lied saying she had no idea where he was. Dawa did not accept this and asked Trisia to see reason as all their lives could be at risk. With a burst of tears Trisia had confessed that Teegue had told her about his plan at their graduation after-party. She told Dawa how angry she had been and begged him not to go. Understandably, Dawa felt the same as Trisia and Dawa had hugged her for telling the truth. She is a good girlfriend to her son and hopes he knows how much she loves him.

Picking up her book she tries to relax and read but her mind won't silence. Thoughts of whether Zenac and Teegue are safe spin through her brain, as well as the advances in the water project she has made this past week. The planet Mazadon is proving fruitful for water and she has signed off on the construction of water pipes to commence next week. She smiles to herself because achieving this milestone of solving the water issue on Arisis is a huge step. Even if they don't find another liveable planet, they can begin saving others from Earth soon because Arisis can house them, there will be enough water now. Placing her book on her bedside shelf, she decides it's time to stop this indulgence and rustle up some breakfast.

"Yum, pancakes. Thanks Mum."

She looks up from the pan to see Braxton straggling into the kitchen, pyjama bottoms dragging along the floor. His blonde locks falling into his eyes makes him look younger. She grins at his boyish charm.

"Grab the blueberries from the fridge and sit down. Is Aria up too?"

"I heard her talking when I walked past her room. She's probably gossiping with her friends again."

Aria was being as much of a pain as her twin. Their teenage angst was overtaking the household and Dawa had had enough. "Aria, breakfast is ready," she shouts.

"Coming," the muffled voice of her daughter reaches her ears. At least she received an answer this time. Aria has been indifferent towards her for some time, being unusually quiet and when questioned by Dawa, being defensive for no real reason. Dawa would rather tackle the issues of Arisis than try to reason with her two older children right now. Both Teegue and Aria seem to be in a world of their own, a very selfish one.

As she walks into the kitchen, Aria is listening to music with her M-Buds in her ears and promptly sits at the table without a word. "A *good morning* would be nice," says Dawa to no one in particular. She can hear the music coming through the buds so there is no way Aria can hear her.

"Hey Mum, don't mind her. What about coming for a bike ride with me?"

She smiles at Braxton, "Sure, eat up and we'll get going."

Back at work the next day she is listening to Sheabz pronounce the Mazadon Water Project open. Dawa feels the warmth and gratitude as the other Luminaries applaud. The crew sent on the second mission with the reinforced rocket made it through the planet's atmosphere without a hitch this time. They remain on Mazadon awaiting other rockets to bring supplies and workers.

"Thank you Sheabz. Now you are all acquainted with the project, are there any questions?"

Both Dawa and Sheabz field questions, which are mainly about the cost and timing but Luminaries 2 and 3 have further concerns about the rockets.

"The rockets are not made for long term use, they are to be used no more than five times. This is how they were designed right? Because of budget constraints," says Tanjaz, "if this water issue is long term, how do we keep transporting water from Mazadon?"

"That is a good point," replies Sheabz, "this is something we will have to consider, however, I am sure our engineers can design better rockets if and when we need them."

Tanjaz and Xzackry both nod as Dawa and Sheabz field more questions. Many of the Luminaries have concerns about no other planet being viable, but she and Sheabz allay their fears. After an hour, there are no more questions and Dawa announces the meeting has ended. When the other Luminaries have left, she asks her father a question, "Of course we can make better rockets, the issue is how do we pay for all this?"

Sheabz walks over to her and placing his arms gently on her shoulders says, "My darling daughter it is time to glean some joy from this victory, the money can be sourced when we need it. For now, go and reward yourself. Do something that will bring you plea-sure because you deserve it."

He is right, it's time to bathe in the success of this project. She decides a relaxing aromatherapy massage is in order later today.

Chapter 30

Leyna

Leyna waits but her patience is wearing thin. Eween said they would arrive soon after midnight, that was two hours ago. She has tried to call him three times without success. There had been no reports of scuffles and this hearing nothing from him is unnerving. She paces the deserted dining area, wringing her hands in frustration. *What could have happened to them?*

Breex walks in shaking his head, "We have been able to come in with thousands and now with less than three hundred they are still not here?"

Leyna sits with a thud, placing her hands in her hair and putting it up in a messy bun. "My worry is they have been ambushed. Maybe we should take some soldiers with us and check. Actually, did you ask the spies in The Enforcers homes?"

"I have and they have heard nothing. What I did find out is that the High Priest has a plan for the merchants' money. There is a reason why he has allowed markets to flourish. He is going to raise taxes and funnel those funds into building a memorial building and statue to himself."

She looks up with a knowing look, "The selfish bastard. There had to be a reason for him to start allowing people to prosper again. So, he ruins historical monuments during the war and now expects people will want to see one of him? Well done for finding that out but right now we have a bigger problem. We need to find Eween, Zenac and the others."

They follow the river to the pick-up point where they split up. With a crew of thirty soldiers, Leyna heads her group towards the side of the wall west of the city. As the wall comes into view, a light rain begins to fall. No one is complaining because the rain is cooling this oppressive summer night. She stretches her right arm straight back towards them indicating they all bend down, as she creeps towards the wall on her own. Then she hears his voice. Eween is shouting and then the gate falls. She starts to run towards him but her soldiers beat her to Eween asking what is going on. Once he explains to the soldiers what has happened he is by her side panting, his left arm dangling by his side.

Arriving back to their compound in Borgo, Eween is sent to the medical unit where they try to save his arm. Leyna is sitting with Breex and Zenac, Fixor has joined them too. Their two guards, Flaiwyn and Asheel also sit with them in the dining area. "How many were lost?"

Zenac, who has only sustained a few scratches and a bruised eye says, "By my rough count maybe fifty."

"We should not have lost any lives. How did you end up in the city?"

"Minutes before we reached the pick-up point, with no one there to greet us, we were ambushed and taken into the city. With my shield protecting me, I managed to kill the soldiers near me and create a diversion. This is when we were able to overthrow them and head into The Enforcers' homes."

Leyna cannot believe what she is hearing, "You what?" she screams standing up and placing her hands firmly on the table, "who gave you the order to do such a thing?"

"It was an opportunity we couldn't waste. We were there and able to enter the area with little force. Most of the families have been eradicated."

"Zenac, are you crazy? Do you think the High Priest is going to let this go? He will target each and every one of us. Before you went in like crazed idiots, he had no idea we were even here."

Zenac laughs and Flaiwyn makes to stand and grab him when Breex stops him. "Leyna is right, you have placed us all in danger."

"Do you really believe the High Priest had no idea? Do you think he blindly allowed thousands of you to enter without noticing? You are crazier than I if you think this to be true. He sets traps, we all know this, and I wanted to stop him before he obliterated all of us."

"And now you have given him the chance to do so," says Breex matching Leyna's anger.

Zenac explains the method behind his madness. By killing off some of his family, the High Priest is now forced to attack and when he does, they will be waiting for him. The High Priest will want to avenge his family, it is a way of weeding him out from behind his protection.

Both Leyna and Breex remain quiet with Leyna asking him to walk with her to the other side of the room. She asks him if what Zenac says will happen They had not thought of bringing the High Priest out into the open.

"It is one way of ensuring we get to him. Maybe we have been given a greater chance of actually capturing him"

They both walk back to where Zenac is seated. "Flaiwyn, show our guest to his quarters. Zenac, we can deal with the other issues tomorrow. Fixor can join us too." She waits until they leave then goes to see how Eween is coping.

Eween is sleeping. She is speaking with the surgeon while waiting for him to wake. He explains to her his arm was severed at the shoulder, the blood loss was substantial, and it could not be saved. He is lucky to be alive. They have given him two pints of blood and it will be weeks before he recovers and then begins rehab. She thanks the surgeon as he walks out and she sits watching

Eween sleep. How did he allow Zenac to take charge? This is their mission.

Groggy and thirsty, Eween asks her for water when he comes too. "There's ice here, that is all you are allowed," she says, placing a piece into his mouth. His chapped lips are blue from bruising and a cut under his chin has been stitched.

He tries to talk once the ice has melted, "I let you down. I'm sorry."

"I am wondering what the hell happened, but don't try to speak now. I came to see you to make sure you are okay, not to discuss where things went wrong."

He nods and closes his eyes again. He will have an explanation and she can wait a few days, for now she will concentrate on more negotiations with Zenac and exactly how they will capture the High Priest.

A week later, she is overseeing the meeting with Eween by her side. With his rehab started his recovery is coming along better than expected, although he is still getting used to only having his right arm. Facing her team she says, "Before The Enforcers regroup we must strike. The High Priest knows we are here and will come for us. We must move now. We are lucky he has not organised his troops already."

"It is unusual. If he knows we are here, why hasn't he attacked yet?" asks Fixor.

They all nod and wonder the same thing when Breex breaks the silence. "Having been ready to do this for some time, I'm waiting to march as soon as you say. The laser is ready. Shall I go with a small crew tonight? And I'll inform our spies, they will be ready to allow us in."

She nods to Breex and then looks over to where Zenac is seated, he gives her a nod of approval as well. Why she needs his blessing is perplexing her, but she wants his support and needs him on their side. "Breex and Zenac summon your soldiers, all of them. They can wait on the eastern wall until you give the signal. We need to make this quick and as painless as possible. I don't want too many casualties. It is not the city folk we are after." She notices both Breex and Zenac punching the dials of their answaes, it is time for the troops to begin their march.

"The High Priest is mine to kill. If any of you capture him, keep guard until I find you. Don't feel the need to kill him yourself because if you do, I will kill you with my bare hands." She stands guard while Breex works with the laser. The flickering light is subdued by soldiers standing near him. Amazed at the power of this tiny instrument, she is asked to look at where Breex has been working on the hole, a hole big enough for them to go through. "Well done. Take as many soldiers as you need Breex, I'll be right behind you."

Keeping guard until the last soldier fits through, she ducks and heads into the city. Finding Breex she falls in with his stride. "Have you heard from Eween?" She is hoping he is doing ok, she had not wanted him to come along, it was too soon after losing his arm. However, he had insisted saying he wanted to be a part of this too. Hopefully he won't do anything stupid like try to be a hero.

A shot fired over their heads pulls her back to reality. Breex pulls her down and indicates with his hand for some of the soldiers to go forward. More shots fling past and the moans of dying soldiers hit their ears. This is not what Leyna had wanted, but if The Enforcers wanted a fight, then bring it on. "All of you head towards The Enforcers' homes and shoot anyone who tries to stop you." With this she charges forward with Breex following.

Leyna keeps heading forward fighting off The Enforcers' soldiers, the only light guiding her is the lit-up windows of the homes. The screams of the dying are all around, but she ignores them because her goal is now so close. A shot skims her shoulder, she ignores it as she is about to enter the gated area where The Enforcers and the High Priest live. Blood drips down her arm and she winces but keeps going. She can hear Breex behind her then sees Eween and Zenac behind pillars. "Hurry, both of you and find shelter. Our spies tell us the Enforcers' specialised armed forces have been deployed. There is no time to waste."

Leyna and Breex hide behind two pillars on the other side of the Great Hall from where Eween and Zenac are. She falls to the floor ripping a piece of cloth from her pants to tie around her wound. Memories of Thadd flood through her mind, he had spoken of the grandness of where he lived. He had not exaggerated. The pillars alone were twenty metres tall, their circumference half that and they are made of white marble. No expense was spared, which makes Leyna gag. While his people suffer, the High Priest indulges his fantasies in this shrine.

The beef and muscle of the specialised armed forces are marching towards them. Their armour is keeping them secure, no bullet will penetrate the reinforced metals. Suddenly, Eween and five other soldiers run out towards the exit, causing a distraction. The armed forces take the bait and march out after him. This may be an idiotic move on his part, but he has now made it easier for her to reach the High Priest.

Zenac is by her side, "You're hurt."

"I'm fine, the bullet grazed my skin. Now let's go. Breex, which one is the High Priest's house?"

Chapter 31

Teegue

Teegue is with the oaf who refuses to tell him his name, so *Oaf* it is. They are creeping around the eastern wall with Teegue wanting to scale the wall. He's heard all the action and wants to be a part of it. The Oaf is holding him down. "Get off me. Don't you understand how much I want to see what my father and Leyna are doing. This is history in the making." All he sees is The Oaf's eyes staring towards the wall totally ignoring him.

Trying to struggle, Teegue gives up. It's no use because his bodyguard is twice his size and is obviously devoted to his mission. Teegue knows not to push it, his father will be angered if this oaf allows him to escape his care. He will bide his time, sunrise is only a few hours away, then he'll make his move.

He can hear Taaz briefing everyone, telling them the signal from Zenac will be sent as soon as the deed is done. The soldiers bring their weapons above their heads in a show of alliance. They are ready.

Once they sit again, The Oaf falls asleep, so Teegue slips from his grip. The sun is breaking through the darkness and he can see the wall. He checks he has a gun, grabs the rope and runs. He will find his father and Leyna, the woman who inspired him to stow away. She is the one person he wants to meet.

He keeps running until he finds a section of the wall with steps. They only reach halfway up, which is enough for him to throw the rope over and abseil down the other side. He manages this easily and as his feet hit the ground, he is confronted by a scene he is not prepared for. Dead soldiers, pools of blood and the stench of rotting flesh attack his nose. He retches.

The sun has brightened the sky to a pale blue, the dawn becoming morning. Wiping his mouth with the back of his hand, he places his cap over his nose and moves forward slowly avoiding the bodies and blood. He has no idea where to go, all the laneways look the same. His compass would be handy, but he had left it on the Salverz. What he finds amazing is no one is alive. Where is everybody?

A hand is on his shoulder making him freeze to the spot. "What the hell are you doing? Do you know the danger you are in?"

It's Taaz. Teegue relaxes, "You're inside the walls, so the High Priest is dead?"

"No, I saw you running. If something happens to you what do you think your father will do to me? Now, come with me you twat, and don't cause any more trouble."

"Aww, come on Taaz, we're here now. Let's go and see what is happening."

"You don't give the orders. Now behave and start walking."

Teegue is pissed off. He was so close to being in the action and now he's back on the other side of the wall with The Oaf watching over him again. There is no way he can escape again because he is being watched closely this time. He wanted to meet Leyna and now he has to work out another plan because he's not going back to Arisis without meeting her.

Chapter 32

Leyna

They are standing at the front door of his home. Leyna is filled with ambition as adrenaline pumps through her body. Her dream of revenge is near. *Thadd, it's happening my darling. You'll see your father soon and you can deal with him however you wish.* She smiles inwardly knowing this is exactly what Thadd wants her to do, his memory has led her here.

"Leyna, move so I can break down the door," says Breex. He gives it a try, but the door doesn't budge. "Holy hell, this door is a fortress all by itself. Time to use the laser again."

The laser works even faster on the reinforced timber door and once inside, Leyna is again confronted with the audacity of the High Priest. The floor is marble, gold taps adorn the kitchen as well as stainless steel appliances. There is also a butler's pantry full of expensive food, condiments and quality utensils. She imagines how many people he would have entertained in this place, all of them agreeing to his ways to stay alive.

Breex and Zenac come back into the kitchen after scouting the house, "He's gone," says Breex, "there's no one here."

"What? That bastard. So much for your idea of drawing him out in the open Zenac."

"He obviously doesn't care about his family as much as I thought. Any idea where he will have gone?"

"He could be anywhere by now. There are secret tunnels out of the Vatican, I'm sure he used one of those to escape. Now we know why we weren't attacked. The coward ran away instead."

"If you're right that he used the tunnels Leyna, the chances of us finding him are remote." She sits on one of the expensive gold adorned dining chairs, her fingers rubbing the 18 carat gold weaved into the timber frame. "We will have to regroup, see how many of our soldiers are injured and bury the dead. Eween and I will take over this house, assuming he is alive. Zenac, call your people into the city, we will need their help with cleaning up. Also, take any prisoners down to the crypts, we can keep them there for now."

"Leyna, we still have the specialised armed forces to deal with, there are one hundred of them."

"Find yourselves accommodation and then gather what is left of your troops and take care of the armed forces."

Breex and Zenac leave her to find their own accommodation. Breex asks her to call him if she needs anything, and to stay put. She needs to rest and look after her shoulder. "We will look for Eween too. If he is alive, we'll have him back with you as soon as we can."

Thanking him, she closes the door behind them. Breex had added the timber square he had taken out of the door back in and sealed it. For now, she is safe. She starts wondering whether Eween is safe too and hoping he is. Although, fighting with one arm would not have been easy. Still, she admires his courage at causing the diversion earlier. When he does eventually come back, he won't be happy to learn that the High Priest has escaped.

Despite her disgust at the opulence of this place, she is hungry so enters the pantry. She needs to keep up her strength. After eating, she tidies up and then heads to have a shower. She needs to clean up her wound and take the blood of the many soldiers she killed off her body. When she walks in, she sees the opulence of the kitchen continues in this bathroom, which is as large as the kitchen. Shaking her head, she wonders whether the High Priest has any morals. Then she laughs to herself, obviously he doesn't.

Two days later, a thin and bedraggled Eween walks into the house. He collapses into her arms. She grabs a pillow to place under his head and goes to the kitchen for water. Bringing the glass to his lips he gags as he tries to drink. "I've been so worried, I'm sorry to see you this way but glad you made it back to me. When you're ready, tell me what happened. I'll go and get some medical supplies."

She proceeds to clean up his wounds. His face is swollen and bruised, his good arm cut in three places, and he is filthy with blood and mud. He needs one of the cuts on his arm stitched and he flinches when she applies the disinfectant. It's deep and already starting to fester.

"I managed to escape from the specialised armed forces down a quiet laneway," he coughs, "more water please?"

"Here," she allows him to drink more this time, "take it easy, don't speak too fast. You're safe now."

"I'll be okay, Leyna. The two idiots who attacked me in the lane are both dead, and the specialised armed forces have been halved."

"I know. Breex and Zenac along with Zenac's soldiers have been cleaning up and our casualties are half those of The Enforcers. Apart from not capturing the High Priest, I count this mission a success."

He nods slightly without answering. Placing his head on the pillow, he begins falling asleep. She lets him be, simply throwing a blanket over him. Having stitched up the more serious deep cut his other injuries are not major, so leaving him on the couch is the best option for him right now.

She busies herself with sending instructions on her compupad as well as messages to her team of what still needs to be done. She also sends out a reward notice for anyone knowing the whereabouts of the High Priest, *Ten Thousand Licdan,* enough to keep a family looked after for at least ten years. This should be enough incentive for someone to come forward. She makes sure to mention the High Priest be brought to her alive.

Eween stirs and she walks over to him. "How are you feeling?"

"Sore and bruised but happy to see your beautiful face," he says, forcing himself to sit up.

Leyna helps him with her hand on his back. "Are you able to stand and walk to the kitchen? Maybe some food will make you feel better? When was the last time you ate?"

"Sounds good and I don't remember. The last few days are a blur of me coming in and out of consciousness."

"Well, you're here with me now and there is ample food in the pantry to feed dozens of people. Can you believe this place?"

He looks around and whistles, "It's fancy, isn't it? No expense spared for our esteemed ruler." He spits these words out with contempt. "Now, what happened? Where is the High Priest?"

"We don't know, he escaped. Presumably through the tunnels underneath the city. He could be anywhere, but apart from Vatican City there is not much left outside of Rome. Italy was bombed into oblivion. There aren't many places left where he can find shelter and have clean water. Isn't it amazing how he didn't think about anyone but himself? He escaped on his own."

"And that surprises you? That man is not human. I'm sure black blood runs through his veins because who would bring such atrocities upon his own people?"

She agrees with him as she brings out some soup from the pantry to heat up for them both. She will not let this go. They will find him and this time she will torture him because killing is too good for a man like him.

Chapter 33

Zenac

Zenac is pacing the floor. He had chosen a house at the back of the compound with the one next door for Taaz and his security team. Safety is his main concern, especially that Teegue is now with him. Angry at him for disobeying the order not to come into The Vatican, Zenac is planning to send Teegue back to Arisis in the next few days. He is waiting on a rocket, one of the super-charged ones, to arrive. He is sitting with Zaydin discussing who will go with Teegue.

"I need Taaz and his team with me so the bodyguard I assigned to Teegue has to stay with us. Who do you suggest?"

"What about Anorea? She knows Teegue well and she is trustworthy."

He thinks about Anorea and the rumours around her helping Leyna and Eween escape Arisis. There is no evidence she did as no one has come forward to claim she is the traitor. Anorea is too good a commando for him to think she may have done such a thing and until he knows anything otherwise, he puts this thought of her betrayal behind him.

"Okay Taaz, you brief Commando5-Anorea and make sure she keeps her eye on Teegue at all times. I don't trust him because he wants to meet Leyna and will do anything to stay here."

Taaz rises from the chair, "As you wish, Sir. I will let you know when the rocket arrives."

He sees Zaydin as well as Taaz and his security team out knowing they won't let him down. Sitting again, he calls Dawa.

When she answers he tells her what has happened and where he is living. She is happy that Teegue is safe even though he was disobedient. She looks forward to seeing him on Arisis and will dole out some punishment then. Surprised to hear the High Priest escaped, she talks of her concern that Zenac will remain on Earth longer now.

"Possibly, Dawa. I should stay near Leyna and Eween, remember they must answer for their escape and stealing the Salverz. So do the others who came with them."

He hears her sighing and saying she understands, then she changes the subject to the success of the Mazadon Water Project. Already, three hundred people live on the planet and most are employed to work on the pipeline. He can hear the pride in her voice.

"Dawa, you deserve all the praise for this. You engaged the Luminaries in this and won their support to keep Arisis a viable planet for us all. When I return, we will begin rescuing more people from Earth if they still want to leave."

He listens to her telling him how things will be different on Earth now the High Priest and The Enforcers no longer rule. Agreeing he says, "We have to organise a new parliament and the people will vote for their own ruler this time. You are right, not everyone will want to leave if the new rulers bring prosperity back to Earth. Darling, we could discuss things all night, but I have to have some rest, tomorrow I must deal with Teegue."

It's morning and Zenac didn't sleep well. The last thing he needs is Teegue causing more fuss.

Slamming the door to the bedroom, Teegue yells at his father, "I'm not going, and you can't make me."

Zenac knew this would be his reaction. Until he meets Leyna, he will not agree to returning to Arisis. He walks out of the front door leaving Teegue to fume. Hopefully he will see reason later.

He is at the house where Leyna and Eween are now living and knocks on the door. When it opens, he sees Eween, "Oh, hi. Glad to see you, but you don't look so good.

"I'm better now. Leyna has nursed me, you should have seen me yesterday. I'm learning to deal with only one arm and it's better than being dead."

"You are right, I guess. At least you have Leyna to help you, is she around?"

She walks in from the bedroom as he speaks. "Hello, Zenac. Have you come to do more negotiating?" she asks, indicating he sits at the table.

"Of sorts. I wanted to ask you to see my son, Teegue. He is fascinated by you and won't return to Arisis until he meets you."

"Your son? You brought your son with you on this mission?"

"Ah no. He stowed away and well, he's here now and won't return until he meets you. What do you say, are you willing to make a young man happy?"

He watches as Leyna thinks about his request. He knows she is thinking how to manipulate this situation to benefit her. She is smart and will always play to her advantage.

"If I do agree to meet him, you have to give me something in return. Leave Eween and I here, we have much work to do."

"You need to pay for your crimes, Leyna. I will look weak to everyone on Arisis if I come home empty handed."

"Then we have nothing further to discuss. Good day, Zenac," she says walking back towards the bedroom.

"Wait. Okay, I agree. But please convince my son to return, he has this idea of staying here to help you restore things. He wants to help in the capture too."

She turns saying, "What an admirable son you have Zenac. He has a good future ahead of him if he feels confident enough to bring stability back to Earth. Which is what Eween and I plan to do."

She walks over to where Eween is seated placing her hand on his shoulder as he looks up at her, "Zenac, we are determined to bring the people of Earth a life they deserve, they have suffered enough at the hands of these tyrants. We need to stay here and finish what we have started. Bring your son back with you tonight and I know he will return after I have time with him."

Zenac returns to the house to find Teegue watching television with a beer and eating snacks. "Where did you find the beer?"

"Dad, there are heaps in the pantry. Haven't you looked?"

Admittedly, apart from heating up some food, he hadn't looked through the pantry or the fridge. Going to get himself a bottle, he falls onto the lounge and clinks the top of his son's bottle wondering why there is alcohol in the High Priest's kitchen when he and The Enforcers did not drink. Or so they let everyone believe.

"Are we good?"

"Only if you let me stay until I meet Leyna."

"Well, you and I are meeting with her tonight. She has agreed to meet you," says Zenac watching disbelief take over Teegue's face. A feeling of calm wafts over him as he hopes Leyna can convince Teegue to leave in a compliant manner.

"Fantastic. She didn't ask for anything in return. Like allowing her and Eween to stay on Earth?"

Zenac is proud of how astute his son is, he thinks ahead, which is the sign of a good leader. "That is exactly what she asked for, yet I am still considering taking them back. Our citizens will want to see them pay."

"I disagree. If Leyna and Eween are elected and do help Earth to recover, no one will want to see them back in prison. Dad, your pride has been hurt, that's all."

Again, Teegue proves he is older than his years. It has been good having him around even though he stowed away, but he can't bend the rules for Teegue, he must return to Arisis as soon as possible.

Chapter 34

Teegue

After making sure his father was telling the truth about meeting Leyna, Teegue goes back into the bedroom to call Trisia.

"If you're calling because I told your mother, she gave me no choice."

"Ha no, I'm past that. I know how convincing my mother can be. I'm calling because I have good news. Leyna has agreed to meet me. Tonight, actually."

"Great, I'm happy for you. After the meeting please come home, I miss you."

"Yes, Father is having a rocket sent down to collect me along with a few others who want to return. I miss you too, but I'm not leaving until I have done something so my name will be in the history books too."

He hears her sighing with frustration, "Teegue you are twenty-years-old, what makes you think your father or Leyna will let you do something. And like what exactly?"

"Capture the High Priest and return him to Leyna. He escaped and is somewhere in hiding. Once I return him, it will mean my name will be blazoned everywhere, including the history books."

Trisia is laughing, "You have got to be joking? You want to achieve something that Leyna couldn't do? Nor any of the army of soldiers down there with you."

"Don't mock me, Trisia. This world is not safe while that man is still alive. I intend to be a part of the group who makes us all safe again, whether we live on Earth or Arisis. Actually, any planet for that matter."

"You have put some thought into this. How do you plan on finding him? I'm sure he has bodyguards"

"No, he escaped on his own. The selfish bastard only saved himself."

"I wouldn't be too sure of that, Teegue. A man like that would have had an escape plan, and to a safe place, one where he is guarded and looked after."

"Possibly, but I will work something out. Listen, I do miss you and will return soon, be patient."

He listens to her as she asks him not to be stupid and to take heed of what his father asks of him. Zenac along with Leyna and Eween have the resources to find and kill the High Priest. She begs him to leave this task to them. The urgency in her voice makes him more determined to do this soon, he wants to kiss those luscious lips once more.

He and Zenac walk in and Teegue takes a breath. This house is even more opulent than the one they are in; how much money did that idiot splurge? The table in front of them is laden with delicacies and Leyna asks them to start eating. "It is nice to meet you Teegue. Your father tells me you stowed away, what was so important that you wanted to come back to Earth?"

"To meet you," he says, stuffing a piece of meat into his mouth. There are two people in the kitchen cooking and there is a waiter serving them. Leyna has laid it on for him and his father.

"Apart from that. I already know you wanted this and now we have met, what else interested you in this mission?"

"You inspired me with your courage. Both you and Eween. I want to be like you, to make a difference. There is much to do here and I want to be a part of helping Earth to recover."

She looks towards Zenac saying, "I told your father you are an admirable young man. He should be proud of you."

"I'll be prouder when he stops disobeying me," scoffs Zenac as the waiter fills his wine glass again.

"Well yes Teegue, your father is correct. An admirable person listens to orders, this is a lesson you have to learn."

He looks towards her with a sheepish look then glares at his father. Teegue doesn't comment, instead remaining silent and allowing the adults to talk. He figures he will learn if he listens to what they have to say and glean some ideas from them he can use.

His father speaks of forming a parliament with the people voting for a leader. Leyna agrees and gives her ideas as to who should form such a team. "Breex is a good leader, I will ask him if he wants to run for one of the ministerial positions. My friend Fixor is also a good leader, I will discuss this with him. Maybe twelve to start with? What do you think Eween?"

"Before we start thinking about this, we need to find the High Priest. I'm not comfortable while he languishes out there, possibly with others. He is not alone."

"I was thinking the same thing, Eween. Why would he escape without having a safe place to go? However, we can begin forming some form of government while sending out soldiers to find him. I don't see a problem, we need to make things better for the citizens as quickly as possible."

"The reward is out there now," says Leyna, "it's incentive enough for someone to bring him to me. My plans for him are as vicious as his have ever been, he will rue the day he ever met me."

Teegue listens as they continue this topic. He will find out who these soldiers are, befriend them and earn their trust. Forget leaving on the rocket heading to collect him. The plan of how to bring the High Priest to Leyna is formulating in his mind. This is going to happen, and it will be him Leyna and his father will look up to. The Licdan reward is only secondary to his cause, it is the recognition he is after.

Chapter 35

Dawa

Trisia is sitting in Dawa's office. Dawa hands her a tissue saying, "Tell me exactly what he said."

Sniffling, Trisia tells her of Teegue's ridiculous idea of him capturing the High Priest, "He says he wants his name in the history books."

Dawa turns away from Trisia so she doesn't see the tears stinging her eyes. That son of theirs is as ambitious as both herself and Zenac, they only have themselves to blame. She remembers the look in his eyes when he implored her to take him with her during the kidnapping, he didn't want her to leave him. That look of determination will be with Teegue forever, she knows he is a leader and will succeed one day. But not like this. He doesn't have the experience of knowing how the High Priest operates that she and Zenac have. His brutality knows no bounds.

Turning back towards Trisia she asks her, "He didn't discuss how he was planning to do this?"

"I don't think he has any idea yet. You don't think he's going to go through with this stupid idea, do you?" Trisia looks up at Dawa pleading. Her face is fearful, showing how much Trisia loves Teegue.

Dawa knows her son is determined enough to at least try, but he will most probably be killed trying. Shivers run through her body at the thought of losing her son. "Thank you for coming to tell me this, Trisia. I will deal with Teegue through his father. Don't worry, we'll make sure he doesn't do anything stupid."

"I know you can stop him. This is why I came to see you. Thanks for listening, and please call me if you need my help with anything."

"You're sweet, but I think I've got this. Go home and don't tell anyone what you know, there is no need to worry your parents or anyone else for that matter."

Trisia walks towards the door and stops, "You are a good mother and Teegue is lucky to have you. I hope he appreciates how much you love him."

And I hope he appreciates how much *you love him*, Trisia, Dawa thinks silently as the door closes.

Her father is pacing in the lounge room. Sheabz is enraged, "How could he be so stupid. He is placing his life at risk and those of everyone on the mission. What is Zenac doing about this?"

"Please calm down," she says, indicating he sit. As he makes himself comfortable in the recliner, she continues, "Zenac told me the High Priest has escaped and he along with Leyna and Eween have taken over the family compound. They are sorting prisoners and burying the dead. Teegue is in the same house as Zenac, he is safe." After her cook places some warming soup on the side table for both of them, she sits next to her father.

"Safe for now. Your son is taking risks and I hope this crazy mission hasn't alerted The Enforcers of our whereabouts. The people of Arisis trust us to keep them safe."

She looks at him, the concern written all over his face. She explains The Enforcer's army has been halved, three of the High Priest's family members remain as prisoners and Zenac said they are formulating a government, the locals will be voting soon. A new leader will be elected with the future looking brighter.

"Leyna will make a good leader," he says, slurping some soup.

"She will be coming back with Zenac. As will Eween. They have to answer for their crime. Although, I agree with you. When I spoke to Zenac about this possibility he said our people will expect them to be punished. He did say that whoever the people of Vatican City vote for will determine the outcome of Leyna and Eween's future. If they are voted in, he will consider giving them a pardon."

"That's wise of him. Now, back to Teegue. What plans do you have for him when he returns?"

She is quiet because she is not sure how to answer this question. Being angry about his actions is one thing, but punishing him for having the courage to assist in this mission, is it necessary? She explains she may speak to Teegue about asking permission rather than secretly stowing away.

"No, Dawa. Teegue must know how much he has pained you and the danger he has placed everyone in by trying to be a hero. Don't be soft on him because you have two other children that will follow in his footsteps if you don't show them right from wrong."

Picking up the soup bowls, she walks to the kitchen and places them on the sink, thanking the cook. Before she walks back in to sit with her father again, she thinks of what he has said. She had not thought of the impact of Teegue's actions on his siblings. The thought of them rebelling like Teegue is frightening.

Chapter 36

Zenac

He is in St Peter's Square walking with Breex and Fixor. The markets are busy with people going about their daily routine. The vibe is calmer because the tension of living under The Enforcers rule has ended. There was always an underlying tension while they lived with the dystopian rules, something that everyone is happy to be free of.

There are still signs of the struggles of the past weeks, many of the paths are still blood-stained and there is rubbish piled up from the damaged houses and buildings. Workers are beginning to rebuild, a sign that things are already mending. It will take years for the atrocities of The Enforcers to be remedied, but Zenac knows the people of this city are resilient. In fact, all humans who survived the tyrannical rule are resilient.

"Yes, I agree with you," says Breex speaking with a vendor, "the High Priest has no morals and it was time he no longer ruled. Voting will happen soon; we are preparing the ballots now and will keep everyone informed."

As they keep walking, many vendors and people thank them for what they have done. They no longer fear for their lives and look forward to the vote. Many mention Leyna and Eween in glowing terms, they are already loved. Others are vocalising how it was about time someone stood up to the tyrants who ruled with such iron fists.

"How humbling to hear these people speak. They have suffered so much; we all did under their rule. All I want is for us to find the High Priest and bring him to justice. Then I can go back to Arisis with my son and anyone else who wants to come back."

"I'm waiting to see what happens with the voting, Zenac. I would be proud to serve the people of Earth if I am voted in. You should probably know that Leyna and Eween will fight you over taking them back, even if Leyna is not voted as leader," says Fixor

Zenac nods but has no desire to discuss this issue with either Fixor or Breex. Eween aided Leyna, and he too needs to be brought to justice. Leyna did ask for a pardon after meeting Teegue, and Zenac had agreed on the night. His mind is not yet made up. However, he is not so determined as he was, Leyna and Eween are succeeding in fixing things. Once Vatican City is working well, there may not be a reason to bring them back, and the citizens will probably not allow him to do so.

He keeps walking with Breex and Fixor thinking about Arisis, he misses Dawa as well as Aria and Braxton. And he misses ruling over his people, he looks forward to being next to Dawa again soon and doing his real job.

When he arrives at his temporary home, Teegue is in the kitchen. There are pots and pans simmering on the cooktop, the table is set for six and he smells an enticing curry. The essence of the aromatic herbs and spices have filtered throughout the house.

"Are we having company?"

"I am. I hope you don't mind, I've invited a few friends over. You can join us for dinner and then… maybe disappear?" asks Teegue with the last two words whispered.

"Gee, thanks. I know when I'm not wanted," he laughs, "but sure, I'll retreat to my bedroom once I've filled my belly with this amazing feast."

"There is so much food still available in this pantry, so we're having chicken korma with rice, naan bread and dahl."

"Sounds fabulous, but who are these friends you've invited?"

"Oh a few boys I've encountered since being here. Some of them have been left orphaned and live together nearby. Wait until you hear the stories they have to tell."

"Sounds interesting," says Zenac as he heads towards his bedroom, "I'll freshen up and come back to help you." Teegue is yet to leave as the rocket taking him home has been delayed. Zenac is pleased he is making friends but this won't stop him sending Teegue back.

He looks around at the four boys, well actually, they are young men, sitting at their table. They are probably the same age as Teegue, but they have seen so much more of life than he. One of them is telling the story of his father who was a locksmith before the war. The Enforcers came into his store and took over. His business was lost just like that. He was told there would be no need for locks in the new world because everyone would be protected by the new rulers. When he came home, he was so ashamed that he let them take his business so easily, his wife found him dead in the bathroom. With five mouths to feed, she didn't know what she was going to do. This is when this boy went out to work in the factories earning what he could so they would survive. His mother died at the hands of The Enforcers only a few years ago because she dared to accuse one of them for being rude to her. She was stoned to death.

The others tell similar stories of how they became vexpersons, orphaned by The Enforcers. Zenac is saddened with what these young men have had to deal with so early in their lives. How lucky were the people of Arisis to have escaped such things?

After Teegue and the boys leave to continue partying, Zenac settles onto his compupad and checks messages. There is one from Dawa, so he calls her.

"How are you? Are you looking forward to Teegue being home in a week?"

"You know the answer to that question. I'm well, as are your other two children who say hello, by the way."

"I miss them, and you as well. I also miss being by your side at the office. You are doing a very capable job without me though," he laughs.

"I still prefer to work with you. How are things going with the voting? Has there been a date scheduled yet?"

He proceeds to tell her things are moving along and maybe in the next few weeks the voting can start. He is pushing things because being home with her is where he wants to be, but procedures have to be set in place and Leyna wants only the best people for her cabinet. She is already talking as if she has won.

"She can be confident," says Dawa, "there is no one else."

"Yes, I guess you're right. My decision of whether to bring her and Eween back will be determined by the citizens of this city." He continues talking to her for hours, asking about Sheabz and the other Luminaries. She confirms they are well, although Sheabz is beginning to show his age. His memory is not what it used to be. It saddens Zenac to hear this, Sheabz is not only Dawa's father, but he is also his confidante when he wants a man's opinion. He asks whether there is any immediate concern and Dawa says no, he is eighty and these things happen. Zenac agrees with her and hopes that Sheabz lives long enough to see the High Priest dead because then he will know that everyone on Earth and Arisis are safe.

Chapter 37

Teegue

Teegue is sitting with his four friends at the newly re-opened café. Four weeks since the attack on the city and the square is beginning to come alive again. People are smiling and the old brown sacks worn during The Enforcers rule are giving way to clothes that were stored away years ago. There is an individuality coming back to people's lives, imagination is making a resurgence and people are breathing easy once more.

The café has indoor and outdoor seating and they have chosen to sit outside in a corner, wanting to remain inconspicuous. The morning is warm and Teegue is speaking to three of them specifically, "Ok, you are all part of the team of soldiers seeking to find the High Priest and I want in. Where is my uniform, Nable?" he asks the boy sitting nearest him. Nable is not going to be part of the team, his disability stops him being a soldier. His hand was cut off by The Enforcers because he refused to sweep the street where the High Priest was to walk. So Nable has been given the task of finding things they will need, speaking to the right people and making sure

Teegue and his three soldiers have all the information to find the High Priest and bring him back to Leyna.

"It's in my backpack, I'll give it to you when it's safe. There are too many people around here. Now, here is the information I was able to find out, he is closer than you think. Maybe only an hour away, he went west. He is in the town of Bracciano at the remains of the medieval Castello Orsini-Odescalchi. There are five others with him."

"Fantastic, well done Nable. I knew he would not be alone. I assume they are armed?"

"Of course. The Castello is basically a one storey fortress now, the five towers didn't survive the war. There are many ways to enter without being detected and night is best."

"Yes, that makes sense. Well, I say we don't wait. Tonight at 23.00 hours, meet me at the end of the Grand Hall. The rocket to take me home arrives in two days, and of course, I won't be on it."

Nable smiles, "Also, I managed to find two answaes, they're old but still working. Teegue, I suggest you take one and I'll keep the other. Keep in touch with me in case anything goes wrong."

"Nothing will go wrong, but thanks. Now, come on boys, let's go and celebrate. Where can we meet some girls?"

It doesn't take long for them to find a young crowd at a park near the entrance to the city gates. Music plays from an old DJ turntable set that Teegue finds out was buried under the rubble of one of the buildings being rebuilt. The music seeps into his body as he moves to the beat. He remembers his parents telling him of festivals they attended during their twenties, this has the same feeling of people his age enjoying themselves and letting loose.

The five of them linger around the edges of the park watching as young people swill drinks and dance without care as their bodies writhe along with the rhythm. The beat of the music melds with the atmosphere of the young people singing along. It is a sound that invites them to join. Teegue can't help smiling, how much has his generation missed out on? He breathes this atmosphere of love, music and dance telling the boys to follow him because it's time to party before their mission goes ahead tonight.

Mingling in the centre of the crowd, sweat and body odour mix with heady adrenaline as Teegue sees two girls dancing towards him.

"Hi," says the blonde, "haven't seen you guys around here before. Are you part of the brave soldiers who freed us?"

Nable speaks before Teegue can answer, "We might be."

"Oh, you're maimed. You can't be part of them, how would you fight?"

"I am able to hold my own," he laughs and takes her aside, away from the crowd.

Teegue smiles as he watches and wonders how often Nable uses his disability to entice girls. The second girl with a shock of dark curls is half his height and is engrossed in the music almost oblivious to him. "Hi, I'm Teegue."

Looking up towards him, he sees her beautiful eyes, a golden brown and as big as unshelled almonds. They are spellbinding as he begins dancing close to her. For a minute he wonders where the other boys are but then figures they can look after themselves. He's going to enjoy himself with this captivating girl.

"Hi, I'm Jzinta." She doesn't say anything further. Instead she keeps dancing in towards the crowd with Teegue following her.

They keep dancing as the music grows louder and more young people join the party.

Later, they are in her home. She definitely is a quiet one. Even as they made love on her four- poster bed, she was quiet. How unusual to see such a bed, the timbers are strong and expensive. How does she afford an item like this let alone a place like this?

Now, they are seated on a settee in a sun-filled lounge room. This apartment is part of a complex of six. The place he and his father are staying at is only two blocks away. She has told him a little about herself and although surprising, he knew there was something different about her look. Jzinta is the love child of the High Priest. One of many probably. She said her mother was a slave from an African country, she doesn't know which one because her mother died during childbirth. She was thrown around from various foster homes to a teen detention centre where one of the guards befriended her. This is his home and he allows her to live here as long as she does chores. Considering her future in detention was bleak, living this way is a better alternative. *This explains the expensive bed and your dark, brooding looks.*

"He's a good man, he treats me well and likes having me around." "Where is he now?"

"At work, he'll be home soon though, maybe you should go."

"Of course, yes. I didn't realise the time. This has been great. You are beautiful and I enjoyed being with you this afternoon."

She bats her huge eyes and smiles, "Thanks, it's been nice meeting you. See you around sometime?"

"Yes, maybe," he says as he opens the door to leave, "I'll find you wherever there is music, I'm sure." He leaves and as he heads home Trisia pops into his head. He decides not to feel guilty because he is a long way from her and Jzinta was a bit of relief before the mission tonight.

The five of them are at the end of the Grand Hall. Nable has given them their weapons and Teegue has the answae. He looks around making sure no one is around.

"You have a long way to go, it's a seven hour walk to the Castello. Take care my friends, I await your good news."

Teegue pulls Nable towards him, slapping his back, "Thank you for all your help, we will be in touch as soon as we succeed."

They walk out of the hall leaving Nable standing there. Each has their head high knowing they are doing a service for humanity.

Four hours in, they stop in an abandoned bunker used during the war to rest and refuel. "We've made good progress, and this full moon has helped," says Teegue after biting into a bread roll. The others remain silent because they are too tired to reply.

Teegue rests his head on his backpack and falls into a restless sleep. Trisia is falling away from him even though he is screaming for her to grab his hand. The shrill of her voice wakes him. Sweating and thirsty, he reaches for his water bottle. Taking a deep breath it takes him a minute to realise where he is.

"You ok? You were thrashing around."

"Just a bad dream, I'm fine. We should probably pack up and head out."

The southern side of Lake Bracciano comes into view and they drop down as a farmer goes past with his cart. "That's our way into the Castello. You two, go and *borrow* his cart. Don't hurt him. Bring him back here because he's going to help us."

Teegue was right, the farmer was willing to help them. In fact, when he heard the High Priest was staying in his hometown, he was more than prepared to help the boys capture him. And now they were five again. Teegue was happy to have another strong man on his team and his body was tensing in a state of excitement. They were going to walk back into the Vatican with the High Priest, and he was going to present him to Leyna.

Chapter 38

Zenac

Zenac's face is burning with rage, he is furious. Breex has walked in with Fixor as well as Flaiwyn and Asheel. Zenac relays what has happened. "He has been trouble ever since he stowed away with us. His friend Nable and a young girl, Jzinta have told me he and his three friends are at the Castello Orsini-Odescalchi in Bracciano. Apparently, the High Priest is there, this is his safe house."

"Is anyone else surprised he has remained so close? He didn't run very far."

"Breex, he probably thought no one would find him. Although this may seem naïve, I'm sure he has a strategy."

"And your son? What does he think he is doing there?"

Zenac proceeds to tell them about the boys Teegue befriended, all of them intent on capturing the High Priest. "Now that Leyna has a reward for his capture, they probably think they can bring him back."

"Not before they are killed trying," says Asheel.

"That is my concern. They may already be dead. We have to go and rescue them and bring back the High Priest ourselves. Teegue was being irresponsible, placing them in danger like this, four young men trying to do the job of experienced soldiers who even with experience, does not guarantee success."

"Okay Zenac, enough talking. I have my Jeep outside and we can be in Bracciano in no time. Come on, let's go."

"Load it up with supplies, Breex and bring your laser along. Fixor, Flaiwyn and Asheel bring along the tools we will need to scale the Castello walls. I'm right behind you," says Zenac as he thinks about what he needs.

Breex parks the car on the southern side of the lake behind a cluster of bushes and they head towards the wall. In the shadow of the late afternoon sun, the wall glows a dirty grey as they throw the ropes over. "Let's split up, Zenac you and Asheel go left towards the back and Flaiwyn, Fixor and I will take the front."

Zenac nods in agreement and thinks about what he will say to his son when he sees him. His anger has escalated in the time it took to arrive here. Teegue was supposed to be on the rocket that arrived this morning and heading back to Arisis, back to safety. If anything happens to him... he tries not to think about his son being hurt in some way, or worse, being dead.

He and Asheel find a back entrance locked with huge chains and an old alarm system. Zenac calls Breex telling him to be careful if he uses the laser, the whole place is probably alarmed. Breex acknowledges telling him Flaiwyn already suspected this, he found plans of the layout that included the electrical and alarm system, he has them with him. Zenac will be informed once Flaiwyn has the alarm disabled.

Zenac blows out a breath full of relief as he and Asheel wait. As they sit on the low stone fence a shiver runs down his spine – the place is quiet, maybe too quiet. It's a couple of hours later when he receives the message from Breex that it is safe to enter. Breex, Fixor and Flaiwyn will be at the back entrance in a few minutes.

When Breex opens the door to allow them in, Zenac is surprised no one stopped them. "Where are the High Priest's protectors? This place looks deserted."

"I thought the same thing, but there are another two floors they could be hiding in. The five towers no longer exist, and only *Sala Isabella* remains, this is the one where the magnificent red tapestry adorned one wall. It was the private bedroom of Isabella De Medici, and there is a trapdoor, they may be holed up down there."

"Or have escaped from there," says Zenac, "let's start by looking in that room first."

They check the whole area from the back entrance to the bedroom, but no one is around. Frustration and fear start to take over as Zenac wonders if they will find his son. "It's time to separate again, we'll take the first floor, you three head to the second. Come on, Asheel," he calls her, indicating with his arm to follow him.

Finding Breex, Fixor and Flaiwyn at the top of the grandiose staircase to the second floor, Breex shakes his head, "I'm sorry Zenac, the place is deserted. What I don't understand is, how did they know we were coming?"

"They may not have known. This is probably part of the High Priest's plan. At least we haven't found any dead bodies, hopefully this means Teegue and his friends are still alive."

A few minutes later they are sitting on the steps contemplating their next move. "We may as well return, there is nothing to see here."

They all move towards the entrance, Zenac letting out a despondent sigh.

"No. This is not true, please Zenac, tell me it's not true. No, no, nooooo."

Dawa's emotional screams are spilling all over him, her voice coming over the answae is filled with the anguish of a distraught mother. He had called her after coming back to the complex. After showering and resting he called because he needed to talk to someone. His own emotions were disturbing; a mix of hate, fear and a gut wrenching anxiety. It was bad enough when the twins were kidnapped, but this is infinitely worse. "I'm feeling the same as you, my darling. I have wavered between wanting to scream at

Teegue and hug him at the same time. How could he be so stupid?"

"He is alive, isn't he? Please tell me he is."

Placing his hand on his forehead he hears himself saying that he is, but he knows this may not be true. Dawa's relieved sighs come through the phone and whether she believes him or not, she doesn't say anything. He is grateful for no more questions because he doesn't want to lie to her. He listens as through tears she tells him she misses them both and wants them home. Until this moment he had not realised how much he wants this too. "Soon. We will find Teegue and his friends and we will be back home straight after. I promise you Dawa, I'm done with Earth, it's time to concentrate on our own planet and forging forward with our plans."

"You don't know how much it pleases me to hear you say this. Zenac, find Teegue and put all of this behind us."

Chapter 39

Dawa

They are sitting at the edge of the lake with a picnic rug laden with food she doesn't feel like eating. The air is clear, and the lake is so still it resembles glass. The mountains on either side are in perfect reflection. Last week's rain has added to the level, but the ground they are sitting on is already bone dry. The lake is forty square kms with two ten-thousand metre mountains on the western and eastern side. These mountains frame the lake and many people sit here taking photos of the spectacular sunrise and sunsets. There are marine animals in the lake, however they are not for human consumption. Many people found this out the hard way by fishing for their own food when they first arrived on Arisis. The animals, some that resemble fish, are poisonous and cause severe digestive problems for months. In some cases, people died. Now there are no fishing signs all around the lake.

It was Sheabz's idea to have a picnic, to come out into nature and help calm her nerves. Aria and Braxton are paddling in the shallows, the cold air not bothering them. She admits being outside seems to alleviate the pressure of thinking about Teegue. She hopes with all her heart he is okay, and that Zenac is right about Teegue being alive. Shirking this thought, she picks at a piece of bread. They will be able to stay out here for two hours, after that they either go back indoors or put their helmets on.

To help with her anxiety, she had baked and prepared all this food herself giving cook the day off. It was too much for the four of them, but she couldn't stop herself. It felt cathartic. The busier she is, the less time she has to think the worst.

"Those two are having a great time. Have they asked about Teegue?"

"Of course they have. Aria misses him but I think Braxton misses him more. They were getting on well, especially with their shared interest in soccer."

"It's only natural they miss him. Please try to remember that Zenac has the resources to find Teegue. Leyna and Eween will help too."

"I know, but what a huge task. It's tearing me apart as well that the last time Teegue and I spoke we had a fight. I don't want those words to be the last words I say to my son."

Sheabz moves closer to her, and she places her head on his shoulder. She stares out past her children's heads to the shimmering lake, her head throbbing with the beginning of yet another headache.

Lying in bed, her compupad pings. Lifting herself and leaning against her pillows, she opens it to find messages from Amallin and Zaydin.

Dawa writes:

Hello, do either of you have more news for me?

Zaydin writes:

Hi Dawa, Zenac hasn't spoken to me yet.

Amallin writes:

We're working on it, Dawa. You have to be patient.

Dawa writes:

I'm trying, Amallin. I feel so helpless, how would you feel if it was your son? Anyway, keep me informed. I'm calling Zenac now.

Zaydin writes:

We will, Dawa. Goodnight.

Amallin writes:

Zenac will ease your mind, I'm sure. Goodnight.

How will Zenac ease her mind when he still has no idea where Teegue has been taken? Still, Amallin is only trying to soothe her fractured nerves and she understands her concern. They are all at a loss. Tears slip down tickling her chin. She lets them fall allowing the pressure she is feeling to be relieved.

Before calling Zenac, she makes herself a cup of tea. With the cup warming her hands, she breathes a sigh looking out into the darkness. This is where she is at right now, in a darkness so thick it is consuming her. Deciding to put these awful thoughts aside, she calls Zenac.

"I haven't briefed Zaydin and Amallin yet, which is why they didn't give you any more information. There is some good news, we know the boys are alive. Teegue sent us a message on an old answae he was given. He managed to hide it in a secret compartment in his backpack. The High Priest's soldiers strip-searched them, went through their bags but obviously didn't look too hard."

"Oh, that's wonderful news. So, did Teegue say where they are?"

"No. They were blindfolded, but they are not too far away from the Castello. They left on foot. Teegue told me there are wine vats where they have been taken. The dungeon they are in reeks of wine."

"There were many wineries in that area, is it possible to search all of them?"

"Not many are left as they were bombed during the war. We're sending troops out in the morning, it shouldn't take too long. Be patient darling, we will find him and his friends."

"You're the second person to tell me to be patient tonight. I suppose there is not much else I can do. I love you, Zenac. Please stay safe."

"I love you too, Dawa. Teegue and I will be home soon."

Placing her head on the pillow she hopes he is right. If anything was to happen to Teegue how could she ever forgive Zenac for going on a mission that was not absolutely necessary? Zenac wants to be a strong leader and make Leyna and Eween pay for their crime. People forget, in years to come they won't even remember what Leyna and Eween did nor that they are escaped prisoners. Closing her eyes, she tries to reflect on the fact their son is alive, this is something positive to think about.

Chapter 40

High Priest

He is standing looking out of the front entrance. The Duomo has
given them refuge for weeks now. They had walked more than eighty
kilometres to arrive here, but it had been worth it. Sitting high atop a
mountain, Orvieto is seemingly impenetrable, or was in medieval
times. Now cars make the trek up bearable, yet they had walked and
were exhausted for days after. He chose this place because he
wanted to be as far away from Leyna and her crew of misfits as
possible, but they were limited to finding a safe place within walking
distance. Losing two of his men along the way was unavoidable, the
terrain is treacherous. Now, with only five men to protect him, he
has to be even more vigilant. Zenac will be wanting his son back, and
with Leyna's help they will do anything to rescue him.

He is keeping the boys safe for now because he needs to entice
Zenac to come to their rescue. The tunnels under this church, and in
fact, the whole of what was once Orvieto, are numerous. There are
also many rooms and caverns coming off the tunnels. The room the
boys are in was once used as a winery and food storage, the old vats

are covered in webs and ancient dust. Whether the wine is still fine to drink, he was not going to try. Even though the Duomo did sustain damage during the war, the main structure has held up well. It is safe for them to live here for as long as they need to.

"Sire, is there anything I can get for you?"

It is his servant, Marzeen, a woman he picked up from the street when they arrived. Beautiful but destitute, he took her in giving her a purpose. She keeps him happy in other ways too, for one so young, her lovemaking is wise and stimulating. Thinking this is making him want her right now.

"You, my sweet. Please come to me."

She walks to him, dropping her robe, all long legs and buxom beauty. He cups her supple breasts, bringing his lips to each one. Her delicate moans please him. There is no one around to see them as he guides her to the stone floor. She effortlessly moves over his body, which is still taut for someone of his age. At sixty-five, he exercises every day and Orvieto's steep streets are perfect for challenging walks. He sighs with pleasure as she performs her magic.

"You are everything I desire, my sweet," he says as they lie together.

"If not for you, I would be dead. I am yours and am grateful."

Kissing her forehead, he smiles and asks her to go and fetch him some wine from his personal stock. It is time for his afternoon snack.

"Sire, I have fresh bread and venison for you as well."

Slapping her rear, he thanks her. He is surprised at how much pleasure he has derived from saving her. Guessing she is only in her late twenties; she is probably right in saying she would have died. When he found her, she was skin and bones, with her long, black hair matted and filthy, dirt covering her whole body. Now, she is blossoming and is eager to please him. He will send out his men again and find more *servants* to save, he is ready for more women like Marzeen.

Walking into the eating hall, he sees his men already sitting enjoying the feast Marzeen has prepared for them. "I see you are all famished. No, please sit, don't get up," he says as he sits at the head of the dining table. How he wishes his twelve Enforcers and their families could be here, but alas there is only these six people he can enjoy food with now. He and his five soldiers. They will have to recruit more, there must be many strapping young people in these parts ready to earn and to serve him.

He looks towards his main man, Eldane saying, "Tomorrow morning organise yourselves and find more soldiers. Men and women, whoever is willing to help. Zenac will come looking for me with renewed force and I will not give him his son willingly."

"As you wish, Sire."

They all remain quiet, each of them faraway with their own thoughts. He looks around this great stone hall with its character similar to The Vatican; the whole church has used the same stone and fittings. Many of the artefacts and paintings are damaged or have been stolen, which is why this Duomo is now derelict.

Reflecting on how much has happened in his life, he was always destined to lead. Born to a court judge and lawyer, he knew the law of his country by the time he was ten. The island of Mauritius had barely escaped climate change by the time the treaty was signed. The GIS – Global Initiative for Sustainability did help the smaller islands with funds, but Mauritius and many of the islands off Africa remained poor. It was his idea to form an army and take on the richer nations, who didn't care about insignificant little islands.

His father had thought him crazy saying, "Dilvant, what makes you think you can topple the mighty powers like America, Britain and China?" He smirks as he wonders what his father would think of what he had accomplished. Now, because of that bitch, Leyna, he is fighting to be returned as ruler. She will pay, they will all pay for their defiance of his power.

Chapter 41

Leyna

Leyna is watching the troops line up at the entrance of the Grand Hall. Zenac is briefing them on what he wants them to do. She listens as his voice commands them. Zenac's voice has authority, it beams out and everyone listens. He has set out a fifty-kilometre radius of area to be searched and they are not to come back empty handed.

Breex, Fixor, Flaiwyn, Asheel and Zaydin stand with each of their troops. They have been assigned north, south, east and west of Bracciano, as well as scouring the area outside the Vatican. Although Leyna thinks this is a waste of time, the High Priest is not stupid enough to hide this close to the city.

Zenac had wanted to join his troops but she had convinced him it would be better to stay here with her and Eween. They could plot their revenge against the High Priest together. He had reluctantly agreed when Leyna told him he could torture the High Priest any way he wished. Along with what she had planned for him, he will beg for his life. Zenac walks to stand near her and Eween as the troops leave. "They will come back with Teegue and his friends, I know it," he says with a wavering voice.

Leyna places her hand on his shoulder, giving him a nod. "Let's go inside, our breakfast will be ready. We need to keep up our strength to defeat that bastard."

The three of them eat in silence. Leyna's thoughts run through what she will do when the High Priest is in front of her. Blazing anger burns her body as she thinks about the first thing she will do. Cut out his tongue? She no longer wants to hear his disgusting words, nor does she want him ever recruiting an army again.

Echoing her thoughts, Eween says, "He will rue the day he ever became leader. I will torture him slowly and hear him beg for mercy. Like he had mercy for all those people he hanged, beheaded and stoned."

"Me too. He will suffer under all three of us and be made an example of in front of the whole city."

"Zenac, Eween, we are taking pleasure in our thoughts of what to do. Maybe we should be a little more humane?"

They both look at her with Eween saying, "What? When was he ever humane, Leyna? No, he will suffer as much as his people have."

"I was just putting it out there in case you two were having second thoughts. Now, are we ready to discuss where to keep him?"

The breakfast dishes are cleared by the servants and Leyna dismisses them, she doesn't want anyone overhearing their plans. They begin discussing what to do and exactly how they will shame the High Priest. Everyone will know he is suffering as much as he has made the world suffer under his rule.

"We have intelligence that he is in Orvieto," announces Leyna.

"That close still? Bracciano and now Orvieto. I thought he would have run further away?" says Zenac.

"I'm sure it pleases you that we don't have to look far for your son. The High Priest has plans we don't know about. I know I have never understood his motivations."

"You're right, Leyna. Well, of course I'm pleased. I will organise more troops and we can head there tomorrow. Although, he is not stupid, Orvieto is set atop a mountain 325 metres above sea level. If he is at the Duomo, then it is a safe location. Without a car the climb up is treacherous."

She continues telling them that he is in fact at the Duomo. There are many tunnels they can escape from, so they have to make sure to capture him this time. Her spies tell her the boys are in one of the rooms off a tunnel and are unharmed for now.

"The sooner we take the High Priest prisoner, the better. Who knows what he will do to those boys if he knows his own life is in danger?"

"He is an unpredictable bastard. You will have to proceed with caution. May I suggest surrounding the area and at least cover all escape routes above ground."

"Leyna, I have already thought of this. You stay here and keep up the work of forming a government. I will look after bringing him back to you. And yes, I know… *alive*," he says as she is about to speak again.

She nods, "May luck be with you. This meeting is over, I will see you and your troops tomorrow afternoon. Zenac, please brief them well, I do not want another escape."

He takes her hand and kisses it, then looking straight into her eyes says, "I promise you with the life of my son to bring him back here and throw him to his knees in front of you."

Eween walks into the bedroom after seeing Zenac out. "I hope they find the boys in time, Zenac told me Dawa will never forgive him if something happens to Teegue."

"It is a dire situation and I would hate to be in their shoes. Teegue may be young but he is not stupid, he knows the High Priest will not harm him because he wants his father to come to the rescue. The question is, will they make it out of there alive?"

"I wouldn't put anything past the High Priest. Now, we have work to do. You want to visit the prisoners, right?"

"Yes, it's time we give them an ultimatum, join us or remain in prison for the rest of their lives."

. . .

Arriving at the catacombs where the prisoners are being held, Leyna speaks to the head warden, "Have you brought the prisoners into the main arena?"

"Hello, Leyna and Eween. Yes, we have fifty of them ready for you, and we will keep sending fifty in as you finish with the ones before."

"Excellent," she says, as she and Eween follow the warden.

Both Leyna and Eween speak to the prisoners and give them the offer. They put forward the pros and cons of them becoming model citizens of Vatican City and joining their cause or dying in prison.

"You know what you can do with your offer. We are loyal to the High Priest, we are his soldiers not yours," yells one prisoner.

Another prisoner yells back, "Hey, who are you speaking for? I do not want to die in prison." Others join the second prisoner shouting the same thing.

Leyna and Eween smile to each other then she puts up her palms, "Please, we will give you all the opportunity to make your choice. There is no need to fight amongst yourselves."

The shouting and yelling subdue to a murmur as Leyna explains how the wardens will help them to fill out the forms being handed to them. "Please add all your details and if you need help, then ask your warden. Anyone who wishes to join us will be allowed to leave the prison once all checks have been completed. We will find housing for you and there are jobs out there as well. Anyone who leaves and then is found to be collaborating with the remaining Enforcers or other prisoners left inside, will find themselves straight back here. Think twice about double crossing us."

In bed after a long day, Eween and Leyna are pleased with how many prisoners took up the offer. They both hope these people will be model citizens and stay on their side. Leyna did make it clear to them if they conform then they will prosper along with everyone else in Vatican City. She hopes she has made the right decision by pardoning over three hundred prisoners so far.

Chapter 42

Zenac

He smiles back towards Leyna as he leaves with his troops. Their army vans are filled with weapons, trackers and night sensory equipment. Zenac has made sure they have everything they will need. It is five in the afternoon now and they will surround the Duomo completely by seven. The troops are briefed and all one hundred of them know the High Priest is a force and as sly as an evil wizard. This is probably why he chose such a place to hide because a derelict, war-damaged Duomo is perfect for one as evil as he.

With only one stop, they reach the Duomo just as the sun begins to set. The troops fall into place and he waits in the Jeep with the others.

"It's very quiet. There is no one around, not even a sentinel keeping watch. He must feel secure in this place."

"We don't know how many he has with him, Breex. Maybe he cannot spare anyone to keep watch from the outer walls. He needs them with him. For now, we wait until the signal arrives from our scouts. Then you go and open a passage for us. The laser is ready?"

"Always."

Zenac nods and feels a comforting force through his body. He will rescue Teegue and his friends, of this he is sure.

"There's the signal," says Breex, "give me about an hour. The stone of these walls will take time for the laser to cut, they are hard and substantial."

Zenac and the others nod, allowing him to leave the Jeep under the cover of darkness. Looking out to the magnificent building in front of him, he wonders why The Enforcers were indiscriminate in their destruction of such structures. It is a tragic waste of human endeavours. The Ancient Romans and Greeks built monuments to last, not to be destroyed by wars. They were built for the pleasure of all generations to come. This one, although obscured in darkness now, is one that has been almost totally destroyed. The façade is still intact albeit with a few ageing features.

Zenac had seen the Duomo many times and the columns with arches intersecting, *The Rose Window*, has the face of Christ surrounded by mosaics. The intricacies of the work took years to create, and one devastating war to deface it. His blood boils when he thinks of how much history The Enforcers have destroyed. His only hope is there are books detailing human history still hidden within The Vatican, maybe not all is lost. His thoughts cease as Breex returns.

"Ok, I have cut a hole big enough for us to enter through one of the tunnels. How many of us should go in?"

"For now, only the five of us. Let the troops know where the entry point is, and they can enter once I give the signal. Too many of us entering could alert the High Priest."

As they enter, Zenac sees the empty plinth where the statue of the *Pietà* once stood. There is an eerie cold throughout this area, it is as if the building is mourning its once brilliant past. Zenac shivers as he walks holding his hand to his pistol holster. He indicates with his left hand to the others to follow him. They step carefully, as the rubble-strewn tiles are treacherous.

He indicates for them to stop and whispers, "When Teegue contacted me he said the area they are in smells of wine. Let's spread out and check the underground areas. The boys will be in one of the many rooms or dungeons."

He takes Asheel and Fixor with him and they head left while the others head right. Still surprised no one has noticed them, he keeps a careful ear on any suspicious noise. The echo in these underground tombs is roaring in his ears. He tells Asheel and Fixor they must tread lightly. As they move along the tunnel, it narrows and the smell of wine is becoming formidable, burning his nose. Looking down, the stone path they walk is stained with wine. Coming towards a narrow area, the light is dim, so he uses the torch on his answae in low-light mode. There is a door at the end. "Follow me," he says.

They reach the door. He hears a noise behind him, feels the blow to his head and blacks out.

"Father. Dad, can you hear me?"

Opening his eyes, they are blurred. Placing his hand on his head where the pain is torturing him, his eyes begin to focus. "Teegue?" His voice is raspy.

"It's me. The High Priest's men cornered you three."

"You're alive," he drawls. "Do you know the angst you have caused your mother and me? The knock on my head has temporarily disabled me, but you are in for a good talking to young man. Are Asheel and Fixor okay?"

"We're right next to you," answer both Asheel and Fixor in unison.

"They hit you first then grabbed both of us and threw us in here with the boys," says Asheel.

His eyes are fully focused now as he sees Teegue and the others staring at him. Looking around, he sees there are two high windows with rusted bars and the only way out is the door they came in from. "I suspected this might happen, it was too quiet. We were able to enter with ease. Teegue, fill us in, what are the High Priest's plans?"

His son begins telling them the High Priest has ordered his five soldiers to recruit the locals into fighting alongside him.

"He would not have had time to recruit and train many yet, we still have a chance," says Zenac.

"Don't underestimate him. He probably has at least another twenty people ready to take your troops on. He has the position of power by being in this church, there are many places to hide and shoot to kill."

"Teegue, there are one hundred troops surrounding the Duomo. What can twenty do against us? However, us being in here with you is a problem. I wonder what has happened to Breex and Flaiwyn"

Asheel answers him, "I received a message from them. They are safe because they made it back to the Jeep. They await your orders."

"Good. Teegue, do you know where the High Priest is hiding?"

"I am not sure, but I have heard footsteps heading towards the Crypt often. He may be there."

"Ok, then that's where we will try first. How often is the door opened and how many of them come in?"

"Twice. Once when they bring our breakfast and then again at dinner. Only one of them brings in the food, dumping it near the door. The other stands guard and the door is never fully opened."

"This is good. When our breakfast is placed in the doorway tomorrow morning, I'll be behind the door ready to ambush. Asheel and Fixor, you back me up as I force the soldier down and take the keys from him. The one standing guard will come in and that's when you boys pounce. We head towards the Crypt once we tie and gag them. Now, all of you get some sleep, tomorrow is going to be a big day."

Zenac finds his answae and sends a message to Breex to be ready to storm the Duomo in the morning. If there are only twenty soldiers they have to deal with, this is the time to make it happen. Breex's message pings back straight away telling him everyone is more than ready.

Walking through the tunnel towards the Crypt, the rough-hewn walls show water marks. Some of these tunnels were used to channel water as well as food storage. Zenac can see why the High Priest chose this place as a safe house; many of these tunnels would have housed people during medieval wars. He will use one of these tunnels if he escapes, but Zenac is determined not to let that happen this time.

"This is it here," whispers Teegue, "this is where the bishops were buried, I learned about this in my history lessons. The Crypt is still intact, the only area that wasn't damaged."

"Unless there is a massive earthquake, these tunnels will be here forever," says Zenac. "Now, I need us all to push this door, we need all our weight combined to budge it." They did as they were told, and the door did fall open. The timber had rotted near the hinges making it easier for them to force it open. Zenac looks around. No one is in this part of the Crypt, so he asks everyone to scout around. As he searches, he admires the fresco of the Crucifixion. Teegue was right, this area is immune to the elements and wars. Although the colours have faded, the fresco is in good condition, as is much of the Crypt.

"Dad, over here."

He follows Teegue's voice and finds him looking down on a woman crouching behind the altar. "Who are you and where is the High Priest?"

She looks up frightened and shivering, "I don't know. He left me here and disappeared. I am Marzeen, I am one of his servants."

"How many servants did he have?"

"There are five of us, I was the first and am... umm, was his confidante," she says with her face showing pride in her status.

"Five of you. Where are the others?"

"They went back to their homes. I have no home to go to, this is my home."

Zenac is annoyed because it seems the High Priest has slipped away again. "You are certain, he didn't say anything to you? You are his confidante after all."

"I am certain."

He takes out his answae and sends a message to Breex to take the Duomo and anyone who has remained in it. They will be their prisoners. He asks him to hold them in the main entrance hall until he arrives. "Right, we need to scour every part of this Crypt and look for clues the High Priest may have left behind." He takes Marzeen with him asking her more questions hoping she may trip up and divulge the High Priest's whereabouts.

Their search is fruitless and as they make their way to the main entrance, Zenac hopes Breex may have some news.

"No, Zenac. We didn't find any sign of him," says Breex as Zenac scans the prisoners kneeling on the floor. They are all young, frightened and stare at him wanting to know their fate.

"Find a room and place these prisoners in there with Flaiwyn standing guard."

"Flaiwyn didn't make it, Zenac. I'm sorry he was killed along with twenty of our troops," says Breex.

"Oh," is all Zenac can say. He hadn't thought about their casualties, but of course the High Priest's soldiers put up a fight, that is what they were trained to do. "Then one of our best is to stand guard." He looks over to Asheel whose face is pale as she averts her eyes from his. She and Flaiwyn were close.

Once the prisoners are locked away, Zenac and his team are all seated on the side benches discussing their next move. Zenac does not want to return to Leyna empty handed.

Chapter 43

Breex

He is standing in the sunshine at the front of the Duomo with Marzeen. It's been three weeks since the High Priest disappeared, and he and Marzeen are enjoying a budding relationship. She managed to escape being imprisoned along with another ten by offering to cook and look after them all. Breex didn't see her as the enemy even though he has kept their relationship secret, not wanting the wrath of Zenac. He had suggested bringing the prisoners into their troops, but Zenac said until one of them confessed to knowing where the High Priest is hiding, they are to remain imprisoned.

Another reason Breex is avoiding Zenac is he and Eween have been in contact. Eween and Leyna were concerned that Zenac had not kept them informed and they wanted to know what was happening. Breex has no alliance to Zenac so told Eween the High Priest had once again escaped.

"That is unfortunate," Eween had said, "Leyna will not be pleased. Zenac's mission was to secure his son's safety, and this has now happened. He will be in no rush to find the High Priest." They had discussed the happenings in Vatican City and how the pre-selections for the Parliament were moving along. Eween and Leyna were the preferred leaders, which is no surprise to anyone. He told Eween how he wants to be part of the parliament as a minister. He would be interested in the ministry of the environment that included the projects of exploring other planets. Eween is pleased to hear this and said that Leyna has already planned for him to be in the running.

The citizens are waiting for the return of the High Priest, they are hungry to see him pay for his crimes. Breex told Eween there are scouts looking and Zenac is still hoping one of the prisoners will betray him and tell them where the High Priest is hiding. As yet, the High Priest eludes them. They both agreed that this time the High Priest had gone where he doesn't want to be found.

Marzeen told Breex he had taken four men with him, but she had no idea where they went. He believes she doesn't know. Breex suspected the High Priest was protecting her, if he had told her she would have been tempted to tell someone. This man may have been a cruel ruler, but he obviously had feelings for his servant. He has led them on a wild goose chase, knowing all along where he was going to end up. What is amazing is he allowed Teegue to live, something Zenac is relieved about. For a man known for his cruelty, the High Priest must have seen something in Teegue and his friends, possibly thinking what they had ventured was brave. For whatever reason, he has shown a surprising weak spot for the young men and his servant. Eween had been sceptical about this news saying the High Priest always had another agenda, he is not to be trusted. They had ended the call with Breex pledging his allegiance to Eween and Leyna.

Zenac is stamping around like a man possessed. Two scouts had returned and informed him no trace had been found. "They are on foot. How can they disappear? The citizens of Vatican City will demand to know how he escaped again, and they have every right to know. While this man remains alive, the whole world is still at risk."

Asheel places her hand on his arm, a little too familiar Breex thinks, but Zenac does calm down. "Giving yourself a heart attack is not going to help. For all we know he may want to disappear and live an easier life. He has only four men to help him, how much harm can they do?"

"This may be a possibility, but history shows the High Priest does not hide. He will reform, probably in another country and will then attack the new Parliament. Leyna and Eween will have to watch their backs, we all will," says Breex as Marzeen places food in front of them all.

"I agree with Breex," says Fixor, "we should probably leave here soon and send all troops back to the city. We have to protect it and everyone there."

Zenac, who is now seated, agrees with them. "You're right, we will all need to be vigilant. I propose we return to Vatican City as you suggest Fixor. We will begin the voting process so we can develop our strength ready for his possible return. When and if he does return, he will have a formidable army with him, of that I'm sure."

They keep discussing and agree to bring the prisoners into their ranks by convincing them they will be safe by joining them. The scouts will be brought back as they will be required to train more soldiers too.

"Once the voting is complete and the new Parliament is formed, Teegue and I will return to Arisis. Then I can come back to Earth with anyone who is interested in helping us."

Breex sees Teegue's face twitch but is glad he is smart enough not to counter his father in front of everyone. He sees a big future for this young man, he knows which battles to pick.

Having finished eating, he eyes Marzeen as she is cleaning up the dishes and she knows this is his signal to meet him in the Crypt when she has finished.

He is on top of her kissing her neck. "You're coming with us, right?"

"If I have a choice I would like to stay here, this is the only home I've ever known. But I know Zenac will not allow me to remain."

"No, he won't and besides, I need you. I have strong feelings for you and want you with me."

She doesn't answer for a few minutes but then eases his mind by saying, "Breex, you are a beautiful man and I too have feelings for you, but these are dangerous times. If the High Priest does return, he will want me again."

"And I will fight him," he says, kissing her passionately. She is the best thing to happen to him, and with his ambition to be part of the parliament, having this stunning woman on his arm will be an asset.

Chapter 44

Dawa

She is hugging her father. "Teegue is safe. Zenac confirmed this morning and I spoke to Teegue as well."

"That is very good news," says Sheabz with tears in his eyes.

They are both in her office. There is a meeting set up with the Luminaries and the Water Foundation of Mazadon to discuss how the water project is coming along. Dawa is to be briefed when the water will be flowing and transported to Arisis. She had called her father in early, needing to tell someone about Teegue. She continues telling Sheabz about how a new parliament is being set up and Zenac promised her he will return with Teegue as soon as everything is settled.

"This will take some time, Dawa. They won't be home in the next few weeks, it will take months to set up a parliament."

"I know but having heard his voice is enough for now. Teegue was only giving me one-word answers, he sounded almost embarrassed. Probably because he was waiting for my reprimand. He will be reprimanded but I didn't want to do it over the phone."

"I will make sure you hold that promise. Teegue is a young, impressionable male. It's obvious he has placed Leyna on a pedestal, the reason he acted irresponsibly."

"Zenac and I will discuss what punishment he receives. If you wish to speak with him about this, please wait until after he has been punished by us."

Sheabz agrees and they discuss other issues at hand until the meeting starts.

Dawa watches on as the five board members of the Water Foundation of Mazadon present their statistics. The head engineer says he is confident water can be shipped back to Arisis within another year. Pipes have been laid end to end for 100kms and the project also includes aqueducts and four dams. It is set to supply Arisis with 200gigalitres of water per year.

"Thank you for your input. I am pleased with the progress. The arrival of this water will be a boost for the citizens of Arisis because our tough water restrictions will be eased."

"Yes Dawa, you are correct. And as more citizens arrive from Earth, we can explore other parts of Mazadon. There will be areas where more pipes can be laid as well as other towns populated."

"This is good news. Let us have the first pipes working well and we can discuss further projects in the future. The Luminaries and I applaud your hard work and quick progress."

"It is an honour to work on this project and I thank you all for your trust in our expertise."

The meeting continues for another hour with other board members presenting budget, logistics and construction reports.

Sheabz and the other Luminaries give her more reports (on edisc) regarding issues pertaining to Arisis, some of which have to wait for Zenac before she can action them. She places these in her *to be actioned* file on her compupad.

"Thank you all for your time, I am pleased we have sorted some of the issues and I ask the team of engineers to keep me informed. Luminaries, I will see you at the next monthly meeting."

Everyone nods, says their goodbyes, and heads back to their respective offices.

Now that the meeting has ended, Dawa's head throbs with all the information. But not even a headache is placing her in a bad mood. Her son is alive and safe, this news has eased the worries of the past few months. She can now look forward to Zenac and Teegue returning. They will be a family again.

Aria sits at the dining table with a scowl on her face. "Why not? I'm old enough. Teegue has been on Earth for months."

Dawa has had enough of this discussion, her head throbbing relentlessly now. Aria had asked to go to Earth because she wants to help Zenac and Teegue. The last thing Dawa needs is another member of her family being placed in the path of the High Priest. "Aria, your father and Teegue will be back soon, and Earth is still a dangerous place while the High Priest is alive. Besides, Braxton and I need you here. And what about work? Aren't you happy being an assistant for the events and bookings of the Ovalaz Luminary Room II?"

"You know I like what I'm doing, Mother. But it's not as exciting as helping Father form a new parliament in Vatican City."

"I'm sorry my answer is no. You will miss your friends too, who will you gossip with there? No more discussion, this conversation is over."

Aria rises from her chair, the scrape piercing through Dawa's head as she watches Aria storm to her bedroom.

"Mum don't worry, she's not going to do something stupid. She's not Teegue."

"I hope you're right Braxton," she replies, "come on, let's help cook to clean up."

After the kitchen is tidy, Dawa pours herself a scotch and calls Zenac. They have a quick discussion about Aria with Zenac adamant that Aria is not to come.

"How the hell is she going to come anyway? There are no spaceships scheduled to come to Earth until after I've returned home with Teegue."

"Honestly, I think she was just venting and had not thought it through. I hear things are going well in the lead up to the election."

Zenac proceeds to tell her about some of the issues, but mostly everything is on track. Breex is one of the candidates along with Fixor, as are Asheel and a young contender, Nable. He explains Nable is a friend of Teegue's, he helped them with equipment and tactics on the mission to find the High Priest.

"Nable is Teegue's age? That's young to be a parliamentarian."

"He's actually the oldest of the friends Teegue has made. Still, at thirty-six, he is young to run for office. However, he is smart and well liked in this city. I think he has a good chance of being a popular politician."

"Ok, I guess I'm caught up on all the Earth news. I am waiting for your return, Zenac, both you and Teegue. The house feels lifeless without you two."

"Patience Dawa. We have to set up the Constitution, laws and departments. Once a leader is elected and everything is in place, then we will leave. Not before."

Dawa already knows the work involved, but this doesn't take away the fact she is missing them. She decides not to reply with how bad she is feeling instead telling him to have a good night and give Teegue a kiss for her. She clicks off her answae knowing it will be months before she sees them again.

Chapter 45

Leyna

Leyna is on the balcony. Eween is by her side. It is a clear summer's morning, the heat of the day not yet biting. She addresses her citizens, her first speech as Madam President. Eween has been elected to the cabinet of Finance, he will give his speech after she finishes her address.

"People of Vatican City, you have had your say and for this we thank you. I, as Madam President, will devote my time to bringing this city back to its former glory. We will be the envy of the world and I guarantee you, other countries will follow in our footsteps. We defeated the authoritarian regime of The Enforcers and the three remaining members of that regime are incarcerated and awaiting trial. I will use all my power to bring the High Priest to justice and the reward money stands, so anyone with information please come forward. I guarantee your safety. Please know you are all safe now, feel free to discuss issues with your newly elected ministers. You no longer need to fear your leader, we are here to lead you to prosperity not to make your lives harder. You now live in a democracy, we will all prosper and know that your leaders are here to make this happen. There is much work to be done to bring this great city and the rest of the world back to a home we will be proud to live in. This is something we must not shy away from and with the environment in mind, we will make our world a beautiful place once more. Our population will grow, we will discover other planets, as Zenac and Dawa have already done. There is no limit to what we can achieve if we all work together for this common goal."

She pauses as she allows the shouts and whistles to sweep over her. The people are in her hands, she and Eween will work together, and her dream will be forged. Leyna bathes in the praise being bestowed on her as she takes Eween's hand and they look up to watch the fireworks and light display.

Eween takes the stand when the fireworks are done and the people cheer once more. They listen again as he speaks to them about his financial plans and how he and his cabinet will work tirelessly to make the Licdan worth more than it ever was in the past. The crowd cheers once more as he smiles at Leyna and they raise their arms in victory. They both bask in the glory.

Back in their home, Zenac, Teegue, Breex and Fixor are sitting with them at the table. Marzeen has insisted on making them a victory meal and is busy in the kitchen. She refused offers for help telling them she was going to surprise them with a feast.

"Our work has only begun," says Leyna.

"Yes, but let's keep this victorious feeling going, even if only for tonight. We will work at a slow and steady pace, as well as concentrate on finding the High Priest. The people will not allow us to forget about him."

"I won't allow us to forget about him, Eween. That man is not safe while I am alive."

Breex smiles, "Leyna, we know how you feel about him. Believe me you are not alone, we all want to see him punished."

They continue discussing plans of where to set up parliament, St Peter's being the likely place, but it will need some refurbishment. Possibly the residences can also be used as the ministries grow and develop. Leyna is pleased with the progress they have made, and she will ensure her cabinet will succeed in making Vatican City the place it once was. Eween has assured her the funds left by The Enforcers will be increased as more countries follow their lead.

Marzeen walks in with their food and asks Teegue to please bring in the large pot. As he places it down, he comments on the smell of the tagine as the middle eastern spices waft amazing aromas throughout the room.

"Enjoy this meal, Teegue, you and I are going back to Arisis after tomorrow."

"What? There is still so much to be done. The High Priest for one..."

"Teegue, you've had your adventure. It is now time to return and become a grown up, you have a job waiting for you. Besides, I'm needed back home."

Leyna takes in the scene between father and son. The tension rises like a dark cloud as Teegue glares at Zenac. She knows Zenac is right, he is the leader of their planet along with Dawa, and she will be waiting for his return. Knowing the huge responsibility of being a leader, Zenac needs to return. Leyna hopes to learn from him and become a respected leader, she wants to emulate his and Dawa's popularity. To her surprise Teegue doesn't argue, he accepts his fate. Given he is lucky to be alive he should listen to his father, the High Priest had every opportunity to kill him and his friends. The fact that he didn't kill them makes her fear for the future. He is out there plotting his revenge, and everyone must be vigilant, it is a certainty he will fight back, the problem is no one knows when.

"Let us all enjoy this meal and tomorrow's festivities at Breex and Marzeen's commitment ceremony," says Leyna raising her wine glass, "and drink in their honour." Smiling, she scans the table as she feels the tension dissipating from Zenac. Teegue on the other hand is another matter, his head is down contemplating his hands.

• • •

Marzeen dazzles as she strides up the grand hall towards where Breex stands at the makeshift altar, which is covered with a dazzling gold and silver cloth. Eween is overseeing the proceedings with some traditions Marzeen has requested. She and Breex will exchange bouquets of traditional wildflowers found near Lake Bracciano. These blue and purple flowers are said to have properties to enhance love and relationships. Leyna finds this a quaint touch to what she believes to be a useless ceremony. Anyone can see they are in love, why do they have to prove it in front of others? Still, Marzeen's beauty is something to behold as she reaches Breex. Her flawless skin beams and the gown embellished by a flowing cloak of deep red and gold matches the one Breex is wearing. Another tradition Marzeen had requested.

Leyna watches on as Eween declares their love to their friends, neither having any family to speak of. They each take their cloaks and cover themselves as they exchange their private wishes. This part of the ceremony is only for the couple, no one else will hear these admissions of love. What a paradox this ceremony is, first you gather everyone to shout out your love for one another, and then you secretly pledge your love. Still, they both glow as their faces light up with happiness once they drop the cloaks and face everyone.

It is now time for another feast with more drinking and celebration. They move out into St Peter's square where the sun is in full glory as they sit at the long table laden with the ceremonial feast.

"They are as much a force as we are," says Eween, raising his wine glass towards Leyna.

She looks at him and clinks her glass to his, "They will be an asset to us."

"This parliament will achieve more than you have dreamed of Leyna, we have a great team and the people are behind us. We cannot lose."

She looks at Eween, who still has his boyish looks even though he is heading for forty. His enthusiasm is sensitive and well-meaning, but she knows there is so much work to be done before they can say they are successful. Especially as the High Priest is hovering around, someone who is not to be trusted. He has a plan, and she knows it will be as devastating as the 20-year war.

Chapter 46

Dilvant
(formerly The High Priest)

He listens as the young leader who introduced himself as Quinan, speaks of the alliance he has formed with the five of them.

"You will not be disappointed, Dilvant. We are strong and young enough to help you regain your rightful place as High Priest Enforcer. We are proud to be your new force and I especially wish to be the leader of your new twelve Enforcers."

Arriving in Heraklion, Crete four days previous, he and his four trusted companions found a place teeming with strapping young people ready to be a part of something big. Little is known of Crete since the devastation of the locust plague of 2275, where the creatures ate everything in their path. To this day, the land has not recovered with regular droughts setting in since then. Attempts to plant crops had failed with most of the six hundred thousand population perishing. Quinan had explained the average age on the island is now forty as many of the elders had died of starvation. Now, with only fifty thousand citizens left, they import much of their food. A cost they can barely afford.

"We have had enough of suffering and want to grow old on our beautiful island, but without someone like you who has the power to help us, our future is grim."

"We thank you for your support. Defeating Leyna and Eween is my one aim, and if I'm able to help your community, then even better. My four companions will instruct you as to how to develop our army, you are to fetch your best people for training."

"Of course," says Quinan, instructing the man sitting next to him to contact his best soldiers and begin the process of forming an army that will be the envy of the world.

"I see you have high hopes, this pleases me. Now, raise your glasses to our alliance and may we profit from our efforts."

The twelve people seated at the table in the centre of the Basilica of St Titus raise their glasses. The Basilica has been converted into the seat of Parliament where decisions are made, such as the one made today that will change the citizens of Crete's lives forever. Dilvant feels the warmth of these people who are desperate for something new, he can see it in Quinan's searching eyes, they have been waiting for this help for years. He will not let them down and he and Quinan will form an army that Leyna and Eween will find formidable, not only because of the youth but also because Quinan will ensure the intelligence of the soldiers is above average. Dilvant will be returned as the High Priest Enforcer by using technology. Once feared by him and destroyed, now he will use it to his advantage. He looks over to the woman seated next to Quinan. Her deep blue eyes pierce his mind as he thinks of Marzeen. He made a mistake by not bringing her with him. Her way of calming his moods, of caressing his needs and listening to his wants, is something he now craves. This allegiance is now formed, it is time to find his next companion.

They all rise and shake on their bond to change the course of history yet again. Quinan walks with him outside, the woman follows behind.

"I present to you once again my sister, Felida," says Quinan.

Everyone at the table had been introduced at the meeting, but Felida remained quiet throughout. "It is my pleasure to meet you, may I invite you both for a celebratory drink?"

"Please go ahead with Felida, I have work to be done. Taxes are not collected by themselves," he laughs.

"Ah, the work of a leader. Yes, of course, I will join you later for dinner," Dilvant replies as he heads towards the Morosini Fountain where Felida is now waiting. His power over women comes from his charm not his looks. With a nose and ears too big for his head, his brown eyes look small. His once dark locks are now thinned grey strands and he allows a salt and pepper stubble to grow on his face. *Distinguished* is how he likes to think of his overall look. Height may have been a problem for him too had his charm not been an asset.

Felida reminds him of Marzeen, her long black hair shines and her lithe body is muscular, showing she works at keeping fit. Smaller in stature than Marzeen, her beauty matches if not surpasses that of his former servant. Felida resembles her brother but is more attractive, her tanned skin glows in the Mediterranean sun. Dilvant will have her, he already feels his body wanting her.

Dinner is at Quinan's home, a rambling villa ten minutes out of Heraklion by car. He is seated next to Felida, her smell still all over him. She had surprised him with her lovemaking, her fitness making her flexible and supple. He can see this going further, for the first time in his life, he only wants one woman. Is this what true love feels like?

Eldane arrives and sits next to him. "These people are incredible," he says, "not only are they young, but they are also intelligent. And fit too. Everyone I trained today was able to give their ideas on how we are going to defeat Leyna and Eween. They are all fit enough to be an asset to the army."

"I agree and I am pleased we decided to come to Crete. I expected to find nothing here and was prepared to look elsewhere to find an army. The reason I chose to come here was that no one ever speaks of Crete, it is a forgotten part of the world so who would bother looking for us here?"

"Oh, I understand," says Eldane, picking up some nuts and placing them in his mouth.

"Tomorrow I will come with you to see the training. These people are keen, and I am happy to have found them. A young army ready and willing is more than I bargained for."

A Greek feast is placed in front of them and Dilvant savours all these treasures, the food as well as the people. Crete is a paradise he didn't know still existed.

<h1 style="text-align:center">Chapter 47</h1>

———————

Teegue

He knocks on the door hoping she is home because he is leaving in a few hours. After some quiet minutes of listening to his own breath, he hears footsteps. It's definitely her.

"Well hello," she says, letting him in.

"Umm, hi. Are you alone?"

"Yes."

He scans the lounge area and finally lets out his breath. He wanted to be alone with her. "I'm ah… sorry I haven't seen you since the dance festival, I have been kind of busy."

She indicates he take a seat and snuggles up next to him, "So I hear. You have been chasing the High Priest. That's some assignment for a kid your age."

"What's age got to do with it? We were close to catching him too. I see news travels fast around here."

She smiles but doesn't let on how she knows. Heading to the kitchen she asks if he wants a drink and comes back carrying the beer he asked for. Sitting next to him again, she rubs her hand on his leg, "We're alone until five so we have a couple of hours to ourselves."

He chugs on the beer, his mouth parched with apprehension. Looking in her eyes he rubs his thumb tenderly over her cheek then he lifts her chin to kiss her rich, full lips. He is aroused as she sits on his lap, her lips blowing soft kisses on his neck. Jzinta is two years older than him, and he likes the fact she is street smart; she is not one to take crap from anyone. After what she has been through, he defies anyone to take her on. Many would be surprised by the power of this diminutive woman.

"Umm, I have to tell you something," he says in between breaths as she is calmly taking off his pants.

"Tell me later, right now I want to ravage you."

He allows her to do so, wanting her more than he realised.

Lying together on the lounge, he brushes a loose hair from her face, "I'm leaving tonight."

"I had a feeling that is what you wanted to tell me. Back to Arisis, I assume?"

"Yes, my father and I are returning now the Parliament has been sworn in. I'm not ready to leave yet, but I have no say in the matter. It pisses me off when he doesn't listen to me."

She looks him directly in the eyes giving him a sly smile. Without a word she walks back into the kitchen as he admires her taut behind. There is nothing like watching a naked, beautiful woman you have just made love to, it is a gratifying feeling and he is treasuring this moment. Jzinta is a different lover to Trisia, she is not only more mature, her experience is evident with how she takes control. His feelings for both women are strong, but this woman who is now walking back towards him has a hold on him he had not expected. She places some snacks on the coffee table and throws a handful of nuts in her mouth.

Teegue proceeds to tell her about his adventure and how he is ready to keep chasing the High Priest. He isn't done with him yet.

"Well, if you stay your father will not be pleased. Maybe return to Arisis with him then come back, this time on your own terms. You are not the only one who wants to see the High Priest dead. I have too want to be rid of him."

"Does he know you exist?"

"Probably, but he has never tried to contact me, nor help me. From what I hear he is not a pleasant man so why would I want anything to do with him?"

"Fair enough. I want to bring him to Leyna, she will deal with him. There is no reason for me to kill him. Besides, I want to be known for finding him and go down in history as the person who rid the world of such vermin."

She turns to him, "Keep talking like that, it's such a turn on. Actually, come with me," she says as he follows her into the bathroom. "I'm horny again, let's do it in the shower."

He grabs her by the bum and kisses her with a passion so strong he craves every inch of her body. She steps into the shower and rubbing her hands over her exquisite breasts, she coaxes him in. He is ready and brings her towards him kissing her then making his way down her wet body. He doesn't want this to end.

As he walks in, he hears his father screaming, "Where have you been?"

"I'm here now, what's the problem?"

"Have you finished packing? We have to leave in fifteen minutes."

"Keep your shirt on, Dad. I packed before I went out, I had a couple of friends to say goodbye to."

"Fine then, come on, let's put these bags in the car."

He follows his father and debates whether he should try and convince him to let him stay. The High Priest is not his only reason to stay now. Jzinta is giving him other reasons to remain on Earth, seeing her again and their passionate tryst has cemented his resolve to stay. This is what he wants but knows it is not possible, not now.

Deciding not to cause more angst with his father, he doesn't ask.

Maybe he will take Jzinta's advice of coming back on his own terms. Being an adult means taking responsibility for your actions, so he will see Trisia and once he sees her, he will know what to do. Maybe Jzinta's charms won't seem so adorable when he is back home.

Chapter 48

Dawa

She is in the kitchen when Braxton walks in asking when they are returning. She turns to look at him, his face alight with expectation. "Only one week to go. Everything is going well according to your father. They'll be back at the scheduled time. Not long now."

He sits at the table with a wide smile, "Oh good. I'm keen to hear all about Teegue's adventure. One day I hope to go back to Earth, maybe it can be a holiday destination?"

"Who knows what the future holds, Braxton. We can only hope things between Earth and Arisis will be amicable. Let's see what your father tells us when he returns, maybe Leyna and Eween are favourable to us. For now, we are safe here," she says hoping things stay that way.

With her tea ready, she sits with Braxton and helps him with his homework. He has a few more years of school and she finds this one-on-one time with him precious. Aria is rarely home and if she is, she is holed up in her room talking to her friends. She misses interacting with her and misses her presence almost as much as Teegue's. Soon they will be a family again and with Teegue home, Aria will be around more – she hopes. Sniffing away a tear as Braxton asks her a question about maths, she decides to concentrate on her youngest for now.

With her head skewed to the side she admires Braxton. His innocent face is in full concentration mode, a look that makes him seem older. She can almost see his brain actively working out the maths problem. Being the third child, he hasn't had the attention of the twins because life became so full, and it was easier to leave him to his own devices. With the twins around to help look after him, Braxton never complained. Now, with Teegue and Aria out on their own, it is time to concentrate on her baby. Time has passed so quickly, he is fifteen next birthday and so much has happened since he was born.

"I could go for some ice-cream, how about you?"

"Good idea. It's time for a break. You have smashed through those problems Braxton, well done."

"Maths comes easy to me Mum, I actually enjoy the logic of it. Numbers are easy."

She's not sure she found maths that easy at school, but now she has people around her who look after the numbers, so she doesn't have to try too hard to remember. Rising from the chair she walks to the freezer to see what ice-cream they have.

"Ooh, brain freeze," laughs Braxton.

"Careful, you don't have to eat it so fast." As she is saying this, she hears her compupad ping. "That might be your father," she says to Braxton as she heads towards her home office.

Zenac appears on screen as she connects, "Hi, how are you?"

"Fine. I was enjoying some ice cream with Braxton, we were in the kitchen. How are you and Teegue?"

"We're fine. He is still a bit peeved with me, what with wanting to stay and all."

"Let him be upset, he has upset us enough. You are due back in three days, are you still on track?"

He tells her they are, from all reports there will be nothing too destructive in their way. She sees his face has lines that were not there when he left, this mission has taken its toll on him. "How are you? You look tired."

"A little. I worry for Earth with the High Priest still at large. Leyna and Eween have set up a parliament that will bring Vatican City back from the brink, they will be concentrating on achieving this, not so much on him."

"Wherever he is it will take time for him to regroup and they will have time to do so as well." Zenac agrees to a point but tells her they need to develop their strategy now along with a stronger army.

"War and violence again. This sort of talk depresses me, and I am so glad you're both coming back and away from the danger."

"Me too, Dawa. I do however feel some guilt about leaving them to deal with everything on their own. You know, I am now fond of them even though they are technically still fugitives. They have proven their worth, I just hope they remain strong."

"I'm glad to hear you are not returning with them. It would have been near impossible given they have been elected."

He continues speaking about the election and the atmosphere of the city now. People are smiling, wearing proper clothes and generally feeling good about the future. She ends the call by saying she is looking forward to having them home and being a family again.

Shutting her compupad, she holds her hand on it for a moment wanting to feel Zenac's presence for a little longer. Then she stands and walks to the kitchen again to help Braxton finish his maths.

Chapter 49

Dilvant

He is with Quinan as they check the troops. They are in the compound where the training took place. It is a thirty-acre property outside of Heraklion, an area where they have been able to house, train and develop their army. Two thousand strong and fit soldiers are in formation as they both walk along, occasionally speaking to one of them. There is a vibrancy to them, they are keen to move on with the mission. As they come to the last of the troops, he and Quinan head to the platform especially built at the front of the arena, they are ready to speak to the army and the citizens who have come to watch.

He steps up and places his hands on the lectern looking over them one more time. He then scans the people, both seated and standing, who are here to celebrate this graduation of sorts. Dressed in his own military uniform, a new one designed and made here in Heraklion, he knows he looks formidable and the troops admire him. They will do whatever he commands, and this power makes him figuratively grow in stature, he can feel their adoration and loyalty.

With his face stern, he begins the speech he prepared to motivate them, although he can now see they will not need to hear all of what he has prepared. They are ready.

"My beautiful people of Crete, I thank you for your dedication to this cause. We are ready to make our move and take back what is mine. Vatican City was my home and I intend to take it away from the traitors. Leyna and Eween, along with their accomplices such as Zenac and his troops, will pay for their treason. We are prepared, our technological weapons are ready and in the coming days you will receive your orders to move out." He stops as cheers rain out and the people in the stands wave their arms and chant, *"You are great Dilvant."*

Continuing he explains their troop masters will give them weapons, one of which can maim a person by using a frequency of high-pitched sounds – loud and consistent. The traitors' ears will bleed and the closer a soldier gets to the machine, they will collapse from the shock. The *Acoustic Moduliser* can blast sounds of up to 120 decibels, enough to make a person deaf. Be sure to be far enough away when this machine is sounded, and always wear your protective ear buds. This time he does not want to kill his people, but he will hurt them enough that they will never betray him again. He looks forward to using this weapon on Leyna and Eween especially.

The other two weapons he is proud of are the *Fotokast*, a machine that projects a hologram of soldiers that look more real the closer you get to them; and the *Saber Concealer*, a laser that surrounds its victims with an invisible shield they cannot escape from. No bullet will be used in this mission unless it is absolutely necessary. He is proud of Quinan and his team, they have devised weapons that will keep his people under his rule once again. As their leader once more, no one will dare to oppose him again because he will have these weapons at his disposal. The world will bow to him again.

Again, cheers and chants swamp him as he finishes. With both hands up he clasps them above his head in a sign of victory. After there is calm, he hands over to Quinan, who will oversee the troops being given the necessary uniforms for each division.

• • •

They are in his bed as she snuggles into his neck, her leg thrown over his. "You have our people in the palm of your hand," she says, "I watched in awe of you today."

He holds Felida close as he thinks himself lucky to have this beauty in his life. It is he who is in awe of her. He is finding this feeling uncomfortable as he is not one to fall this quickly, and he only wants her, she has filled his heart. She is a woman who surpasses every expectation of what a woman should be. Her intelligence is something he finds exciting as much as her beauty. Felida has degrees in psychology, medical science and industrial science. She was part of Quinan's team who developed the technological weapons. Felida is now an integral part of his will to become leader again, he wants her by his side when they win back Vatican City.

"You have an indomitable force, both physically and with your words. Everyone was mesmerised by your speech today."

"I have had many years to perfect my speeches and they have been in front of crowds much larger than today's gathering." He continues recounting his many victories over the years as she listens. His ambition to be a leader began at a young age and has only grown stronger with each victory. Leyna and Eween are his nemeses, they exacted revenge on him, now it is his turn for revenge. He will not allow anyone to beat him and with Quinan, Felida and the whole of Crete by his side, he will not fail.

She straddles him, lightly running her fingers from his chest down to his groin. His eyes take in her modest breasts and tight stomach muscles. Grabbing her shapely arms, he brings her towards him and closing his eyes, he kisses her with a passion he has never felt before.

Chapter 50

Zenac

He sees her running towards him as he steps down from the space-ship. The Valverz had set down two hours early and he was more than pleased to reach out and hug Dawa. Teegue was right behind him, the three of them hugging each other for dear life.

"It's so good to see you both," says Dawa crying.

Aria and Braxton are close behind Dawa, each of Teegue's siblings giving him high-fives. Zenac is happy to see his family together again and gives his children high-fives right back. No one can take the smile off his face. "Let's go, all I want is to be home with all of you."

After collecting his things and saying goodbye to the crew, he says, "Great job everyone. I'll organise a debrief next week. Until then, enjoy your time off." He laughs as they all cheer and head to their respective families who are waiting for them.

They arrive home and he is telling Teegue to go and rest because tomorrow he is to start his job. "What? I don't have any time off?"

Aria and Braxton both head to their rooms sensing there is going to be another *discussion* between their father and brother.

"Time off? You haven't even started working yet and you expect time off?"

"Well, you gave the rest of the crew time off, I thought that meant me too."

"No Teegue, you thought wrong. You were meant to start your job months ago, but seeing as you decided to stow away, you've had your holiday. It's time you start working and learning your trade."

Teegue's face shows how disgruntled he is but he refrains from answering. Zenac is pleased that he has kept quiet because he doesn't have the energy to deal with another argument. Dawa places her hand on his shoulder telling him to go and rest. Happy to oblige, Zenac heads for their bedroom to sleep.

Tossing and turning he gives up. He is too pent up to sleep. His mind is racing with thoughts of the fact he abandoned Leyna and Eween, there is still so much more to do. Rubbing his face with his hand, he decides to shower and go and discuss things with Dawa, he has missed her and their discussions. The decisions he makes have always involved discussions with Dawa first, this time is no different.

"You're up already," she says, shutting her compupad that is sitting on her desk in the home office.

"My mind wouldn't shut off. There are a few things I want to discuss with you. I will rest later." He continues telling her about his feelings and how he wants to have a say in what is happening in Vatican City. "You do realise that if the city improves and the parliament cements its place, other governments will look at their model and emulate it."

"Yes, that is a given. Countries are screaming out for ideas and policies that will improve the lives of their people. But you are needed here, Zenac. I need your help with both the issues affecting Arisis and our children, the twins especially."

He nods knowing he has not focused on his family for some time. Guilt rears up and he knows he has to prioritise time for them. "I know Dawa. You have handled things well, but we are a team and I have let you down lately. But I also know that Leyna and Eween will need help, especially when the High Priest returns." He continues saying he has a vision of being able to go backwards and forwards from Earth, of trading together and people going on holiday to each planet. "This won't happen if the High Priest wins again."

Dawa understands and tells him it is a nice dream for the future, one that can happen if Leyna and Eween keep power. She asks why they will need help when the parliament is strong and they have the people on their side. If the High Priest invades the city, isn't their army equipped enough?

"Possibly," he says, "it will depend on what size the other army is. No one knows where the High Priest is and whether he has the backing of another country. If his army has thousands, say up to ten thousand, then there is no way Leyna and Eween's army will cope. At last count, they had five thousand soldiers."

"So, are you suggesting we send an army down to help them?" Rubbing his chin, Zenac gives a slight nod. "We may need to." "Look, this is a lot to take in, and very speculative at this stage. Try not to make decisions right now. This is something that will need to be discussed with the Luminaries as well as Taaz and his team," she says, taking his hand and leading him back to their bedroom, "I think it's time to rest and you will see this in a different light when you wake."

Zenac allows himself to be led by his wife knowing she is right, no one can predict what the High Priest will do next.

Chapter 51

Leyna

She has returned home from seeing the prisoners again and finds Eween in the kitchen. "Where's cook?"

"I gave the staff the night off. I want to spend time with only you."

She smiles and understands because they have been working ridiculous hours with completing the ministries and setting ministers up in their relevant portfolios. This has paid off, their parliament is now ready for whatever the citizens need. She watches on as he drains the pasta with steam billowing out and throws it into the sauce, the smells tickling both her tastebuds and her hunger. Eween plates up and they move to the lounge, which is where they like to eat when they are on their own.

Once they are comfortable, she tells him some news she overheard while she was with the prisoners. "I was with the wardens about to walk out of the prison yard when the three Enforcer prisoners approached us. You know, the two wives and their handmaiden." Eween nods and she continues telling him they had a proposition to give her news of the High Priest in exchange for their freedom.

"What? How would they know anything while they are locked up?"

"Don't underestimate the prison rumour mill, Eween. And if the High Priest wanted to send someone to give them a message, he would find a way to do so." Again, Eween nods and keeps listening as Leyna progresses with her story. She tells him of a rumour that the High Priest has a strong army and technological weapons, and the one that should worry them the most is that of a laser that imprisons people with an invisible shield. "It's called the *Saber Concealer*, and no one will see it coming.

"So, the one who destroyed technology is now using it in his favour. He obviously has help from another country, there is nowhere in Italy that would be able to build such a weapon."

"He has other weapons too, but this is the only one they mentioned by name. At the moment, we have moved the ladies to a nicer facility until I decide whether to free them. They may be a threat to us on the outside and lead the High Priest back into the city," says Leyna, still not sure what to do with them. She wants to keep an eye on their activities and if they are freed, then that control is gone.

"Keep them in prison but with privileges and dangle their freedom until they give you more information, like where he is."

"Yes, I had thought of that and that's what I will do. They are more valuable to us while they stay in prison. One of them is his preferred wife, the one he married first, and I am sure he will want to rescue at least her. We need to keep her as bait." She stretches and kisses him, "I'm beat. Thanks for a lovely meal. Stay here, I'll put these in the kitchen. Be back in a minute."

Placing the dishes in the sink, she leaves them for the staff in the morning. She wants to return to Eween and make love because she doesn't remember the last time they did. As she walks back towards the lounge, he is already naked waiting for her. "You read my mind," she says as she drops her dress and lays on top of him.

· · ·

She is on the other side of the two-way mirror as Eween interrogates the wife of the High Priest. He is using psychological techniques of preying on her emotions – "Look what he did to you, left you to rot in prison." "If he really loved you, he would have come for you before now." "If you tell us where he is, your freedom is assured."

She raises her head from looking at her hands, "I told your girlfriend everything I know. What are you going to do now? Torture me?"

"We are not like the High Priest. Haven't we been treating you well? I hear you have enjoyed the massages."

She glares at him without answering.

Leyna knows this is useless, obviously she has only been given minimal information. The High Priest is teasing them. She indicates to the guard to tell Eween to stop the interrogation. After a few minutes he is in the room with her.

"It's no use, she doesn't know anything else. We'll keep them in prison with more privileges, if the High Priest wants them, he will know where to find them."

"It's interesting she mentioned torture. I wonder if he tortured members of his own family?"

"Probably. Let's get out of here, I've had enough of this prison for a while." She heads out the security door with Eween following. Outside the gleaming sun warms her. "I'm going to walk back to Parliament," she tells Eween and the security guards.

"I'll join you," says Eween, "I need to stretch my legs after sitting for three hours in that cold room."

They walk in silence. Leyna enjoys the sounds and smells of St Peter's Square. The markets are in full swing stretching the full length on two sides. How she would love to walk through them and browse, but she is already at risk by walking out in the open and the security guards are already on high alert. Her life has changed so much since becoming Madame President, with being guarded every day and not being able to just be herself. She is not complaining, this is what comes with the territory, and she does relish the power she has been bestowed. Placing her face up towards the sun, she feels her stomach rumble and turns to Eween, "I'm hungry and have a desire for a burger. I haven't eaten one in years, it must be the smells of the market that are making me hungry."

"A burger? Okay then let's go and find one."

As they sit at an outdoor table in one of the many cafés with the security guards standing near them, Leyna devours the burger made with a focaccia bun, as well as the fat-cut chips. "Oh my, I didn't know I was so hungry. This is delicious," she says, wiping her chin.

"You certainly enjoyed it. And of course you're hungry, we haven't eaten since breakfast. It's past two now."

"A burger though? Eween, why did I suddenly have an urge to eat one? I haven't eaten one since I was a teenager."

"Nothing wrong with a burger every now and then," says Eween with a mouthful of his double beef burger.

She laughs, "You're enjoying this more than I am." As she looks up, one of the security guards points to his watch and she knows it's time to be an adult again, "I know, time to go back to work."

<h1 style="text-align:center">Chapter 52</h1>

Dilvant

The training has gone well, they have experts in all three weapons. These special troops will be the only ones who handle the Acoustic Moduliser, Fotokast and Saber Concealer. They are now experts on how to use each one – The Acoustic Moduliser is to be used when they are dealing with captured soldiers who are not listening to orders; the Fotokast is for causing distractions and the Saber Concealer is to keep prisoners in one spot while fighting is still going on. The troops will be sent over to Rome by ferries, they will land at Civitavecchia, which is the seaport on the Tyrrhenian Sea. Four ferries have been restored and large enough to fit soldiers as well as ammunition. The largest ferry will house the special troops along with the three technological weapons. Dilvant will travel on this one, he will lead these troops. He is ready to invade and take his rightful place as leader once again.

"Tomorrow at 05:00 hours we will begin our deployment. You all have your orders that must be followed, don't sway from your position, this mission must not fail. All prisoners will be held by the

Saber Concealer until there is a surrender. Leyna and Eween are not to be harmed, they are to be brought to me. Time of arrival is midday. Upon arrival we will set up a surveillance tent, living quarters and ammunition storage units in the port of Civitavecchia. At sunset we will advance towards Vatican City and we will arrive there at approximately 20:00 hours," he says pausing then raising his fist in the air he says with a loud cry, "Dismissed."

He watches on as the troops break formation and head to their respective quarters. Last night they had their last meal, a banquet fit for royalty and were allowed free time into Heraklion. It saddens him that some of these soldiers will not return, but others that survive will be well compensated and live a life full of riches. When you promise people the world, they will follow you till the end of the earth.

Quinan comes up beside him, "Shall we go and celebrate one last time before we leave. I know a brothel that is very discreet."

He looks at his friend, placing his hands on Quinan's shoulders, "My boy, at a time not so long ago I would have come with you and enjoyed the spoils available at such places, but now my answer is no. You go ahead, I am going to see your sister."

"Ah yes, she has mentioned you two are close. I am happy for you, she is a good woman. A warning though, do not betray her or you will be sorry."

"I have no intention of doing such a thing. Your sister has my heart and my soul, and I didn't think I had a soul," he laughs with vigour. He sees Quinan shudder and knows he is still feared, he likes to keep his friends fearful as well as his enemies because he trusts no one.

He arrives at her villa on Heraklion's outskirts. This is her five-acre oasis where she tends her own vines and grows vegetables that tolerate the heat. The home is a modest five-bedroom stone and timber structure in a traditional style, she refurbished it with the help of the best artists and builders on Crete. Admiring it as he walks towards the heavy front timber door, he can see himself living here with her.

"My love, hello. Oh, you look tired."

"It has been a long day checking everything for tomorrow. Now all I want is to be here with you and relax. Have the servants left?"

"Yes," she says, giving him a kiss as he falls into her arms, "and dinner has been prepared, we only need to heat it up."

He whispers in her ear what he would rather do than eat at this minute, and she obliges by taking off her robe and leading him into her bedroom. This upstairs room is the largest in the villa with a balcony opening out to the sea. Her privacy is assured as no one else can build in front, something she ensured when she bought the property. She had a covenant placed on the land in front of this block.

He breathes in her scent as she strips him of his clothes. The freedom he feels, her adulation and this pristine place she lives in combine to elate his feelings. This is love, something he has never felt in his life and the love of this beautiful woman has him entangled and supremely happy. He allows her to kiss his body all over as she gently leads him to her king bed, the silk sheets cool on his skin. Her hair tickles his face as she eases herself onto him, stroking his body and she makes love to him that is both rough and exhilarating at the same time.

He wakes at what he thinks is only a few minutes later. Felida is reading next to him. Placing the book on her lap, she turns to look at him, "You were exhausted, you've been asleep for two hours."

"It only felt like a short time, but then you took the last of my energy away. Mind you, I am happy for you to do that as often as you wish," he says, stroking her face with the back of his hand.

"Well, now you are rested, I want to speak to you about coming with you tomorrow."

He pulls himself back astounded at what she is saying. "No. No way, you are to stay here and wait for me. I will return triumphant and we will rule together."

She moves closer to him placing her hand on his chest, "Dilvant, I want to be with you and see your victory. You need me by your side, and I have made my decision, I'm coming."

Dilvant remembers what Quinan said about not crossing her and he knows of her stubbornness, but it's too dangerous and he has to convince her of that. "My love, all I want is for you to be by my side, together we will rule I promise you this. This mission is dangerous, I cannot allow you to put yourself in such danger. What do you know about war and invasion?"

"Nothing, but you do, and you will protect me. I cannot sit alone on this island and worry about whether you will return. I have waited all my life for someone to show me the world, and now you are here I will not allow you to go without me."

He feels emotional, something he never feels. She is hitting a nerve and he wants her with him as much as she wants to come. He sits up further on the bed looking at her nakedness as a tear drips down his nose. He touches it unconsciously as he pictures her like this every day just as he has done for these last months. His love is overwhelming and knows she cannot come with him. "If something were to happen to you... no, Felida listen to me *please*. Stay here, wait for me. I don't want to lose you. Vatican City will be yours once I have conquered it again. I will return, and you will be my queen. Please do this for me."

Her eyes search his face then she places her head on his chest saying, "I will wait, I don't want to, but I will. Make sure you return to me in one piece, whether you win or lose, I want you back here with me. If you win, we can go and live in Vatican City, but if you lose, we can stay here and hide for the rest of our lives."

"I will not lose and knowing I have you waiting for me will spur me onto victory. I have had enough of hiding, it's no longer for me." He kisses her and this time he makes love to her with gentle caresses, something he is doing for the first time. He floats over her body kissing every inch. Felida brings out his softer side, a side he has never shown anyone else.

Chapter 53

Leyna

They are all sitting in the parliamentary chamber in St Peter's, they set up in the room that is on the right-hand side of the church. These quarters were previously used as a study by the clergy. The library is still intact, something Leyna is grateful for because she has already begun reading the historical tomes. She is at the head of the table with Eween next to her, Breex, Fixor and Nable have joined them along with three other ministers. "I have summoned you here to update you on news of the High Priest," she says as murmurs fill the room.

When she has silence again, she informs them intelligence has reason to believe the High Priest is in Crete and forming another army. This time he is using technology and at present is testing these weapons. "The one we have to worry about is known as a Saber Concealer, it forms an invisible shield no one can escape from. They will use this to capture as many of us as possible."

"So now he likes technology. He had no qualms about destroying the world's technology and now he will use it to destroy us," says Breex.

Eween stands and walks around the room, "An army that has technology behind them is a force we will find difficult to beat. Leyna and I have been discussing what is needed and this is the reason for calling you all here. We want to form an alliance."

"I can already guess with who."

"Yes, we are thinking of Dawa and Zenac, Breex. They have the technology to travel to other planets, their space travel program has been a great success. If we are going to win this, we need their expertise. Our ammunition will not work this time." Eween keeps pacing trying to expend his nervous energy. Unfortunately, he knows the High Priest will be upon them in a few weeks, something he hasn't even told Leyna. The intelligence came to him and he only told her part of the story.

Fixor and the other ministers look at each other with concern, "We knew he was going to be a threat, but this is more than we expected" he says.

"We need to move fast," says Leyna, "we must vote now on this alliance. Eween and I both know it makes sense, but you may have other ideas."

Nable turns towards Leyna, "From what I know we don't have much choice. I have been keeping my own surveillance on our enemy and he is ready. So we must be ready to receive him."

"Nable, we need to know what you have because the more we know of his plans, the more ready for him we will be." Eween sees Nable acknowledge him, "We can talk after this meeting. So, I take it your vote is, *yes*?"

"Yes." With this the others also agree and walk towards Leyna to sign the agreement.

"This is a momentous moment for everyone, Earth and Arisis will join forces and we will be victorious. On behalf of Eween and myself, I thank you." She leaves the chambers with two more books to read and leaves Nable and Eween to discuss all the intelligence. Breex walks with her as the other ministers return to their chambers.

"We have to think about this strategically and also with stealth.

We should ask the citizens to leave the city, they can move to our quarters we left in Borgo. We have to keep them safe."

She mulls this over and knows he is right. With a weapon that can imprison people, if everyone is moved out of the city, this weapon is rendered useless. "Breex, I will discuss this with Eween, but I do think it is a good idea. We will have another meeting and decide what to tell our citizens. They have been through enough and I don't think we should alarm them further."

"We have to move quickly, Leyna. Speak with Eween as soon as possible."

"I know, I will discuss it with him tonight. The situation is dire, with the news the High Priest has the help of Quinan of Crete, he has the advantage of a young army of intelligent people. Any wonder they have been able to develop such sophisticated weapons. Now, Breex if you will excuse me, I have some studying to do," she says pointing to the books.

"Of course, Madame President. I thank you for your indulgence in listening to me."

She smiles at his formality, they have been friends for a long time and she does not expect this from him. Still, this formality is necessary at times. Deciding to walk home instead of going back to her office, she is feeling nauseous and unusually tired. This latest news of the High Priest is not helping.

Sitting on the cool tiles of the bathroom, she wipes her mouth with some toilet paper. Her head throbs having emptied her stomach in a fierce projectile straight into the bowl. She had only confirmed the pregnancy with her doctor yesterday. Until now, she has been fine, she had almost forgotten she was pregnant. Her mouth feels furry and she has a desire for something dry to settle the nausea. Forcing herself up, she washes her face, rinses her mouth then heads to the kitchen.

With a bowl of dry crackers on the coffee table she lays on the lounge, closes her eyes and is asleep within minutes.

She wakes to find Eween sitting on the edge of the lounge watching her.

"You're not well? Since when do you sleep in the afternoon?"

"Oh hi, I felt nauseous after the meeting. I'm fine now, the toilet has the remains of my lunch," she laughs, raising herself up.

"Charming. That explains these crackers. You were smart to come home. Keep resting, I'll have cook rustle something up for me."

"Yes, fine. I'm feeling better but not hungry. Tell me, how did you go with Nable?"

He tells her their intelligence is confirmed, Nable knows Dilvant is in Heraklion with Quinan. Nable will keep listening as his spies are part of the army the High Priest and Quinan have formed.

"What a smart young man he is. He needs to keep us informed, the more we know the better equipped we will be."

Eween assures her Nable will keep their intelligence team updated. "After I eat, we can contact Zenac and Dawa, we need to inform them of our idea. I know Dawa has said she never wants to be involved in another war, but unfortunately, she may have no choice. Zenac will be with us, of this I am sure."

Chapter 54

Eween

"Take only what you need, don't overload yourselves," Eween tells the citizens. They are on the move to Borgo having been told the city may be under attack. Although Leyna had not wanted to tell them of the danger, he and the other ministers had thought it better to tell the truth. Some, once they heard, had decided to stay and help. This pleased everyone, the more help they have the better their chances.

Eween and Leyna had spoken to Zenac and Dawa with Zenac offering to bring his own army to help. Dawa had argued saying there was not enough time, but Zenac had said to leave it to him. Dawa wasn't keen on another war and did not want Zenac to leave for Earth again. Zenac had argued that with the Vespira and the other more sophisticated rockets now in his arsenal, he would leave immediately. Leyna had also given her opinion on the timing, but mentioned she was hopeful they would arrive in time.

They both stand together watching their people nod with despondent urgency as they walk towards their safe houses. Some pick up the pace as they pass. "This is the right thing to do even though they all look dismal, if the High Priest finds the city deserted, he may retreat."

Eween looks at her and with sarcasm says, "And then we'll all live happily ever after. Leyna, he won't stop until he either has this city again or he is dead." He looks at her and knows her statement was ridiculous, but she tells him she only wanted to lighten up the gravity of the situation. Once all the citizens have left, Eween says, "Let's go, we need to rest and wait. Our army has surrounded the city, so no matter which way his army decides to attack, we are ready."

Back in the safety of their home Leyna goes straight to bed. Eween pours himself a scotch and sits with his compupad sussing out what his army is seeing. Picking up the answae, he calls, "Fixor, any movement?"

"No, nothing yet. We know they arrived in Civitavecchia and are on the move. I have a suspicion our spy has been captured or remains back at the camp. We have not heard from him since they began moving."

Eween listens as Fixor informs him about the weapons they are bringing with them, they have no guns, only the three technological weapons. "So, he is intent on capturing and only maiming those who resist. Interesting, I think our High Priest may be softening?"

"According to my spy, he is definitely a different person. He is now known by his name, Dilvant, he is in love with Quinan's sister who is the reason for the change, and he walks freely amongst the citizens. It's strange to say, but he may actually be liked."

Eween runs his hand over his face, sighing, "This may make him even more dangerous, because he has hidden his true self and he could explode at any time. Keep vigilant. I'm beat, send me messages if things change, otherwise I will speak to you in the morning."

"Sure. I'm going to rest too, it's going to be a long few days."

He awakes in a sweat. His hand automatically checks that Leyna is next to him. His breath escapes and settles when he realises it was a nightmare. With his body still shaking, he goes to the bathroom.

Wetting his face with cold water, he stares at his reflection. *It was just a dream, she wasn't being tortured in front of you. He didn't have his filthy hands all over her.*

"Are you okay? Come back to bed."

"I'm fine now that I know I was dreaming. The High Priest had you chained in the square with everyone watching. I was chained only a metre away from you and couldn't help you. Me screaming in the dream woke me."

"Stress is getting the better of you. Come here," she says, patting the space where he sleeps.

Eween obeys and she is slowly caressing his chest, her hand rubbing his body as he becomes aroused. This woman has been by his side through everything and her strength becomes his when he doubts himself. As she makes love to him, he relishes her beauty and knows if she were ever in a situation like the one in his dream, he would do everything in his power to kill the perpetrator.

His compupad beeps and wakes them both. Checking, he sees that Fixor sent a message saying Quinan has been seen by his scouts. He is on the north side of the city with what looks like thousands of soldiers, more than they had anticipated. Eween sends back a message asking him to remain calm, it may be a trick of one of the weapons, the one that sends out holograms. It's possible Quinan is sending out multiple holograms giving the illusion of more soldiers. Fixor sends a message straight back hoping Eween is right because if there are the number of soldiers the scouts saw, they will be dead by the end of the day.

Leyna had also seen the message and looked into Eween's eyes, "I think you're right. There is no way they could have formed an army of many thousands in the time the High Priest has been on Crete."

He takes her hand, "I am sure of it, Leyna. The holograms are a smokescreen to scare our soldiers into surrender. Now, it's time for us to put our plan into place."

. . .

Leyna returns from the prison with the three Enforcer women and chains them to the pillars at the front of the great hall. Eween is waiting for her in his battle uniform. She is already wearing hers with two grenade belts around her waist. Twenty of Taaz's men are with them and they have explosives, machine guns and one tank. Leaving the prisoners, they walk towards the gates of the city.

"Remember, do not resist if you are caught. I do not want any of you maimed and deaf for the rest of your lives. Their army only has three weapons, but they are technologically superior to our armour, this is what we have to deal with. We must think differently and target their feet, maim them before they can maim us. The holograms will look real up close, but you will know they are not real when you shoot and all the soldiers remain standing. Finally, the weapon that imprisons you in an invisible shield will be the easiest to disarm once we defeat them. Be patient and remain calm if you are captured by this weapon."

Leyna stands in front of them next to Eween and places her hand on his shoulder, "We did not come back to Earth to give the High Priest control once more. This fight will be the biggest of our lives and I want our parliament to continue with Eween and myself as leaders, so let them come at us, we are ready to defend our city and our Earth."

Their security team cheers, fist pumping the air. Eween looks around with pride, hoping they have done enough.

They sit and wait. Eween had asked Fixor to send a message when Quinan's army was moving forward, and it arrived with Fixor saying that the enemy army had slain many of their soldiers already. Minutes later, he sends another message that he and hundreds of others were imprisoned in the invisible cell, Quinan's army is heading towards the city's northern gates. Eween takes twenty security guards with him, "Leyna you watch this gate, the northern gate is being attacked." He hugs her with his one arm and kisses her fiercely, "Don't be afraid to go to the bunker, I'll meet you there when this is all over."

Chapter 55

Leyna

Darkness has enveloped them with the city being eerily quiet as they wait. The silence entombs them all. She is impassive to the situation, wanting it to be over. She has had enough of dealing with the High Priest and looks forward to putting him away. For good this time.

She is booted out of her reverie when there is bashing on the other side of the gate and the thunderous sound of battle boots hitting the ground. Leyna is prepared and is with five security guards who have the tank right at the gate. "Wait until I give the signal, everyone is to attack at once."

The gate gives way after an hour of the enemy pushing and shoving it down. She commands her team to rain bullets down on the High Priest's army, who are only a handful to Leyna's surprise. *Where are the rest of them?*

The smell of gunfire mixes with that of blood and death. She was hoping to never have to see this again, but here she is, fighting that bastard once again. She hears him calling her asking her to come down from the tank and surrender. Her men are dead, there are only the five with her left in the tank. She is not surprised, with only a few hundred men on the ground, they were no match to the hundreds who came in with the High Priest. "You will have to kill me. I will never surrender to you."

His evil laugh peels out as his soldiers join him. Humiliation is something she has never felt and this spurs her into hurling two grenades into the darkness. She hears a few grunts but knows she hit nowhere near her target.

"If you do not come down, I will come up there and take you by force. I'm not here to hurt you, or any of your people. I am unarmed, my whole army only has three weapons. Your security guards who lie dead now should not have fought back, my soldiers have orders to spare lives if possible."

She turns to two of the men with her, "The three of us can go down together. I will make sure he leads us to the great hall where he will see his wife chained. There I will cause the distraction and you both go to help Eween. Tell him I was heading for the bunker when you escaped." They both nod with one saying, "Right behind you."

Before leaving, Leyna tells the other two soldiers left with the tank to head forward and rescue anyone from their army left alive, "Bring them back and have them see the medical team." They nod as she heads to meet her nemesis.

Dilvant walks towards her, placing a finger under her chin, "You are a smart woman, Leyna. Now, lead me to Eween and we can finish this. I am the rightful ruler and will be returned, Earth will be restored to my way once more."

She doesn't answer as she feels bile coming up her throat. As she and her two soldiers have their hands chained behind their backs, he forcibly pushes them forward. Pitch darkness makes it hard to see, she walks by memory rather than sight. Something catches her eye on her right side, and she hopes someone in the shadows isn't going to do something stupid. Some citizens had remained to help, but she wasn't hopeful they knew anything about overthrowing a tyrant.

Suddenly, there is a crowd in front of them with flames lit. "We are the citizen army of Vatican City, release Leyna and any other prisoners to us," comes a booming voice of a masked giant, who

Leyna recognises as the voice of The Mechanic, he looks after their fleet of cars. She had no idea he had formed a citizen army.

Then there is a scream from near the great hall, the High Priest's wife is calling him. "My Vimara is alive? Lead me to her."

Leyna speaks with authority, "Citizen army, follow us to the great hall. Do not harm anyone nor place yourselves in any more danger." To her surprise everyone, including the High Priest's army, listens. And her next surprise is the High Priest running towards Vimara the minute he sees her.

"I order you to release her and these other two women immediately." His face glares at her with a fury burning as bright as the flares of the citizen army."

"Not a problem, as soon as you release me and my two guards. Leave us unharmed and you will have your family returned to you."

"You bitch, what makes you think I'm going to release you," he screams, then in a calmer tone, "one of your guards can do it. Give one of them the key, show them where it is." When she refuses to move or say anything, he grabs her by the arm saying in a whisper, "Leyna don't mess with me, your life is in my hands, now give the key to your guard."

The tightness around her arm is making her feel faint and she instructs the guard on her right to take the key out of the longest pocket on her uniform, the on her thigh. She had placed it there so as not to lose it. As he lets go of her arm, she rubs it and takes deep breaths to regain her composure. Being pregnant is not helping her and she feels another wave of nausea. This time she cannot keep it in.

The high priest laughs as he watches the guard unlocking the chains, "I'm scaring you that much. Oh my, poor little Leyna is scared."

She doesn't have the strength to retaliate as she looks towards Vimara who is placing kisses all over his face, "They have kept us in a damp prison like common thieves, I knew you would come back for us."

That woman is delusional if she thinks he came back to rescue them, that he would risk his life for his family. He didn't care about them when he escaped, what makes her think he cares now. But she observes how he seems to care, hugging the three of them. Is he putting on a show? He may have changed and become soft, but she still doesn't trust him, all his evilness is still inside him.

While he is distracted, she nods to the guard standing next to her telling him to run after she does, one of the citizen army will help him. With as much strength as she can muster, she runs down the hall, throwing grenades back at them.

"Follow her you idiots, what are you waiting for?" he yells at his soldiers who were stunned into inaction. As they run, the other guard sneaks away and heads towards where he thinks Eween will be.

Throwing one more grenade at the front of the house they were living in, she heads towards the tunnels. The bunker is down there and, made of solid steel, she will be safe until Eween comes to collect her. As she steps into the bunker, she feels another wave of nausea. Reaching for the crackers on the shelf, she nibbles at them as she creeps down onto the mattress, exhaustion taking over.

<h1 style="text-align:center">Chapter 56</h1>

Eween

His soldiers have been captured, but he managed to escape as he had remained at the back of the formation. With only one arm, he knows not to be on the front line, he is a hindrance.

Something the High Priest and Quinan have not calculated was the disadvantage of having only three weapons is that you can only target three areas at once. If all three weapons are used by separate sections of your army, as they have done, you are left with only one weapon to attack the enemy in front of you. Eween used this to his advantage, and when Quinan was capturing his men with the invisible shield, he was able to make his escape.

As he nears the great hall, he hears voices. He heads towards a crowd with flame torches and recognises The Mechanic who is holding a mask, but he doesn't have time to ask why. Reaching up, Eween taps him on the shoulder, startling him, ,"It's me Eween, put that knife down. What is going on? Where is Leyna?"

The Mechanic tells him there is a standoff between them and the High Priest, he is listening to Leyna's orders of not putting themselves in more danger. She ran, but he doesn't know where she is. He also explains what he is doing there and is ready to fight along with the other citizens.

"Okay, here is what we are going to do. I see he is with his wife and the other two women. We need to capture them. On my order, use your torches to storm his army, there are not many of them, and throw them into prison. Leave the High Priest and his women to me, I will come to them when it is safe. I will wait here and stay out of your way." The Mechanic nods and Eween is always surprised by his bulk, he feels minuscule compared to this man.

As he watches, he is surprised at how the citizens defend themselves. They all have weapons as well as their torches, and with these they defeat the enemy soldiers, which is surprising as they are the more experienced and younger ones. He had been worried when these citizens wanted to stay behind, now he is proud of them and glad they stayed.

The soldiers are gathered together and marched towards the prison. Eween walks towards the High Priest who is now guarded along with the women. "Well, I finally have the pleasure of meeting you. I hear they call you Dilvant."

"That is my name," the High Priest spits out at him.

"No need to be nasty, you're alive aren't you. I gave the order for you and your ladies not to be harmed. Now be careful or I may change my mind." Eween has The Mechanic standing next to him feeling assured of his own safety. "Take them to the tunnels and place them in the first room on the right, the biggest one. I wouldn't want them to suffer in the smaller rooms," he says with sarcasm. Turning away from them, he tells The Mechanic and some of the other citizens to guard the room. Taking others with him, he goes to find Leyna.

As he enters the bunker leaving the citizens on guard, he sees her on the mattress with her face as white as snow. "Leyna," he runs towards her, "what happened to you? Did that bastard hurt you?"

She looks up at him with a groggy focus, "I ah... oh, I'm feeling nauseous again."

"What do you mean again?"

Beginning to focus, she asks him to give her another dry cracker. As she finishes it she says with tears in her eyes, "Eween, I'm pregnant."

"What?" He places his hands on his face in disbelief. Standing up his hands move onto his head as his eyes sparkle with tears. "You are pregnant and you're only telling me now, what the fuck Leyna."

"I'm six weeks and only found out after seeing the doctor last week. The day you found me on the lounge sleeping."

"You have placed yourself in all this danger. If you had told me I would not have let you be a part of all this."

"Eween, I'm fine... okay, apart from the nausea. Look, we're going to be parents, this is even more reason to defeat the High Priest. Speaking of him, has he been captured?"

He still cannot believe what he has been told, he has so many more questions, but they will have time for those later. "Yes, he and his women are in the first room, you know the one... the biggest. The Mechanic is on guard with some of the other citizens. There are a few guarding us too."

"Who would have believed the citizens could do such a thing? I am impressed, that Mechanic is one big brute I wouldn't want to cross."

He laughs, "Good to hear you haven't lost your sense of humour. Now, come here, I want to hug the mother of my child."

Chapter 57

Quinan

Quinan asks his soldiers to move forward. He asks them to find as many citizens as possible and take them prisoner, although there doesn't seem to be many left in the city, the houses are empty.

As they reach the centre of the city, daylight throws light into the square. He sees some of his soldiers strewn about, some injured, others dead. "You there, collect the bodies and place them out of the sun. Take five others with you and identify them. You three, bring the medical supplies with you and attend to the wounded. Everyone else follow me."

He is wary as it is quiet, which is disconcerting. There are some of Leyna's soldiers also dead, he sees a few near the southern gate, but there are more of his soldiers down. Had they underestimated the power of Leyna and Eween's army? "Let's scout around, check all the buildings and houses. Bring anyone who surrenders to the tunnels, I'm heading down there." He remembers from the maps he studied, the ones Dilvant had shown him, the tunnels are at the end of the great hall. Built as an escape route for his family, not many knew of the existence of these tunnels. The catacombs and the crypts of St Peter's Basilica are famous, these ones were only known to a select few.

With a handful of soldiers, he walks down towards the tunnels. He has a handgun that he took from one of the dead soldiers and some of his soldiers were armed as well. As they near the entrance to the tunnels, he hears voices. He turns and indicates to his soldiers following that they move forward. As they approach the voices Quinan hands begin to sweat as he holds onto the rifle and says, "Cover me, then move forward and attack." As he moves, he finds himself standing in front of a monster of a man with a well-armed crowd behind him. They start to attack him and his soldiers and he has no option but to defend himself. The monster pushes him against the wall, his knee pinning him.

"What makes you think I'm going to allow you to go any further?" The Mechanic's voice booms as he hits Quinan with the back of his rifle.

Tasting blood, Quinan flings in and out of consciousness. Coming too he sees one of his soldiers jumping on top of the monster, who simply lobs him to the other wall. Quinan tries to stand but the monster turns and hits him once more. As he falls, he hears guns firing and what he thinks is Dilvant's voice.

The thud in his head is twice as bad this time. He looks down and sees he has been grazed by a bullet, his leg is bleeding. He struggles but manages to stand using the rifle as a prop. He sees many of his soldiers spread out through the tunnel, dead and injured. Others sprinkled in between them are from the crowd. The door to the room is open and he carefully checks, but it is empty. Moving slowly, he finds some of his soldiers further down the tunnel, "Where did the crowd go, especially that huge man?"

"They retreated," says one soldier, "we were struggling but then the man you speak of called them all and they followed. We remained and tried to regroup."

"Maybe they are needed to protect Leyna and Eween. Did you see Dilvant, where is he?"

"I did," says another soldier, "he was injured but the three women with him were carrying him out of the tunnel. When he passed you, he called your name."

"I thought I heard his voice. The women will take him to safety, I hope. Now, we must find where Leyna and Eween are and remember, do not hurt them, bring them to me as I will hand them over to Dilvant." As he speaks, they start moving through the dank tunnel, stepping between the bodies and taking weapons. His head is still throbbing but he has no choice, he wants this finished.

It's not long before they hear voices again. "Halt. This time we need to be more strategic," says Qunian. "You there, take this white rag and wave it towards them in surrender. Your injuries are enough to make them help you. Once you have distracted them, we will attack." The soldier nods and walks further into the tunnel feigning his injuries even more.

Quinan sees his plan working and waves his soldiers forward, he remains behind to adjust his tourniquet on his leg. The bullet that grazed his knee has caused more damage than he first thought and with a tourniquet tightly wound, he is walking with a limp. Suddenly, the monster is in front of him again.

"You again. This time I have had enough," he says, swinging his right arm into Quinan's chin who reels back. "Get up you coward, fight like a man."

This monster is playing with him and Quinan feels around for a rock to throw at him. Finding a stone, he throws it, but it barely makes a dent on the monster's leg. As the monster looks down at his leg, Quinan forces himself up and storms forward into the massive body. The monster sways a little but not enough to allow Quinan to reach his rifle.

The force makes his knee bleed again, his head pulsates with pain as the blow from the monster hits it. Then there is nothing.

Chapter 58

Zenac

Zenac and Taaz reach the city to see soldiers from both sides piled up at the side of the square. Blood, sweat and death reek through the air. "Call the rest of our troops, it's time to finish this," he says as he waits for them to arrive.

They march in formation and Zenac asks them to separate into four groups. "Search every inch of the city, one group come with me to search the tunnels. Taaz, you coordinate another group to treat any survivors no matter whether they are ours or theirs. Set up here and check for survivors in that pile over there."

"Are you sure you don't want me with you, Zenac? I am not a medic."

"I want you to protect the medics in case their soldiers return. The hologram out the front of the city may have been fake, but who knows how many are in the city walls."

"As you wish. Come on, follow me," he says waving his hand towards the group nearest him.

Zenac moves with his men and heads towards the great hall.

When they arrive, he is surprised to find the High Priest with three women in full view. They have made no attempt to hide.

"Well, who have we here?" asks Dilvant, "come all this way to rescue your young protégés have you?"

Looking around thinking this may be a trap, Zenac indicates to some of his troops to scout around. Injured in one foot and with his arm in a sling, he wonders why the High Priest is here, "Why are you not hiding, I am able to take you prisoner with no trouble."

"Go ahead, I'm here for the taking."

This behaviour is puzzling Zenac, what the hell is the High Priest playing at? He moves forward with three other men asking them to each take one of them. "I'll take the High Priest, you three take the women." Moving forward they soon find out why the High Priest is so confident – they are encased in an invisible prison, they have used their own weapon to keep themselves safe.

"Go ahead, touch the shield and see what happens," he says with a smug look.

"Don't touch it," Zenac warns his men, "it's electrified. Twenty of you stay here with me, the others go and find Leyna and Eween. Bring back anyone who has survived."

Asking some of the soldiers to stand guard, Zenac takes the others to check the houses for anyone who may be hiding. They find a few soldiers being held captive by citizens, something he had not expected to see. Leyna had told him all the citizens were moved to Borgo for safety.

"Some of us remained. The Mechanic formed a citizen army and they are now protecting Leyna and Eween in the bunker."

Eween thanks the woman, "Taaz has a medical unit in the square. Take these soldiers there and get yourselves cleaned up." They do as they are told as Zenac keeps checking homes.

He is in the home where he stayed with Teegue when he hears his name. Walking out to the great hall, he sees Leyna and Eween.

She comes running towards him, "You came, I didn't think you would make it in time. Do you know where the High Priest is?"

Eween is right behind her as Zenac hugs them. "He is with three women at the great hall entrance. We can't touch him, he is in an invisible cell that is electrified. I have soldiers guarding them."

"Let's pay him a visit shall we."

Behind her Zenac sees The Mechanic and his motley crew of citizens. Who would have thought these people could help fight the High Priest, but they have, and he knows they could not have done so well without them.

Arriving at the entrance, the High Priest is nowhere to be found and the soldiers are huddled in a cell, their weapons gone. "What the hell happened?" yells Zenac.

"They were asleep and then the next minute we couldn't move. He used some machine on us, how the hell do we get out of here?"

Zenac reflects on how sly the High Priest is, he had every intention of making sure Zenac was confident of leaving him with his soldiers and then making his escape. He may not like the man, but he admires his ingenuity.

"Damn, that bastard has escaped again."

"Yes Leyna, but he is injured, and his army has been diminished to a couple of hundred. Not many of them will return with him."

"He will be well on his way back to Civitavecchia by now and we don't have the resources to chase him."

"No, we don't. What we have to concentrate on is helping everyone who is injured, getting these soldiers out of this cell and cleaning up the city. I would like to commend The Mechanic and his army because their help has given us a victory."

"Zenac is right, Leyna, there is no use chasing after the High Priest, not now. Let's cut our losses and return our citizens from Borgo."

They all head towards the medical tent to find Taaz. Zenac informs him of what has happened and then inspects the work that has been done.

Arriving home to a hero's welcome, Zenac, Taaz and their remaining soldiers wave as they come out of the hangar. Zenac left Leyna and Eween to look after a broken city, yet again, they have their work cut out for them. Leyna asked him to leave, she and Eween had things under control and they would contact him if they needed his help again. Unfortunately, with the High Priest still alive, they all know that time will come again.

He finds Dawa, hugging her to him, "We made it in time, but a citizen army had things under control. Let's go home and I'll tell you all about it.

Chapter 59

Dilvant

He hobbles up the two steps to her villa, she is waiting on the stoop. Propping himself against the wall, she comes to him kissing and hugging him with a passion that envelopes him.

"You said you would return, and you have," she says looking down to where his foot is meant to be.

"I was shot in the foot twice and by the time I returned to Civitavecchia, it could not be saved. But I am alive and happy to see your beautiful face."

She leads him inside taking hold of his walking stick. The place smells of fresh flowers and the sea, so different from what he has been smelling these past weeks. Making sure he is comfortable on the lounge, she heads towards the kitchen, "I have made some soup."

Dilvant doesn't much care what he eats but knows she would have made it herself so it will be tastier than the little food he has had up until now. As he rests, he contemplates how to tell her about Quinan, her older brother won't be returning to Heraklion. Taking in the smells of the Cretan Sea, he finds it calming and looks forward to dipping himself into it in the next few days. A naked dip with Felida will cure him of his grief, he misses Quinan and cannot imagine what she will feel when he tells her.

"No, please tell me it's not true," she says, tears streaming down her face after he gives her the bad news. "Quinan was strong, trained in combat, what happened?"

Hugging her and feeling her pain he says, "The irony is he was killed by one known as *The Mechanic*, a citizen who arranged the citizen army to protect Leyna and Eween. You cannot believe the size of this man, he is a monster." Holding her closer still, he continues with stories of how their young soldiers were ambushed, it was a mistake to leave them fully unarmed. Then he tells her about Zenac coming back with five thousand more troops, which helped their cause, but mostly it was the citizen army that blindsided his soldiers.

Raising her head from his chest she says through her sobs, "We will have a public memorial for Quinan. Where is his body?"

"It's in the morgue along with the other soldiers we managed to bring back with us. But of course you must have a memorial for him."

She nods and takes their plates back to the kitchen. He knows organising this memorial for her older brother will keep her busy and keep their grief at bay for a while. Looking towards the clock, it is noon. He decides that a dip in the sea is called for, "Felida, come with me down to the beach."

They are in the calm waters and he is holding onto her as they both dip themselves into the crystal water. The aquamarine waters surround their naked bodies as they make love. He tastes her tears and his heart is full of love for this woman who has lost the only family she had left.

The sun beams down on the people of Heraklion as they mourn the death of their revered leader. Felida had organised a memorial to the fallen soldiers, which was held yesterday. Today, they are back for Quinan's one. She had wanted a special one for him, this one has his favourite music playing, his beloved football jersey and his soldiers in their full regalia giving him a twenty-one-gun salute.

She had been quiet since he told her the bad news, and Dilvant didn't push her to talk, knowing this was her way of grieving. He is holding her hand as they walk behind the gold coffin, which will remain on display in front of the Morosini Fountain for forty days before being taken to the family tomb. His heart is heavy, and he battles the guilt he feels of not being able to help Quinan, and of coming home alive while bringing his friend home in a box. As they reach the spot where the coffin will rest, Felida collapses but he manages to keep her up with the help of others around them. Someone brings a chair and water, which she takes and sips.

Everyone is now seated as Quinan's colleagues give a eulogy. Dilvant is not surprised to hear of his friend's many accomplishments and the reasons why his people adored him. With five people speaking, the stories are sometimes humorous because Quinan had been full of life with a good sense of humour. At forty years old, he died too young, and he has left a void in Dilvant's heart that will never be filled.

The eleven ministers are seated with Dilvant at the Basilica of St. Titus, the house of parliament. Dilvant had given them a proposal to build a space program, "We will entice the experts from around the world to help us. With this program we will visit Arisis and take down Zenac and Dawa. Then, we will take on Leyna and Eween, but this time we will be ready with technology and armour. Quinan and I wanted to save lives, which is why we only went in with three weapons and no ammunition. This will never happen again, and with this space program we will not only conquer Earth but the galaxy as well."

He waits as this news sinks in and the ministers discuss amongst themselves.

The minister for the interior speaks first, "We have spent much of our budget on the failed attempt, our army has been cut in half and now you want us to play astronauts. This is preposterous, we don't have the knowledge nor the intelligence to run such a program."

"Minister, I beg to differ. Once we find engineers and astronauts willing to be a part of our program, we will find people of similar intelligence amongst our citizens. Cretans are an intelligent race, it is a crime not to use this brain power." Again, he listens to more murmuring.

"Dilvant, it has been a long discussion and we have heard your proposal. Please leave us now to discuss further ideas and vote.

"As you wish, but let me say one last thing, this is something Quinan and I had discussed briefly. He was all for it and we were going to work on it together upon our return. It is in his honour that I would run the project, and will name it, The Quinan Space Project."

"That is very admirable, and we will take this into account. Good day, Dilvant."

He leaves the chambers hoping he has done enough to convince the ministers of his plan. Funds can come from private investors as well as governments, he will begin calling his friends in England and Russia, their space programs are already underway.

Chapter 60

Leyna

She waddles out of their bathroom and sees Eween smiling at her. "What?"

"You look gorgeous... glowing even. Pregnancy suits you."

"If you like it so much why don't you try it?" she says laughing, "the nausea is the best part, believe me." She collapses into his arms glad it is a Saturday and they don't have anywhere to be.

After Zenac left, The Mechanic was named as their head of security and he was receiving training in martial arts from Asheel. They were taking no chances; they want to be even more prepared when the High Priest acts upon his revenge again.

As part of the alliance with Dawa and Zenac, they are investing in a space program to help find more planets that are habitable. Earth still has its challenges, The Enforcers devastated much of the population. Since the fall of the High Priest, Vatican City along with other first-world countries are seeing a baby boom not seen since 2050. Prosperity is motivating citizens to build and grow their businesses and there is healthy exporting and importing happening. Countries like England, USA, China, Canada and even Australia and New Zealand, are all communicating in civil terms again. At the moment, the rest of Italy is still catching up with Vatican City but being the most destroyed country during the 20-year war, they knew things would take time.

She feels a kick and calls Eween, "Here, put your hand on this side."

He does so, but feels nothing for a minute, then he feels the little bump hit his hand, "Wow, he has some strength."

"He? How do you know it's a *he*?"

"Oh, it's a feeling I have," he says taking her onto the lounge, "now, my beautiful Madame President, I think I want to ravish you."

Allowing him his moment, she doesn't argue. Whether they have a boy or a girl, it doesn't matter, as long as their baby grows up in a world that is safe, then she will be happy.

It's Monday and they are all in the chambers at St Peter's Basilica. Breex, Fixor and Nable have given their speeches for the day with their Environment, Finance and Defence portfolios all ticking along well.

Leyna stands and moves over to the hologram showing a complete map of the city. There are still areas in need of repair. "These areas to the east and south are complete, now we must concentrate on the north and west. Borgo is coming along as a centre of manufacturing, so this is where the space program will be based. Eween will fill you in on its progress at our next meeting. By then he will have negotiated with Dawa and Zenac on the funds they are prepared to give to the project. With regard to the north and east sections of the city, Breex will be briefing engineers and builders next week, as he previously mentioned. Eween and I will be inspecting these areas with the selected team when they are appointed. The bigger part of this plan is to expand these building programs to other areas near us. If Italy is to catch up with the rest of the world, we need to give these towns infrastructure similar to what we have in our city."

She lets all this sink in as she sits, her legs giving way to the weight of her pregnancy, then continues, "As you all know, Asheel and The Mechanic along with their security team are training others to be part of our army. News of the High Priest, or Dilvant, as he likes to be known as now, is that apart from losing his right foot, he is in good health. The people of Crete are treated well, however, this is more due to his latest love, Felida. For those of you who don't know her, she is the sister of Quinan, the much-loved ruler who died during our last clash. With this information of our sworn enemy, I end my speech. I wish you all well and bid you a good evening."

She and Eween wait until all the ministers have left before speaking. "I am pleased with how things are going and am especially pleased about our alliance with Dawa and Zenac. This can only be good for our city and Italy as a whole."

"Agreed. Shall we go, I don't want to think about doing any more work. I'll meet you at the car."

"Sure, I'll tidy my desk and be with you soon." Standing, she holds her belly as she feels another small movement. This baby tends to become more active at night, she feels the acrobatics in her sleep.

Walking into her office in the parliamentary rooms, she sees there is a message from Dawa as she opens her compupad.

"I wanted to congratulate you on the good work you are doing in Vatican City. You and Eween escaped Arisis and we were embarrassed by what you did. For a long time, I hated you for doing this to us. How wrong could I have been? You were on a mission to rid Earth of the menace that was The Enforcers and the High Priest. I am so proud of your achievements and also want to congratulate you on your pregnancy, Madame President. Please count me as your friend not your foe, and together with our partners, the alliance we have formed will ensure the safety of Earth, Arisis and any other planet we discover together."

She closes her compupad and carries it with her to the car. Dawa, who was once her enemy, now considers her a friend. Whether they remain friends is yet to be seen because no one knows what the future holds. For now, she will keep both Dawa and Zenac close, with Dilvant still alive, she and Eween will need all the allies they can get. Climbing into the car, she holds onto her bump in a protective show of love because the last thing she wants is for this little one to ever be in danger.

END of Book 2

VOLUME THREE

Xenure Station: The Return

Book 3

Chapter 1

2299

Xenure Station

Leyna

After welcoming the dignitaries to the Ovalaz Luminary Room on Xenure Station and outlining their policy of space exploration, Leyna sits and gives Eween, Zenac and the GIS members the floor. Looking around she is pleased to see how many countries are represented, she and Eween have faith in their alliance with Dawa and Zenac. With this mission having been in the works for four years, their alliance is stronger than ever.

Dilvant has made some murmurings of joining the space race but the finances he expected to come his way have not surfaced because of the mistrust from the rest of the world. Even though she still harbours a want to make him pay for his war crimes this has taken a back step to restoring The Vatican to its former glory and assisting the rest of the world to regroup. For now, Leyna will allow Dilvant to stay in Crete as long as he remains harmless.

The eight members of the GIS board, led by the capable Wilkern and his deputy Sayen, are in attendance. They are a power couple to be reckoned with. Wilkern, as a Biochemist and Environmental Scientist and his partner Sayen as a Psychologist, have the initiative and brain power to run the important work of the GIS - Global Initiative for Sustainability. They run the GIS along with six other environmental scientists and they have done so since the first team was ousted due to falling prey to Dilvant and his Enforcers. They are all specialists in the field of achieving sustainable environments. Other experts in the fields of sustainability are being recruited to work on newly colonised planets. Arisis has the second GIS board working alongside a team of researchers on Mazadon.

Listening to the speeches, Leyna is quietly confident that the delegates will respond to this space project. Earth has a long way to go before it is at full strength again, population growth is on the up and many countries are planning towards financial viability, things are positive. It is in the delegate's interest to have their countries donate as the exploration of other suitable planets for humans to colonise is important for everyone. Earth's environment remains vulnerable and with more population growth, more environmental issues will follow.

"Many thanks to all of you for attending this inaugural meeting of the Universal Space Project headed by Madame President, Minister Eween and our esteemed allies, Dawa and Zenac of planet Arisis. May I reiterate how important it is to keep this meeting confidential until it is announced, which we hope will happen within a month. I now pass you back to Madame President." Wilkern takes his seat next to Eween to thunderous applause giving Leyna a nod and a look of achievement.

"My thanks to you Professor Wilkern and I am sure you will all agree this project is a viable option for humans to conquer space and give us more options for sustainable living. I now invite you all to the dining hall for a celebratory dinner in honour of this meeting. I've been told our chef has organised a culinary feast." Leyna watches on as delegates whisper, shake hands and file out of the Ovalaz room.

Turning to Eween, she takes his hand and follows the others to the dining hall.

Sitting at the head table with Dawa and Zenac as well as Wilkern and Sayen, Leyna is pleased to see that chef and his team do not disappoint. Since their takeover of The Vatican, she and Eween along with their other parliamentarians, have improved the living standards of the city tenfold. Other parts of Italy are following in their footsteps with the rest of the world starting to improve as well. The delegates on Xenure Station for this meeting represent the major powers of the UK, China, Germany, Russia and the developing nations of Australia, New Zealand, Canada, Asia and South America. Along with the GIS, the parliament of The Vatican has been negotiating deals with all these countries, and they have attended this meeting in secret. Until every detail of this project is finalised, and money has been donated as promised, there will be no announcement. All the delegates have signed confidentiality agreements. At this stage, the only countries being difficult are the USA and China. Leyna takes a mouthful of the ocean trout prepared with a delicate Thai sauce and knows if they are able to manage the harmony they have enjoyed these past four years, then this project will not fail.

"Madame President, may I say how lovely you look."

"Thank you Wilkern, but why so formal? The meeting is over, please call me Leyna."

"As you wish, Leyna. I take it Galexia is behaving herself?"

"Ha, I guess so. As much as a three-year-old can. She has her father in the palm of her hand."

Eween laughs, "It's true, she is my everything along with my beautiful wife, of course."

"Oh, what a good save there my man," chuckles Wilkern.

The night is full of discussion about their respective families, political views, where to from here and some salacious gossip. This kept the laughs flowing with enjoyment all round. From the appreciative delegates and general demeanour of the congregation, Leyna is hopeful of a positive outcome for their presentation tonight, the first global project of this harmonised world they have helped create.

Eween is next to her kissing her shoulder, "I am so proud of you, Madame President, you have pulled off the coup of a lifetime."

"Hmm, don't get ahead of yourself, we haven't seen any funds yet. Although, I did feel there was a lot of love in the room. Besides, it wasn't only me, you and the rest of our team had a lot to do with this."

"Without your leadership we would not have come this far. Having the meeting here on Xenure Station has helped keep things quiet, but that won't be possible once funds start rolling in."

"I'll prepare an announcement when we're back on Earth. Dawa and Zenac have told me The Luminaries are committed to the project and will help us to announce it. I'm sure the networks will be pleased to give us airtime."

Technology is another booming business with television and radio stations resurrected in many countries. Compupads and Answaes have been the only technology in service apart from electric cars, but start-up companies are now beginning to produce more affordable products for all citizens. Due to Dilvant and his Enforcers banning all forms of technology during their regime, it has been difficult for companies to produce products affordable for everyone. Now, as countries slowly forge ahead, technology and continuing to save the environment will be the industries that will thrive.

"Of course the networks will give you airtime, what makes you think they won't?"

"The last time I was invited to the Channel 4 political show, *One Power*, I wasn't given enough time to speak and give my point of view."

"That was because the President of the USA wouldn't shut up, he wanted everyone to hear his views."

"Well, he did have a lot to say about Dilvant and how he should be punished. That's not a bad thing."

"Yes, but Dilvant is yours to deal with and we will decide when we take him on again. Anyway, I don't think one incident is going to change the minds of the network executives, you are Madame President after all. You take precedence over any other leader."

She leans over and kisses him warmly, both hands holding his face. "You are right, my love and I love you more for being on my side. Now, today has been a huge day and my weary body needs to rest. Tomorrow we need to discuss donations with each country, which will be another gruelling day."

He turns towards her, kissing her on the lips, "I love you too."

Chapter 2

Dawa

From the viewing platform, Dawa uses the Faemay Telescope to enjoy the immense arena of sparkling gasses, rock and debris surrounding them. Space is a fascinating expanse, and she is privileged to have been a part of the first people to colonise another planet. She, along with Zenac, is one of the pioneers of space exploration. Now, with Leyna and Eween's help, this is going to continue. With the four of them working on it, their proposal to explore new planets suitable for human habitation has solid support. She focuses on the viewing space and is rewarded with a rock-like substance that looks like a meteor. Earth is in for a meteor shower in a few days. As she turns the telescope, she takes in the immense area of blackness speckled with all sorts of space matter.

"Enjoying yourself?"

Turning towards him she smiles, "It's spectacular. I will never tire of the fact I am an observer from this side of the galaxy."

"Well, I'm glad you've had your fun but it's time to help Leyna and Eween with coaxing donations out of the attendees, let's go," says Zenac.

They walk hand in hand to the Ovalaz Luminary Room to find only Leyna and Eween seated on stage.

"Where is everyone?"

"We're not meant to start for another half hour, we wanted to sit in peace for a while Dawa."

"Apologies for disturbing you. We'll sit quietly too."

The four of them enjoy the silence until the dignitaries begin entering, chatting loudly. As they take their seats Leyna stands ready to address them again. She waits until the noise subsides and reassures them that this is the last time they will have to congregate in this room for this project, tomorrow everyone will be heading home. There is polite clapping as she continues asking each delegate to refer to the hologram document in front of them, they are to fill in details of their country's intention and interest in the space project. The final page is to be signed by each delegate showing the amount of Licdan they are willing to donate.

There is complete silence apart from the vents sending filtered air into the room. Each delegate is concentrating on their form. As each one powers down their hologram once completed Leyna waits before she gives them the floor to ask questions. "We have time now for any questions and once everyone is satisfied we will convene for lunch. The rest of the day is free, please enjoy it at your leisure."

To her surprise the four of them are inundated with questions, many having to do with where the spaceships will be built. Three countries – New Zealand, South America and Australia – are keen to bid.

"We will be contacting the countries with an interest in building the necessary parts and machines we require to build the spaceships, the technology required and the country with the most capabilities will be contracted to do the work. We will endeavour to spread the work around a few countries to help with your economic recovery. This is a project for the whole world to benefit from."

As the delegates applaud, the four of them rise from their chairs with Leyna announcing it is time for lunch and a well-earned rest.

Dawa is chatting to Leyna about her children during lunch. She is telling her how Teegue is enjoying working at the Spacedrome, Aria is studying law and Braxton is in his final year of school.

"Law? How is Aria enjoying it? There is much to learn."

"Yes, but she is capable. This being her last year she is finding the workload challenging but fulfilling. She is hoping to go into corporate law."

"That's admirable, maybe one day she will consider political law, we are always looking for good people in that area."

Dawa doesn't answer because the next plate is being placed in front of them. She wonders whether Aria would consider politics, with many political influences around her it may be a good fit. As she is thinking of her children she realises they have been away from them for three weeks. Between visiting Earth and now being on Xenure Station she is glad to be heading home tomorrow. She could do with a hug from them.

After lunch she and Zenac convene with Leyna and Eween in the small room off the Ovalaz Luminary Room. They have some loose ends to fix before leaving and all of them want this project to be flawless before the announcement. As they are discussing and coming to the end of their agenda the subject of Dilvant comes up.

"I still want him to pay for his crimes," says Leyna, "And I want to be the one who administers his punishment."

"You and many others want this to happen. At the moment he is not a threat, so let us have this project underway first. Dilvant will pay soon enough."

"Eween is right, Leyna. Although we do need to keep an eye on him. Our security team has evidence he is wanting to join the space race as well. He has named it 'The Quinan Space Project' in honour of Crete's leader who died during the skirmish at The Vatican."

"One of many who died in what will hopefully be the last fight we have to deal with," says Dawa.

"Unfortunately, I don't think Dilvant has had enough yet, he will want revenge. I'm glad you have him under surveillance Zenac because he is not to be trusted," says Leyna.

They continue with ideas on how to extradite Dilvant back to

The Vatican if necessary as Dawa wonders when their lives will be rid of such a tyrant.

Chapter 3

Dilvant

They are sitting on the balcony, Felida is reading and he is enjoying the view. The aquamarine Sea of Crete can be seen beyond the olive trees. He and Felida have enjoyed many swims in these warm blue waters since his return from the bloody battle for The Vatican. He feels the loss of his power, his family and his friend, Quinan, acutely. Quinan, who was Felida's brother, was the much-loved leader of Crete who died at the hands of the one they call, The Mechanic. This huge man's days are numbered, he is on Dilvant's list, the list of *Revenge*. Felida knows nothing of this list, she has made it clear she wants to live quietly here on Crete with him, she feels no need to avenge her brother's death. He however, wants to return to The Vatican and he hopes to do so soon.

He breathes in the salty air and stretches, "I am heading into parliament, they have news of Quinan's Space Project and I am keen to hear what it is."

Without looking up from her book Felida says, "Ok, I'll see you later."

It upsets him that Felida is not more interested in the space project, something he has named in honour of her brother. He thought this would please her and she would want to be a part of it. Wanting to be the first to find other planets like Earth is occupying most of Dilvant's waking moments. Why isn't she more interested in the project? The space project and wanting to become leader once more are his two most important tasks. Finding funds is the biggest hindrance to the project being successful, but until he has confirmation of such funds, he decides he won't discuss the project with her. He walks into the house leaving her to read.

Arriving at the Basilica, Dilvant walks into the parliamentary chamber. The ministers for Finance and Defence & Home Affairs are waiting for him, as well as the Finance Minister.

"Ah, Dilvant, thank you for seeing us at such short notice."

Dilvant steps down slowly with his slight limp, the prosthetic foot helping him to be independent.

"It's good to see that prosthetic is working for you," says the Minister for Defence.

"It would be better to have my foot," answers Dilvant with contempt, "now what is it you two want to discuss?"

They proceed to tell him they have managed to secure funds for the space project from an unlikely source, his home country of Mauritius. There are more funds needed, but this is a good start.

"Mauritius? I would never have guessed they had the funds let alone interest in the space program. I take it you spoke to the Prime Minister?"

"Yes, but only after speaking with the Treasurer. They have pledged enough to start the project, but you will need to secure more to keep it running. The Prime Minister confirmed the arrangement."

Dilvant sits and proceeds to tell them he has hit a brick wall. "My friends in England and the USA do not have funds to give but they have given me names of Russian parliamentarians, whom I am yet to contact. I have friends in Russia, so I am confident."

The Minister for Defence tells Dilvant that Leyna and Eween

have managed to procure funds from many countries and their project is already underway.

"She is my nemesis," says Dilvant with disgust. "However, I am impressed by her leadership. With her alliance with Dawa and Zenac, she has been able to secure the funds as well as the experts to run her program. I hear countries like England, Australia and New Zealand have facilities already set up to make the elements for the spacecraft. Do you know where they will be built?"

"As far as we know the contract has not been awarded yet. Our spy who was on Xenure Station as a delegate and is now an assistant in their parliament, is keeping us informed. She is a seasoned agent and we will know well in advance what is happening."

This pleases Dilvant, these two ministers are invaluable to him being able to start the project and with a good spy in their enemies' midst they will be kept up to date. He looks forward to the day when he will be back in power, if not at The Vatican then he will rule from here on Crete. Leyna and Eween are right at the top of his revenge list.

"Thank you gentlemen for this news, I will personally call the Mauritian Prime Minister and thank him. Now I will go to my office and see if I am able to make any progress with the Russians."

Sitting behind his desk in his small but adequate office, his title is now Minister for Science and Technology. How ironic for someone who destroyed much of the world's technology when he was leader. He smirks as he adjusts the nameplate on his desk. Opening his compupad, he checks messages before finding the numbers for the Russian ministers. He will try and contact his counterpart in the Russian parliament as well as the treasurer. He has already been informed by his friend in England who told him the Russians are open to heading into space again, they had a successful program last century.

Placed on hold when he finally manages to connect to the Russian government's reception, he raps his fingers on his desk as he waits. The young female voice returns on the line telling him both ministers are occupied, would he like to leave a message? He sighs and asks her to do so. Frustrated, he rises from his chair and decides he has done enough for today. As he makes his way home the afternoon sun is warm and he is looking forward to a swim in the aquamarine water.

Sitting on the lounge they are both watching the news. The main stories are about The Vatican and how things have improved, Leyna and Eween are shown walking amongst the people with security behind them. The Machine is front and centre, the smug look on his face makes Dilvant cringe with distaste. This man is a target and this time he won't survive.

When a commercial comes on he mutes the TV and turns to speak to Felida. "Aren't you going to ask me what I was called in for? It is a Saturday, I don't normally go into parliament on weekends."

"Oh yes, sorry. What was it about?" she asks.

He knows she has no interest in knowing but he tells her anyway. "It was about funds coming in for the space project and you will be surprised when you hear where they came from."

"Ok. This is good news of course?"

"Definitely, it's a start. The country that has donated is Mauritius. Do you believe it? I would never have thought to contact such a small country but sometimes things come from left field."

"That is surprising, your home country is interested in helping, which is a good thing. But where did they find these funds?"

"Their latest Prime Minister is proactive and wants to be more involved in world affairs. When I speak to him I will ask, diplomatically of course, how he managed this. Still, we will need more funds and I have tried contacting two Russian ministers, unfortunately no response from them as yet."

"Russia, they were allies with you during the 20-year war weren't they? Along with China. I'm sure they will be willing to help. Honestly Dilvant, I didn't think you would raise any funds, which is why I feigned not being interested. To have a project named in honour of my brother is huge, but I didn't want to have my hopes raised. You are proving me wrong," she says as she turns towards him, smiling broadly.

"I understand you being hesitant and am glad you are now on board. So, am I able to count on your help?"

She moves closer to him, her eyes pooling with tears, "When you honour my brother you honour me and Crete as a whole. Yes, you can count on me." Placing both her hands on his face, she kisses him passionately and his body reacts to her touch.

Pulling her towards him his anger of her disinterest in the project melts. This motivates him to seek more funds and start this project sooner, he wants to honour Quinan as well as make this a step forward for him to seek his revenge.

Chapter 4

Teegue

Listening to his father speak at the Spacedrome about how he is proud of the progress with the latest spacecraft, Teegue yawns. Not because Zenac is boring, it is because he has been up late every night cramming information about what is happening on Earth. The Universal Space Project that is still top secret, is what he is interested in. He wants to return and assist Leyna and Eween with this project. Even though they have an alliance with his parents, he wants to be on the front line of the project, which he only found out about by accident. He had overheard his parents discussing it after dinner a few weeks ago after they thought he had gone to bed. He was headed to bed but had come back downstairs to get a bottle of cold water. When he heard them talking he stopped and listened.

Dawa and Zenac are helping to facilitate the race to find other planets, but it is on Earth where all the action is taking place. Teegue wants to be an integral part of the processe and be there when the first spacecraft is launched.

His other motivation to return is to see Jzinta again, the beautiful girl he met last time he was on Earth. Dilvant's lovechild had taken his heart. They communicate occasionally, in secret though because he is still seeing Trisia as well. She is his first love straight from school. When he first came home Trisia was ecstatic to see him and their relationship blossomed again. Now, after being home for some years, he feels he wants more from a relationship and doesn't believe Trisia is the woman for him.

"Teegue, are you coming?"

His father's voice brings him back to the present. Having thought of Jzinta he decides he will call her tonight.

"Are you enjoying working here?"

"Dad of course I am, I can't believe you're asking that question. I have learned much about space engineering and I want to fly the latest spacecraft as soon as they are ready."

"I knew you were enjoying working here, I was checking that's all. Glad to hear you haven't become bored. I look forward to you flying your first craft too, your lessons are almost done. Now, let's head home, I'm starving."

"You and me both, Dad."

He's in his room laying on his bed propped up with two pillows, he and Jzinta are chatting. Unfortunately, she has given him bad news.

Teegue writes:

"You're right, it is hard to keep a relationship going when we're living on different planets, but I love you and as soon as the spacecrafts are ready I'll travel to see you."

Jzinta writes:

"Teegue I love you too but you can't expect me to wait, it's been years and I've found someone who is kind, supportive and lives in Italy. Borgo, in fact."

Teegue writes:

I'm shattered Jzinta," he says trying not to feel despair, "I'm happy for you though, you deserve to be loved."

Jzinta writes:

"I miss you terribly and for the first year after you left, I was hopeful of seeing you again. I know you have your work and are learning your craft, which is why you haven't travelled to Earth yet..."

She stops and he imagines she is crying or at least, he hopes she is. He feels like crying too and his eyes begin to well up.

Teegue writes,

"My intentions were to come back after a year, I have told you this, but my work has kept me here. I still want to come to Earth to help Leyna and Eween with something, most of the exciting work is being done there. It may be another six months before I am able to. When I do arrive I hope we can see each other for a drink, I'd like to remain friends."

Jzinta writes:

"Friends, yes that would be nice. How long are you planning to stay?"

Teegue writes:

"As long as I'm needed, I will need to have discussions with Leyna first."

Jzinta writes:

"How do your parents feel about you coming back?"

Teegue writes:

"I haven't told anyone about this plan and especially not them. They will only try to talk me out of it. I won't listen of course because being an adult I am able to do as I please."

Jzinta writes:

"That's true Teegue. Sorry, but I have to go to work now, thank you for understanding."

Teegue writes:

"I'm hurt but do understand why you cannot wait for me. Thank you for being honest and I look forward to having that drink with you."

The screen of his compupad goes black and he slams the lid down swearing. He had waited too long to leave; he was an idiot. Jzinta was the woman he wanted, being away from her had only intensified his love for her.

Placing the compupad aside he stretches and wipes his eyes. The tears had kept flowing during their conversation. Jumping off his bed he punches the pillows and screams inwardly, the ache of losing Jzinta is turning to fury. Fluffy stuffing escapes his pillow as he rips the cover. His breath is short and sharp as he cries again. He hadn't broken things off with Trisia yet, but how is he going to keep seeing her when all he wants is to see Jzinta?

Chapter 5

Felida

The weak sea breeze is only marginally reducing the blistering August heat as she tries to cool her body with her oversized fan. The iced water on the table next to her is almost finished so she stands to go and fetch more. "Would you like another drink, Dilvant? I'm going to refill my water."

"Another beer would be great, thanks." He says this without looking away from gazing towards the sea. She knows this is how he relaxes; the sea is his pacifier. Having been born on an island Dilvant will always have a love for the water, it is appropriate he is now living on another island at this stage of his life. She walks to the kitchen and while refilling her glass she contemplates telling him her plan. Not sure how he will react, she has to be diplomatic and not become emotional. She wants him to be happy with her decision too.

Handing him the ice-cold beer when she returns to the balcony she stands over him for a moment. When he doesn't react, she returns to her rocking chair. "Dilvant, I want to talk to you about something."

"Okay, I'm listening. What is it?"

"How do you feel about being a father again?"

"What the... are you pregnant?"

"No, but I'd like to be. Wouldn't you like an heir? With Thadd..."

"Stop. Don't talk about Thadd, you never knew him, and he betrayed me. Anyway, I have two heirs by two of my ex-wives, two boys as well as a daughter. They survived the takeover of The Vatican because I sent them away."

"What? Why have you not spoken about them? Where are they, why aren't they here with you?"

He begins explaining they are in Milan with family. The boys are eighteen and sixteen. He had asked them to move to Crete but they are happy to live in Milan, both are still studying and have made many friends. He continues telling her how it was a wise move to send them north, considering many of his family members were murdered by Leyna and Eween.

"Yes, there have been tragedies for many at the hands of those two but I'm happy for you, you were smart to do such a thing. However, I would like a child of my own and you would have another heir."

He turns and looks at her for the first time since they have been sitting out here, "Felida, I am too old to father another child. Not that I cannot, but I am wary of bringing another child into the world when I am not the leader. Besides, I don't know how much longer I will live."

She scoffs, "How selfish of you. There is nothing wrong with you, your health is great and you have many more good years ahead of you. Me, I have no one apart from you. This is the reason I want a child, and soon too because at thirty-eight I don't have too much time left to be a mother. Please Dilvant, give me the chance to be a mother."

She watches as he stands staring out. Still gazing out he says, "If this is what you wish, then against my better judgement, I agree."

Rising from the chair she walks towards him, her silk robe flowing behind her. She drops it as she reaches him then turns him towards her placing both hands on his bare chest, "It is my wish to give you a child. You have made me extremely happy." She kisses him and allows her body to melt into his.

Wide awake because of the heat, she slips on her robe and without turning on a light walks out of their bedroom. Overjoyed with Dilvant's approval she has been humming ever since. She had been wary of asking him, knowing he already fathered three boys and two girls. One had unfortunately passed away at only ten years of age, she was always a sickly child. The loss of two children was tragic and he didn't speak of either, the pain too much for him.

This baby will be good for their relationship and she will hire a nanny to take some of the burden away from him as he had mentioned he was weary and old. She didn't believe this but having extra help will mean they have time for their relationship. Dilvant is her lover, her friend and the best thing to happen to her, she wants to keep him interested so he will stay with her. Yes, a baby is going to bring them closer together.

Dropping onto the lounge she decides to try and fall asleep here, this room is cooler. Managing to do so, she wakes to find Dilvant standing over her. "Couldn't you sleep?"

"I was hot and came out to have some water. This lounge was cool, so I stayed here."

"Well I'm happy to hear that, I thought maybe you were unwell," he says as he nudges himself next to her. "I'm sorry if I was blunt yesterday but you caught me off guard."

"Not at all, I was apprehensive about bringing up the subject, so your reaction was not unexpected. Now, I take it you're going into parliament today? How about some eggs before you go? I'll let chef know."

"Two fried eggs with wholemeal toast will be great. I'll have a shower first so give me fifteen minutes," he says, bending to kiss her.

"Sure. I love you."

He turns and winks at her and as he walks away. She sees a skip in his step. Or is that her imagination because she is so happy? She honestly expected to have a fight on her hands, but he obviously loves her. She pulls her robe around her and goes to seek out chef.

Chapter 6

Leyna

It's two in the morning and Leyna is up with Galexia in her arms. Seated on the lounge, she sings a lullaby coaxing her to go back to sleep. She has been unsettled at night for months, which is becoming a real problem. She needs to concentrate on political matters during the day. She and Eween are taking it in turns to pacify her. Some nights are worse than others, tonight is particularly hard because she woke from a night terror. This is the first time she has woken from the traumatising effect of one of these, and it was terrifying to watch.

Their paediatrician had told them not to disturb her when she is in the throes of a night terror, children can usually settle themselves. The awful thing for Leyna is to see her wide-eyed but not seeing as well as screaming, thrashing, and at times crying during an episode. Tonight she woke up and screamed, "Mummy". She was right there but Galexia didn't see her until her eyes focused. That was an hour ago.

She has finally settled and seems to be in a deep sleep, so Leyna carefully stands and takes her back to her bed. As she walks into their bedroom, Eween is up and asks how she is. "Fine now, but it was a bit different tonight. I think it was a nightmare not a night terror. She said she could see me walking away from her and even though she called for me, I didn't turn around. When she has a night terror, she has no memory of it."

"Whatever it is I hope she grows out of it because these broken sleeps are taking their toll on our health."

Slipping into bed next to him she lays her head on his chest. "I know, but it is normal according to the doctors I've spoken to, she is in no danger."

"No, but we are. We're in danger of being zombies due to lack of sleep. I don't remember the last full night's sleep we had."

Raising herself up towards his face she kisses him, "This is the joy of having children. We will have to ride this through, and yes I hope she grows out of it too."

They continue discussing whether to take Galexia to another doctor for a second opinion but decide against it, with all the information they have read as well as been given, it will likely be a waste of time. Besides, their time is precious as they dedicate most of it to the running of The Vatican and the space project.

Leyna walks into the kitchen to see Galexia being fed by her nanny, a young eighteen-year-old student who comes to look after her every day outside of study time.

"Good morning, Ella," she says, giving Galexia a kiss on her sticky cheek. She is having fun feeding herself.

"Good morning Madame President. Um, unfortunately I won't be here this afternoon, I have a family matter to attend to. My apologies."

"Oh, I see. Okay, that's fine, I'll make sure one of us is home after Galexia wakes from her afternoon nap." Leyna hopes Ella doesn't detect the disappointment in her voice. Both Eween and she are busy but one of them will have to be home.

"Thank you, I have to leave as soon as one of you arrives home."

Her breakfast is laid out on the dining table and as she sits, Eween enters and joins her. She tells him about Ella needing time off and he offers to be home in time. "Oh, that's great, I was wondering how I was going to leave to arrive here in time."

"Don't worry Madame President, I've got this covered," he says, kissing her head with an affection that soothes her anxiety.

That is a load off her mind because apart from being exhausted, she didn't need Ella to be away this afternoon. But Eween has come to her rescue. He adores Galexia and is a good father who loves spending time with her. Leyna's maternal instincts don't seem to be as strong. She loves their daughter, of this she is sure, but other priorities need her attention as well. Although, she wonders what these maternal instincts are meant to be? Is it a myth that every woman will be a good mother and know what to do? When Galexia was a baby Leyna struggled with bonding whereas Eween was a natural. As Galexia grew and became more independent Leyna felt more like a mother, more in control of knowing what her daughter's needs were.

"I'll see you at work," says Eween, "I'll leave now seeing as I have to be home early."

"Okay, don't forget to change the meeting time to eleven. That way you won't be rushing to get home."

He nods as he leaves. They have a meeting with private investors who want to be a part of the Universal Space Project and she hopes they will all be ok with the rescheduled time.

Galexia pads over towards her and Leyna collects her in her arms. Her little hands are on Leyna's face, her chubby cheeks wide with a smile. "Love Mummy, I do."

"And mummy loves you more," she says rubbing her nose with Galexia who giggles and quickly slips off her mother's lap to play with her toys. Watching on, Leyna's heart swells with love as Galexia picks up a doll and says, "Love mummy too, you do." She turns to show Leyna the doll. Leyna smiles and blows them both a kiss. The joy of having a three-year-old in the house is wonderful, even when it means you have to endure sleepless nights.

With Galexia cleaned up and settled with her toys, Leyna finishes readying herself for work. Today she has back-to-back meetings with her ministers – Breex, Nable and Fixor as well as Wilkern and Sayen of the GIS. The funds are being organised now and they will have to be administered to the right departments. The Universal Space Project is happening and it's the biggest project of her career.

Chapter 7

Zenac

He places the answae down and swears under his breath. He will talk with Dawa about returning to Earth tonight, Leyna and Eween are making good progress with the Universal Space Project and he feels left out. Wanting to be more hands on, he needs to be at The Vatican and meeting prospective investors face to face. Leyna has agreed with him too, she was the one who had called to discuss a date of arrival.

Sheabz walks in as Zenac is about to check on the progress at the Spacedrome.

"My apologies for entering unannounced, Trisear is not at her desk."

"Not a problem, take a seat." Zenac notices how Sheabz has slowed down in the last few years, his knees seem to be giving way as he holds onto the arm of the chair to steady himself. Still, at seventy-nine he refuses to step down as Luminary1, saying it is work that keeps him going.

"I have been looking at our finances and am worried about the cost of the space program. We need more investors."

Zenac wonders whether Sheabz is psychic, "I spoke to Leyna a few minutes ago about procuring more investors, she wants me to visit them at The Vatican again. I feel it's necessary I am there meeting with investors and helping Leyna and Eween to woo more of them."

"Well, my timing is perfect then. Between the Mazadon Water Project, the new rockets and this space one, we may have too many projects going at once. Financially we are stretching our resources."

"I understand," says Zenac as he stands, "come with me to Dawa's office, we can discuss this with her now. I was going to tell her my concerns tonight anyway."

Zenac leads the way and ignores Sheabz struggling to rise from the chair. He has tried to help before and Sheabz has been offended because he wants his independence. Zenac understands this and while he is not in danger of hurting himself, he backs off.

"Hello, you two," says Dawa looking away from her compupad as they walk in. Zenac tells her about his conversation with Leyna as they make themselves comfortable.

"Yes, I know about this situation. Sheabz, your concerns are right, but we promised to help Leyna and Eween with the space project. Things have started now with the funds we have managed to raise so far."

Zenac proceeds to tell her about visiting Earth again. Leyna and Eween are in the thick of seeing other investors, he needs to be there too.

"Well, we knew you would have to go back at some stage, and it seems the danger has passed, Dilvant is behaving himself."

"And while he is lying low, we need to proceed with the project as quickly as possible. Leyna and Eween need our help, so I will let her know my date of arrival."

Dawa agrees to leave it to him and they keep discussing the financial situation. Sheabz tells them the other Luminaries are also concerned and he will inform them of Zenac's trip, this may ease their minds. Between them, the four leaders are a force of leadership that will convince investors that the Universal Space Project is viable and must be actioned.

Zenac is pleased Sheabz believes in him and that his trip to Earth will appease the Luminaries. "Great, I'm glad to see you are both on board with me going. Now, I must go, the Spacedrome needs my attention." He walks out of Dawa's office leaving father and daughter to keep talking.

Commando1-Zaydin is waiting for him as he walks in. "Ringax and Amallin are waiting for us in the research department."

He joins her and they walk together, "Everything seems to be going well, the new rockets are almost ready." He had commissioned another twenty to be built as they are to be used in the space project.

Zaydin explains the commandos have been able to secure more workers, which is why they are running ahead of schedule. "New recruits for pilots and support staff have also been interviewed, they are ready to start as soon as you give the go ahead."

He remains quiet until they reach the research room where Ringax and Amallin are seated. He and Zaydin join them. They begin discussing the progress of new equipment, rocket launchers and other military rockets being researched. The safety of Arisis and other planets they discover will be a priority, everyone wants peace but while Dilvant is alive, they are cautious.

"Thank you for informing me of these new developments, it is necessary we keep on top of keeping us all safe. Now, I would like to discuss another mission to Earth to take place in the next two weeks. I have yet to confirm a date of arrival with Leyna and Eween, but I need all the commandos to be prepared to leave with me. I will inform those who will be coming, the others will stay here to assist Luminary1-Sheabz from this end. He will be in charge if Dawa joins me, which I know is likely that she will."

Zenac continues discussing with them who he wants as crew, how many rockets will follow the Vespira and who will remain on Arisis to protect it. He listens as they give their ideas on how long they should be on Earth and what supplies will be required. They agree to leave three commandos on Arisis as well as half of Taaz's security team. Zaydin tells them she will inform everyone who needs to know.

"Thanks, that's great Zaydin. Also, if anyone else volunteers to come, we will allow them as long as their skills are needed. Once people find out that another trip to Earth is happening, there will be many who will want to help. This space project is a popular topic around the traps."

The meeting continues for another hour and Zenac notices tension between Zaydin and Amallin. Whenever Amallin makes a suggestion, Zaydin either ignores it or counters with what she thinks is a better suggestion. The feud between these two has escalated since their return from visiting Earth. So far, it has not impacted too seriously on their work, but Zenac decides to keep tabs on both of them because they are both good at what they do. Losing either of them is not an option. He will speak with Donelle about some counselling, she will know how to appease the two of them. Donelle is a seasoned psychologist who has much experience with hot-headed egos.

He and Dawa are seated at the dinner table discussing the events of the day. "And then Zaydin, with eyes glaring, told Amallin what her opinion was. By then, I had had enough and stopped the meeting before things escalated."

"Those two, what are we going to do about them? Or should we let them fight it out?"

"While their feud does not impact their work, leave them to work it out. If things become bad, I will call them both into my office and tell them to keep their personal opinions out of work. They can fight on their own time. If this does not work, I will call in Donelle."

Dawa nods and says this is probably a good idea. Then she tells him about how their children are faring, especially Braxton, who is finding his final year difficult. She has organised another tutor to help him with science and English. His older siblings breezed through their schooling, but Braxton has always struggled.

"Try not to worry, he will be fine once he leaves school and the pressure is off. He told me he is interested in working at the Space-drome too, but not with Teegue. He is interested in metallurgy."

"Yes, he mentioned that to me too. Still, he needs good grades to be accepted. Having us as parents doesn't automatically give him a job."

"Dawa, he knows that. Stop worrying. Now, how about more wine?" he says as he goes to grab another bottle. He tries not to show that he is worried too. Braxton tries hard but he doesn't focus enough, and this has been his downfall. He hopes once school is over, Braxton will find his way.

Chapter 8

Teegue

He is standing at his locker when he hears them. Zaydin and Ringax are discussing a mission to Earth. He moves closer to the voices without letting them know he is listening.

"Two weeks and we will be ready. You make sure all personnel are okay to leave on the date Zenac announces. Tell them to be prepared for a long stay."

"Zaydin, another trip to Earth was always going to happen. I'm sure everyone will be ready."

He listens on but they begin gossiping about Amallin and he loses interest. He has found out what he wanted to know. Since his conversation with Jzinta, he has had a trip to Earth on his mind. Now, he has to find out when his father is planning to leave, and this time he will be part of the team one way or another. He waits until Zaydin and Ringax have left the locker room before leaving for home. He hopes his parents will be discussing the trip.

• • •

He finds Aria and Braxton in the study. "Hey, have either of you heard about Dad going on another trip to Earth?"

"What? Where did you hear this?"

"I was in the locker room at work and overheard Zaydin and Ringax discussing it, Aria. Apparently, he's leaving in two weeks."

"And I suppose you want to go again?" asks Braxton, "if you are, I'm coming with you."

"Brax, you're not eighteen yet and I don't think Dad will let me go let alone you."

"I'm eighteen in three months, that's close enough. I'd enjoy celebrating my birthday on Earth."

"Maybe find out if Dad is actually going to Earth first," says Aria, "then plan your adventures." She continues telling them she hasn't heard their parents talking about another trip and maybe this time their mother will want to go. "The space project is important to both of them."

"You know about the project? I thought it was top secret."

"It is, but you know how rumours spread. So, it is true, you've heard about it too?"

Teegue nods his confirmation and he had not thought about their mother wanting to go on this trip back to Earth. He is sure their father will not want too many onboard, this is not a rescue mission. Finding out more about this trip is his next step, his desire to see Jzinta before her new relationship takes hold is growing every day. He leaves the study and heads to his bedroom.

The compupad pings as soon as he sends the message.

Zaydin writes:

Teegue, what a pleasure. What can I help you with?

Teegue writes:

I heard a rumour about another trip to Earth. Is my father organising one soon?

Zaydin writes:

Why are you asking me this question? Shouldn't you be asking him?

Teegue writes:

Well, normally we are the first to hear about our father travelling. But if he's going in two weeks, why hasn't he said anything?

Zaydin writes:

Another trip to Earth was always going to happen. And there will be many more in future, but I think you need to speak to your father about this. That is, assuming you want to go again.

Teegue writes:

Umm, maybe. Look thanks anyway, I'll wait until my parents let us know what is going on.

Zaydin writes:

Sure Teegue, enjoy the rest of your night.

So, his father is going to Earth again, Zaydin kind of confirmed it. He will try and coax more information from his mother, he needs to know so he can tell Jzinta. A smile lights up his face as he thinks of her. Then it quickly goes when he thinks about having to tell Trisia he will be leaving again.

Closing the compupad, his stomach rumbles as he heads out to join the others for dinner.

"Nice of you to join us," his father says with a mock royal bow.

"Funny Dad, I was busy tidying my room."

"Really? I'm impressed, that's a good excuse to be late for dinner."

His mother gives his father a look that says *leave him be*.

"What's that look for? It's rude to be late for dinner, I'm making a point."

They all sit quietly and eat. Teegue is running questions through his mind wanting to know when the trip is on. He blurts it out before realising what he's done.

"Where did you hear about the trip?"

"So, there is one. I heard some people talking about it while I was in the locker room."

"I'm glad things remain secret around here before they are announced. I may as well tell you now. Yes, I am leaving with a small crew in two weeks."

Both Teegue and Braxton throw questions at Zenac at the same time.

"Whoa, one at a time. Your mother and I haven't even discussed whether she is coming. This is an important trip to help Leyna and Eween secure more investors for a project that is yet to be announced, what will you two offer if you come along? Not that I'm saying you are."

Teegue speaks first, "You know I have always wanted to help. I was of use last time."

"Hmm, some of the time. This time you have no qualifications we need. We want good negotiators like your mother and me. And Braxton, no you will not be coming, you are not old enough nor do you have the experience."

"That's not fair, how do I get experience without going? Teegue was able to go."

"Only because I didn't know about it, Braxton. Now, enough with this discussion. Your mother and I have to discuss what she wants before I consider any other personnel. This trip will be a long one and we have to consider who we leave to look after things here, which includes looking after you three."

By the tone of his father's voice Teegue knows not to argue. But at least he knows he has two weeks to work out how he is going to travel this time. Whether his parents like it or not, he will travel to Earth again because he wants to save his relationship with Jzinta.

Chapter 9

Wilkern

Global Initiative for Sustainability (GIS)

Wilkern looks at the Luminaries then focuses on Dawa and Zenac. They have much to achieve and are yet to secure funds to pay for these projects. The people of Arisis are still paying taxes for the colonisation of this planet and now the Mazadon Water Project as well. All of the parliamentary team and the GIS board has advised against more taxes to pay for the space project. Investors will have to be found.

"Wilkern, what do you say?"

"I will agree with whatever the consensus is as I am sure the rest of my team will."

"Thank you. Then we all agree that the trip to Earth will happen. I will take the Vespira along with three rockets. Upon our return, which is yet to be determined, we will bring anyone from Earth who wishes to migrate to Arisis. We are still able to sustain a larger population. Also, Dawa has agreed to accompany me on this trip, so Luminary 1-Sheabz will be overseeing things here while we are gone. Luminary 2-Tanjaz and Luminary 3-Xzackry will be his deputies."

Sayen stands and disputes the use of three rockets. "Why three rockets? Earth is now a viable place to live, how many people do you think want to migrate?"

"I have been liaising with the immigration department at The Vatican, there are people who are interested in coming to see Arisis and what we have achieved here. It is my hope that they stay after they see what it is like. Remember, many people fear the fact that Dilvant is still alive, they do not want a return of his regime."

"I agree with Zenac, Sayen. And we will support Sheabz and his Luminaries in every way while your team is away."

"Your support is appreciated, Wilkern. Now, Dawa and I will leave you to work out the logistics of what is needed when we are gone. Please brief your staff appropriately. Also, use this Ovalaz room for as long as you need."

Everyone stands as they leave the room. There are murmurs and discussion as the remaining people take a break. Sayen walks over to Wilkern at the coffee station.

"Do you think it's wise for more people to move to Arisis? We have to consider the sustainability of this planet."

"We are nowhere near capacity yet and even though the population here is growing, it is not at an unmanageable rate. Besides, more people living here means more tax revenue and this can only be good for the economy."

"I suppose you're right," says Sayen, stirring his tea.

"You're younger than me and I understand your concerns about sustainability, but with a bit more experience, you will know we are able to populate without compromising the planet."

"Yes, I still have a lot to learn, but sustainability will always be my top priority. I will always voice this concern."

"And that's admirable, I concur. As head of the GIS, it is my priority as well. Have some faith in our leaders, Zenac and Dawa know what they are doing."

Sayen nods and they return to their seats to listen to Sheabz discuss what is required once this mission to Earth is in progress. He also authorises the GIS to announce the Universal Space Project to the population of Earth and Arisis. The colonies of the Moon and Mars will be informed as the project progresses. Their research resources may be required as well, which is something The Luminaries will undertake if and when needed.

They are sitting up in bed together, each on their compupads. Wilkern turns to Sayen and asks him has he heard from his parents.

"No, they haven't accepted our marriage. They didn't bother coming to our wedding, what makes you think I can change their minds now?"

"I was hoping, that's all."

"They not only object to our union, they think you are too old for me."

Wilkern knows about this, he thought the same thing when they met. Sayen had walked up to him at a bar when he first arrived on Arisis. He had just been appointed as the head of the Arisis branch of the GIS. Sayen had already been working as a deputy for six months. The fifteen-year age difference had bothered him from the beginning. But Sayen had pursued him and their love grew despite what others thought of their relationship.

"We have been married for two years, I've given up asking them to approve. We talk occasionally, but honestly I try not to bring up our relationship."

"I know it must be hard, but at least they are still talking to you."

"Sort of. It is always me calling them and they refuse to come here. Actually, I have a lunch date with my mother next week, I forgot to tell you."

"Well, that's positive, how did you get her to agree?"

"It was her idea. Maybe she wants to tell me something, who knows? Still, it will be nice to see her after so long. You know what? Why don't you come along?"

"What? No. You should enjoy your time with your mother, she won't want to see me. No, that's not a good idea."

"Alright then, maybe the next lunch?"

"You enjoy this one first, then we'll see." Wilkern smiles at his partner's optimistic outlook on life. He hopes that one day Sayen's parents will put his happiness over their prejudices.

They are all seated in the Ovalaz room the next day. The Luminaries continue their discussions about the work that needs to be done. The sustainability of the planet is their priority as well and they welcomed Sayen's question from the previous day.

Wilkern sees the proud expression wash over Sayen's face and he gives his hand a squeeze. Sayen looks at him with his eyes glazed with tears. He is an emotional man and cries easily, which makes Wilkern love him more.

"We must always have sustainability in the back of our minds with everything we do. We want to achieve a balance on Arisis, Earth and any other planet we colonise. The Mazadon Water Project is our first sustainable project, we will never take more water than we need. Population growth on Arisis will be closely monitored too."

Both the Luminaries and the GIS are in agreement, which has been the whole point of these meetings. The trip to Earth was an added item to the agenda and if the four leaders are able to secure investors for the space project, then their work on Arisis will be easier. Unfortunately, the success of these projects depends on money. Money that is hard to come by even after years of no Dilvant and his Enforcers.

The discussion moves to financial concerns and Wilkern begins to tune out after an hour of monetary talk. He begins thinking about Sayen's lunch with his mother. Unfortunately, it had not gone well. There will be no second lunch because she asked Sayen to stop contacting them. Sayen's emotions have been on high alert ever since. He wasn't surprised when he cried just now, Sheabz praising him touched a nerve. This is what he wants from his parents, something they are not willing to give.

Chapter 10

Teegue

His hands are on his duffle bag as he crouches watching the launch of the Vespira. His parents had said goodbye to them this morning at five am. Soon after they left for the Spacedrome, he had gathered his belongings and followed them. He left Aria and Braxton sound asleep. Cook and the housekeeper will look after them. Placing his hand over his nose and mouth as the Vespira launches, he is still not used to the sulphuric/kerosene smell of the burning fuels, he says softly, "See you soon Mum and Dad."

After the three rockets are launched, he sneaks over to the small proton rocket. This has been mothballed since they arrived on Arisis. He has spent the last two weeks when no one was around, fixing it so it will make the trip to Earth. He will arrive two weeks after everyone else does but this isn't a problem. His main purpose is to see Jzinta again, and of course help where he is needed.

Sitting in the cockpit he adjusts the necessary controls, checks fuel gauges and launches. He had bribed two engineers to help him launch and they will sign off as he leaves the atmosphere of Arisis.

True to their word, they had not disclosed what he had planned to anyone. Sanuel has always been trustworthy and a good friend to Teegue. He had reservations when Teegue first asked because as one of his parent's top engineers, Sanuel had not wanted to compromise his position. Teegue assured him that he will take all the blame once Zenac and Dawa find out how he managed to leave with this small rocket.

He sits back now having placed the rocket in autopilot and watches space fly by.

Woken by an explosion Teegue rushes to the source. The side of his rocket has been smashed in by what was probably an asteroid or space junk. The damage is minimal but will need repairing. He heads for the cockpit and checks the coordinates. He has been thrown off course and is now heading to Mars. "Shit!"

He can readjust his coordinates, but the damage left on the side of the rocket has to be fixed first. If it is hit with any other space object it will break and his oxygen will be gone. He checked in the cargo bay for a spacesuit and is happy to find one in his size. This was lucky because he had not thought to check on spacesuits because he had not expected to have any hurdles in arriving on Earth. He finds what he needs to do the repair after donning the suit and attaches himself to the tether. Then he unlatches the door. His first time out in space.

With adrenaline rushing through his body, he takes in the scene. Surreal and exhilarating at the same time, he wants to remember this moment. Then practicality takes over, he needs to do this repair before he is blown further off course. He holds onto the sheet that will cover the thirty-centimetre dent and begins soldering. Sweat pours down his face and his mouth is as dry as a dead leaf but he manages to finish and return inside before expiring from heat. The first thing he does once out of the spacesuit is sip water so fast he gags. Taking a deep breath, he hopes he's done enough to stabilise the rocket. Now it's time to fix the coordinates.

. . .

The next few days are not so dramatic, and he is bored. Once he has done all the checks, he has nothing to do. All the books on board have been read, he is sick of playing games on his compupad, especially as it is slow out here. Yet, he still has ten days before he arrives on Earth, the small accident had thrown him out by three days. Things could have been worse, the dent could have broken through and he would not be around now. Shivers run through him as he thinks about what he has undertaken. What was he thinking? He has no experience of flying a rocket with others, let alone on his own. He hopes Jzinta appreciates what he is doing for her.

He thinks about what his father will say when he sees the damage to the rocket. And the fact he has disobeyed him once again, this time he has placed himself in even more danger. This was not something he had factored in; the trips to Xenure Station, Arisis and the last trip to Earth had all been incident-free. Trust his luck that on his first trip on his own he is hit by something hard enough to cause damage. Still, he is proud of himself to have fixed the problem and he is now on the right course.

Picking up his compupad, he decides to contact Jzinta. He had better let her know he is delayed by three days.

Jzinta writes:

Hello. There is a lag, but it is good to hear from you. What happened?

Teegue writes:

Nothing major. The rocket was hit by some flying space junk, only a small dent that I was able to fix. I'm on the right course now.

Jzinta writes:

It was probably a bit crazy of you to come here by yourself, don't you think? I mean, I look forward to seeing you, but not if it means you are in danger.

Teegue writes:

A small glitch that I was able to handle. Please hang in there and I'll see you soon.

Jzinta writes:

Okay, I will count down the days. Please take care of yourself and learn to dodge that space junk.

Teegue writes: Will do, thanks.

He almost writes, *I love you...* then stops himself. But the truth is exactly that, he loves Jzinta.

Trisia's face comes before him and it is tear stained, wet and wild with anger. This is how she looked the last time he saw her. He had visited her to tell her of his departure the night before his launch. She had not taken it well, which he had expected. She was very much in love with him, and always had been since school. It was this that made him feel suffocated, she was demonstrative in showing him how much she loved him. Sometimes it would be notes left in his pockets, other times she would give him a small gift for no reason, but more so it was the holding hands and clutching him whenever they were together. It was like she never wanted to let go. Even though Trisia was his first love and they had enjoyed many good times, he had outgrown their love. He puts thoughts of her away and concentrates on checking his coordinates again. He wants to be with Jzinta as quickly as he can manage.

Chapter 11

Dilvant

Felida is in the bathroom. This is how her mornings start now that she is pregnant. Even though he had had misgivings, when she told him of the pregnancy and seeing her precious face full of love, he was happy to be a father again. He was not happy about how sick she was though, this happened every morning and her skin was sallow, she was thin and ate only dry crackers. How can this be good for the baby?

He had only calmed down when their doctor told him the baby is fine and receiving all the nutrients it needs. He will give Felida vitamins to keep her strength up. She has a condition known as *hyperemesis gravidarum;* it is a severe form of morning sickness. Dilvant had told the doctor he hoped it would pass soon. She is now four months and still throwing up in the mornings.

"I'm going Felida, are you okay?" he says gingerly, "would you like me to get you something?"

"No, leave me alone."

This was their morning routine. It's going to be a long pregnancy.

. . .

Seated with the other ministers in the parliamentary room, Dilvant puts thoughts of Felida's pregnancy to the back of his mind. There are more important things to deal with. He concentrates on what the Minister for Transport is outlining about how he and Dilvant will woo the Russians into funding part of the Quinan Space Project, the money the Mauritians have pledged will only cover a small part of the cost. There are mumblings and a few claps from the ministers as Dilvant is asked to speak.

"It is my honour to accompany our Minister for Transport to Russia. We will not return empty handed." He continues outlining his ideas for the Quinan project, how many people will be involved and who has been employed so far. With three rocket scientists, engineers and ground crew already enlisted to start the project, Dilvant tells them the money from Russia is of vital importance. They listen as he explains where he plans to build the facility and the amount of people that will be employed. "This is a project that will benefit the people of Crete today and in the future."

This time there is applause from all of the ministers, they have waited a long time for a leader who has foresight and the ability to make things happen. Dilvant, as Minister for Science and Technology, had proven his worth. During the last cabinet reshuffle, he had the numbers to go for the leader's position. He had won easily and was beginning to make his mark on the party. The Opposition Leader was a pushover, Dilvant would be leader for some time. He has plans to make the people of Crete trust him to the point they will do everything he says. He has had his citizens in his hands before, he will do it again with the people of Crete.

The rest of the day is filled with meetings and Dilvant and his minister are given their travel papers as well as being briefed on how to deal with the Russians and their culture. Dilvant has dealt with Russians many times and is confident in his ability to converse with them. He speaks six languages, Russian being one of them.

He has always had an affinity with languages, having taught himself French, Italian, Greek, German and Russian over the years.

He has dabbled in Japanese and Mandarin, although is not fluent in these languages. His minister will be of assistance when they meet with the Russians, he is fluent in Russian and German as well.

Finally, the day is free of meetings and he is in his office when the Minister for Transport comes in.

"My apologies for this disruption, I wanted to speak with you about our trip. I feel we need to discuss our position with them."

"Please take a seat. What do you mean? What position?"

"The Russians are a law unto themselves as you know. It might be wise for us to have a plan so we are not bombarded by them. Their tendency to bully is well known."

"Oh, please do not worry yourself. I am well-versed in dealing with the Russians, they were very helpful when The Enforcers and I came to power. They are my allies and always will be."

"I am well aware of how they helped you to power, but where were they this time? Would not an ally have come to your aid by now?"

"You have a point. But Russia has had their own economic problems over the past twenty years, and I have not gone to their aid. This may be the reason."

"We need to be cautious, that is all I am saying."

"I appreciate your warning and will take this into account. Are you ready to leave tomorrow? Do you have everything in hand?"

"My assistant is completing some of the documents as we speak. Everything else, yes, I have it all ready. I thank you for your time, see you at the airport in the morning."

"You will. And please, if you wish to discuss this further, we will have time on the plane."

The minister nods and leaves Dilvant's office. He is a good politician, although at times cautious, he does have a sense of serving his country to the best of his ability. Quinan had told Dilvant he was one of his best ministers and he was right. Dilvant picks up his briefcase and places his compupad into it wishing Quinan was the one travelling with him to Moscow.

. . .

Arriving in Moscow late due to a severe storm, the rain looks like white sheets as it pelts the tarmac. The one-hour flight had taken an extra half hour. Dilvant was not concerned as the meeting with the Russians wasn't until tomorrow at ten. He and the minister had come to an agreement that Dilvant will do the talking and his minister is to speak only when he is addressed. "It will be enough that I speak, remember that I told you I have an understanding with them."

"And that's the third time you have told me," scoffs the minister, "now who is the one worrying?"

"Not worried, I'm making sure we both know our place."

The scour on his minister's face tells Dilvant he is treading on thin ground. It may be time to stop trying to make things perfect and leave this plane.

Their ride from Domodedovo Airport to the hotel is about forty minutes with both of them quiet all the way. Dilvant decides to speak with caution for the rest of this trip, he does not want to make an enemy of his own minister. He stares out the window watching the sparse streetlights become more frequent as they approach Moscow. They had two days to ensnare a pledge, and from all their intelligence, the Russians had no love-lost for Leyna and Eween. This will work to their advantage.

Dilvant had been admiring the Russian White House, which was completed in 1981 and has withstood time for all these years, when a woman walks towards them and introduces herself. She is tall, elegant and blonde, it is a pleasure to take in her beauty. She explains that President Leonid is expecting them.

"President Leonid sends his apologies, he is running a little late for this morning's meeting. He asked that I escort you to the meeting room." The elegant woman has an elegant voice to go with her looks.

Dilvant is disappointed but he makes no comment and only tells her that he and his minister are happy to wait until President Leonid is ready. Silently fuming, he is upset that President Leonid's office had not let them know of this change. So much for diplomacy.

They follow the woman up the central marble staircase to the meeting room. She asks them to take their seats at the long dark timber table and then she excuses herself. The highly polished table has room for twenty, which seems a bit extreme. Why had they not used a smaller meeting room? His question is answered when, along with the same woman, twelve other ministers file into the room.

The tall woman sits at the head of the table and once everyone is seated and quiet, she introduces Dilvant and his minister. Dilvant's anger surfaces again. Is she chairing this meeting? A deputy? She is the youngest minister in this room. How dare the Russian President allow someone of her age to chair an important meeting that deals with large sums of money. A project like Quinan's Space Project is not a small matter.

"Is there a problem, Dilvant?"

As usual his expression had given him away. Dilvant's emotions show instantly on his face and she obviously noticed he was not happy. He needs to be diplomatic now and changes his mood. "Not at all, please go ahead my colleague and I are keen to hear your thoughts about our project."

Her eyes remain on his for longer than needed and Dilvant thinks she may be somewhat confused with his reaction. He will need to be careful because this woman may have more power than he gives her credit for. His minister whispers in his ear and Dilvant assures him everything is fine.

"Once President Leonid joins us, which will be in approximately thirty minutes, you may begin Dilvant, assuming all is well."

"Thank you. Yes, everything is fine," he says as he organises the hologram of the proposal through his compupad ready for when the President arrives. He was wrong, she is not chairing the meeting. Relief floods over him as he had thought the Russians were playing them for fools.

The ministers chat among themselves. Dilvant's nerves begin to wear thin when after thirty minutes there is still no sign of the president. His leg begins to twitch and he fiddles with his nails.

"My apologies distinguished guests," says the president as he walks into the room. This president has a presence the past ones didn't have. His ministers, along with the tall woman, stand and each one greets him warmly. There is an air of authority coming from this man. Dilvant is impressed.

"Please," says the president as he takes Dilvant's and his minister's hand, "Begin because I have kept you waiting long enough."

Dilvant clears his throat, "Thank you President Leonid and also thank you to your ministers who have joined us for this important meeting. He begins explaining what they need and as he does he scans the room to see if any of the ministers react. None, absolutely nothing. Each one of them sits straight backed with impassive faces, the woman included. He continues with his presentation summoning up all his confidence. After he has finished he says, "Now you know all the facts and why we require your assistance, I leave things up for discussion. Any questions?"

The woman stands. "It is common knowledge that you wish to take revenge against Leyna and Eween, but they now have an alliance with Dawa and Zenac who have already found two planets, one of which they have colonised. Are you in a race to beat them to finding another?"

"We plan to run our own race. This project is too important for me to think about revenge, all my focus is on having a viable future for the Quinan Space Project." This is only a half-lie, revenge is always on his mind but now with Felida pregnant, he is not ready to pursue it yet.

The woman continues, "How do you plan to fund this project if we are unable to assist you?"

Dilvant is thrown by this question because he had not thought further than this meeting. He had planned on returning home with the funds secured. "To be frank, without the help of Russian funds, it will be difficult for us to continue with the project. As I outlined earlier, there will be many benefits for both countries – we will need ground staff and qualified personnel and we have begun recruiting for some positions already."

"You have assumed we will be releasing funds to you. This is presumptuous, don't you think?"

Why is this woman grilling him? Dilvant is tiring of these questions and wants someone else to come forward. He need not have worried because she seemed to have read his thoughts.

"We thank you for your answers. I will now allow someone else to ask questions. Ministers, any other questions for our esteemed colleagues?"

Dilvant is pleased to field appropriate questions from the other ministers, questions he knows how to answer. The rest of the meeting is more productive and when it is finished, everyone walks out, but the tall woman remains with Dilvant and his minister.

"What the hell was that all about?" says the Minister for Transport, the first words he has uttered since whispering in Dilvant's ear earlier.

Placing his hand on the minister's arm, Dilvant gives him a scowl. "Remember we are guests here. Please excuse my colleague, he is excitable at times. Will you be joining us for dinner?"

"Unfortunately, no. You will be dining with the President and Vice President and their wives."

"Oh, I see. As this is a social event I thought you may be attending."

"President Leonid will be happy to discuss whatever you wish to talk about."

"Thank you, that is good to hear. I am sure we are in for a pleasant evening."

"You will, now I bid you farewell and thank you for your excellent presentation. We will let you know our decision before you leave."

"Thank you, we appreciate this."

"I bid you a good afternoon gentlemen."

Both men stand watching her leave.

"I thought you said you knew the Russians. Well, you obviously weren't expecting someone like her."

"They have allowed someone who is not qualified to listen in on a confidential meeting and then she questioned us. This is preposterous. I will have something to say to the President tonight."

"Oh, don't be such a stickler for protocol. She is an ambitious

young minister, that's all. If I were you, I would leave it. You'll probably never see her again."

Dilvant muses over what his minister has said, and although this
is strange and somewhat unnerving, he agrees it probably is best left
alone. "I thought there was something strange about her as soon as
we met, she isn't your usual Russian cabinet minister. Not at all like
the ones I'm used to."

"She was definitely pleasant to look at," laughs his minister.

Dinner is announced and the visitors are led into a room next to the
one they were in this morning. They are introduced to the dignitaries
and their chairs are drawn for them. Once seated, President Leonid
acknowledges having met Dilvant before.

"Yes, Mr President, we met when I was planning the overthrow,
one that you were all for. The Enforcers and I ruled the world with
an iron fist, one that was necessary as things were very much out of
hand."

"I agree. The world had become one of the rich and the poor with
no one in between. The situation was not sustainable, nor was the
situation with the environment. But this is all in the past, we have a
future to plan for. Tell me more about this space project. The amount
you are requesting is a substantial amount of money."

"The Quinan Space Project is a substantial project. There will be
long-lasting ramifications for humans for centuries if we manage to
find a planet with Earth's atmosphere."

"That is an admirable reason, but I say enough of this business
talk, let's enjoy this meal for now then you can tell me more. I believe
it is always better to discuss business over a cognac, don't you
agree?"

Both Dilvant and his minister nod. They begin enjoying the food
and the conversation becomes more amicable as more wine is
consumed.

· · ·

They are both standing waiting to board the plane back to Crete. Both have smug looks on their faces.

"I have to congratulate you Dilvant, you were brilliant last night. The President was taken by you."

"I told you I had a way with them. We have a past and I know how they think. Mind you, his beautiful minister had me worried, she was intelligent and asking more questions than I was comfortable with. In the end we had nothing to worry about. President Leonid agreed to help us and that, my friend, is why we came here."

Leyna

Galexia is in a strange mood. When Leyna asked her what was wrong, she shrugged her shoulders and said she had a fight with Teddy. Leyna smiled when she heard her daughter's explanation, Teddy is her favourite soft toy, a cuddly, dark brown bear with a plaid waistcoat. He had been Galexia's constant companion since she was a baby. Even though he had lost an eye, had some fur missing and smelled of mould, Galexia refused to part with him.

"Oh no, that's awful. Are you okay?"

"Yes, but I'd rather not discuss it, Mummy. This issue is between Teddy and me." With this Galexia pads off into her bedroom to collect her school things.

Leyna stifles a smile before Galexia leaves. She is parroting her, this is what Leyna says to Eween when he offers to help her when one or two of the ministers are being obstinate. Leyna walks back to the couch thinking how independent her daughter is and how she is growing up too fast. Eween and she had discussed having another child, but nothing has happened and Leyna has been too busy to look into it further. Galexia hasn't asked for a brother or sister, so Leyna and Eween are not pursuing another pregnancy yet.

Having seen Galexia off to school, Leyna joins Eween in his office. "Have they arrived?"

"Yes, they're waiting for us in the meeting room. Was Galexia okay?"

"Ah ha, she brightened up once I dropped her at preschool. Now, let's go and meet with our allies. This was a lie as she wanted to discuss Galexia with Eween later and didn't want him to worry.

They walk into the meeting room and are pleased to see Zenac and Dawa along with their entourage of ministers, aids and security.

"Welcome, I see you arrived with no issues."

"A dream trip, actually. The Vespira is certainly an improvement and there is more where that spaceship came from."

"I'm glad to hear it, Zenac." Leyna and Eween exchange hand-shakes with everyone and then motion for them to sit.

Eween remains standing. He starts the hologram of where the project is at and explains what needs to happen now. His presentation takes thirty minutes and there are appreciative murmurs throughout the room when he finishes.

"There has been more progress than we expected, especially with the buildings, they are already complete," says Dawa.

"Yes, but this is where we need more funds. Having completed buildings with no funds to fill them with equipment and staff doesn't help us at all. We need your help to secure more."

"This is why we are here, Leyna. We will assist in any way you need us to. I hear that the UK is interested in providing more funds?"

Eween stands again, "There is a story behind this, and it will work in our favour." He walks to and fro with his hands in front of him, palms facing each other. "Our friend, the lovely Dilvant, has secured funds from Russia. He has begun building space facilities on Crete and wants to be the first to find a planet exactly like Earth. The UK Prime Minister called Leyna and I wanting to discuss how we might do better. He has pledged a wonderful sum of money."

"So Dilvant is still a meddler, I didn't think he would simply take in the sea air in Heraklion and while away his time. Then we should take up the UK's offer."

"You're right Zenac, Dilvant had no intention of whiling away his time. And we have already agreed to the UK's offer but if we want to beat Dilvant, we need to secure more funds," continues Eween.

"There is still the USA. And what about Australia, New Zealand and Canada? Will they consider giving more?"

"They are all possibilities, Dawa. If we have to, we may approach China as well. They were interested enough to send delegates to initial meetings."

Everyone in the room begins to voice their views, but Eween puts his hand in the air to calm everyone down. "I know China wants to remain its own entity and does not want to be involved in any space race, war or trade with any other country. They were burnt by Dilvant and The Enforcers when they refused to allow China to rule with them. This was a slap in the face to the Chinese and they will not forget the humiliation. With all the help they gave Dilvant and his regime, he betrayed them. This is something the Chinese Government will never excuse. But it has been many years since The Enforcers ruled, the world has changed for the better, China may want to change with us."

"I say we stick with the other countries first. If we fall short, then approach China. And this is to be done with caution because China will turn on us for the slightest misdemeanour, we all know how proud they are of their society."

"Dawa, the USA is probably the only country who has the funds we are looking for, the others - Australia, New Zealand and Canada, would only be able to give smaller amounts."

"We are looking for 500million Licdan, right? Then we should ask for 350million from the USA and the other countries will fund the rest."

Eween sits and places his elbows on the table looking towards Dawa, "What makes you think the USA will offer so much?

Remember all the money they wasted on the failed Mars missions back in 2050. Will they be willing to invest again?"

"We all know of the failed missions, the Spaniards lost many astronauts, as did the USA. The alliance between Spain and the US was strong back then. But with the success of the UK and European sponsored missions, Mars is now a thriving planet along with the colonies on the Moon. The only downside is their atmosphere, which is why the colonies are smaller than we expected. We can convince the US to try again using our updated technology, much has improved since 2050."

They continue discussing who they will send to speak with the American president and then they keep looking at plans for space-craft, who to hire and how many astronauts will be trained.

Dinner is over and Leyna joins Eween on the couch. She moves his fringe along his forehead saying, "We had a successful day. Dawa and Zenac put forward some worthy points and we have a starting point with the Americans."

Eween shuts his compupad and agrees. He is about to speak when something comes flying through the air and lands at his feet. He looks over to where it came from and sees Galexia standing in the hall with her hands on her hips. Her face is tortured with anger. He looks down to see Teddy has rested on his foot. "Galexia, what is going on?"

"I don't want to see him EVER AGAIN!" She storms back towards her bedroom.

Eween is about to stand when Leyna says, "I'll go, you keep checking your emails."

When Leyna enters Galexia's room she finds her sobbing on the bed, her palms under her forehead. "Do you want to talk about this? It seems to be upsetting you quite a lot."

"I think...," she sobs, "Teddy is too old and he's different. He says he wants me to play with other toys and forget about him. I don't want to, he's my favourite. Mummy, do I have to?"

"Darling, you are right, Teddy is old, but you can still play with him as well as your other toys. Play with a group of them and keep them all company."

"But Teddy says they are all shiny and new and he feels out of place. He's different from them. And so am I. This is what the others are telling me at preschool. They won't play with me."

Leyna wonders where this is coming from. "Galexia, has something happened at school?"

Galexia sits up cross legged and looks at her hands that are resting in her lap, "Maybe. I've tried to be nice to the other kids, but they say I'm different."

"Different, how are you different?"

"I am Madame President's daughter. They say I don't know how they live, and they know I have umm... it's a hard word Mummy... priv-something."

"You mean privilege?"

"Yes, and I don't know what that means."

Leyna thinks for a minute because this is a delicate subject.

Galexia is a privileged child, but her preschool is full of diplomat's and politician's children, they too have privilege. "Listen, I think the other children are misunderstanding their own standing in life, their parents give them privilege too. The only difference is you have a mother who is a leader and maybe this scares them a little. Would you like me to speak to your teachers?"

She nods her head and with sheepish eyes says, "Thank you, Mummy."

Leyna brings her daughter close and kisses her head. She breathes in her fresh, little-girl smell and her insides knot as she wonders why children are so mean. Tomorrow she will walk in with Galexia, speak with her teacher and sort this out. She may be a leader but she is not too busy to help her daughter navigate the complexities of the school yard.

Chapter 13

Zenac

He is looking out of their hotel room window. St Peter's Square is alive with people going about their business, there is a vibrancy to the city now that makes it a place many want to live. The rest of Italy has also progressed since Leyna became Madame President, her government is working towards making it a prosperous country. This is also being mimicked in many other parts of the world where there was affluence once and this is now slowly returning. Everywhere is waking up to this new culture of progress.

He turns when he hears his answae. "Hello."

"Zenac, it's Xzackry, I have some disturbing news. Teegue took the proton rocket with the help of Sanuel and was headed to Earth."

"What the hell was Sanuel thinking? Teegue has disobeyed us once again. And what do you mean, he *was* headed to Earth?"

"Don't blame Sanuel, he told me Teegue said he would take all the blame. Anyway, it was Sanuel who alerted us because he has not been able to contact Teegue. They were keeping in touch every day, but something isn't right. Sanuel has not been able to reach Teegue for thirty-six hours."

Zenac bows his head, his hand rubs his forehead, "Thank you Xzackry, I'll be in touch soon with what I need you to do."

"No problem, Zenac. We await your instructions."

Looking towards Dawa he sees a face of a worried mother, "Teegue has done it again. He tried to follow us here in the proton rocket."

"That rocket wasn't in commission, how did he get it working?"

"Teegue is not stupid and he enlisted the help of Sanuel and one of his engineers. Sanuel is the one who alerted Xzackry there is a problem."

"What's the problem, is Teegue in danger?"

"He could be, but we need more information. Sanuel has been in contact with him every day but hasn't heard from him in the last thirty-six hours."

"What? No, how dare Sanuel help him without telling us. We trust him, why did he not come to us?" Dawa begins pacing, her head in her hands.

"Teegue can be very persuasive, but let's not dwell on this now, we need to find him," says Zenac wondering where the hell to start. "Well, it looks like I won't be going to America." He continues discussing with Dawa what he thinks is the next step of yet another rescue mission. Dawa keeps pacing as Zenac talks, he knows how worried she is. This time Teegue has outdone himself.

Leyna is staring at him wondering how this has happened again. "Your son seems to attract trouble, but of course I understand you have to go. I hope he is safe, anything could have happened to him." says Leyna

Zenac is sitting on the plush black lounge in Leyna's office. Even though it is eleven in the morning, he is gulping down a glass of scotch. "That boy causes us so much pain. He has an independent streak we cannot break."

"Sounds like someone I know," says Leyna, "Look I don't mean to be flippant, this is a serious situation. We can send Dawa with Eween, if she is up to going. You take as many people as you need because this may take some time, who knows where he is floating about."

"This is what worries me. Sanuel told us that Teegue's rocket was hit by space junk, and even though he was able to repair the damage, it seems he went off course anyway. We will take off tomorrow in The Salverz. I will bring Taaz with me and The Mechanic can go with Dawa and Eween. We have to find him, Leyna, we have to."

He drops his head and tears fall. Leyna places her arm around his shoulder and holds him, remaining quiet.

"I will organise everything and will need your best AI to detect signals. I will not return without my son." Zenac's voice drowns to a whisper, the word *son* is hardly audible.

"You take whatever you need. The Salverz is ready with many improvements as well. I will contact my colleagues on Mars and the Moon to see if they have heard anything. We will use all our resources, Zenac. And Breex can go with Eween instead of Dawa to see the US President, we will worry about securing funds. Dawa will need to stay here and assist you with finding Teegue from this end."

He nods, stands and places the empty glass on the side table. The last thing on his mind is the space project and raising funds. Walking out of her office, he turns towards her and is about to say something, but instead turns away again and walks out.

He heads to the airport and security headquarters to organise his team. He will take the Salverz and a reconnaissance craft. Informing Taaz, he tells him to come to the airport with three of his best officers for a briefing.

Taaz arrives within fifteen minutes and two men and a woman tag along behind him. Zenac briefs them on what they need to do before leaving tomorrow morning. "You, along with three of Leyna's security personnel, will be in charge of the AI. Two robots will travel with us, they are trained in finding signals in space even if they are ten billion lightyears away. They can detect danger and if necessary, will fight alongside us. Hopefully it won't come to that, I hope to find my son out there drifting somewhere but not be in any danger."

"We are with you, Zenac. Whatever you need to do, we will be right behind you."

"Thank you. Believe me when I find my son, first I will hug him and tell him how much I love him, then I will ground him for life."

He manages a weak smile as they all walk into the security building to meet the AI.

Exhaustion greets him as he opens the door to their hotel room. He finds Dawa seated at the end of the bed, weeping, tissues strewn in front of her. "Dawa, don't fret, I have everything organised, I will find Teegue."

"I know, Zenac, but something else has happened. I won't be going to America for another reason... Sheabz is dead."

"What, no! Oh Dawa, when? Who told you?"

"Xzackry called again a few hours after you left. I was with Leyna so she already knows I will be returning to Arisis. She will worry about who will go with Eween, she mentioned Breex, who I know will do just fine."

"Of course, he will. And you must return home. How did he die?"

"A brain haemorrhage. Totally out of the blue, he didn't even see it coming. Xzackry said he died on the way to hospital. He called me as soon as it happened and then called me within thirty minutes to say he didn't make it."

Zenac is by her side holding her hand. He too is crying and wipes away his tears that have dampened her hand. Sheabz was like a father to him too as well as a mentor. "I should come back with you, at least for the funeral."

"That is sweet of you, but you need to find Teegue. Sheabz would want you to find him, not waste time on his funeral. You being present will not bring him back. It is enough that I am there to console Aria and Braxton, not only for their Grandfather but also for their brother."

"Yes, you are right. They will be missing both of them. You do need to be back on Arisis, I assume they will wait for you before they decide the date?"

"Yes, I'll go back on the fastest rocket. In the four days it takes me to return, he will reside in state for mourners to grieve for him. Oh Zenac, he was a good man, and I will miss him terribly."

Zenac holds her as she weeps again, this time uncontrollably. They are all at the airport at the same time. Dawa is with her crew of four, Zenac with his crew of twelve plus the two AI. They are hugging each other, both holding on and wishing each other to come home safe.

Dawa lets go of the embrace first. "Zenac, find him please. Losing my father is enough. I refuse to lose both of them."

"I will, I promise you. With Leyna's personnel and AI, we have a lot of resources, we won't fail. You give Aria and Braxton a hug each from me, tell them how much I love them and that I will return with Teegue."

"Contact me as soon as you find him. In fact, keep in touch every day, I will need to hear your voice."

He assures her he will and watches as she enters the rocket. He stands with tears in his eyes as he watches the launch, he wishes Sheabz had waited until they were all home. Brushing aside his tears, he looks for Taaz and his team who are near the Salverz waiting for him. He had farewelled Leyna and Eween the night before, with Leyna asking him to keep in touch because she too will be worried. Had they not organised for Eween to go to America, they would have been at the funeral. Zenac had assured her the space project is too important and Sheabz would have understood. Zenac also tells her that he wants to go to America and do something useful rather than run around the universe rescuing his son again.

"When you find him, don't be too hard on him. He has an adventurous personality just like his father," she had said.

At this moment, Zenac is fuming and does not know what he will do when he finds Teegue, but he certainly hopes this is the last time Teegue will do something this stupid.

Chapter 14

Dilvant

Dilvant is explaining to his ministers how they were able to secure funds from the Russians. Now, they can complete building the space-drome and factories to produce the craft they will need. "The first thing I want to build is a high-speed reconnaissance craft and send it into space to scout for a planet like Earth. We will use a high-powered satellite and we will be the first to colonise the planet. I will rule again and in my way.

There are cheers and congratulations from his ministers. Some ask questions that he is able to answer and then he passes to his finance minister who will outline how the funds will be used. He sits back and sighs because he can see victory in sight once more.

His thoughts turn to Felida, who is no better even though she is six months into the pregnancy. She is difficult to live with as her moods range from a weak sadness to supreme anger when she thinks he is not responding to her needs. It is not easy to know what her needs are when she swings between being excessively tired and wanting to be left alone to wanting him to sit with her and rub her aching back. There have been times when he has suggested a swim, but she refuses to walk down to the beach, "It is too far, my legs won't make it," she has answered him. One of the ministers brings him out of his reverie by asking whether Dilvant will be going on any of the missions.

"I hope to, yes. For now I must concentrate on supporting Felida, she is having a hard time, unfortunately she is ill with morning sickness."

A few other ministers ask more questions about the space project again. He finds himself enjoying the fact they are talking about space exploration rather than Felida and her issues because the project is becoming a reality now thanks to the Russians and the Mauritians. The meeting is animated and productive. He is pleased with the progress and how many of his ministers are keen to have the project continue. Quinan would be proud of such support and it is his memory that keeps Dilvant keen, his body and mind are alive with ideas.

As he walks into the house, he doesn't hear any noise. Is everything okay? Where is Felida? He panics whenever he doesn't know where she is and calls her name over and over. Nothing. No response. He checks every room in the house, their bedroom is a mess of clothes strewn around, the bed unmade. This is not like her, Felida is house-proud.

Walking into the kitchen, he asks the staff if they know where she is, but they say they haven't seen her for hours.

"She didn't say she was going out," says the chef, "maybe she is down at the beach."

"That's where I was headed before I came to speak to you. If she returns before I do, tell her to stay put."

"Of course, Sire."

As he runs down towards the beach, he calls her name many times. Again, no response. The sea air waves over the sand as he looks both ways. There is nothing ahead of him other than the waves lapping the shore. With panic setting in, he heads back to the house and calls her answae while walking up the path. It rings out. Walking back into their bedroom, he sees her mobile on the side table. Picking it up there is his missed call and others. He wonders why she didn't take it with her. He texts some of her friends who say they haven't heard from her but will let him know if they do.

Dilvant starts to pace, where would she have gone without telling anyone? Then he remembers.

He arrives at the crypt to find her dressed in black and kneeling in front of Quinan's coffin. "I'm so sorry, I only remembered now it was his birthday today."

"Yes, he would have been forty-one."

Placing his hand on her shoulder he asks, "How long have you been here?"

She looks up, her eyes ringed with mascara and kohl meshed underneath making her look desperately sad. "I don't know, but I don't want to leave yet."

"Do you mind if I stay with you?"

"Please do," she says, indicating with her hand that he kneel next to her.

They remain silent and he thinks about her brother, his friend. Quinan took to Dilvant the minute they met, and the feeling was mutual. Quinan was his only friend, he had never seen a need for friends, not even with any of The Enforcers. He found Quinan easy to talk to, they laughed joyously together and whenever things were serious, they both consoled each other. How he wishes they had met earlier, Dilvant only knew him for a short time. But in that time Quinan had entered his heart and even though he is not around now, his spirit will always be alive.

It's two hours later when Felida makes a move to leave. She had not said a word in all that time. Dilvant is amazed at the love they had for each other and even though she does not mention him, Dilvant knows she thinks of him every day.

Holding hands, they walk together towards the house. The setting sun throws a red glow on the horizon and the heat has only slightly waned. "We had a very productive meeting today; I think Quinan would be proud of the progress we are making."

She looks up with her blackened eyes, she resembles a tired panda. "That is good news."

"Felida," he says, holding her by the shoulders, "I will make you proud of me and we will rule on a new planet together. We can start a new culture with new values, tell me what you desire, and I will make it happen."

"Dilvant, I am already proud of you. The way you have led our parliament, your ideas and values you have brought to Crete and the people who live here, they love you. When we find another planet, and I know you will, we can make it our own and do things together. I will support you every step of the way. And your son will be proud of you too."

"You know it's a boy?" he asks with a smile he cannot conceal.

"I wasn't going to tell you, but yes, it's a boy. I want to name him, Quinan Jnr, in honour of my brother."

He hugs her with an intensity so fierce it scares him. He is not used to such emotions, but Felida has a way of igniting them in him. "My darling, you have made me the happiest man on Earth. Now all I want is to meet our son."

Chapter 15

Eween

He and Breex are sitting in the Oval Office waiting to see President Werran. This magnificent room has been redecorated by the First Lady. She has used blues and greys, which are not traditional colours, they give a softness that the deep reds and browns did not. The room has an informal feel without losing the grandness that permeates all of the White House.

"Breex, you have the proposal ready?"

"Yes, Eween. Once you begin your presentation, I will hand them over to the president. May I say how wonderful it is to be here with you, if the president agrees, this will be the first time the USA has been in the space race for many years."

"Don't be too excited, Breex, this is going to be an uphill battle. It wasn't easy getting this meeting because of the failures with Spain. Many good people with intelligence beyond their years were lost to the world." Eween is about to keep talking when the door behind them is opened and the president is announced. They both stand.

President Werran is small in stature with a slightly curved back.

Even though he is in his early 60s, this curvature ages him. He shakes their hands and motions for them to be seated. After a bit of small talk, Eween stands and begins his presentation. Breex hands over the proposal to the president and he begins looking through it, then closes it and faces Eween to focus on what he is presenting. He remains animated and interested.

When Eween sits again, the president thanks him for his detailed presentation. He will deliberate with cabinet in the next day or so, but...he coughs into his hand and tells them this is more than they will be able to donate. "Please, enjoy Washington for the next two days, have dinner with my wife and I tomorrow night, and we'll see if we will be able to come to an arrangement."

"Thank you, President Werran, we appreciate your time today."

"Please ask my assistant to help you with where to go and what to see. Thank you, gentlemen."

They gather their things and walk out of the Oval Office. The president's assistant has a folder already prepared for them with information. They thank him and head back to their hotel.

Eween and Breex decide to meet again later, they each have the afternoon free. Eween decides to speak with Leyna.

"Hello, darling."

Leyna asks him how things went at the meeting.

"Hmm, I'm not holding my breath. He listened and seemed interested then said he would consult with cabinet. From the look on his face as we were leaving, he may have lost that interest. He has asked us to stay two days and have dinner with him tomorrow night. It will be good to sit with him and his wife, hopefully in a more informal manner. Maybe I will be able to judge his mood better after a few wines."

"Hopefully. I have heard from Dawa, the funeral was huge and she is very proud of how the people of Arisis handled themselves. It was a sombre yet regal farewell. Sheabz was well-loved by his people," Leyna informs him.

"He deserved a good farewell, he was a brave and admirable man. Has Dawa heard from Zenac?"

"It's early days yet. We probably won't know anything for some time. Teegue has really messed up this time. It's amazing what children will do to anger or worry their parents. Speaking of which, Galexia is now playing with Teddy again. I spoke with her teachers who were aware of the situation with the other children, but they were keeping an eye on it. They were going to mention it to us if things became worse. Although, how much worse I don't know. Anyway, we worked things out with the parents of the boy who was the instigator and now the school yard is one of inclusion and acceptance."

"I hope you told them that if anything like this happens again, they are to come to us immediately. Galexia was traumatised by it all."

"Yes, I did. She has another year at this preschool, and I made sure they understood we do not want something like this to happen again. Oh, here she is now. Galexia, say hello to Daddy."

"Hi, Daddy."

"Hello, my sweet, how are you?"

"I'm good thanks. Teddy says hello too."

"It's good to see you two made up. I miss you and I'll see you in a few days. Put Mummy back on please."

"Okay, bye Daddy, I love you."

"Love you more...oh, Leyna hi. She sounds a lot better."

"I know and I'm grateful she's back to being a little girl who plays with everyone. Now, is there anything you need from me? More information maybe?"

"Not at this stage, maybe after we have dinner I will know more. I'll call you again tomorrow night. Bye my love."

"Ok, goodbye and goodnight. Love you too." Eween looks at his answae for longer than he needs to, he misses his girls. He then places it on the side table. Stretching he rolls over and despite everything on his mind, sleep comes easily.

Breex walks back towards Eween with their lunch, "Here you go, lox on rye complete with lashings of cream cheese."

"Thanks. You know what they say, *when in Rome...* yum," he says unwrapping the sandwich. They are seated on a park bench; the mild day has a slight breeze, and they are enjoying people watching.

"What do you think, do we have a chance?"

"I don't think so, Breex. Since the disasters of 2050 to 2055, the Americans have not been interested in space. They lost many good personnel as did the Spaniards.

"I felt that vibe from the president too. This has been a waste of time."

"Maybe, but if we succeed in finding suitable planets to colonise, there may be a change of heart."

They remain quiet while they eat and keep any further thoughts to themselves.

On their return, Breex's wife Marzeen is at the airport to take them home. She is disappointed with the news they had no luck.

"Leyna won't be pleased that we'll have to find another source," says Eween.

Once they are settled in the car, which is a new electric car with the option to turn it into a flying car in future. Breex is keen to do this, but Marzeen doesn't think the technology is up to scratch yet. "There is not enough evidence that the battery will survive the thrust it needs to make it into the air. I'd rather wait until there is more research. Now, to more important things...I have an idea on where to find more funds, although I don't think you'll like it."

"I'm intrigued," says Eween from the back seat.

"Well, basically we have exhausted all our options. The countries left don't have enough funds even if they do donate some, and the smaller ones aren't interested anyway. There is one country we haven't approached, Russia. Now, I know they are out of the question but there is someone who has approached them and has secured funds."

"Dilvant! You want us to ask Dilvant?"

"We should consider partnering with his project. What is so crazy about that? His operation has the buildings and equipment already set up like we have, he has procured the services of Russia's best and brightest scientists. If we join forces, we will double our capacity and boost our chances of finding suitable planets."

Breex turns to face his wife, "Are you nuts? Why would we want to join forces with Dilvant? Has he suddenly become a saint? Is there something that has happened since Eween and I have been in the USA to change his view on how to be a leader?"

"Wow, any more questions my darling? Look, let's have a meeting with Leyna and discuss this rationally. I don't see many other countries beating at our doors wanting to help out."

Eween shuffles back into his seat and says, "It might be worth discussing. I'll put it to Leyna and see when she has time for a meeting. Dilvant has been quiet since the battle, maybe he has changed, although we don't know for sure what he has planned. He is still someone I will never trust but at this stage, we are running out of options."

They drive the rest of the distance without another word. If they desperately need funds, there are crazier ways of procuring them. Dilvant may be the answer.

Chapter 16

Felida

As she holds their son, she caresses his brow that is knotted with worry. She whispers, "Do not fret Quinan Jnr, you will rise above this, it will not define your life."

Dilvant is discussing with the doctor the *Fibular Hemimelia* his son is born with, "So this bone, the fibula, is it? It is missing on his left leg making it shorter than the other."

The doctor continues informing Dilvant and Felida about their son's deformity. He tells them the leg may not grow straight, it will be weaker than his right and there may be problems with his joints. Having all five toes may help him with walking but he will need physical therapy and possibly surgery. These are all things that will show up as he grows, and surgery will help with giving him two legs the same length. The doctor also tells them they will need many meetings and discussions during his developmental years, but for now he will leave them to enjoy their baby, he is healthy in every other way.

They thank the doctor as he walks out. Felida hands Quinan Jnr to Dilvant. She begins to sob as the information sinks in. "He is going to need help. Why did this happen, what has he done to deserve this?"

"Felida, you know there is no answer to that question. Look at the positive, the doctor said he is healthy and I'm sure his strength as he grows will help him to combat this. Look who he has as parents, surely he has inherited our tenacity? And with my missing foot, he may not feel self-conscious."

She looks at her two boys, a love opening inside her that she grasps with glee. "Yes, he will overcome this, but it feels very unfair right now. He is so innocent, so pure. Life is hard enough without something like this."

"He will have the best of care and the best doctors will do the surgery. We have a lot to deal with in the next few years, but for now, let us enjoy him as a baby. He has time to learn to walk and we will be able to give him so much until then."

Felida begins to cry harder, "You are right, Dilvant. I need to let this out now as I will need all my strength to help him through this."

"Of course, my love. But remember, you will not be alone, we both have love we can shower him with, and this will be a small glitch in his life. Now, I must be going, the ministers are waiting for me. I'll come back later, you try and rest."

She watches him walk out of the hospital room then looks down at Quinan Jnr who is now asleep in her arms. He looks peaceful as she kisses his forehead. She presses the buzzer and a nurse comes in to place him in the bassinet. "May I have some pain killers please?" asks Felida. Although the birth was uneventful, he is a big baby and she had received a few stitches. With the epidural now wearing off, she will need the painkillers to help her sleep. The nurse is back with the pills and Felida takes them then lays back down. Sleep doesn't come easily but eventually she is in a light slumber with Quinan her brother by her side. He tells her he will be by Quinan Jnr's side, the missing bone will not be an issue, he will make sure of it. Tears flow as she falls into a deeper sleep.

•   •   •

They settle into some sort of routine with Quinan Jnr generally doing what all babies do – sleep, eat, poop and grow. His left leg is floppy, and this is the only sign there is something amiss. Their friends who visit don't comment although by now everyone knows little Quinan has a slight disability. The rumour mill was alive with this news within a day of his birth although no one will admit as to who started it. Felida was upset at having her son gossiped about so soon in his life, but Dilvant calmed her.

"This will blow over and there will be different news in a few days. Let them say what they like, Quinan Jnr is oblivious to it all," he had said. Of this, she is thankful. But she dreads the day when he will have to fight his own battles.

She is on the balcony nursing the baby when Dilvant arrives home. "We're out here." He bends down to kiss them both after he finds them. He takes a seat and takes Quinan's left foot into his hand caressing it with fatherly love.

"How are you feeling?"

"Better. Each day I feel stronger, and he is now latching on well. Breastfeeding has become easier, he is feeding properly now. He's chubbier, don't you think?"

"Yes, he is growing, I've noticed. I'm glad feeding is now working for you. Umm, I have some news, and it's unusual." She adjusts herself to see his face clearly and keeps listening. "I have been summoned by Leyna and Eween."

"What?" she says with a look of incredulous alarm.

"They want to talk to us. Myself, our Transport Minister and our Finance Minister have been summoned because they need our help. They have begun their space project just as we have but have run short of funds. They have asked if we would like to collaborate with them."

Felida moves Quinan Jnr to her other breast and once he is settled asks, "After everything that has happened, after wanting to kill you, now they want your help?"

"I know it sounds ridiculous, but they must be in a real bind. Without enough funds their space project will suffer and possibly never get off the ground. As much as I detest them for taking my leadership, this may be good for our project too. We can double our resources. What I don't understand is where did their funds go. I'm sure they were able to raise more than we did."

They discuss this further and Dilvant tells her she is the first person he has told, none of his ministers know about the summons. Obviously, he will have to discuss this with them. She tells him how she worries it may be a trap, she needs him now more than ever. Quinan Jnr needs his father. Dilvant agrees with her but there are no guarantees they will discover a planet on their own, theirs is a small operation compared to the one of The Vatican. And, of course, he will not consider it if he senses any danger. At the moment it is a cordial request.

"And a strange one. I don't trust them, nor Dawa and Zenac. Did you hear that their son is lost somewhere in space? Apparently, he tried to follow his father to Earth and was hit with space junk sending him off-course. Maybe Zenac is behind this request, he wants the project up and running sooner to help find his son?"

Dilvant had heard that news. "I had not considered that Zenac may be the one interested in joining forces." He looks at his son, his hand still holding his little foot. "As a father, I would do anything to save Quinan Jnr if he was in trouble, and my other children if it came to that. I don't blame Zenac for wanting to speed things up."

Quinan unlatches and Felida passes him to Dilvant who expertly places him on his shoulder and begins patting his back. She appreciates the fact Dilvant has experience with babies, she has needed this expertise in the past few months. "I now know what it is to be a mother, and like you, I would do anything to save our son. I hope to never be in Zenac and Dawa's shoes, anything could have happened to their son in space. It will be like looking for a needle in a haystack."

"Still, I will not go into this lightly. Tomorrow I am meeting with all my cabinet to discuss what we will do." Just as he says this, the baby lets out an almighty burp. They both laugh and kiss his chubby cheeks in unison.

"Let me put him down," she says, taking Quinan Jnr in her arms and heading to his nursery. Love warms her body in a way she could never have imagined. She dreads anything happening to him and hugs him closer to her. She feels for Zenac and Dawa, even though they are enemies, no parent should lose a child and the worst of it is, they have no idea where he is or whether he will ever be found.

Chapter 17

Zenac

Four days into their quest to find Teegue and nothing, not even a slight signal. The AI from the craft and from Earth has had no luck either. Both the Moon and Mars colonies are watching out for signals as well. Taaz and The Mechanic come onto the communications deck followed by the robots. "Anything further?"

"No, I'm sorry Zenac. Nothing. We have however noticed more space junk in this area, we may be close to where his proton rocket was hit," says Taaz.

"There is space junk throughout space, but I thank you for your positive thoughts. Now, let's think of other ways to tackle this." The three of them sit at the consoles and discuss ways of detecting signals, they scour the files and communications of thousands of rescue missions. Zenac's answae pings, Leyna wants him to contact her. He leaves his security men to keep scouring the files and heads to his quarters to take her call.

"We have had a faint signal, the Mars colony detected it this morning. It could be something from Teegue. I'll send you the coordinates for you to follow. Don't get your hopes up, it was very faint."

"It's better than we have had so far, thanks Leyna. How are things going with you?"

"We're fine here, you concentrate on finding Teegue. I spoke to Dawa and she is coping without Sheabz but is not coping without Teegue."

"Death is final, so she has to cope without her father, but we don't know if Teegue is dead or alive, that is worse. Of course, she is not coping. I speak to her every day and try to keep her spirits up. She will be happy to hear about this signal."

"Like I said, it may be nothing. But, if it helps Dawa, and you, to cope better, then it's fine to tell her."

"I need to get back to Taaz and The Mechanic and tell them this news. We'll start heading towards that area immediately." Before he leaves his quarters, he sends Dawa a message, they may have found a signal and he will call her when he knows more. Dawa replies saying she awaits his call and won't go to sleep until she hears from him.

After two days of high-speed travel, the Salverz reaches the area indicated by the coordinates Leyna had sent. The amount of space junk in this area was three times the amount they had left behind. "If Teegue was here, I can see how he would have been hit."

"The Salverz has a much tougher exterior, Taaz, so we are safe. But I can see how the smaller proton rocket should not have entered this region. Still, we have no signal."

"The AI tells us there is another faint signal, but it is approximately a billion light years from here."

"Show me where, I have nothing on my screen."

Taaz points to his screen, the AI showing a faint dot on the top right hand of the screen. "Maybe we should head over there?"

"We have to try everything. Punch in the coordinates and have one of the robots keep an eye on it. We all need to have some rest, we won't arrive in the area for at least five days."

They travel for two days and the signal becomes stronger. They keep following it as Zenac begins to hope it's Teegue's rocket. He is scouring files again when The Mechanic calls him to the AI area.

"According to this data, we will arrive in two more days, not three. There seems to be what looks like a rocket, but at this stage, we are not close enough to tell."

"Great, let's hope it's Teegue and he is alive. Keep looking." Zenac moves away from them, his anxiety increasing with the thought they may find Teegue dead... or worse, they don't find him at all.

The two days drag on with Zenac's emotions riding a roller coaster. Every time he communicates with Dawa, he pushes them down because she is distressed enough as it is. He needs to stay strong for her as well as Aria and Braxton.

Lying in his quarters, he sees her face on his compupad. She exudes worry, the lines of her face have deepened since finding out about Teegue's disappearance. "You look shattered."

"I am, I have this bone-crushing tiredness that grips my whole being. This is too much — my father's death is enough to deal with..." She stops as tears begin to flow.

"We have to think positive. We are only two days away from the area where he may be," he says wishing he was by her side. He has an ache to console her, to be with her and his children, all of them. "How are Aria and Braxton holding up?"

Dawa sniffs, her nose red and wet with a mix of tears and runny snot, "They are both angry with him for doing yet another stupid thing, but they miss him. They want both of you back here and they have had enough of this whole thing. Another person who is not holding up is Trisia. She came to see me a few days ago telling me Teegue was headed back to Earth for another woman. Did you know he had someone else?"

"On Earth? No, he never mentioned anyone. Poor Trisia, she doesn't deserve this either. Honestly, what goes through his mind? And if he did have someone on Earth, why didn't he tell us?"

"Teegue keeps these things to himself. Remember when he yelled at Aria for telling us about Trisia? Anyway, he has caused us all a great amount of agony, most of it unnecessary."

"You're right, but us being angry with him doesn't help. We can deal with all of these feelings when we find him and bring him home."

"*If* he is found," says Dawa, wiping her nose with a tissue.

"Like I said Dawa, we have to think positive. Take care please and give Aria and Braxton a hug from me. We all have to stay strong."

Dawa nods, blowing him a kiss. The screen blinks into black.

He flips the lid down and places the compupad on the small desk. Stretching his aching limbs, he does a few exercises before going up to the deck. He hopes Taaz and The Mechanic have some good news.

Arriving on deck, both Taaz and The Mechanic are staring at one of the screens. The two robots are standing behind them, powered down. Zenac wonders why the robots are on the deck at all. "What's going on?"

"Hi Zenac, we were about to call you. The robots were on duty from 00:00 hours as usual and waiting for us before they went back to their stations. They gave me good news, we are thirteen hours away from the spot where the signal came from, and it's Teegue's proton rocket."

"What? Oh, thank the universe. Power them up again, I want to hear what they have to say."

"No need to, Zenac, the transcript is all here on this screen," says Taaz.

Zenac looks down and reads the time of the sighting, sees the grainy photo of what is definitely a rocket, and how the robots and AI have powered the Salverz to arrive at the site ten hours ahead of schedule. "Who authorised them to add power? Not that it's a problem, but..."

"It was me," says The Mechanic, "they signalled me, and I came up to see what they wanted. I didn't bother you or Taaz because I knew you wouldn't have an issue with arriving there ahead of schedule. Also, Zenac, you have enough to deal with."

"I am the commander of this ship, you had no right to go above my head," says Zenac, anger rising inside him.

The Mechanic is taken aback, "I thought I was helping, my apologies. It won't happen again."

Zenac looks away from The Mechanic's embarrassed face, there was no need for him to be reprimanded. Zenac needs to take hold of his emotions. "Right, okay then. These two need to go back to their stations, we're going to need them when we arrive. For us, let's check everything including our suits and make sure there is nothing that is going to make things difficult. As we discussed before, Mechanic, you will stay onboard and Taaz and I will enter the proton rocket with the robots. Are we clear?"

"Yes, sir." Both Taaz and The Mechanic say this as they head towards their quarters ready for what may be a horrible ending or a fantastic reunion.

Zenac is left alone on the deck. His heart is racing with the thought of seeing Teegue. He has to be on that rocket. And alive! Looking down at the screen again, he rereads everything one more time. When he's finished, he thinks about The Mechanic and what he did. He knows he overreacted, but The Mechanic is essentially a civilian and should not be given the power to make decisions. He will know not to do such a thing in future.

Zenac heads to his quarters, it will soon be time to find his son.

Chapter 18

Leyna

The three of them are seated at the kitchen bench having breakfast. Galexia is moving her porridge around with one hand, the other is holding her flopped head. "Come on Galexia, it's time to go to preschool in ten minutes, finish eating."

"It's yucky. I don't want anymore."

Leyna looks at Eween in despair, who smiles and says, "She won't die if she doesn't finish her breakfast." Then turning towards his moody daughter, he picks her up placing her under his arm, "Let's go and fly." With his other arm outstretched he zooms around the bench and then flies to Galexia's bedroom with her laughing hysterically.

Leyna laughs too and is thankful for the light relief Eween brings into these tense situations with Galexia. She sometimes wonders who is harder to deal with, Galexia or her ministers? Most of the time it's Galexia. But she puts this morning's issue aside and heads to her bedroom to collect her things. Today is the day she meets with her nemesis, The High Priest who is now known as Dilvant.

Dawa had been horrified to learn of Marzeen's idea, as had some of the ministers. The Luminaries were not all on board with this either. "How can you even think of entertaining this idea?" Dawa had yelled at the private meeting held a few weeks ago via holograms. Leyna had assured everyone that no agreement will be entered into unless Dilvant proves he can be trusted. Many had asked questions of *"how will we know"* when Eween stepped in asking anyone if they had a better idea. How were they going to fix the shortfall of funds? "Please come forward in the next two weeks if you know of others who will be interested in joining us in this project," he had said. Since that meeting, no one had come forward, so today is the day when The Vatican may fall into bed with its ultimate enemy once more.

Eween is in the meeting room when she arrives. "The ministers are in their offices awaiting your message to join us." He walks towards her and kisses her on both cheeks, "Good luck, Madame President."

She knows he is aware of the importance of this meeting; the International Space Program is in jeopardy without extra funds. They had not expected some changes made to their rockets to be as costly as they were and parts from England became more expensive to manufacture and send to Australia and New Zealand. So, making this unholy alliance seems to be the only answer. "Thanks. Having you by my side keeps me sane."

An assistant is at the door announcing that Dilvant and his ministers have arrived. "Send them in," she says with a quiver in her voice. She clears her throat; she refuses to show any weakness in front of this man.

Dilvant, resplendent in his High Priest robes enters with his ministers, the Minister for Finance as well as the Minister for Defence & Home Affairs. The Minister for Transport declined an invitation to attend. Seeing Dilvant in the uniform of The Enforcers entices rage within her, how dare he wear those hideous robes of their fallen regime. Eween is whispering to her to stay calm, Dilvant has done this on purpose because he wants to intimidate them.

"Madame President, how lovely to see you again. He introduces the two ministers with him and makes apologies for the Minister for the Environment and Space Research, he is unfortunately unwell at this time. And, as you already know, the Minister for Transport declined your invitation."

"Thank you, gentlemen," she nods acknowledging them. "Please be seated."

Eween remains standing, he is the one to make the presentation and recommendations to Dilvant. "Welcome, and we do hope your minister who is ill has a speedy recovery."

Dilvant nods and adjusts his opulent red coat, placing his hands on his knees, "Let us hear what you have to say, it is a pleasure to be in these quarters once more."

Leyna harrumphs and Eween looks over to her as he turns to organise the hologram. She knows he will have something to say about her attitude later.

"Gentlemen," he says turning back towards them, "these are our facilities in Borgo where most of the preliminary work is being done. We have factories in Australia and New Zealand where they are drawing up preliminary designs for spacecraft. We also have a facility in England where parts will be made and then shipped to Australia and New Zealand for construction. With the construction of these facilities over the past ten months, the cost of parts and shipping, most of our funds have been depleted. As you already know, we have been unable to secure the extra fifty billion Licdan to keep the project going. It is for this reason we have called you, the resources and funds you have may be enough for us to complete the required craft and explore space to all our satisfaction." Eween proceeds to show them more images of the facilities, both external and internal. "As you will note, the facilities are of the highest calibre, our production standards will exceed anything ever built before." He remains quiet to let them take in the images.

Leyna stands and moves towards the hologram. With her pointer she indicates the areas of importance and then proceeds to tell them what more needs to be done. "With your help, we will achieve our goals. We know you have also made progress, and we are interested in your high-powered rockets as well as the technology behind them."

Dilvant shifts in his chair placing his elbows on the table, his hands cupped together, "Madame President and Minister Eween, thank you for your presentation. You have given us much to consider, but let me say right at the start, the technology behind our high-powered rockets is top secret, we will never divulge this to anyone."

Leyna and Eween return to their seats with Leyna confronting Dilvant by staring him down, "This will be up for discussion when and if you agree to our proposal, but you are to allow us the use of these rockets, that is not negotiable."

Dilvant stares back at Leyna with a wry smirk, "It seems to me you are in no position to make demands, Madame President, but take it as noted by the three of us."

She holds her ground and keeps staring him down, "My Minister for Finance and the Environment Minister will now come in to join us. They will discuss with you the figures and the breakdown of what is still needed, where the money will be spent and a timeline of when the project will launch. The GIS will be involved in the project launch as well. The Environment Minister will present our plans of how many planets will be checked for human colonisation and the research that will go into finding a suitable planet with a similar atmosphere to Earth." She presses a buzzer under the table and the doors to the room open allowing the ministers to enter.

Three hours later they are standing outside of St Peter's along with Breex and Nable, who are wary of what has happened at the meeting. They are all silent watching the parliamentary car take Dilvant and his ministers to their hotel.

Breex breaks the silence. "What time do you want us at the dinner? I have to let Marzeen know, she is working at the orphanage today."

"I would like everyone seated by seven. Is Marzeen still working, it's late?"

"She finishes at six, but don't worry, we'll make it in time. I want to make sure that man sees everyone of us and show him our strength is in our numbers. He will know we are not to be played."

"This is the attitude we will all carry with us, Breex. Nabel, are you bringing anyone along?" asks Leyna.

"I have a friend, she is a neuroscientist at Central Hospital. We have known each other since school, and she has an interest in the project. She would like to help in some way."

"Being with us is already some help, but please introduce me to her and we can discuss her ideas."

"Mayiss will be delighted to meet you, Leyna."

They stand and talk for a few more minutes then say their good-byes all agreeing to make this dinner the success it needs to be. As much as joining forces with Dilvant is not palatable to any of them, they all know they need his help.

The Vatican dining room is transformed into an elegant space with shimmering gold curtains, white leather chairs, white linen and plates with high-shine gold cutlery resplendent on either side. All the delegates are seated, and Leyna is pleased that everyone who responded to the invitation has attended. There are fifty-two of them and three of the enemy. Every delegate knows what to do with stroking Dilvant's ego, it is to be caressed in every way. Leyna is pleased to see this approach is working because Dilvant is all smiles. But a small blink of disaster crosses her mind, which she will do anything to avoid. This space program has to go ahead, there has been too much money and time being put into it already. Also, the GIS is keen to see other planets colonised because this will give Earth some breathing space to possibly recover even further from the effects of climate change that took hold all those years ago.

Dinner goes smoothly with everyone smiling and mingling with ease. Dilvant is resplendent once again, this time in a black tux with a red checked bow tie. His patent leather shoes shine with an incandescence that reflects his arrogance. Leyna has noticed him watching Marzeen with more than just mild interest. Marzeen had told them all how Dilvant had saved her from a life of living on the street but how she had despised him. She pretended to care for him to ensure she lived. She knows, as they all do, that he will kill someone if he suspects they are a threat. Marzeen made sure she was never a threat to him.

Leyna goes over to Marzeen and asks her to accompany her to the bathroom. When they arrive, she checks there is no one else with them before speaking. "Are you alright, Marzeen? Dilvant has certainly been watching you."

"Yes, I've felt his eyes on me all night. I'm okay because there are others around, and Breex is aware too."

"I'm sorry to put you in this position…"

"Please, Leyna, there is no need to apologise. I did consider not attending tonight but I thought it more important to come and support the cause. As much as I abhor that we need his help, the project is more important."

"Thank you, Marzeen. I will ask Taaz to keep two security guards near you for the next two days that Dilvant is here. You need protection."

"I appreciate it, I don't feel safe with him around. Now, we had better go back before they wonder what's happened to us."

When they return to the table, Marzeen sits with Breex but Leyna is called over by Nable who introduces her to Mayiss. He also calls over Eween, who shakes Mayiss' hand with a smile.

"Pleased to meet you," says Leyna, taking in this striking young woman in an elegant navy-blue gown, her lush, black hair cascading in elegant waves over her shoulders and down her back.

"I appreciate you giving me some of your time, Madame President. You know my father, the surgeon who tried to save Eween's arm."

"Oh yes, Eween and I know him. He is well, I trust."

"He is and sends his best wishes, he too is watching the progress of this project with vigour. I wanted to discuss the idea of medical assistance once the project is underway, but maybe we could have a meeting? There is much to discuss."

"Of course, I will have my assistant contact you with a suitable time. It is lovely to meet you, I look forward to our meeting."

She and Eween watch them walk back to the table, "I had no idea Nable was seeing someone, did you?"

"No, he didn't mention anything to me. Although, he did say she is a friend."

"Leyna, don't be naive, did you see the way he looked at her?"

"Okay, well I'm happy for him. He has no family and deserves someone who loves him. And if he's lucky enough to have someone who looks like her, then good for him. And, she will be an asset to us, I'll make sure we meet with her soon."

Eween agrees as he escorts her back to their seats. The evening is ending and Dilvant and his ministers come to thank them.

"This evening has been pleasurable. My compliments to your culinary staff. As I mentioned at the end of our meeting earlier, we will deliberate your request and will give you our decision before we leave. I must say you have delivered a compelling argument why we should collaborate; however, we have much to discuss amongst ourselves."

"We appreciate that, thank you. I'm glad you enjoyed this evening. Good night," says Leyna, taking each of their hands as they leave. They continue saying goodbye to the other delegates and by the time they arrive home, Leyna is sapped of all her energy. Turning to Eween who is changing out of his clothes at the other side of their bed, she says, "Are we doing the right thing bringing this vulgar man back into our lives?"

"Leyna, if we had another alternative, we would have gone that way. You know this is our last resort."

"Yes, I know, but he is so untrustworthy. I don't think he has changed despite being happy with his partner and becoming a father again."

"Becoming a father will have made some difference, even if it is for the fourth time. Now, stop over-thinking things, come here and give me a hug."

She does as she is told and sinks into his arms wondering what Thadd would think about her collaborating with his father.

Chapter 19

Dilvant

He is sitting in an armchair in his hotel room peering out the window. This was his domain, this is where he had ruled the world. Being back here has heightened his desire to rule once more, and not just on his own planet. He wants it all, even Arisis when he finds it. They will all pay for their disloyalty, he has plans for each and every one of them. But especially Leyna, he will make her suffer and will take pleasure in her screaming for his forgiveness. She will suffer the most because she not only took his leadership, she was the cause of him sending his favourite son to his death. It is her fault he sent Thadd on that suicide mission because she is a vexperson who has forgotten her place in society. He will take delight in seeing her suffer the pain he has suffered of losing Thadd.

Today he will discuss his plan with his ministers, both the ones with him and the others in Crete waiting to hear from him. They will be pleased with what he has in mind because they will all benefit if it comes to fruition. He has no desire to fail, Leyna and Eween along with all their followers will not see it coming. Standing up he heads into the bathroom and showers, the ministers will be waiting for him in the foyer.

While dressing he thinks of Marzeen. She is as beautiful as when he last saw her. His lover and servant was loyal to him, or so he thought. But something still stirs inside him, he must see her before he leaves. Her spell still has a hold on his heart.

He arrives in the foyer and sees his ministers waiting for him. "Gentlemen, shall we go to St Peters and discuss my plan. I have delved into all the information our enemies furnished us with, and with your permission, I think I know what we should do."

"We look forward to hearing all about it," says one of his ministers, "and I do hope this will not cost us more than needed."

"Spoken like a true financier," laughs Dilvant as they head into the parliamentary car.

They arrive in the quiet room at the other end of the parliamentary offices that Leyna promised them. She had assured them of the utmost privacy, "You will not be spied on," she had assured them. Dilvant had laughed inwardly and had requested the help of her assistant to take minutes, who was their envoy anyway. Leyna's assistant had been Dilvant's spy for some time; she had done well to obtain Leyna and Eween's trust.

The four of them make themselves comfortable on the lounge and armchairs, the room is specifically for casual meetings and discussions, but theirs is far from casual. Dilvant asks the assistant to go first.

"Sire, you have the most up-to-date information about what Leyna and Eween have planned. They wish to align themselves with you because you have acquired the best and brightest minds to associate with your Quinan Space Project. As they mentioned, they are interested in the high-power rockets, wanting to use them to find planets in record time."

His ministers squirm in their seats hearing this again when one says, "They will not get their filthy hands on..."

Dilvant stops the minister going further by saying, "It will never happen, I made that clear yesterday." Turning to the assistant, "Now, young lady, is there any more you need to tell me?"

"You have all the information, sire."

"Good, now I need you to keep up with these discussions today, it is extremely important you document everything that is said in this room. Also, the people I ask you to summon, I want to meet in my hotel room on my own. Respil, Marzeen and Vimara are to come individually at the times I ask and are to tell no one of our meeting. Do you understand?" Leyna's assistant will now do his bidding as well. She will be valuable to what he has planned.

"Yes, sire," the assistant replies coyly.

Satisfied she is clear about what is required of her, Dilvant powers up the hologram to his parliament in Crete. "Good morning, it is good to see all of you in attendance." He proceeds to discuss his idea with everyone and some ministers interrupt him with questions. He expected they would query how this plan will work and is happy to discuss ideas on how to improve on his plan. A few ministers congratulate him and are pleased how he has included them all in it. They want to benefit and cheer him on as he speaks.

Respil, one of his prostitutes he had at The Vatican, is the first one to come into his hotel room. "Sire, it is good to see you again." She bows and he helps her to rise by placing a finger under her chin.

"You are as lovely as ever, my sweet. I am glad to see you are being looked after. What is it you do now?"

"I work in a factory where fish is tinned. It is not pleasant, but the pay keeps me with a roof over my head."

He walks towards her and sits her on the bed. "You were very good with my son and I want you to know I appreciate how you kept him happy. I have a job for you if you wish to take it and I will pay you handsomely." He stops for affect and when she doesn't speak, he continues, "I want you to cause problems in Leyna and Eween's relationship. Make yourself available to Eween, have him in compromising situations and take photos." He hands her a camera the size of a golf ball.

"What is this? And how do I get close to Eween, he and Leyna always have security surrounding them."

"This is the camera you will use. Look, you press here, and the photos will be sent to the compupad tablet over there." He points to the coffee table. As long as you have the compupad with you, the photos will automatically upload. Then you send those photos to me."

"Sire, I am not computer literate..."

"My assistant will show you what to do, don't let that worry you. Once I have the photos, you will be paid."

"Umm, okay, I will do my best, but getting close to Eween..."

"My assistant will help you with that as well. She will distract security to give you time to deal with Eween. This should not take you more than a week to achieve, I want to see the damage to their union and the photos I send to the media will be the catalyst. Their relationship will not survive such a scandal."

"As you desire. I am at your disposal and am honoured you trust me with this."

"Respil, you should be rewarded for the services you gave my family, not only what you did for Thadd. What you earn from this job I am asking you to do will keep you well looked after into your old age."

Respil places her hands to her face, one on either cheek, "Oh my, I will not fail, I promise. *Thank you so much*." Her voice quivers with emotion.

"Go now, here are your tools and there is a note in the bag with the details of my assistant and how to contact her. Thank you for helping me with the revenge I have been waiting for."

He watches as she leaves and knows she will not fail him. Now, he has half an hour before his ex-wife Vimara arrives. He lays on the bed and closes his eyes, he can feel a victory is close and this inspires him to keep forging ahead with his plan.

She walks in and he is taken aback at how she has aged. Her once black hair is silver and falls limply about her shoulders. She is also stooped and walks with a cane. "Vimara, what has happened to you?"

"I was surprised when I was summoned, I thought I would never hear from you again. Don't you know I was imprisoned for years? I was only released this month. The cold of that prison room has affected my bones, I am riddled with arthritis."

"I had no idea, I am sorry for your hardship. May I hug you?"

"Gently."

He gives her a light hug about her shoulders and then kisses her cheek, "I am truly sorry, you did not deserve this. But I suppose you're wondering why I summoned you?" She nods and he continues, "I wanted you to know I am a father again, a boy named Quinan Jnr. Would you please let my other children know?"

"I would if I knew where they were. They escaped prison during the first few months we were incarcerated and wanted me to go with them. Unfortunately, I was too ill with fever so they left without me promising to come back. They never did. I assume they are dead. Our other children you sent away have never bothered to contact me," she says her eyes dropping. When she looks up again, her eyes are wet, "But, congratulations, at least you have an heir."

Dilvant is horrified, he has lost his children. Another reason to hate Leyna, another reason for her to pay. "I am... this is devastating. I only have one child now."

"It seems so but it is better than none. May I sit down?"

"Of course, my apologies. Make yourself comfortable."

"So, tell me about your new love? I hear you live in Crete."

"Yes, and her name is Felida. Her brother was ruler of Crete before he was killed helping me to defend my leadership. She is as wonderful a mother as you were."

"I'm happy for you Dilvant, you deserve to be happy. Me, I guess it's too late for me. I live in a small flat on the ground floor of a derelict block on the outskirts of the city. At least it is dry inside."

"This will change. I will buy an apartment for you within the city. You will not suffer any further."

"You will do this for me? Dilvant this is very generous..."

"You are the mother of my children and that will never change. We did have many good times my love and you deserve to have more good times. My assistant will contact you when I have secured a place and you are to move in immediately."

Vimara stands uneasily and falls into Dilvant's arms crying, "Thank you, you are my saviour. I have always loved you."

He remains quiet while holding her and can feel her shoulder bones under his hands. He is pleased with himself that he is able to do this good deed.

It's an hour later when Marzeen appears at his door. "Welcome, I wasn't sure you would come."

"There is a security guard waiting downstairs. He thinks I am coming to see a friend."

"Then you have not lied," he says about to kiss her on the cheek but she abruptly turns away from him.

"Marzeen, don't make me angry. I summoned you here out of the good times we had together. Remember, without me you would still be on the street. You owe me that."

"I have not forgotten, but it was a lifetime ago. I have a completely new life, a husband who loves me the right way and..."

His hand slaps her before she can finish. She reels and he grabs her by the waist throwing her on the bed. He uses a pillow to cover her face so she can't scream. He hears her muffled voice, and this spurs him further. This bitch doesn't appreciate what he did for her and now she will pay. He takes care not to hurt her or leave any bruises but gives her what she deserves.

When he is finished, he tells her to go into the bathroom and clean herself up. Then she is to leave and never to speak to anyone about this. If she does, he will find out and kill her.

After she slinks out without looking at him, he lies on the bed. He has completed the first part of his plan. Making trouble within Leyna and Eween's partnership will be his first reward. His ultimate reward is to be leader of the world...no, the universe. He is ambitious enough to want it all.

Chapter 20

Dawa

Sitting in her office she is finding it difficult to concentrate. Her mind is flooded with scenarios of what has happened to Teegue. Speaking with Zenac last night has not helped either, even though he is adamant he will find Teegue. This gives her some hope, but this hope is as thin as a filament of spider's silk.

She is also still raw and missing Sheabz, the loss of her father while she was on Earth is devastating. She had spoken to him two nights before, and although he said he felt tired, he was otherwise well. Between missing her father and now not knowing where Teegue is or what has happened to him, her body is going into panic mode. This panic feels like a huge lump riding up from her stomach and trying to force its way up her chest. The heaviness is making her gasp for breath.

As she is trying to take in a breath, Trisear walks into her office. "Dawa, oh my, what is going on? You're as pale as snow," he says, rushing to the sideboard and filling a glass with water. He is so nervous the water from the glass spills out. Swearing under his breath he takes the water to Dawa and with his finger gently under her chin, asks her to drink.

After a few minutes Dawa's breathing settles. "I, umm, I had a panic attack. There was a lump in my chest as big as a boulder. Thanks Trisear, I was about to call out when you came in."

"I'm glad I was walking past and noticed you slumped over. Maybe a lie down will help," he says pointing to the lounge. "You are dealing with a lot, is there any better news?"

"I'm afraid not. Although, last night Zenac told me they were close to the area where there is a rocket. It may be Teegue's rocket, I guess I'll know more tonight when we speak again." Laying her head into the deep cushioned lounge, the coolness of the leather feels good on her skin. Her body begins to feel as it should again.

"I do hope you hear better news tonight. Is there anything I can get for you? A tea maybe?"

"No, I'm fine lying here for now. I'll rest for a bit and then head home early. Maybe I'll cook a nice dinner for Aria and Braxton, treat them with something they love. This isn't easy for them either, they miss their brother."

"I can imagine. And that's a good idea. If you need anything, just call. Especially if another attack comes on, I'll have medical help with me this time."

"I'm resting now and should be fine. I need some peace and quiet, that's all."

Trisear nods and walks out leaving Dawa with a glass of fresh water on the side table. Dawa closes her eyes and drifts off into an anxiety strewn slumber.

Aria and Braxton are having a heated dispute over a trivial matter that Dawa isn't interested in. She is still feeling decidedly off kilter after the panic attack and the short sleep she had on the lounge was not restorative, her body is still limp with exhaustion. "Will you two please give it a break, I have a headache."

"Sorry Mum, but he started it."

"What are you twelve?"

"Braxton, I said that's *enough*."

With this stern tone, she finally stops them. She places the tacos in front of them and then she sits. "Now, how about you both tell me something good about your day?"

Braxton starts by telling her about how he is wanting to learn to play guitar, he has been researching how much a guitar costs and about lessons.

"That's great Braxton, it's a good idea to learn an instrument, a nice hobby to have. That is definitely something good, and when you know what you want, we can go and look for a guitar together."

"Oh, thanks Mum, that will be awesome."

"Aria, what about you? Anything new to tell me?"

"Not really. Did you speak to Dad last night?"

Dawa didn't feel like talking about this but she knew they had a right to know. "Yes, they are close to finding the rocket and I'm hoping to find out more tonight."

"This is dragging on and I can tell how much it is affecting you, Mum. Oh, and I forgot to tell you, Trisia called me about a girl on Earth, she said she was the reason Teegue was returning to Earth. Do you know anything about her?"

"So, you did have something to tell me. Trisia called me too and no, I don't know anything about this girl. She must be something special for Teegue to risk his life. When Trisia spoke with me she was distraught, how was she with you?"

"Umm okay, I guess. She thought I may know something about this girl, but I would be the last person Teegue would tell. You know how guarded he is about his personal life."

Dawa knows this only too well. The older Teegue gets, the less she knows about her own son. He has never been much of a talker, so it is not surprising no one knew about his new love interest. They finish their dinner quietly, keeping their thoughts to themselves. She watches both Aria and Braxton and knows their brother's disappearance is weighing on their minds too. Her heart is crumbling with emotions of anger, despair and sheer disappointment with Teegue and his reckless antics. She doesn't want to think about never seeing him again. With this horrible thought, she asks the two of them to place their dishes on the sink, she needs to rest. Kissing them both on the head before going to her bedroom, she doesn't look into their eyes because their sadness is too profound.

Tears have welled in her eyes by the time she is settled and speaking to Zenac. He is saying that they are only an hour away from the rocket. It is definitely the proton rocket. Soon they will prepare to board it and with a lot of luck, Teegue will be on it and okay.

"This is hopeful, Zenac. Does the rocket look damaged?" Her voice sounds detached, it's as if the words are not coming out of her mouth.

"Yes, there is the hole that Teegue looks to have fixed and then some glass has shattered. It doesn't look like it shattered through though, which is good. There should still be oxygen onboard."

"I wish I was there with you, I feel so helpless here and I'm so alone."

"Dawa, you're not alone because Aria and Braxton need you, don't feel like you're doing nothing. Look, I have to go and prepare, please keep your spirits up my love. We can talk again later, and hopefully you can speak with Teegue as well."

She doesn't tell him she does feel alone because Aria and Braxton are busy with their own things, they don't spend much time with their mother. Instead, she says, "That would be wonderful. Please take care, I love you."

Her screen pings to black and she shuts her compupad lid down and an involuntary wail escapes her mouth. This time she is not there to rescue her son and the pain is too excruciating to bear.

Chapter 21

Eween

He is lying comfortably on the lounge waiting for Leyna to return from putting Galexia down for the night. He is thinking about Zenac, they haven't heard from him since he left to find his son. His skin bristles at the thought of both Zenac and Dawa not knowing where their son is, to be lost out there in space, the possibilities of what happened to Teegue are endless.

"You look deep in thought," says Leyna as she sits in the armchair sighing.

"I'm thinking of Zenac and wondering what is happening."

"Oh, we haven't heard, have we? I'll message Dawa tomorrow, although I haven't wanted to contact her because I don't want to upset her any further."

"It is hard to know what to say, but I think you should at least let her know we are thinking of them."

She agrees to do so, and they continue discussing what they think the outcome of their meeting with Dilvant will be. Neither of them has an idea what the decision will be, but other than pride, what reason does Dilvant have not to join forces?

"Imagine how much faster we can move this project along if we combine our resources," says Eween, "He would be stupid not to accept our proposal."

"I agree, and provided he can be trusted... actually, no I don't think we will ever be able to trust him. We, all of us, will need to keep a close eye on him if he does agree. You know what, I've had enough of talking about him, I'm going to bed. Are you joining me?"

"Soon, I might catch some of the late news. Goodnight." She bends down and kisses him before heading to the bedroom. Leyna has met her match with Dilvant, they are both ambitious leaders, the only difference being that Leyna is not a cruel maniac like him. Eween looks down at his emails when a message from an unknown person pings. He opens it in incognito mode. It is from a woman named Respil, someone he doesn't know. He drags the message into the trash.

Eween and Breex are seated at a café in St Peters Square enjoying the end of summer sunshine. Both had wanted a break from being cooped up in their offices and have been discussing their plans for the winter holidays.

"Actually, we may not be going anywhere this winter because Marzeen is pregnant."

"Breex, that's wonderful news."

"Yes, it is but Marzeen is not feeling the best. She is only eight weeks and is throwing up every morning."

"Ah, the dreaded morning sickness. Leyna may be able to help her with some remedies. But great news, so you will have a summer baby."

"Yes, a baby of the new century, the year 2300."

"The year of space exploration like no other, we hope."

They continue talking about their hopes for the future and how both wish to have more children. Galexia has asked for a little sister

Eween tells Breex, but Leyna wants to see the launch of the project before she thinks about pregnancy again.

"After seeing Marzeen and what she is going through so soon into the pregnancy, I don't blame Leyna. Her job as Madame President is not conducive to motherhood."

"True. Leyna seems to be handling it well and having nannies does help. I do hope to be a father again, Galexia is such a joy when she is in a good mood. The love I feel for her is all enveloping, she is everything to me."

"I'll know all about that next year. Now, we had better get back or they'll send a search party out for us," laughs Breex.

As they are walking back, a woman bumps into Eween. His security people run up when she says, "Calm down, my mistake. My apologies, Minister, I was not watching where I was going."

Eween tells security to back down and he falls into pace with Breex again.

Donnelle is in his office discussing her ideas about the mental health program she wants to implement for astronauts. Eween listens as she presents the proposal to him. "I understand what it is you want to do, Donnelle, but we need to discuss this with Leyna. Also, the financing of it all."

"The financials are at the back of the proposal. Of course, Eween, discuss this with as many people in cabinet as you need. I understand funds are tight with the project and do hope it will go ahead."

"We are yet to hear from Dilvant and his ministers, and it is frustrating, but I think this is all part of his tactics. He wants to unnerve us. I'm sorry I didn't catch up with you at the dinner, did you enjoy the evening?"

"Yes, of course. You had many other people to deal with, Eween. I attended as support and was happy to remain in the background. I must say, it was intimidating seeing the High... err, Dilvant up close. He is not as tall as I imagined, and fashion is his forte."

"Yes, he has an air of class about him, which belies who he really is. This has made many women fall into his trap. His latest is Felida, the sister of the deceased ruler of Crete."

"I heard, and the rumours I hear are that he has another son."

"Yes, Quinan Jnr. He was born with a deformed foot, the poor little mite. Although, I am sure he will receive the best of care."

"Well, I've taken up more of your time than I intended. Thank you, I must be going now," she says, rising from the chair, "I will leave all the information with you."

"It was nice to see you, and this proposal has merit. We will let you know whether it will go ahead as soon as funds are confirmed."

After Donnelle leaves, he decides to take the proposal straight to Leyna; she will be interested to see what Donnelle has proposed. With so many astronauts going into space for long stretches of time, they will need to be rehabilitated once back on Earth. With someone like Donnelle looking after them, they are sure to recover well. "Hello my sweet, I have something interesting you may like to see."

"Hi there. Great, I've had enough of looking over these financials. What have you got for me?"

He proceeds to lay out Donnelle's proposal on the office table and tells her about what he thinks. He gives her a few minutes to take in the information and then asks, "Well, what do you think?"

"It has merit, but again it needs money thrown at it. Dilvant is taking his time, isn't he?"

"We know this is how he works, but I think he will come through."

Eween shows her the rest of the proposal and then they sit down to talk over things in general. "Oh, by the way, I have some good news. Marzeen is pregnant."

"Really, that's fantastic."

"Breex told me over coffee, we escaped and caught a few sun rays at a café. He is excited but it means they may not have a winter holiday, Marzeen has morning sickness."

"Oh, I feel for her. I'll call her later and congratulate her. Then I'll commiserate with her too."

"And the baby will be born in the new century, that's exciting too."

"Yes, that is exciting. They're going to be first time parents and they have no idea how their lives will change." They both laugh as Eween heads back to his office.

Chapter 22

Dilvant

Seated in the parliamentary meeting room, Dilvant and his ministers have smug looks on their faces, the look of men who are satisfied with their decision. Leyna and Eween are also seated with Breex and Nable by their side.

"We have deliberated amongst ourselves and with our colleagues in our own parliament in Crete. Personally, I am willing to put any bad blood behind us because as a new father I wish for my son to grow up in a world conducive to prosperity and accord. With this we agree to join your Universal Space Project with the proviso that Quinan's name is added. I propose once everything is finalised, it be named *The Universal Quinan Space Project*, as I want his legacy to go on." Dilvant's smugness is now palatable.

He notices the faces of his four enemies remain impassive. Maybe he should not consider them enemies any longer, but that bad blood runs deep, he will never forget what they did to him. Having lost his family, his leadership and his dignity, Dilvant is only agreeing to this union because it serves a purpose for him. The sooner he finds a planet to colonise with his followers, the sooner he can exact his revenge. This time there will be no coming back for Leyna, Eween, Dawa and Zenac; the famous four will be no more.

"Well, this certainly is an exceptional day. We will have to discuss amongst ourselves regarding the name change, but essentially we accept that you wish to join forces with us," says Leyna still with an impassive look on her face.

Eween stands and extends his hand to the three of them, "Welcome aboard, gentlemen. We trust this will be a new era of not only space exploration but also one of peace and trust among all humans."

They all stand and exchange handshakes. Leyna calls her assistant to bring in the paperwork and they prepare to sign the necessary documents to seal the deal. As her assistant is laying out the papers, Dilvant gives her a smile, indicating she is doing a good job. He will talk to her before they leave.

Breex suggests they open a bottle of champagne but Dilvant and his ministers decline saying they need to return to the hotel and prepare to go to the airport. They are keen to return to their families. This is understood by everyone and once all the signatures are complete, this extraordinary meeting is closed.

She walks into the hotel room. Dilvant admires this young spy, her golden red curls, and her green eyes. With her quiet demeanour she has managed to secure the trust of Madame President and her ministers, something Dilvant had not expected of one so young. But she had insisted she would prove her worth, and she has.

"Sire, I am pleased to have been of service. I look forward to further instructions."

"For now, continue as you have been. Once I return to Crete and settle into this new norm, I will send you your orders. It is strange to be in bed with my enemies, but I have bigger plans for them."

"I look forward to being a part of your grand plan. It was obvious to me you would want more from this arrangement."

"The reason I called you here is I wanted to privately thank you for your service. Please take this as appreciation for your work," he says handing her an envelope.

She opens it and gasps when she sees the glistening, gold card.

"You are... Sire, you are giving me a gold credit card, this is very generous..."

"And for the first year you will be compensated because I will be paying your bills. Consider it a gift for being a loyal subject."

"My parents were loyal to you when they were alive, I am continuing in their legacy. I am honoured you think highly of me and my work. I will not disappoint you, no matter what assignment you send my way."

Dilvant walks over to where she is seated and places his hands on her shoulders, kissing both her cheeks. "It is people such as you who give me the reasons to keep our cause going. My vision of power to a few with everyone else doing our bidding will happen once more. The Enforcers will return and be twice as powerful as before."

With his hands still on her shoulders, she stands and kisses him back on both cheeks. Then she tucks the gift into her jacket pocket, "I look forward to the day you rule once more."

"Not much longer to wait, you will see. Now, I have to organise myself to return home. See yourself out and enjoy spoiling yourself, you deserve it."

She leaves with a huge smile on her face, and once again, he is happy to have done a good deed. He is surprised at how satisfying it is to help people who are loyal to him, his followers will never defy his cause. The ones closest to him will always benefit from his generosity.

Quinan Jnr gives him a gummy smile as he picks him up from his crib. "How I missed you," Dilvant says, kissing his chubby cheeks. As he turns to Felida, he kisses her as well. "And you, too."

"Dilvant, you were only away for three days, I doubt Quinan Jnr even noticed you were gone."

They both laugh as they make themselves comfortable on the

balcony. It is late afternoon with the sea still a shade of blue and as still as ice. Dilvant had missed this view as well.

"So, what happens now?"

"We are in bed with my enemies. I have earned their trust, we will collaborate and make both space projects one great success."

"It amazes me you are being so glib about this, what is your agenda?"

"Felida, why are you asking such a question? I want to lead again, remember? By having their trust, I will be able to take over with them not suspecting anything untoward."

"I understand that, but how are you going to lead? The people of Crete are used to a certain lifestyle, they will not allow you to go back to how you led before."

"Have faith in me Felida, I will lead my people as a true leader," he says kissing and tickling Quinan Jnr who laughs with glee. Felida looks at him with a look of distrust, which he ignores. She will not dictate to him what type of leader he will be. Besides, he will always look after those he loves, and she and Quinan Jnr will always be cared for.

He locks his office door as his ministers walk in. It is time for their secret talks.

"Settle yourselves, gentlemen. A drink before we start?"

They both ask for a scotch. Dilvant pours three glasses and places them on the table between them along with the bottle. He proceeds to tell them that once the GIS announces the date of the launch of the high-power rockets, he will send two of their brightest astronauts into space as soon as the announcement is made. "They will probably announce a date a few weeks before launch, and I want to beat everyone to finding a planet."

"I do hope it is not too difficult to find one similar to Earth. Has there been any research to date?"

"Yes, two scientists were employed by me for this purpose alone. Since I implemented the Quinan Space Project, they have been working on the best way to explore space." He places his hand on his compupad, "you will soon see the results of their research, but first I need you both to sign disclosure statements, this is top secret and if word of what we are doing happens to escape this room, I will kill you both."

Both ministers quiver at his directness.

Dilvant continues by placing the documents in front of them, "Please take your time to read through and then sign where indicated. Please do not be fearful, you are safe as long as you disclose none of what we speak of today." The two men seem to visibly relax as they both read what is expected of them.

Relaxing back into his chair, Dilvant downs the scotch and pours himself another one as the two men read. He had chosen these two, the transport minister and finance minister, as his trusted allies. He has outlined every detail of what he expects of them and once they finish reading, they will have no doubt of what needs to be done. Dilvant added extra security to these documents by typing them himself, this plan is not to fail and the less people who know about it, the better.

They finish reading the documents, sign them and hand them back to Dilvant. He will store them in the fireproof safe later. "Now, gentlemen, sit back and observe the brilliance of my plan that I have orchestrated with the help of the research findings of the two scientists."

He powers up the hologram and within minutes the eyes of both his ministers watch in awe. They see how he plans to colonise a planet and then set up an army to capture the other colonies, including Earth. He will be the ultimate ruler of the known Universe and his followers will be rewarded. By the look on their faces, Dilvant knows he has them in the palm of his hands.

Chapter 23

Dawa

She is holding him with tears pouring down her face. His shoulder is wet with them. Zenac has returned without Teegue and Dawa is devastated. The minute he walked off the Salverz she knew. Her body is wracked with sadness and despair, how can this be happening?

"Dawa, we found his rocket but there was no sign of him. There were no signs of any struggle and all his equipment and suits were gone. We can still investigate the planets near where we found his rocket, he may have somehow survived on one of them."

Her eyes turn to look at his face, which is full of despair as well. "You're going back to look for him? This isn't the end of the search?"

"I'm not prepared to give up yet. We have come back to restock and make repairs to the Salverz. Please have faith, we both have to believe Teegue is still alive."

Looking into his eyes she sees them glisten with unshed tears, "I have to believe that and this time I will come with you."

Zenac nods, "You may be the good luck charm we need."

They turn and walk together to their waiting car. "Aria and Braxton are waiting for us at home, we'll need to break the news with care."

"I've missed them Dawa, this is another reason we came home, we were all missing our loved ones."

The children were as devastated as Dawa when Zenac told them the news. Aria and Braxton remained silent for a few minutes after being told and then hugged their parents. The four of them held onto each other and cried for what seemed hours. When they eventually came apart, Zenac told them of his plan to return.

"We're coming with you," they said in unison.

"At this stage we don't even know whether your mother is able to come along, but in all fairness, you two need to stay home and keep your lives as normal as possible."

"We worry as much as you do, Dad," says Aria with her pleading eyes.

Zenac tries to appease them as Dawa heads towards her room, she suddenly needs to be on her own. She plonks on her bed with her head in her hands as she lets out a muffled scream. On her bedside table are photos of all of them and three framed photos of the children as babies. She picks up the one of Teegue and clutches it close to her heart. "You are out there, aren't you? Please help us to find you, send us a signal." She lays down still holding the photo to her chest. Even though it is only the middle of the day, she sleeps.

He is in front of her. She reaches out to him and her hand moves through him. "Teegue, what is happening?" He doesn't answer. She moves closer and he disappears. "Nooooo, Teegue, please come back." She feels a hand on her shoulder. Her eyes open.

"Dawa, you were screaming. Bad dream?"

Struggling to wake, Zenac comes into focus, "Umm, yes I guess so. Teegue was in front of me but my hand went right through him. When I came closer, he disappeared. Wha... what time is it?" she says, stifling a yawn.

"It's four, you've been asleep for hours. We didn't want to disturb you, but your scream shattered the silence in the house."

"It felt real, Zenac. But..."

"Dawa, don't torture yourself, we will find him. Now, we need to keep things as normal as possible for Aria and Braxton. Let's take them out for a burger, it will take our minds off this for a little while." She nods and accepts his invitation to help her into the shower. Even though she is walking into the bathroom, her body feels like it has remained lying on the bed. The act of walking is too much for her, all she thinks about it going back into that dream. There her son is real, or at least as real as a dream can be.

Zenac's idea of going out for dinner did relieve the tension for the time they were out, but when they arrived home, the house felt as empty as it had for the weeks since Teegue's disappearance. Dawa took herself to their bedroom saying good night in a whisper. She heard Zenac asking the children to go to bed as well, he wanted to stay up a little longer. She was happy for him not to follow her because she wanted to be alone again.

The days following are a blur of crying, arguing and despair for the four of them. Dawa went to work, as did Zenac, but she found she could not concentrate for a whole day. She came home to the sanctuary of her bedroom every day and dreamt of Teegue. After two weeks of this, Zenac asks her to talk to him.

"I'm worried about you, Dawa. This can't go on. You need to stay strong."

"Why?" she screams, "what for? I miss him with all my being, what is the point of me staying strong? Will that bring Teegue back?"

"Please calm down, screaming isn't helping. Look, why don't you go and speak to someone, or at the very least, start a yoga class or maybe meditation."

She looks at him and knows he is concerned, but this is worse than when Teegue and Aria were kidnapped. They had a chance of finding them back then, no one knows where Teegue is, or if he's even alive. This thought makes her break down again.

"Dawa," he says hugging her to him, "this is difficult but as I said when I arrived home, we have to have faith he is alive. You are spiralling into depression and it isn't helping any of us."

She knows he is right. This is a situation no parent would ever want to face, the loss of a child, and Teegue is still a child to her, he is barely in his twenties. "I'll look into yoga or meditation, give me time to grieve first."

He turns to walk out of their bedroom but not before she sees his face contorted with concern. This is different for him, he is looking at going out again and finding their son, he has this to focus on. What is her focus? All she can think of is that they may never see Teegue again. The heaviness of this thought makes her body crumble as she lays on the bed in a foetal-like state.

"Mum, where are you?"

She can hear Braxton calling for her, she hasn't moved in over an hour. Rising she pulls her hair back, takes a deep breath and says, "Coming." She doesn't want him seeing her like this, so she goes into the bathroom, brushes her hair and washes her face.

"There you are. I saw your car parked outside, I thought you'd be at work."

"I was but came home because of a headache, what did you want?" She could see by his face he didn't believe her excuse, but he doesn't mention it.

"Nothing really, just making sure you're okay. Can I go to my friend's place? He has a new video game we want to try."

"Yes, of course. Ask our driver to take you if you like."

"No need, I'm going to Krosy's place, he's only two streets away." She is taken aback that he is friends with someone who was the school bully and wants to ask how? Why? Deciding not to interfere, she is happy her youngest child is smart enough to know people grow up. This small act gives her a glimmer of hope as a semblance of a smile breaks her tortured look.

"Great, thanks Mum. I'll be back for dinner."

She watches as he strides off. What an ordinary, everyday thing to be doing. Her son is going to be with a friend. When was the last time she spent time with her friends? The ones who have contacted her since finding out about Teegue, the ones who want to help but don't know how. She wonders when she will feel like doing something as ordinary as seeing her friends again.

The days turn into months. Zenac has not left yet because he has been helping Leyna and Eween finalising the treaty with Dilvant. The thought of them dealing with that deviant terrifies her, but she doesn't have the strength to argue nor the inclination. She must trust that they know what they are doing.

She had finally taken Zenac's advice and found an outlet for her depression. It was not yoga or meditation; instead she found solace in painting. Her watercolours of objects around her – flowers, trees and landscapes – are what keep her sane. When she is in the painting zone, everything else disappears. The darkness that befalls her is always that little bit lighter when she paints.

Also, she started seeing her friends again, for coffee and chats. All she could handle were small amounts of time with them before she needed to be by herself again. Everyone, including Zenac, had accepted this.

As the months became a year, the pain of not seeing her son was no less, but she hoped that Zenac's trip to find him would bring him home. Zenac had finally set a date for another rescue mission, a year to the day Teegue went missing.

Chapter 24

Eween

He is walking to his gym locker when a woman sidles up to him. "I'm wanting to wish you luck, Minister."

"Umm, okay. Thank you, I guess. Who are you?" He looks around wondering what she is doing in the men's locker room.

She places her hand on his shoulder looking where his arm should be. "It's awful that this happened to you. Many people were maimed during the scuffle to rid us of that scourge, Dilvant." She jumps up and kisses his cheek and manages to take a photo.

"What the hell. Did you take a photo? Delete it immediately."

"My name is Respil and I want a memory of you. Please don't make me delete it."

"I don't know who you are or why you want a photo of kissing me, but I insist you delete it. Now, I have much to do." He walks away from her and washes his face. He has taken up playing indoor soccer socially, mainly to keep up his fitness but also to ease the stress of their life. Being the partner of Madame President has its perks sure, but the tension is beginning to show. He has been especially worried since receiving that message from some woman, it had rattled him. And now, here she is.

"Get out of the men's locker room. And leave me alone or I will call security."

"Oh, the nice man who was standing out the front? He was called away and he won't be back because of a personal issue."

"You bitch, what the hell do you want?"

"I want to be your friend."

He grabs her arm, and she looks down at where his hand is tightening, "Bruise me and I'll go to the police. How will that look?"

Eween let's go and walks out of the room to join his team. He plays with the fury inside him. She watches from the sideline taking photos. After the game, he contemplates telling security about the situation, but decides to leave it until she becomes a real problem. He will need evidence that she is the one causing issues.

Arriving home, Galexia runs up to him, "Daddy, look what I did," she says, swinging a large piece of art board around. When she finally stops swinging it he sees it's a painting of what he thinks is something prehistoric. "Wow, what is that animal?"

"It's a prehisteric bird. I painted it today."

Leyna walks in and kisses him, "Prehistoric," she laughs, "she's been waiting for you to come home so she could show it to you. Now, come on Galexia, time for bed."

He smiles. This is his real life, and he will do everything to protect it. Whatever this Respil woman is trying to do, he won't allow it to happen.

He is heating up some food when Leyna walks into the kitchen. She pours herself a wine and offers him one. He nods and they sit at the bench.

"You okay?"

"Tired. It was a good match, though. I'm glad I started soccer, and no one even asks about my arm now. Although, they say I have an advantage over them with handball."

"Well, you do," she smiles, "it's good you have an outlet. Things are crazy right now."

They discuss the current situation with Dilvant and his agreeing to join them. Eween knows it is not ideal and they have made a deal with the devil, but hopes between the four of them, they can keep him under control. Leyna tells him about her day and how many of the ministers are expressing concern with this agreement. "But no one is coming forward with a better solution, and I told them until someone does, this is the way forward."

Eween nods. He rises from the stool and places his plate in the sink. "Listen, I'm beat and headed for a shower then bed."

"I'll join you in bed soon, I have a few loose ends to deal with first."

Leaving her to it, he heads to their bedroom. After his shower, he lies down and opens his compupad. There is another message from Respil. This time it's a photo of him missing the ball at tonight's game. She captioned it, 'Minister Eween is off his game' and then added two 'xx' with a lip emoji. Slamming down the lid of his compupad, he throws it to the floor. Then, thinking twice, he steps out of bed and collects it, placing it on his bedside table. Leyna would think it weird to find it on the floor.

The following evening Eween has a drinks night with his team. They meet at a local bar once a month to discuss strategy and have a social drink. He enjoys these evenings, they help him relax as much as playing indoor soccer does. After a few hours of drinking, he needs the bathroom. As he walks towards it, she is standing in front of the door. "Move."

"You're not happy to see me?"

He makes a move to enter the men's room without answering. Having had a lot to drink he sways and misses the door.

"Here, let me help," she says, opening the door.

Walking in, he avoids looking at her. This woman is thirty-something and not unattractive. Had he been single, he may have had a fling with her. But right now, she is a nuisance.

He is at the sink washing his hands when she walks in. Before he can move, she is forcing herself onto him. Someone behind them clicks a camera. He hears the shutter click several times.

With as much force as he can muster with one arm, he pushes her off him. "Get away from me you bitch."

She runs out of the bathroom laughing with the other girl. He begins to chase after them, but they are out of the bar before he can reach them.

"Eween, what the hell? Who were those girls?" asks one of his teammates.

"No one, just a couple of troublemakers. I'm done here guys, see you all next week."

His teammates say their goodbyes as Eween heads outside to hail a cab.

The next morning the photo is being circulated by all of Earth's media.

Chapter 25

Zenac

With the space program about to be launched, Zenac had received information from Leyna and Eween that the name will remain the same - International Space Program. It will have a SubName of 'Featuring Quinan High-Powered Rockets'. Dilvant had agreed to this somewhat reluctantly then saw it as an honour to his friend because the manufacture of high-powered rockets was their idea, an idea he discussed with Quinan before he died.

They were all waiting in the hangar. Zenac had procured one of Dilvant's powerful rockets, the fastest rockets ever made, and they were admiring it. He hears whispers of admiration within his crew and he too is amazed at what they have been able to achieve. They may be in bed with a madman, but joining forces had not been as stupid (or dangerous) as it first seemed.

There is a small crowd waiting for them to launch when he returns to the launch pad. It's mainly the crew's family and his family are at the front with Dawa looking solemn and dispossessed as always. How he wants to please her. With all his heart he hopes to find Teegue because watching his wife wither away into her dark world is terrifying. He himself has his own struggles, but he is doing his best to keep up appearances. He has a duty to his people to uphold his status as a leader. Dawa has too, but she has cast this aside to grieve for her son.

"Thank you all for coming today even though it is a solemn occasion. I say *solemn* with hesitancy because there is always hope, hope that Teegue will be found." He stops as there is intermittent clapping then continues, "With this amazing new rocket, which travels at fifteen miles per second, we will shorten our time in space. I will have your loved ones back before they are even missed." Again, he stops as there is laughter and more applause.

"Just come back safe and with your son," comes a shout from the back of the crowd.

"I intend to and thanks for your concern. Now, we bid you farewell," he says as he turns towards the rocket with his crew following.

Zaydin and Amallin are on their consoles ready for their instructions. Taaz and the Mechanic are seated and strapped in. The other crew members are strapped into their seats in their section, everyone is ready and waiting for Zenac. He turns to his console and gives the order, "Let's go and find my son."

"Sir, there is a signal and it's strong. It's coming from this planet, unnamed but within ten thousand light years from us."

Zenac moves over to Zaydin after checking his own screen. "Yes, I saw it too. Set coordinates to head towards it. The signal should become stronger." Zaydin acknowledges him and resets the coordinates.

"Taaz, Mechanic, follow me," says Zenac.

As they walk into the meeting room, Zenac closes the door behind them. He offers them both a drink, but they decline. He pours himself a scotch into the drinking pouch then turns to speak to them, "Please sit, this is a briefing about what I expect of you both should we find something hostile when we land."

"We assumed this is why you brought us along," says Taaz.

"No one has ever journeyed this far into the universe, this high-powered rocket is allowing us to break barriers and explore more than we've ever been able. What we don't know is what dangers lie in front of us. Security personnel will be needed more than ever, so I want the two of you to head a recruitment drive to train a super security taskforce."

"I will be glad to, Zenac, as I'm sure Mechanic will too," says Taaz. The Mechanic nods his head in agreement.

"We all know Dilvant is not trustworthy even though he has helped us thus far. I, actually we, that is, Dawa and myself, want to be prepared should Dilvant revert to his old ways." Zenac makes it clear that Dawa is still a part of his leadership team even though it may not seem like it right now.

"This planet will give us an idea of how many recruits will be needed."

"Yes Taaz, and we can always recruit every few years depending on what happens. Now, if there is antagonism towards us when we land, I need you two to take all the soldiers on this rocket and protect it. If my son is being held prisoner, then we need soldiers to rescue him." His voice chokes in his throat so he sips deeply on the pouch.

"We understand, Zenac and we won't let you down."

"I know, now please go and brief your soldiers."

Taaz and the Mechanic turn and walk out. Zenac has faith in their abilities, what he doesn't have faith in is what they will find on this planet. Is the signal coming from Teegue?

He places the pouch down and sits. With his elbows on his knees, he cups his hands under his chin. They have been away from Arisis for three weeks and he worries about Dawa every minute he is absent. His mind is full of scenarios of what they might find, but the one he wants to hang onto is the one where Teegue is safe and they will be able to bring him home.

He returns to the communications console and as he enters Zaydin and Amallin are arguing. "Hey, what's going on? Zaydin, take your hands off Amallin." Zaydin had her hands around Amallin's neck in a choke hold. "Are you two crazy?"

"She insulted my family," spits out Zaydin.

"You called me a hick because I'm from midwest America."

"You're both acting like children, we have an important job to do. Now, how close are we Zaydin?"

Their faces redden with humiliation as they turn to their consoles. Zaydin brings up the coordinates and reports, "My estimation is we have two more days of travel. The signal is coming from the plaque recorder from Teegue's rocket. It's likely to be from him."

"Finally, some good news. Both of you research the planet. Find out if there are any lifeforms, what the atmosphere is like... anything that will help us when we land. And both of you keep your personal feelings away from this mission. Leave your issues for when we arrive home."

"Absolutely, sir," they reply in unison.

They all walk down the cargo plank with full space suits as Zaydin and Amallin had found that the hydrogen levels on this planet are high, so they had recommended wearing the suits for their protection.

Zenac looks around. The planet resembles the surface of the moon, desolate and bland. There are pockets of scrub-like plants with thorns and tortured branches. The temperature is fifteen degrees Celsius, and the sky has a brown tinge around the horizon. They are armed as they walk around looking for where the signal is coming from.

Taaz and Mechanic, along with their soldiers, walk ahead scouting for any danger. After three hours they find nothing. Zenac tells them to take a break, he needs to think. As he walks towards the spaceship, he sees Zaydin and Amallin in an embrace. Shaking his head, he can't understand these two, one minute they are fighting, the next they are lovers. He smiles as he is happy they have worked things out. He hopes this relationship has longevity because they are both good at their job and he doesn't want to lose either of them.

After an hour's break, he summons them again. "Time to begin our hunt again, let's go."

"It's down there."

"What is Zaydin?"

"The signal is coming from down there. Look, isn't that a tunnel?"

They gather their things and head towards it. When they arrive they find it is a tunnel. Actually, it's a cave that's been fashioned into a tunnel. The entrance is lined with what looks like steel and a name is carved into one panel. 'Welcome to Granada.'

Zenac lets out a gasp, "Granada as in Spain? Could there be survivors here?"

They enter and walk down the cobbled path. Bright tiles line parts of the walls and lights are fixed to some of them. As they walk deeper into the tunnel, the lights are more frequent, and the temperature rises.

"Zenac, my readings show there is oxygen down here, we should be able to remove our helmets."

With this, they all remove them and keep walking.

Two robots greet them at the end and stop them from entering. A massive steel door is behind them. The robots, both at least eight feet, tower over them. Nothing happens for some time, they all stand there looking at each other.

"We are not here to harm anyone. I am looking for my son, Teegue. Are you able to help us find him?"

There is no reaction from the robots, but a small lock being unlatched is heard. Then a small flap is lifted. Minutes later the door opens with a screech of metal on metal. They lift their hands to their ears trying to muffle the sound.

"Sorry about that, this door doesn't get opened often. Welcome strangers," says an elderly man with a slight Spanish accent. "Please come in."

They walk into a paradise of trees, babbling brooks and squawking birds – all artificially lit. Their heads turn to look around, the smell is fresh with a hint of cedar.

"My name is Zenac and this is my crew. We have come from Arisis but originally we are from Earth."

"I am Elvardo, I will take you to our King."

They remain quiet as they follow the stooped man, who should be walking with a walking stick. Instead, he is using his left hand moving it backwards and forwards with every step, this is keeping him in balance.

Arriving at an opening, in front of them is a row of small terraces with a double storey one in the middle. Elvardo turns to them, "Please wait here. I will return once I know the King is available."

"How far down do you think we are? This place is tropical, nothing like the surface."

"Don't know Taaz, but I think I prefer it down here. Even the artificial light is soft and welcoming."

"The King will see you now," shouts Elvardo who is standing at the entrance of the double storey terrace.

Chapter 26

Eween

Two months after the offending photo, Eween is in the courtroom. Respil and her accomplice have been brought to trial for harassment, bribery and offensive behaviour against him. The past two months have been hell for him and Leyna.

He thinks about the last time he had seen this bitch. It had been at the end of the meeting when Dilvant had agreed to join forces with them. Eween had asked Leyna to wait as he had to go to the bathroom. As he walked towards it, he felt someone was following him. When he turned, there was no one there.

As he came out of the bathroom, she was waiting for him. "Another photo, Minister?"

He glared at her but decided to ignore her. Walking back towards where Leyna was sitting, Respil taps his shoulder. "What? What is it you want?"

"I think highly of you, that's all. Please, let's be friends."

"Thanks, but I have enough friends. Now, if you don't stop, I will call security."

"Let me take another photo and I will stop."

"Sure, so you can blackmail me again? Do you think I'm stupid? Now, leave me or I will call security." He turns and is about to shout...

"I'm going, it's fine," she says brushing her hand on his face, "no need to be so unfriendly."

Now, Respil, along with her accomplice, is being tried and will be sent to jail, he will make sure of it.

When the photo of the two of them in the men's room had surfaced, the shame it brought with it was immense. He had to explain to Leyna he was being set up. She had wanted to believe him, but then when the other photos were also published, she found it hard to believe him. They fought and Galexia heard many of their arguments. This had broken his heart; he was losing both his girls.

"What were you thinking?" Leyna had yelled at him.

"She was pursuing me. You have to believe me Leyna, and I have no idea why she is targeting me."

"To ruin you, of course. And take me along with you."

"There is someone behind this, I'm sure. She is not working alone. Her face is familiar. I know I've seen her before."

Leyna had wanted to throw him out. She was embarrassed by his behaviour and both their reputations were on the line. The two months of hell felt like a lifetime and he had to prove his innocence.

During the two months before the trial, Eween tried to remember where he had seen her before. The detectives looking after the case had told him she was hired by Dilvant when he was the High Priest. She worked as a prostitute keeping him and The Enforcers happy. Then it clicked, he had seen her at Dilvant's mansion. The judge would not look favourable on the fact she sold herself for a living, this will be his trump card.

In the end, two of his teammates had recognised Respil as the girl who watched their indoor soccer games. One of them had seen her go into the men's locker room when Eween was in there. Both girls were jailed for five years.

His solicitor congratulated him as they walked out of the court building. Eween thanked him for his service and walked over to where his two teammates were standing. "You two are the best, thanks for having my back." They both told him they couldn't watch his life being trashed and were glad to help.

He walked into his home. It was quiet, Leyna was still at work and Galexia would not be home until Leyna picked her up. He grabbed a scotch bottle and poured himself a double shot. After the girls were convicted, a weight was released from his shoulders, but the issues this situation had caused with his relationship with Leyna would take some time to fix. This was his mission, he would do everything in his power to regain her trust, especially because he didn't do anything wrong.

Chapter 27

Leyna

Her relationship with Eween was slowly being repaired. They both knew Dilvant had asked Respil to compromise Eween, and this made it all the sweeter that they were still together. It was obvious Dilvant had wanted to do some damage but had not succeeded. Eween is with her as the announcement is being made.

Wilkern and Sayen are both at the podium. St Peter's square is at capacity with citizens as well as dignitaries from countries around the world.

"We are proud to announce the official launch date of the *International Space Program* to be the 1st of May 2300. The featured program of high-powered rockets will be named, *The Quinan High-Powered Rockets Project*. This space exploration initiative will bring our world closer together with the technology required being manufactured by various countries, bringing us together in one common goal – that of finding suitable planets for humans to live and prosper."

Loud applause explodes throughout the crowd. High pitched whistles and cheers echo through the square. After all the speeches and accolades are done, the dignitaries are escorted into The Vatican ballroom for a celebratory cocktail function.

Dilvant is flanked by his ministers, five of them this time, as Leyna and Eween welcome them in. "Zenac, Dawa, they are not present?"

"Zenac is still searching for his son," informs Leyna, not wishing to give anything further away. She does not want Dilvant to think there is something wrong with their alliance.

"I am sorry to have missed them. Please send Zenac my heartfelt wishes for a successful search."

She cringes inwardly at his insincerity but keeps the smile on her face.

Once all the dignitaries have been welcomed, she and Eween walk to where Breex and Marzeen are standing. Taking a champagne from the offered tray Leyna says, "Marzeen you look radiant."

"Ha, you're being kind. I'm the size of a rhino."

They all laugh and Leyna can see Marzeen is struggling with the extra weight, her legs are twice their normal size. As much as she loves her daughter, seeing her friend struggle is a reason not to fall pregnant again.

She falls into a relaxed chat with many of the dignitaries, they come and go with amicable friendships being forged even stronger. The hype with which they built up this space project has lived up to its name, there was every possibility that planets will be found, or, at least, one that will be suitable for colonisation. The high-powered rockets are being tested and the results are promising. Each rocket has the name Quinan with a number after it. There are twenty in the first production with Quinan-1 already purchased by Zenac.

Her thoughts turn to him and Dawa. She knows Dawa is struggling and had turned down the invitation to come to this announcement ceremony for medical reasons. Leyna has contacted Dawa on many occasions in the past year and has watched her age with each conversation. Her resolve has been hit hard, losing her son to the unknown must be unbearable. The last conversation they had was after Zenac left on Quinan-1. She spoke of her hopes that Teegue will come home this time. Leyna had seen a light in her eyes, a glimmer of hope, for the first time since the disappearance.

Dilvant is in front of her taking her out of her reverie. "Madame President and Eween, may I say how proud I am to be involved in this project. The Quinan rockets are testing well and from what I have gathered tonight, Zenac has had no issues with Quinan-1."

Eween speaks as he can feel Leyna tensing up, "It is a successful project, one our citizens are fully behind and impressed with the progress. The rockets seem to be working as expected. We shall see once they start going out on missions. Our astronauts are ready and waiting to launch."

Leyna is grateful that Eween stepped in because she would have said something about Respil had she answered Dilvant.

Dilvant accepts a drink and a hors d'oeuvre from the attendant. "We have all placed much emphasis on this project, so for this reason it will not fail. The citizens of Earth deserve to have the security of another planet, or two, while this one is still recovering from climate change. I am abhorred that there were so many deniers in our past."

"The GIS have it all in hand, climate change is something that will never happen again," says Eween.

"Of this I have been assured by your colleagues at the GIS. We trust what they say is true."

"We have no reason to believe it isn't. They work hard to maintain the integrity of emissions and keep companies accountable."

"This is good to hear. Now, I bid you all goodnight, I must go and check on my family."

They all watch as he and his henchmen leave.

"*We trust what they say is true.* I was ready to punch him when he said that. He hasn't changed, I'm telling you we have to keep a close watch on him."

"We know, Breex. But this is something we don't need to worry about right now, how about another drink?"

"I'm with Breex on this one, Dilvant makes me nervous every time I see him," says Fixor.

"We'll not let our guard down. Thanks for the offer of another drink Eween, but we had better make tracks too. Marzeen is tired and we still have lots of work to go through on Monday."

Eween nods in agreement as Leyna smiles and gives Breex and Marzeen a kiss goodbye, "Look after yourself Marzeen and call me if you need anything."

"Will do, thanks. Come on Breex before I collapse."

Closing her compupad having briefed Dawa on the events of the day, she turns to Eween who is reading. "He is a dick, isn't he?"

"Dilvant? Yes, of course," says Eween in a mocking tone, "he thinks the world owes him a living and he will never bow down to the likes of us or Dawa and Zenac."

She kisses his cheek, "Goodnight, my love." Rolling over and plumping her pillow she thinks about how far they have come. Once fugitives they now rule The Vatican with much of the world as their allies. They have enough power that Dilvant had wanted to destroy Eween with a former prostitute taking compromising photos of him. Their success has come from treating humans with respect and showing them what a real leader can do. Dilvant's attempt to ruin this was a mere blip. The space project will bring further unison to a world that was once so fractured it almost destroyed itself. Now, with the GIS and their alliance with Dawa and Zenac, the future for all humans is looking bright. She drifts off to sleep with a sense of achievement because the children of today will inherit a better future.

Chapter 28

Dilvant

He walks around it. His ministers follow him, their mouths agape. This rocket is twice the size of the Quinan ones being built; it has a capacity of taking a thousand people at a time.

"It is our turn to rescue humans. With this rocket, Quinan-Gold, I will colonise a new planet in my own indomitable way. My close followers will rejoice in being the chosen ones to help me rule. The Enforcers shall be selected once more, and we will make the life of the famous four leaders miserable."

The rocket is housed in a secret tunnel outside the walls of the cemetery. Dilvant has picked this spot as he felt close to Quinan here. No one other than the three of them know of its whereabouts, and even then, he takes a different route each time he brings them with him. He is taking every precaution that they don't tell anyone what he has planned. So far, they have been loyal to him.

"Have you set a date for launch?"

"Yes, I have. As you know, the launch of the International Space Project has been set for 1st May, I intend to launch Quinan-Gold with a select few onboard two weeks earlier. This rocket has a force field that is impenetrable, it will not be detected on any radar. I will personally select the people coming with me, then you will follow with others including Felida and Quinan Jrn," he points to the finance minister. "Then, it will be your turn to bring more with you next," he indicates to the transport minister, "and between the three of us, we will colonise and lead this new planet."

His two ministers beam from ear to ear. They love to hear that they will be leaders of a whole planet, not just an island in the Mediterranean. "Now let us return to parliament where I will summon the few who will join us on this flight."

Quinan Jnr toddles over to his father. Dilvant scoops him up and smothers him with kisses, "What has my big boy been doing today?"

Felida smiles as she gives Dilvant a kiss, "He's been busy doing his exercises after his operation, the one you missed because you were at The Vatican."

He notices the tone of scorn in her voice but chooses to ignore it, "Yes, that was unfortunate timing. But I'm home now and am happy for lots of cuddles," he laughs pretending to chase Quinan Jnr who hobbles around on his knees, his leg dragging behind him. The strength will come Dilvant tells himself, they are spending a lot of money making sure his legs will be the same length once he stops growing.

He watches as Felida takes him to have a bath and his heart explodes with love. *Thadd you haven't been replaced, he is you in another form.* He looks around as if Thadd is in the room and brushes a tear from his eye.

Felida returns in an hour to find Dilvant on their bed. "He's finally asleep."

"That's good. Come here my love, I've missed you." She falls on top of him, he is naked and has been waiting for her. "I have something to tell you."

He proceeds to tell her about the Quinan-Gold rocket and his plan to colonise another planet. How he will rule in the old ways and make this new planet an ode to his teachings.

"Well...that is amazing," she says, clearing her throat.

"You doubt my ability?"

"No, of course not. It's, wow...it's a lot to take in. I had no idea, I thought you were happy to have an alliance with the rest of the world."

"A world that betrayed me? No, I will show them all, and especially the famous four, that I will not be made a mockery of."

"Please calm yourself," she says, kissing him, "I am right here by your side and I know you will achieve whatever you wish for."

He does calm down and brings her face down to his, kissing her with fervour. He takes in her smell and enjoys the release he feels as they make love. He hopes her hesitancy at his news is his imagination playing tricks on him.

Quinan-Gold is ready for launch. The select few that know about this secret project are at the hangar waiting for his instructions. Dilvant's hands are sweating because this is big, the biggest thing he has undertaken. Under the nose of the rest of the world he will find a planet with similar qualities to Earth, he will be the ultimate leader once more.

With him are his trusted two ministers along with Eldane, who has protected Dilvant since before the days of his defeat. They, along with three female engineers, are the discovery team. With the power of Quinan-Gold, they will be in space for as long as it takes to find a suitable planet. He will not return to Earth until they find the right one.

Felida kisses him farewell and he gives Quinan Jnr a cuddle. "I'm doing this for you. This new planet will be yours to rule in the future, it will be your safe haven away from the tragic past of Earth."

Quinan Jnr smiles and gurgles as Felida takes him into her arms, "Be careful," she says to Dilvant.

"I will return victorious. I can feel it, there is a new world for us out there. You will be my queen." She gives him a half smile and he knows this is not what she wants. Felida wants a quiet life in Heraklion, but he will show her a new life, a life of riches and freedom she could never have imagined.

The people of Crete will follow him. He knows there are some who will not want to leave, but they will pay. He will make it clear to all the citizens that they must follow him and make a new world.

Then they will help him to take over the universe. He will not take no for an answer.

They step into Quinan-Gold and ready themselves for launch. Dilvant stands at the console and activates the protection shield. They will go into orbit undetected by anyone on Earth, the Moon or Mars colonies and this space race is theirs to win. He and his team will go down in the history books as the first astronauts to discover another planet where humans can survive just as they do on Earth.

Chapter 29

Marzeen

Marzeen looks at the face of her newborn and for a split second sees the resemblance of the High Priest. His eyes, forehead...so much like Dilvant. Fear grips her heart but before it takes hold, she brushes this aside and looks up towards Breex, he is the father of her son.

Edsel was born without any fanfare. He came into the world quickly, Marzeen's labour was only two hours. This was a blessing as he is a big baby and Marzeen was carrying more weight than her body could handle. These last few weeks had been spent on the lounge because she found it difficult to move.

The only significant thing about Edsel's birthdate is that it is the same day as the launch of the space program. Marzeen had gone into labour a few weeks after arriving home from the cocktail event. Edsel was born at 11.30pm on May 1, 2300.

The space program was something Breex had been working on with Leyna and Eween. And, of course, Dilvant. She tries not to think about him and what he did to her, she never wants to remember that awful afternoon. Edsel will celebrate his birthday with the advent of humans discovering the universe, this is what she will concentrate on. This will be a more important event that will obscure her mind and diminish her memories of Dilvant.

Breex is holding Edsel but he's stiff and awkward.

"Relax, you won't hurt him. Babies are stronger than you think."

"Marzeen, he is perfect," he says as he brushes his finger lightly over his son's face.

"Well let's see if you think the same way when he screams to be fed and keeps us awake at night."

"You seem to know things about newborns."

"There are two three-month-old babies at the orphanage, I have learnt some things about little ones since working there."

"Of course. Well, that knowledge will come in handy," says Breex as Edsel begins to fidget.

"Oh dear, here you go, I have no idea what to do."

Marzeen laughs, "I hope you relax by the time we have him home. I'm going to need your help at times."

Breex shrugs his shoulders, "I'll watch you and learn I guess."

Edsel keeps fidgeting and begins to cry. Marzeen unclasps her bra and attempts to have him latch on. His mouth is open, but he keeps missing the nipple. "Come on," coaxes Marzeen, squeezing a little liquid for him to smell. This works, he finds the nipple and begins suckling. "That's better, well done."

Breex is sitting next to them and working on his tablet. He has been at the hospital for two nights and has said he doesn't want to go home without them. Marzeen had explained that someone has to bring more baby clothes and do mundane chores like the washing.

"What is the maid for?"

"I gave her a week off knowing I wasn't going to be home. You can handle a bit of washing. Now, grab that bag in the cupboard and I'll give you a list of what you need to bring."

He does as he is told and Marzeen sends him off with a smile. Edsel is finished feeding when a nurse comes in to take him to the nursery. She tells Marzeen to have a rest and she'll bring Edsel back again when he needs his next feed. Marzeen gratefully accepts the nurse taking Edsel because she is exhausted. This feeding takes it out of her.

After freshening up in the bathroom, she closes the blinds and makes the room as dark as possible. Lying down she stares at the ceiling for some time before sleep finally arrives.

"Edsel, come on, come to mummy." She begins to panic when he doesn't come, "Edsel, please...where are you?"

"He's mine, how dare you keep him for himself, you bitch. Look at him, he looks like me. I know he belongs to me."

"Dilvant, noooooo. Stop, please don't take my son away. Let's discuss this. Breex and I..."

"You keep your filthy husband out of this. My son will be raised my way. Edsel come to daddy, that's a good boy."

"Nooooo," she screams but she can't hear her own voice. What is going on?

Suddenly she is sweating, then she's cold and clammy. Then the room is filled with light and the sounds of a baby crying.

Taking deep breaths she says, "Oh, someone is hungry. Don't worry little one, your mummy is here." Marzeen pushes herself up, accepting her baby from the nurse. It was a nightmare, just a horrible nightmare. She lets out a sigh of relief as Edsel nuzzles into her. She looks forward to taking him home.

Watching Edsel as he coos in his bassinet, Marzeen decides to have a quick shower while he is happy and safe. It's midday and she hasn't had a chance to do anything for herself until now. Breex has promised to be home early every afternoon since they brought their baby home, and so far, he'd kept that promise for two out of three nights. The space project is in full swing and he is needed, but he had said being with his son was more important.

Stepping out of the shower, she can hear Edsel fidgeting already. It's time for another feed, this baby has an insatiable appetite. The rest of the afternoon flies by and Marzeen wonders where the time has gone. The maid comes into the nursery asking if she needs anything else before she leaves. "Oh, umm, no, I think I'm fine for now. Thank you, I'll see you tomorrow." With a nod the maid leaves just as Edsel begins screaming to be fed again.

She is still feeding when Breex arrives home.

"Look at you, you're an expert at this now. Hello my darlings."

"Edsel, Daddy's home and early too. Isn't he a good Daddy?"

Breex bends to kiss her and then Edsel on his head. "How has he been today?"

"The day is a blur of feeding and nappy changes. Honestly, his appetite is incredible."

"I guess that's a good thing isn't it? It means he's healthy and growing."

"Yes, it does but I don't have a minute to myself. Also, my brain is going stale, please tell me what's going on in the outside world." Breex laughs and then proceeds to tell her that there is still no word from Zenac about finding Teegue and this worries Leyna and Eween. The space project is moving along well, and the first group of astronauts have left. "They launched this morning and have two months of reconnaissance then they report back. Depending on what they find, the other astronauts will follow. Everyone is on edge as to what they will (or won't) find."

Marzeen settles Edsel and walks to Breex giving him a hug, "I'm glad you're home, this conversation makes me feel like I'm still an adult. I guess we have to think positive that there is more out there for us, otherwise there has been lots of money spent for nothing."

"There are rumours going around that some citizens are sceptical about the amount of money being poured into the project. Apparently, Mauritius donated money to Dilvant's Quinan project and the people of that island are not happy. They are saying that he is an unworthy deviant and should not be given any money. They do not trust him."

Marzeen cringes at the mention of his name. Will this ever stop? Shaking it off she says, "Well they aren't wrong, are they? I know it was my idea and I understand why Leyna and Eween needed to join forces with him, but it still leaves a bad taste in my mouth."

Breex doesn't answer and she knows why. He hates talking about

Dilvant. Knowing she has a past with that man makes Breex wary even though she has given Breex her undivided love. That man is trouble, so she understands why Breex feels the way he does. "How about a drink to relax before dinner?" she asks, trying to clear the air.

Chapter 30

Zenac

The soldiers are at ease and remain under shade while they wait for their superiors to come back from the king's house. Zenac is ushered into a room along with his three colleagues. The room is comfortable but certainly not regal. There is a fireplace, which seems unnecessary. It's not ornate, just plain black tiles with a timber mantle. Photo frames adorn it and Zenac sucks in his breath when he sees one of them contains a photo of Teegue. He has one arm around a woman who is holding a baby. The other three see it too and exchange glances.

"Please sit, I will summon some beverages for you," says Elvardo, leaving them.

"Zenac, are you okay?" asks Zaydin.

"I'm not sure. At least I know Teegue is alive, but he has a family? I... I'm not sure what to think."

"Maybe wait for the King, he might explain," says Amallin. As Amallin finishes talking King Setiago enters the room. A middle-aged man with a smooth, bald head, he neither looks like a king nor sounds like one. His voice is placid and quiet.

"Welcome to Granada." There is no hint of a Spanish accent. "May I ask why you are here?"

Zenac stands and offers his hand, but the King doesn't reciprocate. Clearing his throat, he says, "I'm looking for my son Teegue." He looks at the photo, his face lined with worry.

"Teegue came to us almost two years ago. He has been very helpful and is an honourable man. I assume you want to see him?"

"Of course, my partner and I have missed him very much, as have his two siblings. May I see him now?"

The King sits and places his hands on his lap, "I understand how you must have missed him, but he is married to my daughter, Elira. They have a daughter, Joaque."

Zenac is not sure what he is playing at but answers amicably, "I understand. May I please see him?"

Elvardo enters with two women bearing drinks that are welcomed by all of them. As they leave the King says, "I will leave you to hydrate, please excuse me."

"Not a man of many words, is he?" says Taaz.

Downing the sweet beverage, Zenac answers, "I hope this isn't going to be messy, I will not leave without Teegue."

"Dad." Teegue runs to Zenac, hugging him with a force that almost knocks them both down.

"Oh, Teegue, you're alive." Zenac holds him away by the shoulders, "You look well, too." His voice cracks as he says this and his emotions are welling up, his body is unsure yet whether to be relieved. The situation is still so uncertain.

"Hello," Teegue greets the others. Taaz slaps him on the shoulders with tears glistening in his eyes.

"I have a lot to tell you all." He proceeds to recount how the signal he was sending finally reached Granada and they sent a rescue rocket, their one and only, to find him. "As you probably have guessed, these people are descendants of the failed Spanish/USA mission of 2050. The three ships all made it here, and of the one hundred people who landed here, there are now ten thousand Granadians. I don't want you to worry, they are peace-loving people, so Taaz and Mechanic, relax.

"The soldiers outside were a precaution, Teegue."

"I appreciate that Taaz, thanks. Dad, I wanted so much for you to receive the signal, which I haven't stopped sending out as you know, or you wouldn't be here. When they rescued me, at first, they were wary that more might follow and were not sure why I was out in space alone. I was imprisoned until I made a pact." He moves over to the mantle and picks up the photo frame, "This is Elira and her daughter, Joaque."

"Her daughter? She's not yours?"

"Elira was pregnant when I arrived. She fell in love with a man her father did not approve of. He has since disappeared. I offered to marry Elira and give Joaque a father in return for my freedom. Elira is the heir to the throne, and I belong beside her."

Zenac stands and begins pacing, his anger is beginning to take hold.

"The Spaniards are not known for wanting a royal family, how do they have a royal family now?" asks Zaydin.

"When they landed here there was chaos. Someone needed to take charge, and for want of a better title, called himself King. They are not rich royals or revered as such, it is a title only. King Setiago is a fair man."

Zenac explodes, "A fair man! Are you brainwashed or something? You are still a prisoner, he is not allowing you to come home."

"Please stay calm, shouting is not appreciated here, they are a calm race. Do you think I have kept the signal going for nothing? Of course I want to come home, it's a little more complicated now I have a family, that's all. I will work on him, the King will listen to me."

"So, you have gained his trust?" asks Amallin, "that was wise."

"Yes. I knew I had to, and marrying his daughter was part of earning that trust. The other way is that I have given them my skills in technology and helped them with improving the atmosphere here in this layer where they live. The surface is uninhabitable, but here they are safe. When I arrived, there was a danger that the hydrogen would enter this area, so the reinforced steel door was made stronger and we added the steel at the cave's entrance."

Elvardo enters again and invites them all to dine with the King.

They move into a dining room with a steel floor and chairs with steel legs.

"I am happy you agreed to join me, please make yourselves comfortable." When the king sits, he is joined by Elira. The photo does not do her justice, she is definitely queen material. With long, blonde locks to her shoulders, blue eyes and high cheekbones, she smiles and greets them all with grace. Teegue takes his place next to her.

One big happy family. Zenac is not sure what to think, although he agrees with Teegue, this is an added complication.

After dinner Zenac sends the others back to the ship with the soldiers outside. "I want to spend some time with my son." He watches as they leave then returns to the table. He and Teegue talk about the situation. King Setiago, Elira and Elvardo had all retired to bed.

"How does Elvardo figure in this family?"

"He is the king's uncle and is extremely loyal to them. He helped me to convince the king I was an honourable man. Elira is a good mother and she too is loyal to her father. Joaque is a delight. Honestly Dad, I was headed to Earth to help you but also to see a girl I had met. Obviously, the universe had other ideas. I met Jzinta during all the strife at The Vatican. She is a lovechild of Dilvant's and I loved her. Actually, I still do."

"You left Arisis because of the love of someone fathered by Dilvant? You're crazier than I thought. Maybe it's better you ended up here. Now tell me more about the King and what he has over you?"

Teegue was visibly angered by his fathers comments but instead of arguing he proceeds to tell him about the Granadians. He tells him how private the Granadians are and there is still anger about the fact they were left to their own devices. The Spanish and US governments never bothered to look for them. So, they carved out an existence that led them to live on this third layer, six layers from the core of this planet. Each king has improved their lot and soon they forgot about Earth. Until he came along. The current king has allowed Teegue to live with them despite being concerned that there may be dangerous elements out there. Elvardo had convinced him Zenac and his crew were not a threat.

"They have done well considering the circumstances, but this doesn't mean you have to stay. We are not a threat and you cannot be kept prisoner here."

"I don't consider myself a prisoner, I will find a way to come home. Maybe not for good but I want to secure rights to visit."

"Teegue, you are breaking my heart. How do you expect me to explain this to your mother? Do you love Elira?"

Teegue doesn't answer immediately, which tells Zenac he did what he did to survive. In Zenac's mind, Teegue is definitely still a prisoner.

"It's late, leave things with me for now. I will deal with the king. Don't worry, I'll come home at some stage."

"If I return home without you your mother will be devastated. I'll wait until you are ready."

Teegue nods and stands, "As you wish, Dad," he says as he leaves the room, "Elvardo will organise an escort to take you back to the ship."

Chapter 31

Dawa

She is standing at the window staring out to the lake. The water sparkling in the midday sun consoles her withered heart. Teegue did not return with his father. He's alive, and she is grateful, but he has remained on Granada like a prisoner. She and Zenac had argued last night with Dawa telling him he had not fought hard enough to bring their son home. He had defended himself by saying Teegue was the one who wanted to stay.

Something doesn't add up. Why would Teegue not come on his own, he could visit and then return? What does this King have over their son? It amazes her how Teegue is able to find trouble wherever he goes.

"Dawa, they are ready for you."

Turning away from the view, she readies herself for yet another meeting about the space project. Its success has buoyed everyone's spirits. She is trying to focus on good things, but Teegue's situation clouds her judgement.

Luminary 1-Tanjaz is chairing the meeting, which she is grateful for because her mind is not on political matters right now. Tanjaz was awarded the position forty days after Sheabz's death. This was the ritual, tradition meant that whoever was in the position of Luminary 2 automatically rose to the top position. Tanjaz is a capable candidate and will serve the Luminaries well.

She is only half listening until the discussion turns to a rumour, one about Dilvant. "Intelligence has informed me that Dilvant seems to have found a planet that is like Earth. It has two moons, is smaller and is five million light years away. So far this is all we know."

"How reliable is this rumour, Tanjaz?"

"We are still finding out more about this. I'll keep you and Zenac informed Dawa."

Tanjaz continues to discuss the space project and the success of the high-powered rockets. Astronauts are praising the reliability and comfort as well as the ease of control. As much as everyone had reservations about Dilvant and including him in their project, no one can deny it has been worthwhile.

Dawa tunes out again as her thoughts turn to Teegue once more. Maybe the King doesn't have a hold on him, it might be his love for the woman and her daughter that is keeping him there. Teegue does have an honourable streak and he must feel an obligation to this new family. This eases her pain slightly, but she needs to see him, Teegue has been gone for too long.

Aria and Braxton are discussing whether Teegue has done the right thing by staying on Granada. "What's the problem?" asks Aria, "we can always visit."

"Yeah, I'd like to see this planet. And how fascinating that they live underground." Braxton's eyes light up with awe.

"I'm still in discussion with Teegue. And you all heard him on the chat last night, he is happy for us to visit him while he works on the King to change his mind. I don't see any reason why Teegue and his family can't visit us."

"It was good to see his face, Zenac. For me, I still want to see him in person. Why don't we go to Granada then?"

"That might be an option if the King remains stubborn. I think he is protecting his daughter and granddaughter."

"Obviously, just like we want to protect Teegue. I say we go as soon as possible, I need to see him and give him a hug. Then I will scold him for giving us all this grief once again."

"You already did that last night, Dawa. I'll see what I can do about the four of us going."

Later, while they are both lying in bed, Dawa starts on Zenac. "It would have been easier if you had returned with Teegue. Us traipsing over to Granada is pandering to the King, someone we know nothing about."

"They are peace-loving people, I've told you this already. I did my best to bring Teegue home, but he is stubborn. And he seems happy to be there."

"How can he not miss us?"

"He didn't say he didn't. He kept the signal going so we would eventually find him. Doesn't that tell you he missed us?"

Dawa remains quiet. She still thinks Teegue is being selfish but keeps this to herself. She decides to change the subject to the rumour. "I wouldn't put it past Dilvant to try and beat everyone else to finding a suitable planet. I know it's a rumour for now, but I suspect he wants to rule again. My worry is that he will return to his archaic ways, something the people of Crete would not want to return to."

"*If* they travel to this new planet. There is no reason for people to remain on Earth now. With the Moon, Mars and Arisis colonies, population growth can be managed along with the environment. The GIS will never allow Earth to be ravaged by climate change as it was in the past."

"You're right, but I wouldn't put it past Dilvant wanting to ravage Earth once more and rule with more Enforcers. He will want to rule all the colonies, I am sure of it." Dawa shudders at the thought but knows it is a possibility. If Dilvant has found a planet suitable to colonise, then he will rule it his way and then invade the rest. His obsession with being the High Priest once more is frightening.

· · ·

Tanjaz and Xzackry are in her office reporting on the Mazadon Water Project. This is another successful project, one Dawa is proud to have watched grow from an idea she had put forward. Arisis is a sustainable planet now and tourism and trade has been booming with the other colonies. The rate of people moving to Arisis has slowed, this is due to Leyna and Eween taking power and bringing civility back for all humans.

As Tanjaz and Xzackry leave, Zenac walks in. "Good reports on Mazadon?"

"Yes, everything is going to plan. At least something is working out well in my life."

"Don't be so pessimistic, Teegue is alive, you have this to celebrate. Besides, I have a date, we travel to Granada next week."

She runs towards him embracing him in a hug, "Oh, Zenac how wonderful. The four of us are going?"

"Yes, we will consider it a family holiday. We haven't had one since the children were little, I think it's a little overdue."

"Hmmm, I don't think I would have picked Granada for a holiday, but it will be interesting. Oh, I can't wait to see him, Zenac. Thank you."

"It's nice to see you smiling again. I'm heading to the Spacedrome to finalise everything, I'll see you at home later."

She watches him walk out. He had done his best to bring Teegue home, she should not have been so hard on him. There is something she has to remember, their children are adults now and have a mind of their own.

Chapter 32

Dilvant
Crete

He is on the podium overlooking the citizens of Heraklion. Felida is by his side and they both take in the cheers of their people.

"Six months," he shouts as the cheers die down, "this is all it took to be the first to find a planet like Earth. Our rockets designed and manufactured by us, by you the people of Crete, have served us well. The planet Dilvant-1 was discovered in record time, and we will colonise it. I will lead you to the greatest planet in this universe. There we will flourish and be a power to be reckoned with."

Cheers rain out, and although he hears a few disgruntled yells, Dilvant knows his people are behind him. He will entice them with land and a prosperity they can only imagine. Once they have settled in the capital, Quinan City, Dilvant will begin forming his new army along with his ten new Enforcers. His chosen few, the family he has collected for himself, will rule with the iron fist he believes is the only way to rule. He keeps watching as the crowd begins to disband. He whispers to the minister standing near him as he steps off the podium, "Find the citizens who are against me and take them to prison. No one is allowed to remain here because I need all the people with me to overthrow the famous four."

The other remaining ministers and Eldane, his most trusted minister, are by his side having been a part of this announcement to the people of Crete. Along with Eldane, these three men will be Enforcers. Dilvant already has the others in mind, they are all loyal to him and are prepared for the riches he will bestow on them and their families. His power has a way of enticing people to obey him and this keeps them loyal to the cause.

He watches her as she bangs kitchen drawers and mutters under her breath. Felida had not been impressed with his new planet. She was annoyed he named it, named the capital after her brother and all without consulting anyone, not even his ministers, let alone her.

"Honestly, how selfish of you. This achievement is for all of us, we have all helped you along the way. How could you not consult us on such an important thing? Naming the planet after yourself is absurd."

Now he's had enough, she has been moaning about this for days. No one else seems to be upset about the naming, in fact, many have praised him for honouring Quinan again. "Absurd! What are you whining about, Felida? I have every right to name the planet anything I bloody well like. And I've yet again included your brother. Don't you think he would like a capital city named after him?"

"Of course, he would be pleased, and I thank you for including his memory in all of this. But you're missing the point. I'm saying you were selfish in making the decision on your own."

"Felida, you had better back off. This is all on me, I came up with the idea of exploring other planets and I have found one that is most suitable. I had every right to choose the name." He yells and can feel the veins in his neck strain. Taking himself onto the deck to cool off, he breathes in the salty air. If she doesn't stop this nonsense, he will do something he will regret. Holding onto the rail, his knuckles turn white from the pressure. He lets go and shakes his hands vigorously. He has to rid himself of this pent-up anger and decides to go for a swim. He heads to the bedroom to change.

Coming out of the room he fears Felida will ask if he wants company. She turns to him but he keeps walking and ignores her because if he tells her what he is feeling, she will be shocked.

Leaving his towel on the sand, he jumps into the clear water. It is cool and he feels his body relax as the buoyancy takes his body. With strong strokes he swims until his body aches and allows the azure water to soothe him.

When he returns, he has calmed considerably. She is watching the news as he walks to her and places his hands on her shoulders. "I'm sorry, I needed some time to myself."

Turning her head up to look at him, he sees she has been crying. Walking around to her he bends to kiss her wet cheeks. "You must understand I had to make decisions quickly, I need this project to be up and running immediately. From now on I will consult you all as we have much work to do setting us this new world."

She nods and pats the lounge next to her. He sits and she places her head on his shoulder and continues to watch the news.

The transport minister has his crew ready. They are taking three hundred people with them to begin the building of Quinan City. Eldane will follow with others who have the skills to fill the necessary jobs. Dilvant wants to move everyone from Crete by the end of the year, they are to populate Quinan City and then he will have them working on building other areas of the planet. Nine hundred thousand people will follow him to Dilvant-1, he has already committed to this. He will also concentrate on developing his army again because it is now time for Leyna, Eween and their allies to pay for what they have done.

The first people to live permanently in the new city are the three hundred from the first rocket. Dilvant will move Felida and Quinan Jnr permanently in the next month as he wants them safely away from Earth before he starts his plan. Eldane and a few of his soldiers are the only ones who know of his desire to take over leadership of Vatican City once more. He will rule both Earth and Dilvant-1 at first because this is his destiny. Then, he will invade the other colonies.

As he oversees the progress of Quinan City becoming a reality, his heart swells with emotions he hasn't felt for a long time. His power is back, and his citizens will know this power in the coming months. He walks onto the land that will have his new home built on. From this vantage point, he sees the two moons shining over the sea, the spread of their light shimmers from the horizon and he knows he is finally home.

Chapter 33

Zenac

Along with Dawa, Zenac is travelling to Earth again. After two years of surveillance their intelligence team has discovered where the planet Dilvant-1 is situated. They now know Dilvant is planning more trouble. Zenac wants to help Leyna and Eween with a plan to stop him. And this time stop him once and for all.

"Teegue offering his help is interesting, don't you think?"

"Yes, for a peace-loving people, the fact they have offered to help fight Dilvant shows how much they despise him as well."

"With what he has done, pretending to join forces with us and then going off on his own, there are many people now who don't trust him just as much as we do." As Dawa says this her compupad pings. "It's Felida. She sent me a message last week and wants to speak with us." She presses to answer, "Hello," says Dawa cautiously.

"Is Zenac there with you?" When Dawa confirms this, Felida continues, "Now that you know about Dilvant-1, I need your help. Or, actually, I'm offering to help you. Dilvant is becoming more and more ambitious, in fact, he is crazy with desire to destroy you, The Vatican and anyone who opposes him. I'm worried for my son because I don't want him to experience war. If you agree, I will feed you information about Dilvant's plans because my people are not used to living this way. For the past six months, Dilvant has added more draconian rules, worse than what we had on Earth previously."

Zenac looks at Dawa with raised eyebrows, "You are taking a risk contacting us, you're placing your life in danger."

"I know Zenac, but there is no other way. Dilvant has to be stopped. I've watched him descend into madness over the past 2 years and I don't want Quinan Jrn to see his father like this."

"But aren't you all living together in Quinan City?"

"We were. I brought Quinan Jnr home to Heraklion two months ago. The education and medical system in Quinan City is not set up yet. I used this as an excuse to bring us home. Dilvant is so engrossed in his plan I don't think he is even missing us. Am I able to count on you both?"

"We're on our way to Earth to meet with Leyna and Eween. We'll contact you when we arrive, the four of us will discuss what we can do for you."

Felida pings out with a thank you.

"Is she trustworthy?"

"Maybe, Dawa. Her brother was not an ally, but he never caused trouble. And from what our intelligence tells us about Felida, she wants a quiet life on Crete. We can discuss this with Leyna and Eween, and between us we'll find a way."

As soon as they arrive they head to parliament. In the meeting room with Leyna and Eween they discuss Felida's offer. After looking at all the evidence laid in front of them, they all decide she is being genuine. Felida has no reason to betray them, but she has every reason to betray Dilvant. She is protecting her son. Zenac points out the information they have about Felida is that she is a woman who loves her country and had met Dilvant when he was pretending to be someone he wasn't. He tricked both Felida and her brother Quinan into believing he was an honourable man.

"That man has no honour," spits out Dawa, "so let's agree to accept Felida's information and defeat Dilvant, this time for good."

Zenac admires the fire that has returned in Dawa. Ever since they visited Teegue on Granada and met Elira and Joaque, Dawa was her old self again. During the time they thought they would never find Teegue, Zenac had worried about her, he had never seen her depressed and thought she may not recover if Teegue wasn't found.

Eween stands and begins pacing, "It's not so much that I don't trust Felida, our intelligence shows she is a good woman with much more honour than Dilvant. It is Dilvant that worries me. What do you think he has planned this time?"

Zenac stands up as well and places his hand on Eween's shoulder, "I understand your concern, but we need her help if we are going to defeat Dilvant again. From what I have been told, he has amassed another army, more weapons and wants to lead all the colonies."

"All of them?" Leyna slams the table. "He is truly mad. We have lived a peaceful existence with the Moon and Mars colonies, I will not stand to see that disrupted."

"Then, as I said, we accept Felida's help. And we must be the attackers on his soil. Earth has seen enough wars."

They all agree with Dawa as Leyna calls in her new assistant to draw up the necessary papers. Dilvant's spy, Leyna's previous assistant, was discovered months ago. She escaped and hasn't been heard of since. They all assume she is on Dilvant-1 helping Dilvant with his awful plan.

Zenac also summons Breex, Nable and Fixor to be briefed. They will need everyone on board for this mission, another one in trying to defeat the menace that is Dilvant.

After Leyna has returned to her office with Dawa, Eween and Zenac remain in the meeting room. Zenac speaks to the ministers and is waiting for their reaction. They fidget for a while, then Fixor breaks the silence.

"Zenac, do you realise how crazy this is? First, we make this ridiculous alliance with that madman, and now you want to accept the word of his partner?"

He proceeds to restate their case, and the fact that Felida has more to lose if she stays on Dilvant-1. "Her son, Quinan Jnr, has special needs because of his foot. The education and medical systems are not yet worthwhile on that planet, so she has returned to Heraklion. Why else would she offer to give us information? She fears for the life of her son as well as hers."

"It's a trap. Dilvant is using his family to give us false information and then he will strike."

Breex stands up and says, "Fixor, you are a pessimist. Zenac has explained why Felida is doing this, and you as a parent must feel the same way."

"I am wary, that's all. Blind trust will get us nowhere."

Eween takes the floor, "Fixor, we are all wary of Dilvant and what he is capable of, which is why we should strike first. With Felida's help we will have an advantage. I think she is doing this out of desperation because she is seeing what is happening to her people. They had a good life on Crete, and many didn't want to move to Dilvant-1. Who knows what Dilvant threatened them with if they didn't? And what he is doing to them now is even worse."

Fixor remains quiet and fidgets again.

Zenac proceeds to fill them in on the information Felida has already supplied. There will be no need for Dilvant to come back to Earth because Earth's army will attack first. "Our shields will keep us undetectable and we already know his weapons are still the ones he used last time with some added, mainly high-powered guns. We know how the technological ones work and understand how to disarm them. Even with his other procured weapons, with stealth, we will outwit his army."

Fixor nods but Zenac can see he is not convinced. Not that this matters, he is not one of the soldiers going to fight.

Continuing to discuss what still needs to be done, he also briefs them on what is required for the next step of the space project. With Dilvant already winning the space race, their project will concentrate on finding planets with resources that will help Earth and the other colonies. The GIS has again agreed to be involved and they will take a larger role this time. If in the meantime another suitable planet is found, then this will be a bonus. He ends the meeting by asking for the existing troops to be put on notice and for more recruits to be conscripted.

As the ministers file out of the room Zenac sighs.

"He is hard work but we don't have anything to worry about. Fixor doesn't have the numbers behind him to block us," says Eween.

"I'm not sure that is true. No one wants another war and Fixor is trying to avoid it. But things have gone too far, it's too late to back out now. Dilvant must be stopped."

Eween nods and collects his papers. They walk out of the meeting room and decide to join Leyna and Dawa for a late lunch.

Chapter 34

Leyna

Six months after the agreement to accept Felida's help, Leyna walks along the line of troops who stand at attention before her. Eween is following behind along with Dawa and Zenac. The new recruits were found from all over the world and have been trained. They join the existing army. Earth is ready to attack. This is the most formidable army they have ever had, a combination of men and women from all their allied countries. The world has combined in this fight against the tyranny that is Dilvant.

Felida has given them valuable information about the layout of Quinan City, and she has temporarily returned to be their contact on Dilvant-1. She has a small group of followers who will also help. Quinan Jnr is being cared for in Heraklion and she has said that she hopes this mission will be quick as she wants to return to look after her son. Dilvant thinks their son has remained because of treatment for his foot. This is enough for Felida to keep Dilvant away from him because Dilvant's obsession clouds his thoughts, and he is becoming more dangerous every day. Felida fears he might attack soon and has asked Leyna to hurry and send Earth's troops.

Leyna's last contact with Felida was a few weeks ago and she told Felida to be patient, but with the help of their allies, this army is now ready for the task. They have been briefed on the stealth attack to be launched in two days. It has been explained to them that minimal damage should be done, and the people of Quinan City are not to be harmed. The aim is to capture Dilvant and bring him back to The Vatican for trial.

As they reach the podium, she stands and adjusts the microphone. "At ease my loyal troops. I can see we are ready for yet another mission against Dilvant. For the last time, I hope. The three rockets that will transport you all to Dilvant-1 have been fitted with undetectable shields and there are people in Quinan City ready to help you with this task. Please stay safe and do your job with the utmost precautions. Thank you all for your service and I look forward to welcoming you back victorious."

Eween takes the podium and goes over the timeline. Then Zenac explains how Taaz, The Mechanic and their security forces will also help with this operation. Once they finish, the troops are sent back to their barracks as they all head back to parliament.

After more briefings and meetings, Leyna buzzes Eween. "Let's have some lunch. It's been a huge morning."

"Sure, I'll ask Dawa and Zenac too. And I want to go out, I need some fresh air."

The four of them head to a restaurant in the piazza with security in tow and are greeted by the owner, "Madame President, such a pleasure." He seats them at a corner table away from the few other diners.

This is one of her favourite restaurants for dinner, usually for special occasions, and they occasionally come here for lunch. It might be premature, but she feels this is a special occasion, it's not every day you organise your army to invade another planet. The ambience is modern chic, with high backed chairs in luxurious black leather, crisp white linen and crystal glasses. The menu is small because only fresh, seasonal produce is used. Today she is feeling like one of their seafood dishes, maybe a crab dish.

"This is a great restaurant, but what are we celebrating?"

"No reason, Dawa. I'm feeling like things are going to change for the better and wanted to share this feeling with you."

"That's good enough for me," laughs Zenac.

They continue their banter, some of it about the task ahead but mostly they talk about their families. The relaxed ambience of the place combines with their buoyant conversation.

"I hear that Teegue has offered to help. I've always liked your son," says Leyna.

"Yes, he will provide a peacekeeping army once our work is done. Teegue has great regard for you too, Leyna. It is wonderful that we found him, and the fact we have a granddaughter now is an added bonus."

"She is gorgeous," says Dawa, "I love her to bits. Aria and Braxton enjoy playing with her when they visit. Now that the King trusts us, Teegue and Elira visit often." She looks at Zenac and he nods with love awash in his face.

"Actually, it's still early but we can't keep this news in any longer. Elira is pregnant."

"Oh, what wonderful news. Congratulations." Both Leyna and Eween smile with this news.

"It was a worry when you didn't know where Teegue was, but the universe protected him by leading him to Granada. Things are all well now and with two grandchildren, your family is expanding."

"Yes, Leyna. I went through a terrible time when he was lost as you know. I lost a part of myself during that time. A new baby will heal this part of me."

"Of course, and no need to worry about Teegue anymore, Dawa. He is safe and all going well, the universe will be safe again soon. We will also have another planet to colonise in our own way. Our citizens want to feel safe, and without Dilvant around, they will be." She is sure of this, Dilvant will not escape again. She will not let Felida down and the people of Crete will be rescued and returned home. As leader of the free world, she will ensure peace will reign for all the colonies for the distant future.

Her thoughts drift away as her mind comes back to the conversation. Leyna places her hand on Eween's arm, laughing at something Zenac has said. Her feeling that something great is coming for all of humanity is growing.

Chapter 35

Felida

"Mummy loves you and I'll be home soon." Felida clicks off her compupad with tears streaming down her face. She hopes she hasn't lied to her son. It has taken the Earth team more time to organise an army than anticipated and she has stayed in Quinan City longer than she had anticipated. What she has seen in her time here horrifies her. Dilvant has tightened restrictions and placed curfews on his citizens, everyone is to be home by nine pm. Many are asking why and being thrown into prison if they persist. She has tried to ask him the reason, but he brushes her aside and says he will lead how he wants. He told her if she insisted on this line of questioning, she too would end up in prison.

Two days later Felida is given confirmation that Earth's army is on their way. She contacts her own team and asks them all to be on guard. That evening she is on her best behaviour with Dilvant, she gives herself to him and praises him for his efforts.

"This is more like it, Felida. You have come to your senses."

"Yes, my love," she coos, "I have decided that you know best and only have the interests of our citizens in what you do."

He kisses her then brushes her hair aside, "When we bring our son back, we will be a family again and I will groom Quinan Jnr in my way of being a leader. This is all his to inherit."

A cold shiver takes over her body at the thought and she hopes he cannot sense how she is feeling. To be sure, she kisses him passionately because she needs him to trust her for a while longer.

Dusk is descending and it's cold even though it's only five o'clock. She sees her three security guards at their checkpoint and nods to each one. Each is camouflaged with balaclavas and long coats, for keeping out the cold as well as being incognito. She hears a whistle signalling there has been a landing. Looking around, the street is deserted and even the police have gone home for dinner. The next crew won't be on until five thirty, they have to move fast.

"What the...? Leyna, what are you doing here?"

Even though she was dressed in the same camouflage as her own guards, Felida would recognise those wide eyes anywhere.

"You didn't think I was going to let you have all the fun," she jokes, "I'm here to both protect you and personally bring him back with me."

"Madame President, you are putting yourself at great risk. But we don't have time to argue, we must move. Dilvant is in his office at parliament, security will be changing over in the next thirty minutes."

"Taaz, Mechanic, follow us. Send some of your troops ahead of us to run reconnaissance," orders Leyna, as Felida starts walking.

"We are only two streets away, so my guards will arrive first. As soon as they see the parliamentary guards move, they will scale the wall. We will only proceed when they say the area is safe."

They walk with reticence, the security staff in silence as Felida and Leyna whisper to each other.

"It's freezing."

"Yes, and many people are not used to it. Dilvant did do one thing right though, all the homes and offices have heating."

"He gives one concession and then takes so many others away."

"He wasn't like this when my brother and I met him. He was charming and willing to help. All our ministers warmed to him as well. But in the past 2 years, he has shown his true colours. I fear for Quinan Jnr, which is why I came to you."

"We know, Felida. Dilvant does have a charming side and he uses it to his advantage when he needs to. Don't feel bad for falling for him, many have done so before you."

"I feel so cheated. I want him to be the man I first met."

Taaz interrupts them, "There, the guards are moving. Stay alert." Felida sees the look on Leyna's face. She knows why. "It's enormous, isn't it?"

"What was he thinking? Why would he need a parliament building this huge? There are only nine hundred thousand citizens." "And he has used reinforced steel throughout along with concrete and all the windows are double-glazed. He has installed a security system that he says is not hackable, but with the help of your security team, our team has worked out how. They will disarm the system before they enter. Then they will summon us," adds Felida.

They remain hidden and quiet until the signal arrives. Felida turns to Leyna, "You have been instructed what to do. I'll go in first with the story that I needed to collect some things from my office. Which is what I will do beforehand. If he sees files in my hands, he won't suspect anything. Then, I will suggest we go home together as I have a special meal prepared for us."

"Yes, I understand. I'll be waiting outside with Taaz and Mechanic. Be quick, we only have fifteen minutes left before the guards are back on duty."

Felida walks in behind her security guards, then they step aside and make way for her to enter the building and then her office. Inside, she collects some random files and then taking a deep breath, she heads to Dilvant's office.

Knocking, she pries open the door a little, "Hi, I'm not disturbing you, am I?"

"Well, hello my love. What brings you here at this time?"

She lifts the files, "Had to pick these up, I want to work on them tonight." As she finishes, two of his henchmen grab her from behind. She tries to scream but a hand is on her mouth before she can.

"You bitch, did you think I am so stupid as to not know what you were doing? My army has the building surrounded."

There is gunfire and a commotion in the hallway. The war they were trying to avoid has begun.

He comes close to her and with a face of evil, he places his hand under her chin holding her arm firm, "No one double crosses me. Take her to the vault along with anyone else you capture."

The files she was holding scatter to the floor as she is brutally escorted out of his office.

When she is thrown into the vault, Leyna is already there along with three of her guards. She has been shot in the leg.

"Oh no, you need medical help."

"It's okay, the tourniquet is fine for now. How the hell did he know?"

"There must be a mole in my ranks," Felida spits out angrily, "they will pay, I promise you."

The muffled sounds of the war raging outside can be heard. They sit in silence until Felida remembers something.

"Wait, there is a secret escape from this vault. I overhead Dilvant speaking of it to the engineers and architects when he was designing this building. He wanted a secret door so he could escape quickly if he needed to."

"Why would he put us here if he knows we can escape from here?"

"I don't know, maybe his mind was clouded with rage. But who cares, you three, help me to find that door. Look for something that looks out of place."

The walls are polished concrete, there are no windows, and the steel door is reinforced. From what Felida can see, there is nothing unusual. As the four of them scan the room, the door is opened, and food is placed on the floor for them.

"Well how nice of him, he wants us kept alive," scoffs Leyna. She winces as she tries to make herself comfortable.

"Take it easy, I'll bring the food to you," says Felida.

"Felida, do you have any idea who would betray you?" asks Leyna as they eat the slop they have been given.

"It could be any one of the thirty who say they are loyal to me. But I will find out when we get out of here." What she doesn't say aloud is *if* they get out.

They eat in silence. Then Leyna asks them all to look up. There they see a patch of concrete, approximately a metre in length, that is a shade darker than the rest of the ceiling. "It's only slight, but it's definitely different. Could this be the secret door?"

"It could be," says Felida, "and the only way to find out is if the three of you stand on each other's shoulders." She points to each of the security guards.

Within seconds they are doing as they are told. The guard on top tells them there is a small channel that needs to be prised open.

"Try using my fork," says Leyna.

"It's plastic," says Felida, "it won't be strong enough. We need to trick one of the guards when they come back for the tray. I'm sure they will have something sharp we could use."

"Ok then, we wait," says Leyna as the guards jump off each other's shoulders.

The five of them sleep for a few hours, but the escalating war outside wakes them. Felida turns to Leyna and sees she is sweating. Placing her hand on Leyna's forehead, she gasps. "We have to call the guards, Leyna has a fever." Walking towards the door, she screams.

A voice booms from the other side, "What is it?"

"We have an emergency here. Madame President needs medical attention. Please go and find a doctor." There is no response.

"Do you think he has gone to find one?" asks one of the guards.

"I hope so, she is becoming delirious." Looking at Leyna's leg, Felida can see it is puffed with redness and is oozing. "If they don't hurry, she will lose this leg. Or worse, she will die."

What seems like hours pass, there is no way of knowing what

time it is. All their possessions were confiscated when they were imprisoned. Felida is anxious for help and begins screaming again. "Hey," she yells as she bangs both hands on the door, "have you no morals, there is a woman in here in agony. She is the leader of the free world, do you know what will happen to all of you if she dies?" Felida breaks down and cries. She should have sent Leyna home.

The guard who spoke before comes over and takes her by the shoulders, "They aren't stupid, someone will be here soon."

She looks up into his caring eyes and hopes he is right.

More time passes but then the door opens. A doctor is sent in and begins work on Leyna's leg as soon as he sees her. The smell from the wound takes over the room as he takes off the bandages.

"Will... will she be okay?" asks Felida.

"Give me a minute, let me do my work. I'll let you know when I know."

Felida feels stupid for asking but her nerves are escalating. If anything happens to Leyna it will be her fault and she will never forgive herself. She paces while the doctor works. Then, an idea comes to her. While the doctor is distracted with tending to Leyna, Felida takes two tools from the doctor's open bag. The doctor doesn't notice and Felida slips them to the guard watching her.

When Felida turns back towards the doctor, she asks her to help her get Leyna up to a more comfortable position. Felida can see she is tired from being bent down and on her knees the whole time. Also, she looks to be in her fifties, Dilvant actually sent someone with lots of experience.

"Here are some antibiotics, give them to her three times a day. I have cleaned the wound for now, but she will need surgery. Unfortunately, her leg may not be saved. Make sure she drinks lots of water, I'll have the guard bring extra for you."

They thank her as she is allowed out the door.

"Right, do you have the tools?"

"Yes, but aren't we meant to get more water? Maybe we should wait until after that."

"Okay, you're right," says Felida, "but if they don't come soon, we have to risk it."

Leyna moans and Felida grabs a water bottle and puts it to her parched lips. "We're going to have you home soon. I promise not to let anything else happen to you."

"You're an optimist, how can you promise that?"

Felida glares at the guard, "Because I believe it."

The guard keeps quiet as the other two snicker and slap him on the back.

Time is going slowly for Felida and her nerves are shot. "That's it, we're not waiting any longer. Come on you three, get up there. We need to have our Madame President back home as soon as possible." The three guards look at each other. "Now," yells Felida.

The guards jump up and the one on top uses both tools to pry the channel open. He balances with precision and manages to open the small door.

"Yes! Well done." Then Felida hears the door. She runs to it and pushes it closed. "Wait, we have an issue here. I'll tell you when to open the door."

The guards are incredulous, and Felida whispers, "What are you looking at? Get Leyna up there and then come back for me. Hurry!"

"We need to come in, we have water for you."

"Not long now, I order you to give us more time." Felida hears some scuffles on the other side of the door but nothing more is said.

When Leyna has been lifted, with difficulty, Felida makes her way up and then the guards follow. The final guard is helped up by the other two making a chain and allowing him to scramble over them.

By the time Dilvant's guards are in the vault, the secret door is closed, and they are left looking into an empty room.

Chapter 36

Dilvant

Holed up in his office, Dilvant barks orders to his army. He is yelling at one of his head generals when the guard who was guarding the vault runs in puffing, "They're gone."

"Breathe man, what are you saying?"

"The prisoners, they escaped."

Dilvant slams his fist on his desk. "Damn, that secret door, they found it. I should have thought this through. How did they get up there? Wait, don't answer that, I figured it out, those guards were tall enough to reach if they stood on each other's shoulders." Slamming his fist onto the intercom this time, he yells instructions to find the prisoners, "Don't harm them, I need them for bargaining power. Bring them back to me alive." Then he turns to the guard and tells him to go back to his post and find two others to help once the prisoners are returned.

His anger at his own stupidity for putting them in that room won't allow him to stay in his office any longer. He calls for two security guards and the three of them grab guns and head out to where the action is happening.

Night has descended but there is enough light from both moons to see, it is more like twilight than night. They step over corpses and rubble, there has been more than handguns used in the fighting. Heading towards a group of soldiers, Dilvant hears that they are using the Acoustic Moduliser, the sound being emitted can make anyone's ears bleed. He grabs three ear protectors as he approaches the group, "Here you two, put these on quickly." Then the three of them crouch down and watch the carnage.

The Earth army is being attacked by the high-pitched sound being emitted by the Acoustic Moduliser, many of them holding their ears and screaming but Dilvant knows they hear no noise coming out of their mouths. The soldiers following behind don't know why they are holding their ears until they are closer to the sound.

As Dilvant watches on with glee when a message is given to him that a rocket is heading back to Earth with the two women.

"Argh, that bitch has managed it," he screams. She has escaped from his clutches and right now there is nothing he can do about it. He indicates to two of his men to follow him. They head back to his office.

When they arrive in his office, he fires a message to Eween telling him that Felida is his and he will come back to find her. Then he sends another one to Dawa and Zenac telling them he is winning this war and will come to Arisis next. He stands up and rubs his chin as he thinks about what to do next. As he is thinking his office door is swung open and six soldiers stand with their weapons pointing straight at him.

One of them speaks, "Dilvant, in the name of Madame President and the people of Earth and their colonies, we arrest you for inciting violence causing a war. Put your hands up."

Dilvant does as he is told. The soldier summons another behind him to bring Dilvant over to the group. With his arms behind his back and blindfolded, Dilvant is ushered out of his office. The group heads to where Taaz and Mechanic are waiting for them near the rocket.

"Take him to the cell and make sure three well-armed guards are posted outside," orders Taaz, as he watches them escort Dilvant into the rocket. Next, he sends a message to Eween about the capture of their ultimate enemy.

He sits on the filthy mattress and eats his breakfast. Dilvant has been imprisoned in a Roman prison since his capture two weeks ago. The war came to an end with his capture and Dilvant-1 is now controlled by Earth's army and they are waiting on Granada's peacekeeping force to assist them. This is what he has been told by Eween, who has also told him his trial will begin soon. Eween said he wants to bring back the death penalty but Leyna won't allow him. "Death is an easy way out," she had told him, "Dilvant needs to suffer as he has made others suffer." Eween had not argued with her and told Dilvant as much. Dilvant had remained defiant and not answered.

Two days later, Dilvant is dressed in a suit and sitting in a courtroom.

They are all asked to rise as the judge enters the courtroom. As Dilvant stands he looks around and sees Leyna in a wheelchair. Her left leg is only a stump. She was injured during the fight on Dilvant-1. Both she and Eween have been maimed by war, Eween lost an arm and now Leyna a leg. This gives him some solace that they have suffered as well, and he smiles.

He wonders what Quinan Jnr has done to be in the disabled club. His young son didn't do the things he and his enemies have done. It is unfair that he will suffer his whole life with an affliction he does not deserve. Felida is seated next to Leyna and gives him a cold hard stare. He lurches forward trying to get to her, but he is held back by court security. The courtroom erupts.

"Order. I will have order in my court. You," he says pointing at Dilvant, "will behave yourself or I will send you back to the cells and we will proceed without you."

As quiet descends once more, the trial of the world's most hated leader begins.

Weeks pass and Dilvant is informed by guards that news of the trial is filling the news channels and is all people are talking about. Dilvant knows he won't be coming out of this cell. Seeing Felida in the courtroom every day is screwing with his mind. She betrayed him and she is free while he is rotting in this disgusting place. He lies down and tries to rest but sleep eludes him just as it has for the past week. How did he end up here? He had Enforcers doing his bidding, he was a leader that ruled the world and now... He rolls off the mat and pulls the sheet off the filthy mattress.

An alarm sounds as guards are running towards the cell. The three guards who had stood outside Dilvant's cell door had discovered his limp body. The news that the High Priest Enforcer was dead was on the airwaves within thirty minutes.

Chapter 37

Teegue

He takes in his reflection in the small mirror in his quarters on the rocket heading to Dilvant-1. The outfit doesn't suit him, but it is necessary for what he and his peacekeepers have been asked to do. The dull grey uniform has been designed for practicality and ease of wear. Every one of them will wear the same, there is no rank in his army. He thinks about his unborn child and Joaque, his stepdaughter. It will be good for their generation to know the reasons for this mission. Peace will prevail for all, and this is good for young and old.

Teegue had convinced the King it was important for Granada to be involved in this mission if they want to be a part of the colonies. "It is time for you to stop hiding and make your people a part of the universe that incorporates Earth with all its allies." The King had agreed to the mission as long as it was for peacekeeping purposes only. Teegue had explained to him that as Dilvant was no longer alive, there was no reason to use force. He is about to leave his room when his answae rings.

"Hello."

"Hi, I have some important news."

"What is it, Dad?"

"Our scientists have found something interesting about Dilvant-1. The planet is in a phase of freezing over the next fifty years, so your mission to have all citizens safely returned to Crete is more important than ever."

"As peacekeepers we will now have to ensure the safe return of all citizens, is this what you're asking us to do? This will take some time; how long do we have?"

"This ice phase started a few years ago, the planet is becoming colder by two degrees per season. The core is hardening, and this process is accelerating. In the next two years the average temperature during the day will be five degrees Celsius. Snow and ice will overtake eventually. This is not sustainable to human life in the long term."

"It only took Dilvant nine months to move the population of Crete to Dilvant-1, I'm sure you'll find they are keen to return to Earth. We won't need two years to rescue everyone."

"I hope not, but we have to keep the planet's changing temperature in mind. The unpredictability is what worries me."

"So, after all that, Dilvant was not the first person to discover a liveable planet like Earth."

"No, I guess not. I must go but I also wanted to wish you luck. You have done a good service to the people of Granada by bringing them into our alliance, this will help all humans in the long term."

"Dad, I always had the intention of doing something about Granada's situation. There is no need for them to worry any longer. Also, it is only the King and a few elders who hold a grudge against the governments of the US and Spain for not sending help back then. Many of the citizens of Granada are happy to be able to help. Goodbye Dad, we'll come and visit you on Arisis soon."

Teegue and his peacekeeping army arrive on Dilvant-1 with everyone still talking about Dilvant taking his own life. Walking into the melee, he sees Taaz and his security forces. He heads towards them with his team in tow.

"Well look who we have here, Mr Troublemaker himself."

"Nice to see you too, Taaz."

They both hug each other and laugh amicably. "Only joking, it is good to see you. I'm proud of how you have handled a tough situation. Let's get comfortable, we have much to discuss."

Teegue follows Taaz to a tent where the smell of coffee twitches at his nose. He asks only two of his team to follow him, the others are to wait with the security forces for further instruction.

"A good hot coffee will go down well right now, it's freezing."

"Coming right up," says Taaz, asking the others what they would like. "Okay then, four coffees, one tea, thanks." His order is punched into the compupad till and the girl behind the counter tells him she'll bring them over.

When he's back at the bench with the others he says, "Right, Teegue, you've heard the news?"

"Yes, we heard the news before we left Granada. So does this change what we need to do?"

"Not really, but it might speed things up because basically the war is over before it even began. Dilvant was the driving force behind taking over the universe, no one else is that crazy. Also, the people want to go back to Crete. They have heard the news of this planet becoming colder and want the warmth of their island again. Now, here's what I need you and your army to do..."

Teegue nods and looks around, still listening but taking in his surroundings at the same time. There are heaters every few metres, but his feet are chilled. Everyone has their coats, parkas and scarves on, and many are holding mugs of hot beverages with gloves still on. From the little he has seen of this planet so far, he would not like to live here. Granada is much more inviting even if they are living underground.

"Okay, have you understood all that?"

"Not a problem. We'll begin working as soon as I have my army settled." As he finishes speaking, he sees a girl at the counter who looks like... no, really? Is it her? "Umm, please excuse me Taaz. You two please return to the others, I'll be with you soon. I have someone I must say hello to."

"Jzinta?" She turns to look at him and her amazing eyes are still as beautiful as he remembered. "It is you, how are you? What are you doing here?" he blabbers.

"Teegue." She jumps into his arms and kisses both his cheeks, "I was wondering when you were arriving."

He holds her at arm's length and admires her. "So, you knew about the peacekeeping force?"

"Everyone does, it's all everyone on Earth is talking about. How you have brought Granada into the alliance and how you have earned the King's trust. I hear you have a daughter, congratulations."

"Stepdaughter, but yes. Her name is Joaque and she has me tied around her little finger. I adore her to bits. Elira is also pregnant. I have three people who will be safe because of what has happened here. Tell me about you, what's been happening since we last spoke?"

"Congratulations, I'm happy for you. I told you I was seeing someone. We are still together and happy. And the reason I'm here is to help out with getting people home. I figure Dilvant, who was my father after all, caused all these problems, so I may as well try to fix part of it."

"Very noble. It's great to see you Jzinta, but I had better get back to my post and organise everyone so we can start work too. See you around, okay?"

"Sure, you'll find me here every day at this time."

He kisses both her cheeks again and holds onto her for longer than he probably should, but she is mesmerising. He now remembers why he was going back to Earth to be with her. Still, that was a lifetime ago, he has a family to care for now. Rushing back to his post, he puts thoughts of anything happening with Jzinta out of his mind.

People are crowding the area and shoving to reach the front. Teegue is near the rocket's entrance with a microphone, "Please keep calm, there are three rockets leaving this morning. Anyone found not keeping in line will be removed and your departure will not happen today." He kept his voice as authoritative as possible, although the mass of people was disconcerting. Taaz had warned him this might happen, the citizens have had enough of this planet, especially the ones who arrived first.

The security forces are doing a reasonable job of keeping the crowd in order and Teegue sees The Mechanic coming towards him. He introduces himself.

"I know who you are, Mechanic, your reputation precedes you. It's good to finally meet you in person."

"Your reputation is well known too, Teegue. Taaz has asked me to give you a break, he said to meet him in the mess."

Teegue thanks him and gladly hands over the microphone. After four hours of standing and yelling out instructions his voice is raspy, a break will do him good. Arriving at the mess, the smell of food and coffee mingle with the chatter of security and peacekeeping personnel enjoying their lunch break. He sees Taaz and heads towards him.

"Hi, how was your first morning?"

"Tougher than I thought. The amount of impatient people, honestly. There were a few times there when I almost lost control. But your personnel and my army stepped in and did my job for me."

"That's what they're meant to do. Now, how about some food?" asks Taaz indicating they head to the service bar.

With their food trays in hand, they sit at the same bench and eat. Jzinta walks up and says hello. Teegue introduces her to Taaz, explaining how they know each other.

"I wanted to give you this," she says, handing Teegue a note before disappearing into the crowd. He unfolds it and then places it in his pocket.

"She's a stunner. An old flame?"

"Sort of. We had a thing for a short time while I was on Earth. But we have both gone our separate ways."

"Life has a way of doing that. I hardly see my family these days. My partner and I split after Leyna and Eween took power."

"Sorry to hear that, Taaz."

He doesn't answer and Teegue feels sorry for this six-foot-four hulk who looks like he's never shed a tear. He can see he's trying hard not to cry right now.

"Well, time for me to head back. Keep up the good work, Teegue."

"Will do, thanks Taaz." Teegue watches as he walks away sniffing.

Taking out the note, he reads it again. *Meet me at the Covo Bar tonight. Would like a drink with my old friend.* His body tingles with anticipation as he heads back to work.

The muted lighting is coming more from the heaters than the lights as he enters the bar. He strains to see until his eyes adjust. She is seated towards the back of the room in an off-the-shoulder top and jeans. Looking around, everyone is dressed to party, so he takes off his coat and undoes a few buttons of his shirt. He kisses her cheek as he sits on the stool next to her.

"I had to see you on your own. Would you like some of this?" she says, showing him the bottle of vodka. He nods and she pours him a shot. They both drink and he feels the warmth of the liquid coat his throat. He indicates he wants another.

"I can't believe I've seen you again so soon. I was going to look you up once I arrived on Earth. I am planning to take my family there soon." He places his hand on her knee and she smiles. Their attraction is mutual, and he knows where this night is headed.

They talk as if they've never been apart, and the bottle of vodka is emptied by the time the bar closes. Jzinta takes his hand, and they are both warmly drunk. "My place isn't far."

Holding her hand his body begins to react to her touch. As they walk, he pushes her up against a wall and kisses her. She falls into place with him, her passion as ripe as his. He is powerless to stop what is going to happen once they arrive at her home.

His answwae rings, Elira is calling him. He looks over and Jzinta is still asleep. Rising carefully from her bed, he heads to the kitchen to take the call. "Hello, my darling."

"Hi, I wanted to hear your voice. How are things going, when do you think you'll be home?"

"We'll be here for a few months yet. Is everything alright, how are you feeling? How is Joaque?"

"I'm feeling well. Pregnancy seems to agree with me. And Joaque, like me she is missing you, but don't fret, we are fine. The house is quiet without you here, that's all."

"We will be finished sooner than first thought if that helps. With Dilvant dead, our peacekeeping duties have taken a giant leap forward to getting people off the planet safely."

"Is it as cold as they say?"

"Yes, but all indoor areas are heated. It's not so bad." As he is speaking, Jzinta comes in and begins boiling the jug. "Look, I have to go but it is good to hear your voice. I'll do a face-call soon, when I find time to sit at my compupad."

"That would be good. I love you."

"Me too. Bye." He places the answae down on the kitchen bench.

"I take it that was Elira. Don't feel bad, this was us saying goodbye to each other. And it was long overdue."

"I know, and it can never happen again," he says with guilt rising up.

"You look so cute when you think you've done something wrong. It won't happen again, the chances of us meeting again are minimal."

Looking at her as she stands there in a man's shirt, probably her partner's, he hopes she is right. But he has a family and responsibilities now, this is something he does not want to jeopardise no matter how much he thinks he's still in love with Jzinta.

Chapter 38

Leyna and Eween

Her speech is telecast throughout the world and news centres on the other colonies, including Granada, cover it as well. Leyna promises to keep the Universal Space Project funded and the exploration of the universe will be her legacy. Along with Eween, she also thanks Dawa and Zenac for their help in not only this project, but for defeating Dilvant now and during their takeover of The Vatican. She outlines her government's plans for the future and announces there will be another election within the next two years. She has ministers who are young and ambitious, so she wants to give them a chance to prove their worth. Breex and Marzeen are included with these ministers. She knows Breex would make a good leader. Also, with another baby due in six months, Leyna wants to spend more time with her growing family. Eween has put his name in the ballot too, so she looks forward to the outcome. Whether Breex or Eween become leader, she knows the world will be fine. Leyna is grateful of the opportunities she has been given and now it's time to let the next generation of politicians continue her work.

She ended up with two operations on her left leg, but the infection had done too much damage and the leg was amputated from just above the knee. The prosthetic she has now is her third one and the most comfortable. She had needed a lot of rehabilitation to learn to use the prosthetic and get her head around having one and half legs. The strange thing is, she still feels like she has two. And, she has Eween to console her, with him losing his arm and her having lost her leg, they each help each other with what the other can no longer do.

Once the transmission is finished, the floor manager asks her to wait until the microphone is removed before she can leave. Eween comes over and kisses her, "Well done, Madame President."

Dawa and Zenac

She watches with tears in her eyes as Braxton boards the rocket headed for Earth. The excitement oozed out of him from the minute he heard he had a job as a metallurgist with the space project. So, she and Zenac had lost one son to Granada, and now their youngest was on his way to Earth to another life independent from his parents. Both pride and sorrow mix to mottle her emotions.

Zenac, who is next to her, senses she is not coping and holds her hand, "He's going to be fine," he whispers.

"I know, but he will always be my baby."

They keep holding hands until after the rocket launches. Aria looks at the two of them and says, "He hasn't died guys, don't look so sad. Come on, let's go home."

When they arrive home, Aria asks if she can have Teegue's room now, "It's the biggest bedroom and I have lots of stuff."

"Sure, when Teegue visits there is plenty of space in your room," says Dawa wanting to please Aria because she wants her around as long as possible. Since the passing of Granada's King, Teegue has moved to Granada permanently. He and his family did move to

Arisis for a short time to show his daughter and son both Arisis and Earth, his heritage. Dawa and Zenac had relished their time with their son, daughter-in-law and their two grandchildren, who were now six and three. Elira, being the sole heir, is now Queen of Granada and must live there. Teegue will visit Arisis at times, but mainly on his own and this is very different to him having lived here, she had been used to having him around again.

For the immediate future, she along with Zenac and Aria will be staying on Arisis and be a part of the space race from here. She is in no rush to leave; this is where her father is buried and where they were safe from Dilvant and The Enforcers for a long time.

Felida

Quinan Jnr is quietly playing with his toys after a small tantrum. He had wanted his father and it is only now Felida is realising that he will never know his father. He will know of him, but not who he was, or what he was really like. She will tell him about the man she met, how loving and caring he was. She wants to minimise the impact of all the bad things he will hear about Dilvant and to appease her mind that she didn't fall in love with a monster.

Now that they are back in Heraklion, she wants to give Quinan Jnr as normal a life as possible. She herself wants a quiet life even though the parliamentary ministers have asked her if she wants to pursue a life in politics. She contemplated this for about five minutes but decided to devote her life to bringing up her son. Being his mother is enough for her and this will be her focus. What she has decided to do is to volunteer with the space project and help families who lose loved ones when rockets go missing or blow up. This inevitably happens when rockets are sent to areas of the universe that are unknown. This is how she will help and it is her way of giving back to the community she loves.

She, Leyna and Dawa keep in touch every so often and once a

year they meet up in Vatican City. Occasionally Marzeen joins them when she can. With Breex as President, she is not always available. Their lives have intertwined because of one madman, so their friendship comes from a place of anguish. Their sisterly bond now keeps them sane and can never be broken.

The End

More about Xenure Station

The short story (Book 1) was written in the early 2000s when my two children started school. At the time I was writing online for a site called, Hubpages and working part-time for a public relations company.

After September 11, people were still coming to terms with what this new millennium was to bring. Fear and paranoia were rife. The internet was growing and becoming a part of our everyday lives. Mobile phones were also increasing in popularity. Technology was taking a hold and although many people were wary of big brother watching over us, most people embraced the latest tech device that came along.

This is when the seed for Xenure Station came to me. With technology moving so fast and permeating every part of our lives, what would happen if we suddenly had to live without it? Or if it was only available to a select few?

The other theme in this science fiction story is that of Climate Change. By the time my story starts, the world has managed to stop the world from overheating, but another menace is to take its place – The Enforcers. A group of twelve zealous, power-hungry men form a dictatorship of all the developed nations and force people to follow their draconian rules.

The Enforcers came to power promising safety for all. After a 20-year war, they overthrew all governments standing in their way and became a one-world power regime. Assets and finances are controlled by them and everyone knows their place. They delivered on their promise – everyone was safe but at the same time everyone was also controlled.

The first instalment *Xenure Station: A Billion Light Years* is a short story available on Amazon Kindle as an eBook. It has also been combined with *Xenure Station: The Revenge Book 2* and *Xenure Station: The Return Book 3*. This is the complete Trilogy and is available online as well as various bookstores and various libraries.

Glossary

Answae – Restored communication devices. These were used during the 20-year war but then most were destroyed once The Enforcers came to power.

CMPV – Commando Mission People Vehicle. A vehicle restored along with the Salverz. It travelled within the Salverz along with other equipment.

Commando – A soldier assisting Zenac and Dawa.

Commando-(number) – An elite soldier who protects Zenac, Dawa and Luminaries.

Licdan – Global currency on Earth. Controlled by The Enforcers.

Loope card – Currency on Arisis

Luminaries – Ten highly educated people who advise Zenac and Dawa.

The Enforcers – Twelve men from five of the world's poorest nations. They form an alliance and take over the world.

The GIS – Global Institute for Sustainability. Now working under The Enforcers regulations. Global warming targets are still adhered to. A new branch is formed on Arisis.

Acoustic Moduliser - Weapon used by High Priest. Blast sounds of up to 120 decibels, enough to make a person deaf.

Fotokast - Weapon, machine that projects a hologram of soldiers that look more real the closer you get to them.

Saber Concealer - Weapon, laser that surrounds its victims with an invisible shield they cannot escape from.

Munitions depot – series of tunnels in Sahara Desert near Morocco.

Salverz – spaceship that gets them to Xenure Station

Vespira – second spaceship like The Salverz

Mazadon – Planet with water (near Arisis)

Heredan – Planet near Arisis with similar atmosphere

Xeradyn – Planet further away but atmosphere similar to Earth

Spacedrome – where spaceships/rockets are built on Arisis

Parliament Row – houses of parliament on Arisis

Universal Space Project – Leyna and Eween's space project

The Quinan Space Project – Dilvant's space project in honour of Felida's deceased brother. He was the leader of Crete.

Granada – planet where Teegue is found

Acknowledgments

Writing is so much a part of me that I lose myself in my characters and stories. This was definitely the case with Xenure Station. The premise for this story is what would life be like without technology and how would people react when sadistic, zealous men take over the world. Many of us, including myself, make a living from the internet. What would a world without this mean? What would I do with myself if I couldn't write and publish?

As a fan of science fiction and fantasy stories, I began formulating this story in the early 2000s when technology and the internet were becoming embedded in our lives. How did we ever live without all this information in the palm of our hands? To anyone born after 1995, yes, we did live without mobile phones and if we wanted information we went to a library.

There are a few people I need to thank for helping me to publish this story. Firstly, my family. Tony, Sebastian and Alessia, you are always encouraging and supportive of my creative pursuits. You allow me the time I need to reach my goal of publishing my stories.

To my fellow creatives – Mark, Joseph and Andre. Your help with the covers, cover photo and reading my early drafts has been great. Mark, I thank you for allowing me to bounce ideas off you and for your constructive criticism.

To my wonderful friends. Thanks for being patient when I talked about my stories (incessantly at times) as I was nutting out the storylines. Your feedback was invaluable, as is your friendship. Special mention to the All Hallows mums and my BC group, we have all bonded through a love of reading and the occasional dinner and drinks.

And lastly, to everyone who has reviewed my stories. I am beyond pleased that you enjoy my work, a writer without readers is just a writer. Thank you for taking the time to read and review my books, I appreciate your thoughts and I hope my stories keep you entertained for many years to come.

Happy reading
    Maria P Frino

About the Author

Maria has made a career of using words to communicate. Working at a TV station, her first paid job nurtured Maria's love of words. A move to Sydney to study Communications gave her the opportunity to work with advertising & public relations agencies, corporate companies and newspapers. She has written PR, ads and newsletters for products from food to jewellery, fashion and interiors as well as garden and building products. For both traditional print media and digital. When she is not writing website content or as a Senior Reviewer for the online site, Weekend Notes, she works on her short stories and novels.

Her first published story, *The Studio* is a crime short story. *Xenure Station: A Billion Light Years* is Maria's second short story. Both are available online.

The Decision They Made, Maria's debut novel, is available online, in selected bookstores and various libraries.

Two Men in a Shed, is a contemporary adult novel by Maria and is available now online, from bookstores and in various libraries.

If your local bookshop or library does not have my books on their shelves ask them to stock a copy.

Contact the author
www.mariapfrino.com

mariapfrino@gmail.com

twitter.com/frino_mp
instagram.com/mariapfrino